Praise for *The Essential Peter S. Beagle*, *Volumes I & II*

"Master enchanter Peter S. Beagle is best known for his novel *The Last Unicorn*, a book which has charmed generations of readers. But the briefer enchantments collected in these two volumes also brim with the deepest and truest of his magical powers: with laughter, with wisdom, and with the ineffable pleasure of the imaginary memories he shares. From the gradually refined focus of 'Professor Gottesman and the Indian Rhinoceros' to the crankily slipped-and-skewed perspective of 'Vanishing,' these are visions of an inner world all of us need to visit again and again. Each tale is a spell welcoming our hearts to their real home: wonder."
—Nisi Shawl, author of *Everfair*

"Stepping into a Peter Beagle story is like stepping out your front door into an alternate, but entirely logical, world: Your girlfriend seems to be a werewolf, the evening news is anchored by the Angel of Death, dreadful poetry is a lethal weapon, and a Berkeley traffic cop has to negotiate a depressed dragon out of an intersection. But then, what else to expect from a wizard of mischief like Beagle? Two perfect volumes that should come with a warning: When you try and go back inside your house, all its rooms will have changed."
—Laurie R. King, author of *The Beekeeper's Apprentice*

"Having all these Peter Beagle stories collected together is pure joy. His writing has amazed me my whole life. You'd think I'd be used to it by now, but the amazement is ongoing."
—Carrie Vaughn, author of the Kitty Norville series

"This was an amazing collection, and I cannot recommend it enough for existing fans of Mr. Beagle or fans of fantasy shorts or cozy fantasy."
—*All Booked Up*

"Peter S. Beagle's short stories tap into the sweetest sap of the soul and leave their mark forever. He always makes me cry in the most wonderful and necessary way."
—Delilah S. Dawson, author of *Wicked as They Come*

"*The Essential Peter S. Beagle Volumes I & II* are everything I hoped for and wanted them to be. Beagle's clever and utterly whimsical storytelling is evident in every story, and I love jumping from tale to tale and exploring the facets of his mind. The writing is fun and explores the unique while keeping one foot in the familiar, making it perfect for readers of all ages. I highly recommend these charming volumes!"
—Charlie N. Holmberg, author of *Keeper of Enchanted Rooms*

Praise for Peter S. Beagle

"One of my favorite writers."
—Madeleine L'Engle, author of *A Wrinkle in Time*

"Peter S. Beagle illuminates with his own particular magic such commonplace matters as ghosts, unicorns, and werewolves. For years a loving readership has consulted him as an expert on those hearts' reasons that reason does not know."
—Ursula K. Le Guin, author of *A Wizard of Earthsea*

"Peter S. Beagle has both opulence of imagination and mastery of style."
—*New York Times Book Review*

"At his best, Peter S. Beagle outshines the moon, the sun, the stars, the entire galaxy."
—*Seattle Times*

"Peter Beagle deserves a seat at the table with the great masters of fantasy."
—Christopher Moore, author of *Lamb* and *The Serpent of Venice*

"Not only one of our greatest fantasists, but one of our greatest writers, a magic realist worthy of consideration with such writers as Marquez, Allende, and even Borges."
—*The American Culture*

"We all have something to learn—about writing, about humanity, about hope—from Peter Beagle."
—Seanan McGuire, Hugo Award-winning author of the Wayward Children series

"Peter S. Beagle is (in no particular order) a wonderful writer, a fine human being, and a bandit prince out to steal readers' hearts."
—Tad Williams, author of *Tailchaser's Song*

"Peter S. Beagle is a master of the magical."
—Kurt Busiek, author of *Astro City* and *The Avengers*

"[Beagle] has been compared, not unreasonably, with Lewis Carroll and J. R. R. Tolkien, but he stands squarely and triumphantly on his own feet."
—*Saturday Review*

"Peter S. Beagle is the magician we all apprenticed ourselves to."
—Lisa Goldstein, author of *The Red Magician*

"One of the all-time greats."
—*The Guardian*

"There are other authors who can write a sentence as well as Beagle, but there are very few who keep inventing sparkling fantasy ideas for decade after decade."
—*SF Commentary*

Praise for *The Overneath*

[Starred] "Beagle's latest collection of short stories includes 13 fantasy gems and features many previously uncollected and never-before-published works. . . . A masterful collection from a short story master—a must-read for Beagle fans."
—*Kirkus*

[Starred] "With sharp, lean elegance, Beagle effortlessly chronicles the lives of unicorns, trolls, magicians, and adventurers in 13 poignant stories, many of which caution readers about magic gone awry and temperamental creatures. . . . This enchanting collection employs simple humor and affectionate sarcasm and will enchant any reader who still believes in magic."
—*Publishers Weekly*

[Starred] "Beagle's strong and versatile talent is well on display here, and fantasy readers will be missing out if they don't give it a look."
—*Booklist*

"Verdict: For fantasy fans, Beagle should be a staple."
—*Library Journal*

Praise for *Sleight of Hand*

"Wise, warm and deep."
—*The New York Times*

"This 13-story anthology will entice even the most jaded reader to read long hours into the night . . . *Sleight of Hand* will beguile and enchant."
—*New York Journal of Books*

"Beagle still has the power to surprise . . . a new collection of stories by one of the all-time greats."
—*The Guardian*

Also by Peter S. Beagle

Fiction

A Fine and Private Place (1960)
The Last Unicorn (1968)
Lila the Werewolf (1969)
The Folk of the Air (1986)
The Innkeeper's Song (1993)
The Unicorn Sonata (1996)
Tamsin (1999)
A Dance for Emilia (2000)
The Last Unicorn: The Lost Version (2007)
Return (2010)
Summerlong (2016)
In Calabria (2017)
The Way Home (2023)

Short fiction collections

Giant Bones (1997)
The Rhinoceros Who Quoted Nietzsche and Other Odd Acquaintances (1997)
The Line Between (2006)
Your Friendly Neighborhood Magician: Songs and Early Poems (2006)
We Never Talk About My Brother (2009)
Mirror Kingdoms: The Best of Peter S. Beagle (2010)
Sleight of Hand (2011)
The Overneath (2017)

Nonfiction

I See By My Outfit (1965)
The California Feeling (with Michael Bry, 1969)
The Lady and Her Tiger (with Pat Derby, 1976)
The Garden of Earthly Delights (1982)
In the Presence of Elephants (with Pat Derby and Genaro Molina, 1995)

As editor

Peter S. Beagle's Immortal Unicorn (with Janet Berliner, 1995)
The Secret History of Fantasy (2010)
The Urban Fantasy Anthology (with Joe R. Lansdale, 2011)
The New Voices of Fantasy (with Jacob Weisman, 2017)
The Unicorn Anthology (with Jacob Weisman, 2019)

THE ESSENTIAL
PETER S. BEAGLE
VOLUME I

TACHYON PUBLICATIONS
SAN FRANCISCO

The Essential Peter S. Beagle: Volume I

Cover art and interior illustrations by Stephanie Law
Cover design and interior layout by Elizabeth Story

Tachyon Publications LLC
1459 18th Street #139
San Francisco, CA 94107
415.285.5615
www.tachyonpublications.com
tachyon@tachyonpublications.com

Series editor: Jacob Weisman
Project editor: Jaymee Goh

Print ISBN: 978-1-61696-388-0
Digital ISBN: 978-1-61696-389-7

Printed in the United States by Versa Press, Inc.

First Edition: 2023
9 8 7 6 5 4 3 2 1

THE ESSENTIAL
PETER S.
BEAGLE
VOLUME I
LILA THE WEREWOLF
AND OTHER STORIES

Table of Contents

Peter Beagle: Bottling Talent

by Jane Yolen

Peter Beagle and I are almost the same age. Born in the same place—New York City. Okay, confession—I am two months older, a hard admission because I have always prided myself on hitting the professional writing stage early. But, lest you think this is a simple older sister/baby brother contest, let me tell you that he was miles ahead of me, miles ahead of most American writers of that time, getting his BA a year before I did and winning major Fellowships along the way—Stanford Creative Writing fellowship in 1960 and the Guggenheim (1970) among them—while the rest of us had only barely tried authoring a book.

And *what* a first book his was . . . when he had turned barely twenty one the month before. His novel *A Fine and Private Place* was published in 1960 by Viking, a top literary publisher of the day. The book—urban fantasy before there was any such designation. It was a calling card thrown down into the middle of the Major Players' game by a mere boy. The novel is about the journey between life and death and a man not ready to die, who nevertheless has died. He is trapped between life and death, searching for an escape, his only companions in the graveyard in which he finds himself an accommodating raven and an eccentric man who lives in the mortuary and talks to the dead. He stays there until love enters the equation.

I was working in publishing then, a young editor, and read the book with great delight. I became a major fan of his, although far too shy to write and say so.

I guess this introduction changes all that.

But Beagle turned the world of fairy—unicorns and wish granters and angels both of life and death—into literary masterpieces that ring with authentic voices, stretching the definition of urban and rural fantasy in novels, novellas, and short stories. His work is a weird combination of Isaac Bashevis Singer, William Butler Yeats, a Borscht Belt comedian, and a wise-ass New York Jewish kid. His stories simply ring out with magic, tragicomedy, and the lyric line. NO one else even comes close!

Most people my age became Beagle fans when *The Last Unicorn* appeared. And although I love that book, I loved *A Fine and Private Place* and *I See by My Outfit* even more. They fit right into my emotional playlist, while *Unicorn* was just another great fantasy novel that I devoured on the way to the next and the next.

As I began writing this introduction, nineteen children and two teachers were murdered by a crazed eighteen-year-old in two attached schoolrooms in Texas. I read the news at the same time I was reading the stories in this book, not only because the deadline was closing in (no horrific pun intended) but because once I started reading (and, in some cases, rereading) the stories, I realized that the news could have been written (with more elegance and truth) by Beagle himself. His kind of story. His kind of darkness. His kind of hoped for redemptions. His dabbling in the wrong side.

The first story I began was new to me: "Uncle Chaim and Aunt Rifke and the Angel," an alternately brilliantly funny and dangerously sad story that did not take the edge off the news of the school shooting but somehow magnified the story in a way that made me weep as I read the ending. But that was only a precursor for the next one I settled into—"We Never Talk About My Brother." And as I read, I was beginning to see a pattern that—if I hadn't already been in awe of Beagle's breadth as a writer—would have assured it. It certainly explained his work—and, in some ways, the horrendous TV news.

Both those stories and others in the book utilize Yiddishkeit notions as well as trying to quantify the American experience. Stickball, and New York City streets, and the interplay of local schoolboys and witches. Urban spooks. Odd kings. Still, somehow the tales are also underpinned by knowledge of Torah, world history, the rules of stickball, philosophy, classic literature and—surprisingly—bad poetry. Yet the voice of each story, the delineation of characters, is different enough that one might be fooled into thinking that not one but two or more authors had written them.

For example, "Professor Gottesman and the Indian Rhinoceros" in other hands might have been a smug put-down (or windup) of academia. But here, although there is humor, there is pathos as well and—I expect—a heavy nod to the classes Beagle must have taken in philosophy in college. But it is so much more than that. It is about friendships and unlikely partners and the ability to believe in the impossible. Besides that, it is a paean to old professors and odd academics that I—as an old academic and widow of one as well—find so moving. First published in 1985, nearly forty years ago and before Beagle would have known or worried much about aging, at least not as he might well do today, being in his 80s. But boy! Does it resonate.

And so it goes, through the entire collection—all the stories are, by tone, by characterization, by any other measure, definitely Peter Beagle's, but also so wildly (and so ecstatically) different, it can feel as if another author must have a hand in them as well. Yet I know—we know—the editors, the fans know—that it is all Beagle's work. Breadth, texture, tonal quality, humor, and pathos intermixed, and that great free fall into depth.

I'm especially fond of the odd but—even when hopelessly wrong—endearing characters, like Uncle Chaim painting the angel over and over, like Esau Robbins, who wants to be a nice God but can't be, like the love-possessed ghost who proposes a duel of bad poetry, like King Pelles, a man of peace who purposely creates a war. And dear, benighted Professor Gottesman seeing a rhino but understanding, in the end, that it's a unicorn. Plus the countless others who all belong to us now but owe their authority—paintbrush and crown and horn and all—to the incomparable Peter Beagle.

If only we could bottle and sell this talent to would-be writers, the world of American letters would be a better place.

Professor Gottesman and the Indian Rhinoceros

"Professor Gottesman and the Indian Rhinoceros" is still one of my favorites of my own stories. René Auberjonois, a splendid actor and a good friend, always wanted to play Professor Gottesman, if it ever became a movie. When I mentioned that the Professor is Swiss-born, René responded immediately, "Well, I'm Swiss!" I borrowed the character's name from a dentist who had his office in the Bronx building where I grew up. A very nice, funny man who didn't believe in Novocain. Scarified my entire childhood, he did. . . .

Professor Gustave Gottesman went to a zoo for the first time when he was thirty-four years old. There is an excellent zoo in Zurich, which was Professor Gottesman's birthplace, and where his sister still lived, but Professor Gottesman had never been there. From an early age he had determined on the study of philosophy as his life's work; and for any true philosopher this world is zoo enough, complete with cages, feeding times, breeding programs, and earnest docents, of which he was wise enough to know that he was one. Thus, the first zoo he ever saw was the one in the middle-sized Midwestern American city where he worked at a middle-sized university, teaching Comparative Philosophy in comparative contentment. He was tall and rather thin, with a round, undistinguished face, a snub nose, a random assortment of sandy-ish hair, and a pair of very intense and very distinguished brown eyes that always seemed to be looking a little deeper than they meant to, embarrassing the face around them no end. His students and colleagues were quite fond of him, in an indulgent sort of way.

And how did the good Professor Gottesman happen at last to visit a zoo? It came about in this way: his older sister Edith came from Zurich to stay with him for several weeks, and she brought her daughter, his niece Nathalie, along with her. Nathalie was seven, both in years and in the number of her there sometimes seemed to be, for the Professor had never been used to children even when he was one. She was a generally pleasant little girl, though, as far as he could tell; so when his sister besought him to spend one of his free afternoons with Nathalie while she went to lunch and a gallery opening with an old friend, the Professor graciously consented. And Nathalie wanted very much to go to the zoo and see tigers.

"So you shall," her uncle announced gallantly. "Just as soon as I find out exactly where the zoo is." He consulted with his best friend, a fat, cheerful, harmonica-playing professor of medieval Italian poetry named Sally Lowry, who had known him long and well enough (she was the only person in the world who called him Gus) to draw an elaborate two-colored map of the route, write out very precise directions beneath it, and make several copies of this document, in case of accidents. Thus equipped, and accompanied by Charles, Nathalie's stuffed bedtime tiger, whom she desired to introduce to his grand cousins, they set off together for the zoo on a gray, cool spring afternoon. Professor Gottesman quoted Thomas Hardy to Nathalie, improvising a German translation for her benefit as he went along:

> This is the weather the cuckoo likes,
> And so do I;
> When showers betumble the chestnut spikes,
> And nestlings fly.

"Charles likes it too," Nathalie said. "It makes his fur feel all sweet."

They reached the zoo without incident, thanks to Professor Lowry's excellent map, and Professor Gottesman bought Nathalie a bag of something sticky, unhealthy, and forbidden, and took her straight off to see the tigers. Their hot, meaty smell and their lightning-colored eyes were a bit too much for him, and so he sat on a bench nearby and watched Nathalie perform the introductions for Charles. When she came back to Professor Gottesman, she told him that Charles had been very well-behaved, as had all the tigers but one, who was rudely indifferent. "He was probably just visiting," she said. "A tourist or something."

The Professor was still marveling at the amount of contempt one small girl could infuse into the word *tourist*, when he heard a voice, sounding almost at his shoulder, say, "Why, Professor Gottesman—how nice to see you at last." It was a low voice, a bit hoarse, with excellent diction, speaking good Zurich German with a very slight, unplaceable accent.

Professor Gottesman turned quickly, half-expecting to see some old acquaintance from home, whose name he would inevitably have forgotten. Such embarrassments were altogether too common in his gently preoccupied life. His friend Sally Lowry once observed, "We see each other just about every day, Gus, and I'm still not sure you really recognize me. If I wanted to hide from you, I'd just change my hairstyle."

There was no one at all behind him. The only thing he saw was the rutted, muddy rhinoceros yard, for some reason placed directly across from the big cats' cages. The one rhinoceros in residence was standing by the fence, torpidly mumbling a mouthful of moldy-looking hay. It was an Indian rhinoceros, according to the placard on the gate, as big as the Professor's compact car, and the approximate color of old cement. The creaking slabs of its skin smelled of stale urine, and it had only one horn, caked with sticky mud. Flies buzzed around its small, heavy-lidded eyes, which regarded Professor Gottesman with immense, ancient unconcern. But there was no other person in the vicinity who might have addressed him.

Professor Gottesman shook his head, scratched it, shook it again, and turned back to the tigers. But the voice came again. "Professor, it was indeed I who spoke. Come and talk to me, if you please."

No need, surely, to go into Professor Gottesman's reaction: to describe in detail how he gasped, turned pale, and looked wildly around for any corroborative witness. It is worth mentioning, however, that at no time did he bother to splutter the requisite splutter in such cases: "My God, I'm either dreaming, drunk, or crazy." If he was indeed just as classically absent-minded and impractical as everyone who knew him agreed, he was also more of a realist than many of them. This is generally true of philosophers, who tend, as a group, to be on terms of mutual respect with the impossible. Therefore, Professor Gottesman did the only proper thing under the circumstances. He introduced his niece Nathalie to the rhinoceros.

Nathalie, for all her virtues, was not a philosopher, and could not hear the rhinoceros's gracious greeting. She was, however, seven years old, and a well-brought-up seven-year-old has no difficulty with the notion that a rhinoceros—or a goldfish, or a coffee table—might be able to talk; nor in accepting that some people can hear coffee-table speech and some people cannot. She said a polite hello to the rhinoceros, and then became involved in her own conversation with stuffed Charles, who apparently had a good deal to say about tigers.

"A mannerly child," the rhinoceros commented. "One sees so few here. Most of them throw things."

His mouth dry, and his voice shaky but contained, Professor Gottesman asked carefully, "Tell me, if you will—can all rhinoceri speak, or only the Indian species?" He wished furiously that he had thought to bring along his notebook.

"I have no idea," the rhinoceros answered him candidly. "I myself, as it happens, am a unicorn."

Professor Gottesman wiped his balding forehead. "Please," he said earnestly. "Please. A rhinoceros, even a rhinoceros that speaks, is as real a creature as I. A unicorn, on the other hand, is a being of pure fantasy, like mermaids, or dragons, or the chimera. I consider very little in this universe as absolutely, indisputably certain, but I would feel so much better if you could see your way to being merely a talking rhinoceros. For my sake, if not your own."

It seemed to the Professor that the rhinoceros chuckled slightly, but it might only have been a ruminant's rumbling stomach. "My Latin designation is *Rhinoceros unicornis*," the great animal remarked. "You may have noticed it on the sign."

Professor Gottesman dismissed the statement as brusquely as he would have if the rhinoceros had delivered it in class. "Yes, yes, yes, and the manatee, which suckles its young erect in the water and so gave rise to the myth of the mermaid, is assigned to the order *sirenia*. Classification is not proof."

"And proof," came the musing response, "is not necessarily truth. You look at me and see a rhinoceros, because I am not white, not graceful, far from beautiful, and my horn is no elegant spiral but a bludgeon of matted hair. But suppose that you had grown up expecting a unicorn to look and behave and smell exactly as I do—would not the rhinoceros then be the legend? Suppose that everything you believed about unicorns—everything except the way they look—were true of me? Consider the possibilities, Professor, while you push the remains of that bun under the gate."

Professor Gottesman found a stick and poked the grimy bit of pastry—about the same shade as the rhinoceros, it was—where the creature could wrap a prehensile upper lip around it. He said, somewhat tentatively, "Very well. The unicorn's horn was supposed to be an infallible guide to detecting poisons."

"The most popular poisons of the Middle Ages and Renaissance," replied the rhinoceros, "were alkaloids. Pour one of those into a goblet made of compressed hair, and see what happens." It belched resoundingly, and Nathalie giggled.

Professor Gottesman, who was always invigorated by a good argument with anyone, whether colleague, student, or rhinoceros, announced, "Isidore of Seville wrote in the seventh century that the unicorn was a cruel beast, that it would seek out elephants and lions to fight with them. Rhinoceri are equally known for their fierce, aggressive nature, which often leads them to attack anything that moves in their short-sighted vision. What have you to say to that?"

"Isidore of Seville," said the rhinoceros thoughtfully, "was a most learned man, much like your estimable self, who never saw a rhinoceros in his life, or an elephant either, being mainly preoccupied with church history and canon law. I believe he did see a lion at some point. If your charming niece is quite done with her snack?"

"She is not," Professor Gottesman answered, "and do not change the subject. If you are indeed a unicorn, what are you doing scavenging dirty buns and candy in this public establishment? It is an article of faith that a unicorn can only be taken by a virgin, in whose innocent embrace the ferocious creature becomes meek and docile. Are you prepared to tell me that you were captured under such circumstances?"

The rhinoceros was silent for some little while before it spoke again. "I cannot," it said judiciously, "vouch for the sexual history of the gentleman in the baseball cap who fired a tranquilizer dart into my left shoulder. I would, however, like to point out that the young of our species on occasion become trapped in vines and slender branches that entangle their horns—and the Latin for such branches is *virge*. What Isidore of Seville made of all this . . ." It shrugged, which is difficult for a rhinoceros, and a remarkable thing to see.

"Sophistry," said the Professor, sounding unpleasantly beleaguered even in his own ears. "Casuistry. Semantics. Chop-logic. The fact remains, a rhinoceros is and a unicorn isn't." This last sounds much more impressive in German. "You will excuse me," he went on, "but we have other specimens to visit, do we not, Nathalie?"

"No," Nathalie said. "Charles and I just wanted to see the tigers."

"Well, we have seen the tigers," Professor Gottesman said through his teeth. "And I believe it's beginning to rain, so we will go home now." He took Nathalie's hand firmly and stood up, as that obliging child snuggled Charles firmly under her arm and bobbed a demure European curtsy to the rhinoceros. It bent its head to her, the mud-thick horn almost brushing the ground. Professor Gottesman, mildest of men, snatched her away.

"Good-bye, Professor," came the hoarse, placid voice behind him. "I look forward to our next meeting." The words were somewhat muffled, because Nathalie had tossed the remainder of her sticky snack into the yard as her uncle hustled her off. Professor Gottesman did not turn his head.

Driving home through the rain—which had indeed begun to fall, though very lightly—the Professor began to have an indefinably uneasy feeling that caused him to spend more time peering at the rearview mirror than in looking properly ahead. Finally, he asked Nathalie, "Please, would you and—ah—you and Charles climb into the backseat and see whether we are being followed?"

Nathalie was thrilled. "Like in the spy movies?" She jumped to obey, but reported after a few minutes of crouching on the seat that she could detect nothing out of the ordinary. "I saw a helicopiter," she told him, attempting the English word. "Charles thinks they might be following us that way, but I don't know. Who is spying on us, Uncle Gustave?"

"No one, no one," Professor Gottesman answered. "Never mind, child, I am getting silly in America. It happens, never mind." But a few moments later, the curious apprehension was with him again, and Nathalie was happily occupied for the rest of the trip home in scanning the traffic behind them through an imaginary periscope, yipping "It's that one!" from time to time, and being invariably disappointed when another prime suspect turned off down a side street. When they reached Professor Gottesman's house, she sprang out of the car immediately, ignoring her mother's welcome until she had checked under all four fenders for possible homing devices. "Bugs," she explained importantly to the two adults. "That was Charles's idea. Charles would make a good spy, I think."

She ran inside, leaving Edith to raise her fine eyebrows at her brother. Professor Gottesman said heavily, "We had a nice time. Don't ask." And Edith, being a wise older sister, left it at that.

The rest of the visit was enjoyably uneventful. The Professor went to work according to his regular routine, while his sister and his niece explored the city, practiced their English together, and cooked Swiss-German specialties to surprise him when he came home. Nathalie never asked to go to the zoo again—stuffed Charles having lately shown an interest in international intrigue—nor did she ever mention that her uncle had formally introduced her to a rhinoceros and spent part of an afternoon sitting on a bench arguing with it. Professor Gottesman was genuinely sorry when she and Edith left for Zurich, which rather surprised him. He hardly ever missed people, or thought much about anyone who was not actually present.

It rained again on the evening that they went to the airport. Returning alone, the Professor was startled, and a bit disquieted, to see large muddy footprints on his walkway and his front steps. They were, as nearly as he could make out, the marks of a three-toed foot, having a distinct resemblance to the ace of clubs in a deck of cards. The door was locked and bolted, as he had left it, and there was no indication of any attempt to force an entry. Professor Gottesman hesitated, looked quickly around him, and went inside.

The rhinoceros was in the living room, lying peacefully on its side before the artificial fireplace—which was lit—like a very large dog. It opened one eye as he entered and greeted him politely. "Welcome home, Professor. You will excuse me, I hope, if I do not rise?"

Professor Gottesman's legs grew weak under him. He groped blindly for a chair, found it, fell into it, his face white and freezing cold. He managed to ask, "How—how did you get in here?" in a small, faraway voice.

"The same way I got out of the zoo," the rhinoceros answered him. "I would have come sooner, but with your sister and your niece already here, I thought my presence might make things perhaps a little too crowded for you. I do hope their departure went well." It yawned widely and contentedly, showing blunt, fist-sized teeth and a gray-pink tongue like a fish fillet.

"I must telephone the zoo," Professor Gottesman whispered. "Yes, of course, I will call the zoo." But he did not move from the chair.

The rhinoceros shook its head as well as it could in a prone position. "Oh, I wouldn't bother with that, truly. It will only distress them if anyone learns that they have mislaid a creature as large as I am. And they will never believe that I am in your house. Take my word for it, there will be no mention of my having left their custody. I have some experience in these matters." It yawned again and closed its eyes. "Excellent fireplace you have," it murmured drowsily. "I think I shall lie exactly here every night. Yes, I do think so."

And it was asleep, snoring with the rhythmic roar and fading whistle of a fast freight train crossing a railroad bridge. Professor Gottesman sat staring in his chair for a long time before he managed to stagger to the telephone in the kitchen.

Sally Lowry came over early the next morning, as she had promised several times before the Professor would let her off the phone. She took one quick look at him as she entered and said briskly, "Well, whatever came to dinner, you look as though it got the bed and you slept on the living room floor."

"I did not sleep at all," Professor Gottesman informed her grimly. "Come with me, please, Sally, and you shall see why."

But the rhinoceros was not in front of the fireplace, where it had still been lying when the Professor came downstairs. He looked around for it, increasingly frantic, saying over and over, "It was just here, it has been here all night. Wait, wait, Sally, I will show you. Wait only a moment."

For he had suddenly heard the unmistakable gurgle of water in the pipes overhead. He rushed up the narrow hairpin stairs (his house was, as the real-estate agent had put it, "an old charmer") and burst into his bathroom, blinking through the clouds of steam to find the rhinoceros lolling blissfully in the tub, its nose barely above water and its hind legs awkwardly sticking straight up in the air. There were puddles all over the floor.

"Good morning," the rhinoceros greeted Professor Gottesman. "I could wish your facilities a bit larger, but the hot water is splendid, pure luxury. We never had hot baths at the zoo."

"Get out of my tub!" the Professor gabbled, coughing and wiping his face. "You will get out of my tub this instant!"

The rhinoceros remained unruffled. "I am not sure I can. Not just like that. It's rather a complicated affair."

"Get out exactly the way you got in!" shouted Professor Gottesman. "How did you get up here at all? I never heard you on the stairs."

"I tried not to disturb you," the rhinoceros said meekly. "Unicorns can move very quietly when we need to."

"*Out!*" the Professor thundered. He had never thundered before, and it made his throat hurt. "Out of my bathtub, out of my house! And clean up that floor before you go!"

He stormed back down the stairs to meet a slightly anxious Sally Lowry waiting at the bottom. "What was all that yelling about?" she wanted to know. "You're absolutely pink—it's sort of sweet, actually. Are you all right?"

"Come up with me," Professor Gottesman demanded. "Come right now." He seized his friend by the wrist and practically dragged her into his bathroom, where there was no sign of the rhinoceros. The tub was empty and dry, the floor was spotlessly clean; the air smelled faintly of tile cleaner. Professor Gottesman stood gaping in the doorway, muttering over and over, "But it was here. It was in the tub."

"What was in the tub?" Sally asked. The Professor took a long, deep breath and turned to face her.

"A rhinoceros," he said. "It says it's a unicorn, but it is nothing but an Indian rhinoceros." Sally's mouth opened, but no sound came out. Professor Gottesman said, "It followed me home."

Fortunately, Sally Lowry was not more concerned with the usual splutters of denial and disbelief than was the Professor himself. She closed her mouth, caught her own breath, and said, "Well, any rhinoceros that could handle those stairs, wedge itself into that skinny tub of yours, and tidy up afterwards would have to be a unicorn. Obviously. Gus, I don't care what time it is, I think you need a drink."

Professor Gottesman recounted his visit to the zoo with Nathalie, and all that had happened thereafter, while Sally rummaged through his minimally stocked liquor cabinet and mixed what she called a "Lowry Land Mine." It calmed the Professor only somewhat, but it did at least restore his coherency. He said earnestly, "Sally, I don't know how it talks. I do not know how it escaped from the zoo, or found its way here, or how it got into my house and my bathtub, and I am afraid to imagine where it is now. But the creature is an Indian rhinoceros, the sign said so. It is simply not possible—not possible—that it could be a unicorn."

"Sounds like *Harvey*," Sally mused. Professor Gottesman stared at her. "You know, the play about the guy who's buddies with an invisible white rabbit. A big white rabbit."

"But this one is not invisible!" the Professor cried. "People at the zoo, they saw it—Nathalie saw it. It bowed to her, quite courteously."

"Um," Sally said. "Well, I haven't seen it yet, but I live in hope. Meanwhile, you've got a class, and I've got office hours. Want me to make you another Land Mine?"

Professor Gottesman shuddered slightly. "I think not. We are discussing today how Fichte and von Schelling's work leads us to Hegel, and I need my wits about me. Thank you for coming to my house, Sally. You are a good friend. Perhaps I really am suffering from delusions, after all. I think I would almost prefer it so."

"Not me," Sally said. "I'm getting a unicorn out of this, if it's the last thing I do." She patted his arm. "You're more fun than a barrel of MFA candidates, Gus, and you're also the only gentleman I've ever met. I don't know what I'd do for company around here without you."

Professor Gottesman arrived early for his seminar on "The Heirs of Kant." There was no one in the classroom when he entered, except for the rhinoceros. It had plainly already attempted to sit on one of the chairs, which lay in splinters on the floor. Now it was warily eyeing a ragged hassock near the coffee machine.

"What are you doing here?" Professor Gottesman fairly screamed at it.

"Only auditing," the rhinoceros answered. "I thought it might be rewarding to see you at work. I promise not to say a word."

Professor Gottesman pointed to the door. He had opened his mouth to order the rhinoceros, once and for all, out of his life, when two of his students walked into the room. The Professor closed his mouth, gulped, greeted his students, and ostentatiously began to examine his lecture notes, mumbling professorial mumbles to himself, while the rhinoceros, unnoticed, negotiated a kind of armed truce with the hassock. True to its word, it listened in attentive silence all through the seminar, though Professor Gottesman had an uneasy moment when it seemed about to be drawn into a heated debate over the precise nature of von Schelling's intellectual debt to the von Schlegel brothers. He was so desperately careful not to let the rhinoceros catch his eye that he never noticed until the last student had left that the beast was gone, too. None of the class had even once commented on its presence; except for the shattered chair, there was no indication that it had ever been there.

Professor Gottesman drove slowly home in a disorderly state of mind. On the one hand, he wished devoutly never to see the rhinoceros again; on the other, he could not help wondering exactly when it had left the classroom. "Was it displeased with my summation of the *Ideas for a Philosophy of Nature?*" he said aloud in the car. "Or perhaps it was something I said during the argument about *Die Weltalter.* Granted, I have never been entirely comfortable with that book, but I do not recall saying anything exceptionable." Hearing himself justifying his interpretations to a rhinoceros, he slapped his own cheek very hard and drove the rest of the way with the car radio tuned to the loudest, ugliest music he could find.

The rhinoceros was dozing before the fireplace as before, but lumbered clumsily to a sitting position as soon as he entered the living room. "Bravo, Professor!" it cried in plainly genuine enthusiasm. "You were absolutely splendid. It was an honor to be present at your seminar."

The Professor was furious to realize that he was blushing; yet it was impossible to respond to such praise with an eviction notice. There was nothing for him to do but reply, a trifle stiffly, "Thank you, most gratifying." But the rhinoceros was clearly waiting for something more, and Professor Gottesman was, as his friend Sally had said, a gentleman. He went on, "You are welcome to audit the class again, if you like. We will be considering Rousseau next week, and then proceed through the romantic philosophers to Nietzsche and Schopenhauer."

"With a little time to spare for the American transcendentalists, I should hope," suggested the rhinoceros. Professor Gottesman, being some distance past surprise, nodded. The rhinoceros said reflectively, "I think I should prefer to hear you on Comte and John Stuart Mill. The romantics always struck me as fundamentally unsound."

This position agreed so much with the Professor's own opinion that he found himself, despite himself, gradually warming toward the rhinoceros. Still formal, he asked, "May I perhaps offer you a drink? Some coffee or tea?"

"Tea would be very nice," the rhinoceros answered, "if you should happen to have a bucket." Professor Gottesman did not, and the rhinoceros told him not to worry about it. It settled back down before the fire, and the Professor drew up a rocking chair. The rhinoceros said, "I must admit, I do wish I could hear you speak on the scholastic philosophers. That's really my period, after all."

"I will be giving such a course next year," the Professor said, a little shyly. "It is to be a series of lectures on medieval Christian thought, beginning with St. Augustine and the Neoplatonists and ending with William of Occam. Possibly you could attend some of those talks."

The rhinoceros's obvious pleasure at the invitation touched Professor Gottesman surprisingly deeply. Even Sally Lowry, who often dropped in on his classes unannounced, did so, as he knew, out of affection for him, and not from any serious interest in epistemology or the Milesian School. He was beginning to wonder whether there might be a way to permit the rhinoceros to sample the cream sherry he kept aside for company, when the creature added, with a wheezy chuckle, "Of course, Augustine and the rest never did quite come to terms with such pagan survivals as unicorns. The best they could do was associate us with the Virgin Mary, and to suggest that our horns somehow represented the unity of Christ and his church. Bernard of Trèves even went so far as to identify Christ directly with the unicorn, but it was never a comfortable union. Spiral peg in square hole, so to speak."

Professor Gottesman was no more at ease with the issue than St. Augustine had been. But he was an honest person—only among philosophers is this considered part of the job description—and so he felt it his duty to say, "While I respect your intelligence and your obvious intellectual curiosity, none of this yet persuades me that you are in fact a unicorn. I still must regard you as an exceedingly learned and well-mannered Indian rhinoceros."

The rhinoceros took this in good part, saying, "Well, well, we will agree to disagree on that point for the time being. Although I certainly hope that you will let me know if you should need your drinking water purified." As before, and so often thereafter, Professor Gottesman could not be completely sure that the rhinoceros was joking. Dismissing the subject, it went on to ask, "But about the scholastics—do you plan to discuss the later Thomist reformers at all? St. Cajetan rather dominates the movement, to my mind; if he had any real equals, I'm afraid I can't recall them."

"Ah," said the Professor. They were up until five in the morning, and it was the rhinoceros that dozed off first.

The question of the rhinoceros's leaving Professor Gottesman's house never came up again. It continued to sleep in the living room, for the most part, though on warm summer nights it had a fondness for the young willow tree that had been a Christmas present from Sally. Professor Gottesman never learned whether it was male or female, nor how it nourished its massive, noisy body, nor how it managed its toilet facilities—a reticent man himself, he respected reticence in others. As a houseguest, the rhinoceros's only serious fault was a continuing predilection for hot baths (with Epsom salts, when it could get them). But it always cleaned up after itself, and was extremely conscientious about not tracking mud into the house; and it can be safely said that none of the Professor's visitors—even the rare ones who spent a night or two under his roof—ever remotely suspected that they were sharing living quarters with a rhinoceros. All in all, it proved to be a most discreet and modest beast.

The Professor had few friends, apart from Sally, and none whom he would have called on in a moment of bewildering crisis, as he had called on her. He avoided whatever social or academic gatherings he could reasonably avoid; as a consequence, his evenings had generally been lonely ones, though he might not have called them so. Even if he had admitted the term, he would surely have insisted that there was nothing necessarily wrong with loneliness, in and of itself. "I *think*," he would have said—did often say, in fact, to Sally Lowry, "there are people, you know, for whom thinking is company, thinking is entertainment, parties, dancing even. The others, other people, they absolutely will not believe this."

"You're right," Sally said. "One thing about you, Gus, when you're right you're really right."

Now, however, the Professor could hardly wait for the time of day when, after a cursory dinner (he was an indifferent, impatient eater, and truly tasted little difference between a frozen dish and one that had taken half a day to prepare), he would pour himself a glass of wine and sit down in the living room to debate philosophy with a huge mortar-colored beast that always smelled vaguely incontinent, no matter how many baths it had taken that afternoon. Looking eagerly forward all day to anything was a new experience for him. It appeared to be the same for the rhinoceros.

As the animal had foretold, there was never the slightest suggestion in the papers or on television that the local zoo was missing one of its larger odd-toed ungulates. The Professor went there once or twice in great trepidation, convinced that he would be recognized and accused immediately of conspiracy in the rhinoceros's escape. But nothing of the sort happened. The yard where the rhinoceros had been kept was now occupied by a pair of despondent-looking African elephants; when Professor Gottesman made a timid inquiry of a guard, he was curtly informed that the zoo had never possessed a rhinoceros of any species. "Endangered species," the guard told him. "Too much red tape you have to go through to get one these days. Just not worth the trouble, mean as they are."

Professor Gottesman grew placidly old with the rhinoceros—that is to say, the Professor grew old, while the rhinoceros never changed in any way that he could observe. Granted, he was not the most observant of men, nor the most sensitive to change, except when threatened by it. Nor was he in the least ambitious: promotions and pay raises happened, when they happened, somewhere in the same cloudily benign middle distance as did those departmental meetings that he actually had to sit through. The companionship of the rhinoceros, while increasingly his truest delight, also became as much of a cozily reassuring habit as his classes, his office hours, the occasional dinner and movie or museum excursion with Sally Lowry, and the books on French and German philosophy that he occasionally published through the university press over the years. They were indifferently reviewed and sold poorly.

"Which is undoubtedly as it should be," Professor Gottesman frequently told Sally when dropping her off at her house, well across town from his own. "I think I am a good teacher—that, yes—but I am decidedly not an original thinker, and I was never much of a writer, even in German. It does no harm to say that I am not an exceptional man, Sally. It does not hurt me."

"I don't know what exceptional means to you or anyone else," Sally would answer stubbornly. "To me it means being unique, one of a kind, and that's definitely you, old Gus. I never thought you belonged in this town, or this university, or probably this century. But I'm surely glad you've been here."

Once in a while she might ask him casually how his unicorn was getting on these days. The Professor, who had long since accepted the fact that no one ever saw the rhinoceros unless it chose to be seen, invariably rose to the bait, saying, "It is no more a unicorn than it ever was, Sally, you know that." He would sip his latté in mild indignation, and eventually add, "Well, we will clearly never see eye to eye on the Vienna Circle, or the logical positivists in general—it is a very conservative creature, in some ways. But we did come to a tentative agreement about Bergson, last Thursday it was, so I would have to say that we are going along quite amiably."

Sally rarely pressed him further. Sharp-tongued, solitary, and profoundly irreverent, only with Professor Gottesman did she bother to know when to leave things alone. Most often, she would take out her battered harmonica and play one or another of his favorite tunes—"Sweet Georgia Brown" or "Hurry on Down." He never sang along, but he always hummed and grunted and thumped his bony knees. Once he mentioned diffidently that the rhinoceros appeared to have a peculiar fondness for "Slow Boat to China." Sally pretended not to hear him.

In the appointed fullness of time, the university retired Professor Gottesman in a formal ceremony, attended by, among others, Sally Lowry, his sister Edith, all the way from Zurich, and the rhinoceros—the latter having spent all that day in the bathtub, in anxious preparation. Each of them assured him that he looked immensely distinguished as he was invested with the rank of *emeritus*, which allowed him to lecture as many as four times a year, and to be available to counsel promising graduate students when he chose. In addition, a special chair with his name on it was reserved exclusively for his use at the Faculty Club. He was quite proud of never once having sat in it.

"Strange, I am like a movie star now," he said to the rhinoceros. "You should see. Now I walk across the campus and the students line up, they line up to watch me totter past. I can hear their whispers—'Here he comes!' 'There he goes!' Exactly the same ones they are who used to cut my classes because I bored them so. Completely absurd."

"Enjoy it as your due," the rhinoceros proposed. "You were entitled to their respect then—take pleasure in it now, however misplaced it may seem to you." But the Professor shook his head, smiling wryly.

"Do you know what kind of star I am really like?" he asked. "I am like the old, old star that died so long ago, so far away, that its last light is only reaching our eyes today. They fall in on themselves, you know, those dead stars, they go cold and invisible, even though we think we are seeing them in the night sky. That is just how I would be, if not for you. And for Sally, of course."

In fact, Professor Gottesman found little difficulty in making his peace with age and retirement. His needs were simple, his pension and savings adequate to meet them, and his health as sturdy as generations of Swiss peasant ancestors could make it. For the most part, he continued to live as he always had, the one difference being that he now had more time for study, and could stay up as late as he chose arguing about structuralism with the rhinoceros, or listening to Sally Lowry reading her new translation of Cavalcanti or Frescobaldi. At first he attended every conference of philosophers to which he was invited, feeling a certain vague obligation to keep abreast of new thought in his field. This compulsion passed quickly, however, leaving him perfectly satisfied to have as little as possible to do with academic life, except when he needed to use the library. Sally once met him there for lunch to find him feverishly rifling through the ten Loeb Classic volumes of Philo Judaeus. "We were debating the concept of the logos last night," he explained to her, "and then the impossible beast rampaged off on a tangent involving Philo's locating the roots of Greek philosophy in the Torah. Forgive me, Sally, but I may be here for awhile." Sally lunched alone that day.

The Professor's sister Edith died younger than she should have. He grieved for her, and took much comfort in the fact that Nathalie never failed to visit him when she came to America. The last few times, she had brought a husband and two children with her—the youngest hugging a ragged but indomitable tiger named Charles under his arm. They most often swept him off for the evening; and it was on one such occasion, just after they had brought him home and said their good-byes, and their rented car had rounded the corner, that the mugging occurred.

Professor Gottesman was never quite sure himself about what actually took place. He remembered a light scuffle of footfalls, remembered a savage blow on the side of his head, then another impact as his cheek and forehead hit the ground. There were hands clawing through his pockets, low voices so distorted by obscene viciousness that he lost English completely, became for the first time in fifty years a terrified immigrant, once more unable to cry out for help in this new and dreadful country. A faceless figure billowed over him, grabbing his collar, pulling him close, mouthing words he could not understand. It was brandishing something menacingly in its free hand.

Then it vanished abruptly, as though blasted away by the sidewalk-shaking bellow of rage that was Professor Gottesman's last clear memory until he woke in a strange bed, with Sally Lowry, Nathalie, and several policemen bending over him. The next day's newspapers ran the marvelous story of a retired philosophy professor, properly frail and elderly, not only fighting off a pair of brutal muggers but beating them so badly that they had to be hospitalized themselves before they could be arraigned. Sally impishly kept the incident on the front pages for some days by confiding to reporters that Professor Gottesman was a practitioner of a long-forgotten martial arts discipline, practiced only in ancient Sumer and Babylonia. "Plain childishness," she said apologetically, after the fuss had died down. "Pure self-indulgence. I'm sorry, Gus."

"Do not be," the Professor replied. "If we were to tell them the truth, I would immediately be placed in an institution." He looked sideways at his friend, who smiled and said, "What, about the rhinoceros rescuing you? I'll never tell, I swear. They could pull out my fingernails."

Professor Gottesman said, "Sally, those boys had been *trampled,* practically stamped flat. One of them had been *gored,* I saw him. Do you really think I could have done all that?"

"Remember, I've seen you in your wrath," Sally answered lightly and untruthfully. What she had in fact seen was one of the ace-of-clubs footprints she remembered in crusted mud on the Professor's front steps long ago. She said, "Gus. How old am I?"

The Professor's response was off by a number of years, as it always was. Sally said, "You've frozen me at a certain age, because you don't want me getting any older. Fine, I happen to be the same way about that rhinoceros of yours. There are one or two things I just don't want to know about that damned rhinoceros, Gus. If that's all right with you."

"Yes, Sally," Professor Gottesman answered. "That is all right."

The rhinoceros itself had very little to say about the whole incident. "I chanced to be awake, watching a lecture about Bulgarian icons on The Learning Channel. I heard the noise outside." Beyond that, it sidestepped all questions, pointedly concerning itself only with the Professor's recuperation from his injuries and shock. In fact, he recovered

much faster than might reasonably have been expected from a gentleman of his years. The doctor commented on it.

The occurrence made Professor Gottesman even more of an icon himself on campus; as a direct consequence, he spent even less time there than before, except when the rhinoceros requested a particular book. Nathalie, writing from Zurich, never stopped urging him to take in a housemate, for company and safety, but she would have been utterly dumbfounded if he had accepted her suggestion. "Something looks out for him," she said to her husband. "I always knew that, I couldn't tell you why. Uncle Gustave is *somebody's* dear stuffed Charles."

Sally Lowry did grow old, despite Professor Gottesman's best efforts. The university gave her a retirement ceremony, too, but she never showed up for it. "Too damned depressing," she told Professor Gottesman, as he helped her into her coat for their regular Wednesday walk. "It's all right for you, Gus, you'll be around forever. Me, I drink, I still smoke, I still eat all kinds of stuff they tell me not to eat—I don't even floss, for God's sake. My circulation works like the post office, and even my cholesterol has arthritis. Only reason I've lasted this long is I had this stupid job teaching beautiful, useless stuff to idiots. Now, that's it. Now, I'm a goner."

"Nonsense, nonsense, Sally," Professor Gottesman assured her vigorously. "You have always told me you are too mean and spiteful to die. I am holding you to this."

"Pickled in vinegar only lasts just so long," Sally said. "One cheery note, anyway—it'll be the heart that goes. Always is, in my family. That's good, I couldn't hack cancer. I'd be a shameless, screaming disgrace, absolutely no dignity at all. I'm really grateful it'll be the heart."

The Professor was very quiet while they walked all the way down to the little local park, and back again. They had reached the apartment complex where she lived, when he suddenly gripped her by the arms, looked straight into her face, and said loudly, "That is the best heart I ever knew, yours. I will not let anything happen to that heart."

"Go home, Gus," Sally told him harshly. "Get out of here, go home.

Christ, the only sentimental Switzer in the whole world, and I get him. Wouldn't you just know?"

Professor Gottesman actually awoke just before the telephone call came, as sometimes happens. He had dozed off in his favorite chair during a minor intellectual skirmish with the rhinoceros over Spinoza's ethics. The rhinoceros itself was sprawled in its accustomed spot, snoring authoritatively, and the kitchen clock was still striking three when the phone rang. He picked it up slowly. Sally's barely audible voice whispered, "Gus. The heart. Told you." He heard the receiver fall from her hand.

Professor Gottesman had no memory of stumbling coatless out of the house, let alone finding his car parked on the street—he was just suddenly standing by it, his hands trembling so badly as he tried to unlock the door that he dropped his keys into the gutter. How long his frantic fumbling in the darkness went on, he could never say; but at some point he became aware of a deeper darkness over him, and looked up on hands and knees to see the rhinoceros.

"On my back," it said, and no more. The Professor had barely scrambled up its warty, unyielding flanks and heaved himself precariously over the spine his legs could not straddle when there came a surge like the sea under him as the great beast leaped forward. He cried out in terror.

He would have expected, had he had wit enough at the moment to expect anything, that the rhinoceros would move at a ponderous trot, farting and rumbling, gradually building up a certain clumsy momentum. Instead, he felt himself flying, truly flying, as children know flying, flowing with the night sky, melting into the jeweled wind. If the rhinoceros's huge, flat, three-toed feet touched the ground, he never felt it: nothing existed, or ever had existed, but the sky that he was and the bodiless power that he had become—he himself, the once and foolish old Professor Gustave Gottesman, his eyes full of the light of lost stars. He even forgot Sally Lowry, only for a moment, only for the least little time.

Then, he was standing in the courtyard before her house, shouting and banging maniacally on the door, pressing every button under his hand. The rhinoceros was nowhere to be seen. The building door finally buzzed open, and the Professor leaped up the stairs like a young man, calling Sally's name. Her own door was unlocked; she often left it so absentmindedly, no matter how much he scolded her about it. She was in her bedroom, half-wedged between the side of the bed and the night table, with the telephone receiver dangling by her head. Professor Gottesman touched her cheek and felt the fading warmth.

"Ah, Sally," he said. "Sally, my dear." She was very heavy, but somehow it was easy for him to lift her back onto the bed and make a place for her among the books and papers that littered the quilt, as always. He found her harmonica on the floor, and closed her fingers around it. When there was nothing more for him to do, he sat beside her, still holding her hand, until the room began to grow light. At last he said aloud, "No, the sentimental Switzer will not cry, my dear Sally," and picked up the telephone.

The rhinoceros did not return for many days after Sally Lowry's death. Professor Gottesman missed it greatly when he thought about it at all, but it was a strange, confused time. He stayed at home, hardly eating, sleeping on his feet, opening books and closing them. He never answered the telephone, and he never changed his clothes. Sometimes he wandered endlessly upstairs and down through every room in his house; sometimes he stood in one place for an hour or more at a time, staring at nothing. Occasionally the doorbell rang, and worried voices outside called his name. It was late autumn, and then winter, and the house grew cold at night, because he had forgotten to turn on the furnace. Professor Gottesman was perfectly aware of this, and other things, somewhere.

One evening, or perhaps it was early one morning, he heard the sound of water running in the bathtub upstairs. He remembered the sound, and presently he moved to his living room chair to listen to it better. For the first time in some while, he fell asleep, and woke only when he felt the rhinoceros standing over him. In the darkness he saw it only as a huge, still shadow, but it smelled unmistakably like a rhinoceros that has just had a bath. The Professor said quietly, "I wondered where you had gone."

"We unicorns mourn alone," the rhinoceros replied. "I thought it might be the same for you."

"Ah," Professor Gottesman said. "Yes, most considerate. Thank you."

He said nothing further, but sat staring into the shadow until it appeared to fold gently around him. The rhinoceros said, "We were speaking of Spinoza."

Professor Gottesman did not answer. The rhinoceros went on, "I was very interested in the comparison you drew between Spinoza and Thomas Hobbes. I would enjoy continuing our discussion."

"I do not think I can," the Professor said at last. "I do not think I want to talk anymore."

It seemed to him that the rhinoceros's eyes had become larger and brighter in its own shadow, and its horn a trifle less hulking. But its stomach rumbled as majestically as ever as it said, "In that case, perhaps we should be on our way."

"Where are we going?" Professor Gottesman asked. He was feeling oddly peaceful and disinclined to leave his chair. The rhinoceros moved closer, and for the first time that the Professor could remember, its huge, hairy muzzle touched his shoulder, light as a butterfly.

"I have lived in your house for a long time," it said. "We have talked together, days and nights on end, about ways of being in this world, ways of considering it, ways of imagining it as a part of some greater imagining. Now has come the time for silence. Now, I think you should come and live with me."

They were outside, on the sidewalk, in the night. Professor Gottesman had forgotten to take his coat, but he was not at all cold. He turned to look back at his house, watching it recede, its lights still burning, like a ship leaving him at his destination. He said to the rhinoceros, "What is your house like?"

"Comfortable," the rhinoceros answered. "In honesty, I would not call the hot water as superbly lavish as yours, but there is rather more room to maneuver. Especially on the stairs."

"You are walking a bit too rapidly for me," said the Professor. "May I climb on your back once more?"

The rhinoceros halted immediately, saying, "By all means, please do excuse me." Professor Gottesman found it notably easier to mount this time, the massive sides having plainly grown somewhat trimmer and smoother during the rhinoceros's absence, and easier to grip with his legs. It started on briskly when he was properly settled, though not at the rapturous pace that had once married the Professor to the night wind. For some while he could hear the clopping of cloven hooves far below him, but then they seemed to fade away. He leaned forward and said into the rhinoceros's pointed silken ear, "I should tell you that I have long since come to the conclusion that you are not after all an Indian rhinoceros, but a hitherto unknown species, somehow misclassified. I hope this will not make a difference in our relationship."

"No difference, good Professor," came the gently laughing answer all around him. "No difference in the world."

Come Lady Death

"Come Lady Death" is the one bit of fiction salvaged from the year I spent at Stanford, in a writing class that included Larry McMurtry, Ken Kesey, Judith Rascoe, and my Kentucky buddy Gurney Norman. I did write an entire novel there, about which the less said, the better. But this short story, sold to *The Atlantic*, keeps being reprinted hither or thither to this day and was turned into an opera I'm still proud of. I wrote the libretto, David Carlson of San Francisco wrote the music, and *The Midnight Angel*, as our opera was entitled, was produced in St. Louis, Sacramento, Cooperstown, and most recently in Milwaukee. In some ways, I actually like it better than the original story!

This all happened in England a long time ago, when that George who spoke English with a heavy German accent and hated his sons was King. At that time there lived in London a lady who had nothing to do but give parties. Her name was Flora, Lady Neville, and she was a widow and very old. She lived in a great house not far from Buckingham Palace, and she had so many servants that she could not possibly remember all their names; indeed, there were some she had never even seen. She had more food than she could eat, more gowns than she could ever wear; she had wine in her cellars that no one would drink in her lifetime, and her private vaults were filled with great works of art that she did not know she owned. She spent the last years of her life giving parties and balls to which the greatest lords of England—and sometimes the King himself—came, and she was known as the wisest and wittiest woman in all of London.

But in time her own parties began to bore her, and though she invited the most famous people in the land and hired the greatest jugglers and acrobats and dancers and magicians to entertain them, still she found her parties duller and duller. Listening to court gossip, which she had always loved, made her yawn. The most marvelous music, the most exciting feats of magic put her to sleep. Watching a beautiful young couple dance by her made her feel sad, and she hated to feel sad.

And so, one summer afternoon she called her closest friends around her and said to them, "More and more I find that my parties entertain everyone but me. The secret of my long life is that nothing has ever been dull for me. For all my life, I have been interested in everything I saw and been anxious to see more. But I cannot stand to be bored, and I will not go to parties at which I expect to be bored, especially if they are my own. Therefore, to my next ball I shall invite the one guest I am sure no one, not even myself, could possibly find boring. My friends, the guest of honor at my next party shall be Death himself!"

A young poet thought that this was a wonderful idea, but the rest of her friends were terrified and drew back from her. They did not want to die, they pleaded with her. Death would come for them when he was ready; why should she invite him before the appointed hour, which would arrive soon enough? But Lady Neville said, "Precisely. If Death has planned to take any of us on the night of my party, he will come whether he is invited or not. But if none of us are to die, then I think it would be charming to have Death among us—perhaps even to perform some little trick if he is in a good humor. And think of being able to say that we had been to a party with Death! All of London will envy us, all of England."

The idea began to please her friends, but a young lord, very new to London, suggested timidly, "Death is so busy. Suppose he has work to do and cannot accept your invitation?"

"No one has ever refused an invitation of mine," said Lady Neville, "not even the King." And the young lord was not invited to her party.

She sat down then and there and wrote out the invitation. There was some dispute among her friends as to how they should address Death. "His Lordship Death" seemed to place him only on the level of a viscount or a baron. "His Grace Death" met with more acceptance, but Lady Neville said it sounded hypocritical. And to refer to Death as "His Majesty" was to make him the equal of the King of England, which even Lady Neville would not dare to do. It was finally decided that all should speak of him as "His Eminence Death," which pleased nearly everyone.

Captain Compson, known both as England's most dashing cavalry officer and most elegant rake, remarked next, "That's all very well, but how is the invitation to reach Death? Does anyone here know where he lives?"

"Death undoubtedly lives in London," said Lady Neville, "like everyone else of any importance, though he probably goes to Deauville for the summer. Actually, Death must live fairly near my own house. This is much the best section of London, and you could hardly expect a person of Death's importance to live anywhere else. When I stop to think of it, it's really rather strange that we haven't met before now, on the street."

Most of her friends agreed with her, but the poet, whose name was David Lorimond, cried out, "No, my lady, you are wrong! Death lives among the poor. Death lives in the foulest, darkest alleys of this city, in some vile, rat-ridden hovel that smells of—" He stopped here, partly because Lady Neville had indicated her displeasure, and partly because he had never been inside such a hut or thought of wondering what it smelled like. "Death lives among the poor," he went on, "and comes to visit them every day, for he is their only friend."

Lady Neville answered him as coldly as she had spoken to the young lord. "He may be forced to deal with them, David, but I hardly think that he seeks them out as companions. I am certain that it is as difficult for him to think of the poor as individuals as it is for me. Death is, after all, a nobleman."

There was no real argument among the lords and ladies that Death lived in a neighborhood at least as good as their own, but none of them seemed to know the name of Death's street, and no one had ever seen Death's house.

"If there were a war," Captain Compson said, "Death would be easy to find. I have seen him, you know, even spoken to him, but he has never answered me."

"Quite proper," said Lady Neville. "Death must always speak first. You are not a very correct person, Captain," but she smiled at him, as all women did.

Then an idea came to her. "My hairdresser has a sick child, I understand," she said. "He was telling me about it yesterday, sounding most dull and hopeless. I will send for him and give him the invitation, and he in his turn can give it to Death when he comes to take the brat. A bit unconventional, I admit, but I see no other way."

"If he refuses?" asked a lord who had just been married.

"Why should he?" asked Lady Neville.

Again it was the poet who exclaimed amidst the general approval that it was a cruel and wicked thing to do. But he fell silent when Lady Neville innocently asked him, "Why, David?"

So the hairdresser was sent for, and when he stood before them, smiling nervously and twisting his hands to be in the same room with so many great lords, Lady Neville told him the errand that was required of him. And she was right, as she usually was, for he made no refusal. He merely took the invitation in his hand and asked to be excused.

He did not return for two days, but when he did, he presented himself to Lady Neville without being sent for and handed her a small white envelope. Saying, "How very nice of you, thank you very much," she opened it and found therein a plain calling card with nothing on it except these words:

Death will be pleased to attend Lady Neville's ball.

"Death gave you this?" she asked the hairdresser eagerly. "What was he like?" But the hairdresser stood still, looking past her, and said nothing, and she, not really waiting for an answer, called a dozen servants to her and told them to run and summon her friends. As she paced up and down the room waiting for them, she asked again, "What is Death like?" The hairdresser did not reply.

When her friends came they passed the little card excitedly from hand to hand, until it had gotten quite smudged and bent from their fingers. But they all admitted that, beyond its message, there was nothing particularly unusual about it. It was neither hot nor cold to the touch, and what little odor clung to it was rather pleasant. Everyone said that it was a very familiar smell, but no one could give it a name. The poet said that it reminded him of lilacs, but not exactly.

It was Captain Compson, however, who pointed out the one thing that no one else had noticed. "Look at the handwriting itself," he said. "Have you ever seen anything more graceful? The letters seem as light as birds. I think we have wasted our time speaking of Death as His This and His That. A woman wrote this note."

Then there was an uproar and a great babble, and the card had to be handed around again so that everyone could exclaim, "Yes, by God!" over it. The voice of the poet rose out of the hubbub, saying, "It is very natural, when you come to think of it. After all, the French say *la mort*. Lady Death. I should much prefer Death to be a woman."

"Death rides a great black horse," said Captain Compson firmly, "and wears armor of the same color. Death is very tall, taller than anyone. It was no woman I saw on the battlefield, striking right and left like any soldier. Perhaps the hairdresser wrote it himself, or the hairdresser's wife."

But the hairdresser refused to speak, though they gathered around him and begged him to say who had given him the note. At first they promised him all sorts of rewards, and later they threatened to do terrible things to him. "Did you write this card?" he was asked, and "Who wrote it, then? Was it a living woman? Was it really Death? Did Death say anything to you? How did you know it was Death? Is Death a woman? Are you trying to make fools of us all?"

Not a word from the hairdresser, not one word, and finally Lady Neville called her servants to have him whipped and thrown into the street. He did not look at her as they took him away, or utter a sound.

Silencing her friends with a wave of her hand, Lady Neville said, "The ball will take place two weeks from tonight. Let Death come as Death pleases, whether as a man or woman or strange, sexless creature." She smiled calmly. "Death may well be a woman," she said. "I am less certain of Death's form than I was, but I am also less frightened of Death. I am too old to be afraid of anything that can use a quill pen to write me a letter. Go home now, and as you make your preparations for the ball, see that you speak of it to your servants, that they may spread the news all over London. Let it be known that on this one night, no one in the world will die, for Death will be dancing at Lady Neville's ball."

For the next two weeks Lady Neville's great house shook and groaned and creaked like an old tree in a gale as the servants hammered and scrubbed, polished and painted, making ready for the ball. Lady Neville had always been very proud of her house, but as the ball drew near she began to be afraid that it would not be nearly grand enough for Death, who was surely accustomed to visiting in the homes of richer, mightier people than herself. Fearing the scorn of Death, she worked night and day supervising her servants' preparations. Curtains and carpets had to be cleaned, goldwork and silverware polished until they gleamed by themselves in the dark. The grand staircase that rushed down into the ballroom like a waterfall was washed and rubbed so often that it was almost impossible to walk on it without slipping. As for the ballroom itself, it took thirty-two servants working at once to clean it properly, not counting those who were polishing the glass chandelier that was taller than a man and the fourteen smaller lamps. And when they were done she made them do it all over, not because she saw any dust or dirt anywhere, but because she was sure that Death would.

As for herself, she chose her finest gown and saw to the laundering personally. She called in another hairdresser and had him put up her hair in the style of an earlier time, wanting to show Death that she was a woman who enjoyed her age and did not find it necessary to ape the young and beautiful. All the day of the ball she sat before her mirror, not making herself up much beyond the normal touches of rouge and eye shadow and fine rice powder, but staring at the lean old face she had been born with, wondering how it would appear to Death. Her steward asked her to approve his wine selection, but she sent him away and stayed at her mirror until it was time to dress and go downstairs to meet her guests.

Everyone arrived early. When she looked out of a window, Lady Neville saw that the driveway of her home was choked with carriages and fine horses. "It all looks like a funeral procession," she said. The footman cried the names of her guests to the echoing ballroom. "Captain Henry Compson, His Majesty's Household Cavalry! Mr. David Lorimond! Lord and Lady Torrance!!" (They were the youngest couple there, having been married only three months before.) "Sir Roger Harbison! The Contessa della Candini!" Lady Neville permitted them all to kiss her hand and made them welcome.

She had engaged the finest musicians she could find to play for the dancing, but though they began to play at her signal, not one couple stepped out on the floor, nor did one young lord approach her to request the honor of the first dance, as was proper. They milled together, shining and murmuring, their eyes fixed on the ballroom door. Every time they heard a carriage clatter up the driveway, they seemed to flinch a little and draw closer together; every time the footman announced the arrival of another guest, they all sighed softly and swayed a little on their feet with relief.

"Why did they come to my party if they were afraid?" Lady Neville muttered scornfully to herself. "I am not afraid of meeting Death. I ask only that Death may be impressed by the magnificence of my house and the flavor of my wines. I will die sooner than anyone here, but I am not afraid."

Certain that Death would not arrive until midnight, she moved among her guests, attempting to calm them not with her words, which she knew they would not hear, but with the tone of her voice, as if they were so many frightened horses. But little by little, she herself was infected by their nervousness: whenever she sat down, she stood up again immediately, she tasted a dozen glasses of wine without finishing any of them, and she glanced constantly at her jeweled watch, at first wanting to hurry the midnight along and end the waiting, later scratching at the watch face with her forefinger, as if she would push away the night and drag the sun backward into the sky. When midnight came, she was standing with the rest of them, breathing through her mouth, shifting from foot to foot, listening for the sound of carriage wheels turning in gravel.

When the clock began to strike midnight, everyone, even Lady Neville and the brave Captain Compson, gave one startled little cry and then was silent again, listening to the tolling of the clock. The smaller clocks upstairs began to chime. Lady Neville's ears hurt. She caught sight of herself in the ballroom mirror, one gray face turned up toward the ceiling as if she were gasping for air, and she thought, "Death will be a woman, a hideous, filthy old crone as tall and strong as a man. And the most terrible thing of all will be that she will have my face." All the clocks stopped striking, and Lady Neville closed her eyes.

She opened them again only when she heard the whispering around her take on a different tone, one in which fear was fused with relief and a certain chagrin. For no new carriage stood in the driveway. Death had not come.

The noise grew slowly louder; here and there people were beginning to laugh. Near her, Lady Neville heard young Lord Torrance say to his wife, "There, my darling, I told you there was nothing to be afraid of. It was all a joke."

"I am ruined," Lady Neville thought. The laughter was increasing; it pounded against her ears in strokes, like the chiming of the clocks. "I wanted to give a ball so grand that those who were not invited would be shamed in front of the whole city, and this is my reward. I am ruined, and I deserve it."

Turning to the poet Lorimond, she said, "Dance with me, David." She signaled to the musicians, who at once began to play. When Lorimond hesitated, she said, "Dance with me now. You will not have another chance. I shall never give a party again."

Lorimond bowed and led her onto the dance floor. The guests parted for them, and the laughter died down for a moment, but Lady Neville knew that it would soon begin again. "Well, let them laugh," she thought. "I did not fear Death when they were all trembling. Why should I fear their laughter?" But she could feel a stinging at the thin lids of her eyes, and she closed them once more as she began to dance with Lorimond.

And then, quite suddenly, all the carriage horses outside the house whinnied loudly, just once, as the guests had cried out at midnight. There were a great many horses, and their one salute was so loud that everyone in the room became instantly silent. They heard the heavy steps of the footman as he went to open the door, and they shivered as if they felt the cool breeze that drifted into the house. Then they heard a light voice saying, "Am I late? Oh, I am so sorry. The horses were tired," and before the footman could reenter to announce her, a lovely young girl in a white dress stepped gracefully into the ballroom doorway and stood there smiling.

She could not have been more than nineteen. Her hair was yellow, and she wore it long. It fell thickly upon her bare shoulders that gleamed warmly through it, two limestone islands rising out of a dark golden sea. Her face was wide at the forehead and cheekbones, and narrow at the chin, and her skin was so clear that many of the ladies there—Lady Neville among them—touched their own faces wonderingly, and instantly drew their hands away as though their own skin had rasped their fingers. Her mouth was pale, where the mouths of other women were red and orange and even purple. Her eyebrows, thicker and straighter than was fashionable, met over dark, calm eyes that were set so deep in her young face and were so black, so uncompromisingly black, that the middle-aged wife of a middle-aged lord murmured, "Touch of a gypsy there, I think."

"Or something worse," suggested her husband's mistress.

"Be silent!" Lady Neville spoke louder than she had intended, and the girl turned to look at her. She smiled, and Lady Neville tried to smile back, but her mouth seemed very stiff. "Welcome," she said. "Welcome, my Lady Death."

A sigh rustled among the lords and ladies as the girl took the old woman's hand and curtsied to her, sinking and rising in one motion, like a wave. "You are Lady Neville," she said. "Thank you so much for inviting me." Her accent was as faint and almost familiar as her perfume.

"Please excuse me for being late," she said earnestly. "I had to come from a long way off, and my horses are so tired."

"The groom will rub them down," Lady Neville said, "and feed them if you wish."

"Oh, no," the girl answered quickly. "Tell him not to go near the horses, please. They are not really horses, and they are very fierce."

She accepted a glass of wine from a servant and drank it slowly, sighing softly and contentedly. "What good wine," she said. "And what a beautiful house you have."

"Thank you," said Lady Neville. Without turning, she could feel every woman in the room envying her, sensing it as she could always sense the approach of rain.

"I wish I lived here," Death said in her low, sweet voice. "I will, one day."

Then, seeing Lady Neville become as still as if she had turned to ice, she put her hand on the old woman's arm and said, "Oh, I'm sorry, I'm so sorry. I am so cruel, but I never mean to be. Please forgive me, Lady Neville. I am not used to company, and I do such stupid things. Please forgive me."

Her hand felt as light and warm on Lady Neville's arm as the hand of any other young girl, and her eyes were so appealing that Lady Neville replied, "You have said nothing wrong. While you are my guest, my house is yours."

"Thank you," said Death, and she smiled so radiantly that the musicians began to play quite by themselves, and with no sign from Lady Neville. She would have stopped them, but Death said, "Oh, what lovely music! Let them play, please."

So the musicians played a gavotte, and Death, unabashed by eyes that stared at her in greedy terror, sang softly to herself without words, lifted her white gown slightly with both hands, and made hesitant little patting steps with her small feet. "I have not danced in so long," she said wistfully. "I'm quite sure I've forgotten how."

She was shy; she would not look up to embarrass the young lords, not one of whom stepped forward to dance with her. Lady Neville felt a flood of shame and sympathy, emotions she thought had withered in her years ago. "Is she to be humiliated at my own ball?" she thought angrily. "It is because she is Death; if she were the ugliest, foulest hag in all the world, they would clamor to dance with her, because they are gentlemen and they know what is expected of them. But no gentleman will dance with Death, no matter how beautiful she is." She glanced sideways at David Lorimond. His face was flushed, and his hands were clasped so tightly as he stared at Death that his fingers were like glass, but when Lady Neville touched his arm, he did not turn, and when she hissed, "David!" he pretended not to hear her.

Then Captain Compson, gray-haired and handsome in his uniform, stepped out of the crowd and bowed gracefully before Death. "If I may have the honor," he said.

"Captain Compson," said Death, smiling. She put her arm in his. "I was hoping you would ask me."

This brought a frown from the older women, who did not consider it a proper thing to say, but for that Death cared not a rap. Captain Compson led her to the center of the floor, and there they danced. Death was curiously graceless at first—she was too anxious to please her partner, and she seemed to have no notion of rhythm. The Captain himself moved with the mixture of dignity and humor that Lady Neville had never seen in another man, but when he looked at her over Death's shoulder, she saw something that no one else appeared to notice: that his face and eyes were immobile with fear, and that, though he offered Death his hand with easy gallantry, he flinched slightly when she took it. And yet he danced as well as Lady Neville had ever seen him.

"Ah, that's what comes of having a reputation to maintain," she thought. "Captain Compson, too, must do what is expected of him. I hope someone else will dance with her soon."

But no one did. Little by little, other couples overcame their fear and slipped hurriedly out on the floor when Death was looking the other way, but nobody sought to relieve Captain Compson of his beautiful partner. They danced every dance together. In time, some of the men present began to look at her with more appreciation than terror, but when she returned their glances and smiled at them, they clung to their partners as if a cold wind were threatening to blow them away.

One of the few who stared at her frankly and with pleasure was young Lord Torrance, who usually danced only with his wife. Another was the poet Lorimond. Dancing with Lady Neville, he remarked to her, "If she is Death, what do these frightened fools think they are? If she is ugliness, what must they be? I hate their fear. It is obscene."

Death and the Captain danced past them at that moment, and they heard him say to her, "But if that was truly you that I saw in the battle, how can you have changed so? How can you have become so lovely?"

Death's laughter was gay and soft. "I thought that among so many beautiful people, it might be better to be beautiful. I was afraid of frightening everyone and spoiling the party."

"They all thought she would be ugly," said Lorimond to Lady Neville. "I—I knew she would be beautiful."

"Then why have you not danced with her?" Lady Neville asked him. "Are you also afraid?"

"No, oh, no," the poet answered quickly and passionately. "I will ask her to dance very soon. I only want to look at her a little longer."

The musicians played on and on. The dancing wore away the night as slowly as falling water wears down a cliff. It seemed to Lady Neville that no night had ever endured longer, and yet she was neither tired nor bored. She danced with every man there, except with Lord Torrance, who was dancing with his wife as if they had just met that night, and, of course, with Captain Compson. Once he lifted his hand and touched Death's golden hair very lightly. He was a striking man still, a fit partner for so beautiful a girl, but Lady Neville looked at his face each time she passed him and realized that he was older than anyone knew.

Death herself seemed younger than the youngest there. No woman at the ball danced better than she now, though it was hard for Lady Neville to remember at what point her awkwardness had given way to the liquid sweetness of her movements. She smiled and called to everyone who caught her eye—and she knew them all by name; she sang constantly, making up words to the dance tunes, nonsense words, sounds without meaning, and yet everyone strained to hear her soft voice without knowing why. And when, during a waltz, she caught up the trailing end of her gown to give her more freedom as she danced, she seemed to Lady Neville to move like a little sailing boat over a still evening sea.

Lady Neville heard Lady Torrance arguing angrily with the Contessa della Candini. "I don't care if she is Death, she's no older than I am, she can't be!"

"Nonsense," said the Contessa, who could not afford to be generous to any other woman. "She is twenty-eight, thirty, if she is an hour. And that dress, that bridal gown she wears—really!"

"Vile," said the woman who had come to the ball as Captain Compson's freely acknowledged mistress. "Tasteless. But one should know better than to expect taste from Death, I suppose." Lady Torrance looked as if she were going to cry.

"They are jealous of Death," Lady Neville said to herself. "How strange. I am not jealous of her, not in the least. And I do not fear her at all." She was very proud of herself.

Then, as unbiddenly as they had begun to play, the musicians stopped. They began to put away their instruments. In the sudden shrill silence, Death pulled away from Captain Compson and ran to look out of one of the tall windows, pushing the curtains apart with both hands. "Look!" she said, with her back turned to them. "Come and look. The night is almost gone."

The summer sky was still dark, and the eastern horizon was only a shade lighter than the rest of the sky, but the stars had vanished and the trees near the house were gradually becoming distinct. Death pressed her face against the window and said, so softly that the other guests could barely hear her, "I must go now."

"No," Lady Neville said, and was not immediately aware that she had spoken. "You must stay a while longer. The ball was in your honor. Please stay."

Death held out both hands to her, and Lady Neville came and took them in her own. "I've had a wonderful time," she said gently. "You cannot possibly imagine how it feels to be actually invited to such a ball as this, because you have given them and gone to them all your life. One is like another to you, but for me it is different. Do you understand me?" Lady Neville nodded silently. "I will remember this night forever," Death said.

"Stay," Captain Compson said. "Stay just a little longer." He put his hand on Death's shoulder, and she smiled and leaned her cheek against it. "Dear Captain Compson," she said. "My first real gallant. Aren't you tired of me yet?"

"Never," he said. "Please stay."

"Stay," said Lorimond, and he, too, seemed about to touch her. "Stay. I want to talk to you. I want to look at you. I will dance with you if you stay."

"How many followers I have," Death said in wonder. She stretched her hand toward Lorimond, but he drew back from her and then flushed in shame. "A soldier and a poet. How wonderful it is to be a woman. But why did you not speak to me earlier, both of you? Now it is too late. I must go."

"Please, stay," Lady Torrance whispered. She held on to her husband's hand for courage. "We think you are so beautiful, both of us do."

"Gracious Lady Torrance," the girl said kindly. She turned back to the window, touched it lightly, and it flew open. The cool dawn air rushed into the ballroom, fresh with rain but already smelling faintly of the London streets over which it had passed. They heard birdsong and the strange, harsh nickering of Death's horses.

"Do you want me to stay?" she asked. The question was put, not to Lady Neville, nor to Captain Compson, nor to any of her admirers, but to the Contessa della Candini, who stood well back from them all, hugging her flowers to herself and humming a little song of irritation. She did not in the least want Death to stay, but she was afraid that all the other women would think her envious of Death's beauty, and so she said, "Yes. Of course I do."

"Ah," said Death. She was almost whispering. "And you," she said to another woman, "do you want me to stay? Do you want me to be one of your friends?"

"Yes," said the woman, "because you are beautiful and a true lady."

"And you," said Death to a man, "and you," to a woman, "and you," to another man, "do you want me to stay?" And they all answered, "Yes, Lady Death, we do."

"Do you want me, then?" she cried at last to all of them. "Do you want me to live among you and to be one of you, and not to be Death anymore? Do you want me to visit your houses and come to all your parties? Do you want me to ride horses like yours instead of mine, do you want me to wear the kind of dresses you wear, and say the things you would say? Would one of you marry me, and would the rest of you dance at my wedding and bring gifts to my children? Is that what you want?"

"Yes," said Lady Neville. "Stay here, stay with me, stay with us."

Death's voice, without becoming louder, had become clearer and older—too old a voice, thought Lady Neville, for such a young girl. "Be sure," said Death. "Be sure of what you want, be very sure. Do all of you want me to stay? For if one of you says to me, no, go away, then I must leave at once and never return. Be sure. Do you all want me?"

And everyone there cried with one voice, "Yes! Yes, you must stay with us. You are so beautiful that we cannot let you go."

"We are tired," said Captain Compson.

"We are blind," said Lorimond, adding, "especially to poetry."

"We are afraid," said Lord Torrance quietly, and his wife took his arm and said, "Both of us."

"We are dull and stupid," said Lady Neville, "and growing old uselessly. Stay with us, Lady Death."

And then Death smiled sweetly and radiantly and took a step forward, and it was as though she had come down among them from a very great height. "Very well," she said. "I will stay with you. I will be Death no more. I will be a woman."

The room was full of a deep sigh, although no one was seen to open his mouth. No one moved, for the golden-haired girl was Death still, and her horses still whinnied for her outside. No one could look at her for long, although she was the most beautiful girl anyone there had ever seen.

"There is a price to pay," she said. "There is always a price. Some one of you must become Death in my place, for there must forever be Death in the world. Will anyone choose? Will anyone here become Death of his own free will? For only thus can I become a human girl."

No one spoke, no one spoke at all. But they backed slowly away from her, like waves slipping back down a beach to the sea when you try to catch them. The Contessa della Candini and her friends would have crept quietly out the door, but Death smiled at them and they stood where they were. Captain Compson opened his mouth as though he were going to declare himself, but he said nothing. Lady Neville did not move.

"No one," said Death. She touched a flower with her finger, and it seemed to crouch and flex itself like a pleased cat. "No one at all," she said. "Then I must choose, and that is just, for that is the way I became Death. I never wanted to be Death, and it makes me so happy that you want me to become one of yourselves. I have searched a long time for people who would want me. Now I have only to choose someone to replace me and it is done. I will choose very carefully."

"Oh, we were so foolish," Lady Neville said to herself. "We were so foolish." But she said nothing aloud; she merely clasped her hands and stared at the young girl, thinking vaguely that if she had had a daughter, she would have been greatly pleased if she had resembled the Lady Death.

"The Contessa della Candini," said Death thoughtfully, and that woman gave a little squeak of terror because she could not draw her breath for a scream. But Death laughed and said, "No, that would be silly." She said nothing more, but for a long time after that the Contessa burned with humiliation at not having been chosen to be Death.

"Not Captain Compson," murmured Death, "because he is too kind to become Death, and because it would be too cruel to him. He wants to die so badly." The expression on the Captain's face did not change, but his hands began to tremble.

"Not Lorimond," the girl continued, "because he knows so little about life, and because I like him." The poet flushed, and turned white, and then turned pink again. He made as if to kneel clumsily on one knee, but instead he pulled himself erect and stood as much like Captain Compson as he could.

"Not the Torrances," said Death, "never Lord and Lady Torrance, for both of them care too much about another person to take any pride in being Death." But she hesitated over Lady Torrance for a while, staring at her out of her dark and curious eyes. "I was your age when I became Death," she said at last. "I wonder what it will be like to be your age again. I have been Death for so long." Lady Torrance shivered and did not speak.

And at last Death said quietly, "Lady Neville."

"I am here," Lady Neville answered.

"I think you are the only one," said Death. "I choose you, Lady Neville."

Again Lady Neville heard every guest sigh softly, and although her back was to them all, she knew that they were sighing in relief that neither themselves nor anyone dear to themselves had been chosen. Lady Torrance gave a little cry of protest, but Lady Neville knew that she would have cried out at whatever choice Death made. She heard herself say calmly, "I am honored. But was there no one more worthy than I?"

"Not one," said Death. "There is no one quite so weary of being human, no one who knows better how meaningless it is to be alive. And there is no one else here with the power to treat life"—and she smiled sweetly and cruelly—"the life of your hairdresser's child, for instance, as the meaningless thing it is. Death has a heart, but it is forever an empty heart, and I think, Lady Neville, that your heart is like a dry riverbed, like a seashell. You will be very content as Death, more so than I, for I was very young when I became Death."

She came toward Lady Neville, light and swaying, her deep eyes wide and full of the light of the red morning sun that was beginning to rise. The guests at the ball moved back from her, although she did not look at them, but Lady Neville clenched her hands tightly and watched Death come toward her with little dancing steps. "We must kiss each other," Death said. "That is the way I became Death." She shook her head delightedly, so that her soft hair swirled about her shoulders. "Quickly, quickly," she said. "Oh, I cannot wait to be human again."

"You may not like it," Lady Neville said. She felt very calm, though she could hear her old heart pounding in her chest and feel it in the tips of her fingers. "You may not like it after a while," she said.

"Perhaps not." Death's smile was very close to her now. "I will not be as beautiful as I am, and perhaps people will not love me as much as they do now. But I will be human for a while, and at last I will die. I have done my penance."

"What penance?" the old woman asked the beautiful girl. "What was it you did? Why did you become Death?"

"I don't remember," said the Lady Death. "And you, too, will forget in time." She was smaller than Lady Neville, and so much younger. In her white dress she might have been the daughter that Lady Neville had never had, who would have been with her always and held her mother's head lightly in the crook of her arm when she felt old and sad. Now she lifted her head to kiss Lady Neville's cheek, and as she did so, she whispered in her ear, "You will still be beautiful when I am ugly. Be kind to me then."

Behind Lady Neville the handsome gentlemen and ladies murmured and sighed, fluttering like moths in their evening dress, in their elegant gowns. "I promise," she said, and then she pursed her dry lips to kiss the soft, sweet-smelling cheek of the young Lady Death.

Lila the Werewolf

"Lila the Werewolf" is the second of my Joe Farrell adventures, and one of only two I've ever written—forty years apart!—about werewolves. Which is odd, when you think about it, as fascinated as I've always been with shapeshifters. The producer I sold it to managed to sell it simultaneously to two other producers before his death. I've never begrudged him the scam—he bought me great lunches and told me wonderful jokes in Yiddish, which I almost understood.

Lila Braun had been living with Farrell for three weeks before he found out she was a werewolf. They had met at a party when the moon was a few nights past the full, and by the time it had withered to the shape of a lemon, Lila had moved her suitcase, her guitar, and her Ewan MacColl records two blocks north and four blocks west to Farrell's apartment on Ninety-eighth Street. Girls sometimes happened to Farrell like that.

One evening, Lila wasn't in when Farrell came home from work at the bookstore. She had left a note on the table, under a can of tuna fish. The note said that she had gone up to the Bronx to have dinner with her mother, and would probably be spending the night there. The coleslaw in the refrigerator should be finished before it went bad.

Farrell ate the tuna fish and gave the coleslaw to Grunewald. Grunewald was a half-grown Russian wolfhound, the color of sour milk. He looked like a goat, and had no outside interests except shoes. Farrell was taking care of him for a girl who was away in Europe for the summer. She sent Grunewald a tape recording of her voice every week.

Farrell went to a movie with a friend, and to the West End afterward for beer. Then he walked home alone under the full moon, which was red and yellow. He reheated the morning coffee, played a record, read through a week-old "News of the Week in Review" section of the Sunday *Times,* and finally took Grunewald up to the roof for the night, as he always did. The dog had been accustomed to sleeping in the same bed with his mistress, and the point was not negotiable. Grunewald mooed and scrabbled and butted all the way, but Farrell pushed him out among the looming chimneys and ventilators and slammed the door. Then he came back downstairs and went to bed.

He slept very badly. Grunewald's baying woke him twice; and there was something else that brought him half out of bed, thirsty and lonely, with his sinuses full and the night swaying like a curtain as the figures of his dream scurried offstage. Grunewald seemed to have gone off the air—perhaps it was the silence that had awakened him. Whatever the reason, he never really got back to sleep.

He was lying on his back, watching a chair with his clothes on it becoming a chair again, when the wolf came in through the open window. It landed lightly in the middle of the room and stood there for a moment, breathing quickly, with its ears back. There was blood on the wolf's teeth and tongue, and blood on its chest.

Farrell, whose true gift was for acceptance, especially in the morning, accepted the idea that there was a wolf in his bedroom and lay quite still, closing his eyes as the grim, black-lipped head swung towards him. Having once worked at a zoo, he was able to recognize the beast as a Central European subspecies: smaller and lighter-boned than the northern timber wolf variety, lacking the thick, ruffy mane at the shoulders, and having a more pointed nose and ears. His own pedantry always delighted him, even at the worst moments.

Blunt claws clicking on the linoleum, then silent on the throw rug by the bed. Something warm and slow splashed down on his shoulder, but he never moved. The wild smell of the wolf was over him, and that did frighten him at last to be in the same room with that smell and the

Miro prints on the walls. Then he felt the sunlight on his eyelids, and at the same moment he heard the wolf moan softly and deeply.

The sound was not repeated, but the breath on his face was suddenly sweet and smoky, dizzyingly familiar after the other. He opened his eyes and saw Lila. She was sitting naked on the edge of the bed, smiling, with her hair down.

"Hello, baby," she said. "Move over, baby. I came home."

Farrell's gift was for acceptance. He was perfectly willing to believe that he had dreamed the wolf; to believe Lila's story of boiled chicken and bitter arguments and sleeplessness on Tremont Avenue; and to forget that her first caress had been to bite him on the shoulder, hard enough so that the blood crusting there as he got up and made breakfast might very well be his own. But then he left the coffee perking and went up to the roof to get Grunewald. He found the dog sprawled in a grove of TV antennas, looking more like a goat than ever, with his throat torn out. Farrell had never actually seen an animal with its throat torn out.

The coffeepot was still chuckling when he came back into the apartment, which struck him as very odd. You could have either werewolves or Pyrex nine-cup percolators in the world, but not both, surely. He told Lila, watching her face. She was a small girl, not really pretty, but with good eyes and a lovely mouth, and with a curious sullen gracefulness that had been the first thing to speak to Farrell at the party. When he told her how Grunewald had looked, she shivered all over, once.

"Ugh!" she said, wrinkling her lips back from her neat white teeth. "Oh baby, how awful. Poor Grunewald. Oh, poor Barbara." Barbara was Grunewald's owner.

"Yeah," Farrell said. "Poor Barbara, making her little tapes in Saint-Tropez." He could not look away from Lila's face.

She said, "Wild dogs. Not really wild, I mean, but with owners. You hear about it sometimes, how a pack of them get together and attack children and things, running through the streets. Then they go home and eat their Dog Yummies. The scary thing is that they probably live right around here. Everybody on the block seems to have a dog. God, that's scary. Poor Grunewald."

"They didn't tear him up much," Farrell said. "It must have been just for the fun of it. And the blood. I didn't know dogs killed for the blood. He didn't have any blood left."

The tip of Lila's tongue appeared between her lips, in the unknowing reflex of a fondled cat. As evidence, it wouldn't have stood up even in old Salem; but Farrell knew the truth then, beyond laziness or rationalization, and went on buttering toast for Lila. Farrell had nothing against werewolves, and he had never liked Grunewald.

He told his friend Ben Kassoy about Lila when they met in the Automat for lunch. He had to shout it over the clicking and rattling all around them, but the people sitting six inches away on either hand never looked up. New Yorkers never eavesdrop. They hear only what they simply cannot help hearing.

Ben said, "I told you about Bronx girls. You better come stay at my place for a few days."

Farrell shook his head. "No, that's silly. I mean, it's only Lila. If she were going to hurt me, she could have done it last night. Besides, it won't happen again for a month. There has to be a full moon."

His friend stared at him. "So what? What's that got to do with anything? You going to go on home as though nothing had happened?"

"Not as though nothing had happened," Farrell said lamely. "The thing is, it's still only Lila, not Lon Chaney or somebody. Look, she goes to her psychiatrist three afternoons a week, and she's got her guitar lesson one night a week, and her pottery class one night, and she cooks eggplant maybe twice a week. She calls her mother every Friday night, and one night a month she turns into a wolf. You see what I'm getting at? It's still Lila, whatever she does, and I just can't get terribly shook about it. A little bit, sure, because what the hell. But I don't know. Anyway, there's no mad rush about it. I'll talk to her when the thing comes up in conversation, just naturally. It's okay."

Ben said, "God damn. You see why nobody has any respect for liberals anymore? Farrell, I know you. You're just scared of hurting her feelings."

"Well, it's that too," Farrell agreed, a little embarrassed. "I hate confrontations. If I break up with her now, she'll think I'm doing it because she's a werewolf. It's awkward, it feels nasty and middle-class. I should have broken up with her the first time I met her mother, or the second time she served the eggplant. Her mother, boy, there's the real werewolf, there's somebody I'd wear wolfsbane against, that woman. Damn, I wish I hadn't found out. I don't think I've ever found out anything about people that I was the better for knowing."

Ben walked all the way back to the bookstore with him, arguing. It touched Farrell, because Ben hated to walk. Before they parted, Ben suggested, "At least you could try some of that stuff you were talking about, the wolfsbane. There's garlic, too—you put some in a little bag and wear it around your neck. Don't laugh, man. If there's such a thing as werewolves, the other stuff must be real, too. Cold iron, silver, oak, running water—"

"I'm not laughing at you," Farrell said, but he was still grinning. "Lila's shrink says she has a rejection thing, very deep-seated, take us years to break through all that scar tissue. Now if I start walking around wearing amulets and mumbling in Latin every time she looks at me, who knows how far it'll set her back? Listen, I've done some things I'm not proud of, but I don't want to mess with anyone's analysis. That's the sin against God." He sighed and slapped Ben lightly on the arm. "Don't worry about it. We'll work it out, I'll talk to her."

But between that night and the next full moon, he found no good, casual way of bringing the subject up. Admittedly, he did not try as hard as he might have: it was true that he feared confrontations more than he feared werewolves, and he would have found it almost as difficult to talk to Lila about her guitar playing, or her pots, or the political arguments she got into at parties. "The thing is," he said to Ben, "it's sort of one more little weakness not to take advantage of. In a way."

They made love often that month. The smell of Lila flowered in the bedroom, where the smell of the wolf still lingered almost visibly, and both of them were wild, heavy zoo smells, warm and raw and fearful, the sweeter for being savage. Farrell held Lila in his arms and knew what she was, and he was always frightened; but he would not have let her go if she had turned into a wolf again as he held her. It was a relief to peer at her while she slept and see how stubby and childish her fingernails were, or that the skin around her mouth was rashy because she had been snacking on chocolate. She loved secret sweets, but they always betrayed her.

It's only Lila after all, he would think as he drowsed off. Her mother used to hide the candy, but Lila always found it. Now she's a big girl, neither married nor in graduate school, but living in sin with an Irish musician, and she can have all the candy she wants. What kind of a werewolf is that? Poor Lila, practicing "Who Killed Davey Moore? Why Did He Die? . . ."

The note said that she would be working late at the magazine, on layout, and might have to be there all night. Farrell put on about four feet of Telemann laced with Django Reinhardt, took down *The Golden Bough*, and settled into a chair by the window. The moon shone in at him, bright and thin and sharp as the lid of a tin can, and it did not seem to move at all as he dozed and woke.

Lila's mother called several times during the night, which was interesting. Lila still picked up her mail and most messages at her old apartment, and her two roommates covered for her when necessary, but Farrell was absolutely certain that her mother knew she was living with him. Farrell was an expert on mothers. Mrs. Braun called him Joe each time she called and that made him wonder, for he knew she hated him. Does she suspect that we share a secret? Ah, poor Lila.

The last time the telephone woke him, it was still dark in the room, but the traffic lights no longer glittered through rings of mist, and the cars made a different sound on the warming pavement. A man was saying clearly in the street, "Well, *I'd* shoot'm. *I'd* shoot'm." Farrell let the telephone ring ten times before he picked it up.

"Let me talk to Lila," Mrs. Braun said.

"She isn't here." What if the sun catches her, what if she turns back to herself in front of a cop, or a bus driver, or a couple of nuns going to early Mass? "Lila isn't here, Mrs. Braun."

"I have reason to believe that's not true." The fretful, muscular voice had dropped all pretense of warmth. "I want to talk to Lila."

Farrell was suddenly dry-mouthed and shivering with fury. It was her choice of words that did it. "Well, I have reason to believe you're a suffocating old bitch and a bourgeois Stalinist. How do you like them apples, Mrs. B?" As though his anger had summoned her, the wolf was standing two feet away from him. Her coat was dark and lank with sweat, and yellow saliva was mixed with the blood that strung from her jaws. She looked at Farrell and growled far away in her throat.

"Just a minute," he said. He covered the receiver with his palm. "It's for you," he said to the wolf. "It's your mother." The wolf made a pitiful sound, almost inaudible, and scuffed at the floor. She was plainly exhausted. Mrs. Braun pinged in Farrell's ear like a bug against a lighted window. "What, what? Hello, what is this? Listen, you put Lila on the phone right now. Hello? I want to talk to Lila. I know she's there."

Farrell hung up just as the sun touched a corner of the window. The wolf became Lila. As before, she only made one sound. The phone rang again, and she picked it up without a glance at Farrell. "Bernice?" Lila always called her mother by her first name. "Yes—no, no—yeah, I'm fine. I'm all right, I just forgot to call. No, I'm all right, will you listen? Bernice, there's no law that says you have to get hysterical. Yes, you are." She dropped down on the bed, groping under her pillow for cigarettes. Farrell got up and began to make coffee.

"Well, there was a little trouble," Lila was saying. "See, I went to the zoo, because I couldn't find—Bernice, I know, I *know*, but that was, what, three months ago. The thing is, I didn't think they'd have their horns so soon. Bernice, I had to, that's all. There'd only been a couple of cats and a—well, sure they chased me, but I—well, Momma, Bernice, what did you want me to do? Just what did you want me to do? You're always so dramatic—why do I shout? I shout because I can't get you to listen to me any other way. You remember what Dr. Schechtman said—what? No, I told you, I just forgot to call. No, that is the reason, that's the real and only reason. Well, whose fault is that? What? Oh, Bernice. Jesus Christ, Bernice. All right, *how* is it Dad's fault?"

She didn't want the coffee, or any breakfast, but she sat at the table in his bathrobe and drank milk greedily. It was the first time he had ever seen her drink milk. Her face was sandy-pale, and her eyes were red. Talking to her mother left her looking as though she had actually gone ten rounds with the woman. Farrell asked, "How long has it been happening?"

"Nine years," Lila said. "Since I hit puberty. First day, cramps; the second day, this. My introduction to womanhood." She snickered and spilled her milk. "I want some more," she said. "Got to get rid of that taste."

"Who knows about it?" he asked. "Pat and Janet?" They were the two girls she had been rooming with.

"God, no. I'd never tell them. I've never told a girl. Bernice knows, of course, and Dr. Schechtman—he's my head doctor. And you now. That's all." Farrell waited. She was a bad liar, and only did it to heighten the effect of the truth. "Well, there was Mickey," she said. "The guy I told you about the first night, you remember? It doesn't matter. He's an acidhead in Vancouver, of all places. He'll never tell anybody."

He thought: I wonder if any girl has ever talked about me in that sort of voice. I doubt it, offhand. Lila said, "It wasn't too hard to keep it a secret. I missed a lot of things. Like I never could go to the riding camp, and I still want to. And the senior play, when I was in high school. They picked me to play the girl in *Liliom*, but then they changed the evening, and I had to say I was sick. And the winter's bad, because the sun sets so early. But actually, it's been a lot less trouble than my goddamn allergies." She made a laugh, but Farrell did not respond.

"Dr. Schechtman says it's a sex thing," she offered. "He says it'll take years and years to cure it. Bernice thinks I should go to someone else, but I don't want to be one of those women who runs around changing shrinks like hair colors. Pat went through five of them in a month one time. Joe, I wish you'd say something. Or just go away."

"Is it only dogs?" he asked. Lila's face did not change, but her chair rattled, and the milk went over again. Farrell said, "Answer me. Do you only kill dogs, and cats, and zoo animals?"

The tears began to come, heavy and slow, bright as knives in the morning sunlight. She could not look at him; and when she tried to speak, she could only make creaking, cartilaginous sounds in her throat. "You don't know," she whispered at last. "You don't have any idea what it's like."

"That's true," he answered. He was always very fair about that particular point.

He took her hand, and then she really began to cry. Her sobs were horrible to hear, much more frightening to Farrell than any wolf noises. When he held her, she rolled in his arms like a stranded ship with the waves slamming into her. I always get the criers, he thought sadly. My girls always cry, sooner or later. But never for me.

"Don't leave me!" she wept. "I don't know why I came to live with you—I knew it wouldn't work—but don't leave me! There's just Bernice and Dr. Schechtman, and it's so lonely. I want somebody else, I get so lonely. Don't leave me, Joe. I love you, Joe. I love you."

She was patting his face as though she were blind. Farrell stroked her hair and kneaded the back of her neck, wishing that her mother would call again. He felt skilled and weary, and without desire. I'm doing it again, he thought. "I love you," Lila said. And he answered her, thinking, I'm doing it again. That's the great advantage of making the same mistake a lot of times. You come to know it, and you can study it and get inside it, really make it yours. It's the same good old mistake, except this time the girl's hang-up is different. But it's the same thing. I'm doing it again.

◦

The building superintendent was thirty or fifty: dark, thin, quick, and shivering. A Lithuanian or a Latvian, he spoke very little English. He smelled of black friction tape and stale water, and he was strong in the twisting way that a small, lean animal is strong. His eyes were almost purple, and they bulged a little, straining out—the terrible eyes of a herald angel stricken dumb. He roamed the basement all day, banging on pipes and taking the elevator apart.

The superintendent met Lila only a few hours after Farrell did; on that first night, when she came home with him. At the sight of her the little man jumped back, dropping the two-legged chair he was carrying. He promptly fell over it, and did not try to get up, but cowered there, clucking and gulping, trying to cross himself and make the sign of the horns at the same time. Farrell started to help him, but he screamed. They could hardly hear the sound.

It would have been merely funny and embarrassing, except for the fact that Lila was equally frightened of the superintendent, from that moment. She would not go down to the basement for any reason, nor would she enter or leave the house until she was satisfied that he was nowhere near. Farrell had thought then that she took the superintendent for a lunatic.

"I don't know how he knows," he said to Ben. "I guess if you believe in werewolves and vampires, you probably recognize them right away. I don't believe in them at all, and I live with one."

He lived with Lila all through the autumn and the winter. They went out together and came home, and her cooking improved slightly, and she gave up the guitar and got a kitten named Theodora. Sometimes she wept, but not often. She turned out not to be a real crier.

She told Dr. Schechtman about Farrell, and he said that it would probably be a very beneficial relationship for her. It wasn't, but it wasn't a particularly bad one either. Their lovemaking was usually good, though it bothered Farrell to suspect that it was the sense and smell of the Other that excited him. For the rest, they came near being friends. Farrell had known that he did not love Lila before he found out that she was a werewolf, and this made him feel a great deal easier about being bored with her.

"It'll break up by itself in the spring," he said, "like ice."

Ben asked, "What if it doesn't?" They were having lunch in the Automat again. "What'll you do if it just goes on?"

"It's not that easy." Farrell looked away from his friend and began to explore the mysterious, swampy innards of his beef pie. He said, "The trouble is that I know her. That was the real mistake. You shouldn't get to know people if you know you're not going to stay with them, one way or another. It's all right if you come and go in ignorance, but you shouldn't know them."

A week or so before the full moon, she would start to become nervous and strident, and this would continue until the day preceding her transformation. On that day, she was invariably loving, in the tender, desperate manner of someone who is going away; but the next day would see her silent, speaking only when she had to. She always had a cold on the last day, and looked gray and patchy and sick, but she usually went to work anyway.

Farrell was sure, though she never talked about it, that the change into wolf shape was actually peaceful for her, though the returning hurt. Just before moonrise she would take off her clothes and take the pins out of her hair and stand waiting. Farrell never managed not to close his eyes when she dropped heavily down on all fours; but there was a moment before that when her face would grow a look that he never saw at any other time, except when they were making love. Each time he saw it, it struck him as a look of wondrous joy at not being Lila anymore.

"See, I know her," he tried to explain to Ben. "She only likes to go to color movies, because wolves can't see color. She can't stand the Modern Jazz Quartet, but that's all she plays the first couple of days afterward. Stupid things like that. Never gets high at parties, because she's afraid she'll start talking. It's hard to walk away, that's all. Taking what I know with me."

Ben asked, "Is she still scared of the super?"

"Oh, God," Farrell said. "She got his dog last time. It was a Dalmatian—good-looking animal. She didn't know it was his. He doesn't hide when he sees her now, he just gives her a look like a stake through the heart. That man is a really classy hater, a natural. I'm scared of him myself." He stood up and began to pull on his overcoat. "I wish he'd get turned on to her mother. Get some practical use out of him. Did I tell you she wants me to call her Bernice?"

Ben said, "Farrell, if I were you, I'd leave the country. I would." They went out into the February drizzle that sniffled back and forth between snow and rain. Farrell did not speak until they reached the corner where he turned towards the bookstore. Then he said very softly, "Damn, you have to be so careful. Who wants to know what people turn into?"

May came, and a night when Lila once again stood naked at the window, waiting for the moon. Farrell fussed with dishes and garbage bags and fed the cat. These moments were always awkward. He had just asked her, "You want to save what's left of the rice?" when the telephone rang.

It was Lila's mother. She called two and three times a week now. "This is Bernice. How's my Irisher this evening?"

"I'm fine, Bernice," Farrell said. Lila suddenly threw back her head and drew a heavy, whining breath. The cat hissed silently and ran into the bathroom.

"I called to inveigle you two uptown this Friday," Mrs. Braun said. "A couple of old friends are coming over, and I know if I don't get some young people in we'll just sit around and talk about what went wrong with the Progressive Party. The Old Left. So if you could sort of sweet-talk our girl into spending an evening in Squaresville—"

"I'll have to check with Lila." She's *doing* it, he thought, that terrible woman. Every time I talk to her, I sound married. I see what she's doing, but she goes right ahead anyway. He said, "I'll talk to her in the morning." Lila struggled in the moonlight, between dancing and drowning. "Oh," Mrs. Braun said. "Yes, of course. Have her call me back." She sighed. "It's such a comfort to me to know you're there. Ask her if I should fix a fondue?"

Lila made a handsome wolf: tall and broad-chested for a female, moving as easily as water sliding over stone. Her coat was dark brown, showing red in the proper light, and there were white places on her breast. She had pale green eyes, the color of the sky when a hurricane is coming. Usually she was gone as soon as the changing was over, for she never cared for him to see her in her wolf form. But tonight she came slowly towards him, walking in a strange way, with her hindquarters almost dragging. She was making a high, soft sound, and her eyes were not focusing on him.

"What is it?" he asked foolishly. The wolf whined and skulked under the table, rubbing against his leg. Then she lay on her belly and rolled and as she did so the sound grew in her throat until it became an odd, sad, thin cry; not a hunting howl, but a shiver of longing turned into breath. "Jesus, don't do that!" Farrell gasped. But she sat up and howled again, and a dog answered her from somewhere near the river. She wagged her tail and whimpered.

Farrell said, "The super'll be up here in two minutes flat. What's the matter with you?" He heard footsteps and low frightened voices in the apartment above them. Another dog howled, this one nearby, and the wolf wriggled a little way towards the window on her haunches, like a baby, scooting. She looked at him over her shoulder, shuddering violently. On an impulse, he picked up the phone and called her mother.

Watching the wolf as she rocked and slithered and moaned, he described her actions to Mrs. Braun. "I've never seen her like this," he said. "I don't know what's the matter with her."

"Oh, my God," Mrs. Braun whispered. She told him. When he was silent, she began to speak very rapidly. "It hasn't happened for such a long time. Schechtman gives her pills, but she must have run out and forgotten—she's always been like that, since she was little. All the thermos bottles she used to leave on the school bus, and every week her piano music—"

"I wish you'd told me before," he said. He was edging very cautiously towards the open window. The pupils of the wolf's eyes were pulsing with her quick breaths.

"It isn't a thing you tell people!" Lila's mother wailed in his ear. "How do you think it was for me when she brought her first little boyfriend—" Farrell dropped the phone and sprang for the window. He had the inside track, and he might have made it, but she turned her head and snarled so wildly that he fell back. When he reached the window, she was already two fire-escape landings below, and there was eager yelping waiting for her in the street.

Dangling and turning just above the floor, Mrs. Braun heard Farrell's distant yell, followed immediately by a heavy thumping on the door. A strange, tattered voice was shouting unintelligibly beyond the knocking. Footsteps crashed by the receiver and the door opened. "My dog, my dog!" the strange voice mourned. "My dog, my dog, my dog!"

"I'm sorry about your dog," Farrell said. "Look, please go away. I've got work to do."

"I got work," the voice said. "I know my work." It climbed and spilled into another language, out of which English words jutted like broken bones. "Where is she? Where is she? She kill my dog."

"She's not here." Farrell's own voice changed on the last word. It seemed a long time before he said, "You'd better put that away."

Mrs. Braun heard the howl as clearly as though the wolf were running beneath her own window: lonely and insatiable, with a kind of gasping laughter in it. The other voice began to scream. Mrs. Braun caught the phrase *silver bullet* several times. The door slammed, then opened and slammed again.

Farrell was the only man of his own acquaintance who was able to play back his dreams while he was having them: to stop them in mid-flight, no matter how fearful they might be—or how lovely—and run them over and over, studying them in his sleep, until the most terrifying reel became at once utterly harmless and unbearably familiar. This night that he spent running after Lila was like that.

He would find them congregated under the marquee of an apartment house, or romping around the moonscape of a construction site: ten or fifteen males of all races, creeds, colors, and previous conditions of servitude; whining and yapping, pissing against tires, inhaling indiscriminately each other and the lean, grinning bitch they surrounded. She frightened them, for she growled more wickedly than coyness demanded, and where she snapped, even in play, bone showed. Still they tumbled on her and over her, biting her neck and ears in their turn; and she snarled but she did not run away.

Never, at least, until Farrell came charging upon them, shrieking like any cuckold, kicking at the snuffling lovers. Then she would turn and race off into the spring dark, with her thin, dreamy howl floating behind her like the train of a smoky gown. The dogs followed, and so did Farrell, calling and cursing. They always lost him quickly, that jubilant marriage procession, leaving him stumbling down rusty iron ladders into places where he fell over garbage cans. Yet he would come upon them as inevitably in time, loping along Broadway or trotting across Columbus Avenue towards the Park; he would hear them in the tennis courts near the river, breaking down the nets over Lila and her moment's Ares. There were dozens of them now, coming from all directions. They stank of their joy, and he threw stones at them and shouted, and they ran.

And the wolf ran at their head, on sidewalks and on wet grass, her tail waving contentedly, but her eyes still hungry, and her howl growing ever more warning than wistful. Farrell knew that she must have blood before sunrise, and that it was both useless and dangerous to follow her. But the night wound and unwound itself, and he knew the same things over and over, and ran down the same streets, and saw the same couples walk wide of him, thinking he was drunk.

Mrs. Braun kept leaping out of a taxi that pulled up next to him; usually at corners where the dogs had just piled by, knocking over the crates stacked in market doorways and spilling the newspapers at the subway kiosks. Standing in broccoli, in black taffeta, with a front like a ferryboat—yet as lean in the hips as her wolf-daughter—with her plum-colored hair all loose, one arm lifted, and her orange mouth pursed in a bellow, she was no longer Bernice but a wronged fertility goddess getting set to blast the harvest. "We've got to split up!" she would roar at Farrell, and each time it sounded like a sound idea. Yet he looked for her whenever he lost Lila's trail, because she never did.

The superintendent kept turning up too, darting after Farrell out of alleys or cellar entrances, or popping from the freight elevators that load through the sidewalk. Farrell would hear his numberless passkeys clicking on the flat piece of wood tucked into his belt.

"You see her? You see her, the wolf, kill my dog?" Under the fat, ugly moon, the Army .45 glittered and trembled like his own mad eyes.

"Mark with a cross." He would pat the barrel of his gun and shake it under Farrell's nose like a maraca. "Mark with a cross, bless by a priest. Three silver bullets. She kill my dog."

Lila's voice would come sailing to them then, from up in Harlem or away near Lincoln Center, and the little man would whirl and dash down into the earth, disappearing into the crack between two slabs of sidewalk. Farrell understood quite clearly that the superintendent was hunting Lila underground, using the keys that only superintendents have to take elevators down to the black sub-sub-basements, far below the bicycle rooms and the wet, shaking laundry rooms, and below the furnace rooms, below the passages walled with electricity meters and roofed with burly steam pipes; down to the realms where the great dim water mains roll like whales, and the gas lines hump and preen, down where the roots of the apartment houses fade together, and so along under the city, scrabbling through secret ways with silver bullets, and his keys rapping against the piece of wood. He never saw Lila, but he was never very far behind her.

Cutting across parking lots, pole-vaulting between locked bumpers, edging and dancing his way through fluorescent gaggles of haughty children, leaping uptown like a salmon against the current of the theater crowds, walking quickly past the random killing faces that floated down the night tide like unexploded mines, and especially avoiding the crazy faces that wanted to tell him what it was like to be crazy—so Farrell pursued Lila Braun, of Tremont Avenue and CCNY, in the city all night long. Nobody offered to help him, or tried to head off the dangerous-looking bitch bounding along with the delirious gaggle of admirers streaming after her; but then, the dogs had to fight through the same clenched legs and vengeful bodies that Farrell did. The crowds slowed Lila down, but he felt relieved whenever she turned towards the emptier streets. *She must have blood soon, somewhere.*

Farrell's dreams eventually lost their clear edge after he played them back a certain number of times, and so it was with the night. The full moon skidded down the sky, thinning like a tatter of butter in a skillet, and remembered scenes began to fold sloppily into each other. The sound of Lila and the dogs grew fainter whichever way he followed. Mrs. Braun blinked on and off at longer intervals; and in dark doorways and under subway gratings, the superintendent burned like a corposant, making the barrel of his pistol run rainbow. At last he lost Lila for good, and with that it seemed that he woke.

It was still night, but not dark, and he was walking slowly home on Riverside Drive through a cool, grainy fog. The moon had set, but the river was strangely bright: glittering gray as far up as the Bridge, where headlights left shiny, wet paths like snails. There was no one else on the street. "Dumb broad," he said aloud. "The hell with it. She wants to mess around, let her mess around." He wondered whether werewolves could have cubs, and what sort of cubs they might be. Lila must have turned on the dogs by now, for the blood. Poor dogs, he thought. They were all so dirty and innocent and happy with her.

"A moral lesson for all of us," he announced sententiously. "Don't fool with strange, eager ladies, they'll kill you." He was a little hysterical. Then, two blocks ahead of him, he saw the gaunt shape in the gray light of the river, alone now, and hurrying. Farrell did not call to her, but as soon as he began to run, the wolf wheeled and faced him. Even at that distance, her eyes were stained and streaked and wild. She showed all the teeth on one side of her mouth, and she growled like fire.

Farrell trotted steadily towards her, crying, "Go home, go home! Lila, you dummy, get on home, it's morning!" She growled terribly, but when Farrell was less than a block away, she turned again and dashed across the street, heading for West End Avenue. Farrell said, "Good girl, that's it," and limped after her.

In the hours before sunrise on West End Avenue, many people came out to walk their dogs. Farrell had done it often enough with poor Grunewald to know many of the dawn walkers by sight, and some to talk to. A fair number of them were whores and homosexuals, both of whom always seem to have dogs in New York. Quietly, almost always alone, they drifted up and down the Nineties, piloted by their small, fussy beasts, but moving in a kind of fugitive truce with the city and the night that was ending. Farrell sometimes fancied that they were all asleep, and that this hour was the only true rest they ever got.

He recognized Robie by his two dogs, Scone and Crumpet. Robie lived in the apartment directly below Farrell's, usually unhappily. The dogs were horrifying little homebrews of Chihuahua and Yorkshire terrier, but Robie loved them. Crumpet, the male, saw Lila first. He gave a delighted yap of welcome and proposition (according to Robie, Scone bored him, and he liked big girls anyway) and sprang to meet her, yanking his leash through Robie's slack hand. The wolf was almost upon him before he realized his fatal misunderstanding and scuttled desperately in retreat, meowing with utter terror.

Robie wailed, and Farrell ran as fast as he could, but Lila knocked Crumpet off his feet and slashed his throat while he was still in the air. Then she crouched on the body, nuzzling it in a dreadful way.

Robie actually came within a step of leaping upon Lila and trying to drag her away from his dead dog. Instead, he turned on Farrell as he came panting up, and began hitting him with a good deal of strength and accuracy. "Damn you, damn you!" he sobbed. Little Scone ran away around the corner, screaming like a mandrake.

Farrell put up his arms and went with the punches, all the while yelling at Lila until his voice ripped. But the blood frenzy had her, and Farrell never imagined what she must be like at those times. Somehow she had spared the dogs who had loved her all night, but she was nothing but thirst now. She pushed and kneaded Crumpet's body as though she were nursing.

All along the avenue, the morning dogs were barking like trumpets. Farrell ducked away from Robie's soft fists and saw them coming; tripping over their trailing leashes, running too fast for their stubby legs. They were small, spoiled beasts, most of them, overweight and short-winded, and many were not young. Their owners cried unmanly pet names after them, but they waddled gallantly towards their deaths, barking promises far bigger than themselves, and none of them looked back.

She looked up with her muzzle red to the eyes. The dogs did falter then, for they knew murder when they smelled it, and even their silly, nearsighted eyes understood vaguely what creature faced them. But they knew the smell of love, too, and they were all gentlemen.

She killed the first two to reach her—a spitz and a cocker spaniel—with two snaps of her jaws. But before she could settle down to her meal, three Pekes were scrambling up to her, though they would have had to stand on each other's shoulders. Lila whirled without a sound, and they fell away, rolling and yelling but unhurt. As soon as she turned, the Pekes were at her again, joined now by a couple of valiant poodles. Lila got one of the poodles when she turned again. Robie had stopped beating on Farrell, and was leaning against a traffic light, being sick. But other people were running up now: a middle-aged Black man, crying; a plump youth in a plastic car coat and bedroom slippers, who kept whimpering, "Oh God, she's eating them, look at her, she's really eating them!"; two lean, ageless girls in slacks, both with foamy beige hair. They all called wildly to their unheeding dogs, and they all grabbed at Farrell and shouted in his face. Cars began to stop.

The sky was thin and cool, rising pale gold, but Lila paid no attention to it. She was ramping under the swarm of little dogs, rearing and spinning in circles, snarling blood. The dogs were terrified and bewildered, but they never swerved from their labor. The smell of love told them that they were welcome, however ungraciously she seemed to receive them. Lila shook herself, and a pair of squealing dachshunds, hobbled in a double harness, tumbled across the sidewalk to end at Farrell's feet. They scrambled up and immediately towed themselves back into the maelstrom. Lila bit one of them almost in half, but the other dachshund went on trying to climb her hindquarters, dragging his ripped comrade with him. Farrell began to laugh.

The Black man said, "You think it's funny?" and hit him. Farrell sat down, still laughing. The man stood over him, embarrassed, offering Farrell his handkerchief. "I'm sorry, I shouldn't have done that," he said. "But your dog killed my dog."

"She isn't my dog," Farrell said. He moved to let a man pass between them, and then saw that it was the superintendent, holding his pistol with both hands. Nobody noticed him until he fired; but Farrell pushed one of the foamy-haired girls, and she stumbled against the superintendent as the gun went off. The silver bullet broke a window in a parked car.

The superintendent fired again while the echoes of the first shot were still clapping back and forth between the houses. A Pomeranian screamed that time, and a woman cried out, "Oh my God, he shot Borgy!" But the crowd was crumbling away, breaking into its individual components like pills on television. The watching cars had sped off at the sight of the gun, and the faces that had been peering down from windows disappeared. Except for Farrell, the few people who remained were scattered halfway down the block. The sky was brightening swiftly now.

"For God's sake, don't let him!" the same woman called from the shelter of a doorway. But two men made shushing gestures at her, saying, "It's all right, he knows how to use that thing. Go ahead, buddy."

The shots had at last frightened the little dogs away from Lila. She crouched among the twitching splotches of fur, with her muzzle wrinkled back and her eyes more black than green. Farrell saw a plaid rag that had been a dog jacket protruding from under her body. The superintendent stooped and squinted over the gun barrel, aiming with grotesque care, while the men cried to him to shoot. He was too far from the werewolf for her to reach him before he fired the last silver bullet, though he would surely die before she died. His lips were moving as he took aim.

Two long steps would have brought Farrell up behind the superintendent. Later he told himself that he had been afraid of the pistol, because that was easier than remembering how he had felt when he looked at Lila. Her tongue never stopped lapping around her dark jaws; and even as she set herself to spring, she lifted a bloody paw to her mouth. Farrell thought of her padding in the bedroom, breathing on his face. The superintendent grunted and Farrell closed his eyes. Yet even then he expected to find himself doing something.

Then he heard Mrs. Braun's unmistakable voice. *"Don't you dare!"*

She was standing between Lila and the superintendent: one shoe gone, and the heel off the other one, her knit dress torn at the shoulder, and her face tired and smudgy. But she pointed a finger at the startled superintendent, and he stepped quickly back, as though she had a pistol, too.

"Lady, that's a wolf," he protested nervously. "Lady, you please get, get out of the way. That's a wolf, I go shoot her now."

"I want to see your license for that gun." Mrs. Braun held out her hand. The superintendent blinked at her, muttering in despair. She said, "Do you know that you can be sent to prison for twenty years for carrying a concealed weapon in this state? Do you know what the fine is for having a gun without a license? The fine is Five. Thousand. Dollars."

The men down the street were shouting at her, but she swung around to face the creature snarling among the little dead dogs.

"Come on, Lila," she said. "Come on home with Bernice. I'll make tea and we'll talk. It's been a long time since we've really talked, you know? We used to have nice long talks when you were little, but we don't anymore." The wolf had stopped growling, but she was crouching even lower, and her ears were still flat against her head. Mrs. Braun said, "Come on, baby. Listen, I know what—you'll call in sick at the office and stay for a few days. You'll get a good rest, and maybe we'll even look around a little for a new doctor, what do you say? Schechtman hasn't done a thing for you, I never liked him. Come on home, honey. Momma's here, Bernice knows." She took a step towards the silent wolf, holding out her hand.

The superintendent gave a desperate, wordless cry and pumped forward, clumsily shoving Mrs. Braun to one side. He leveled the pistol point-blank, wailing, "My dog, my dog!" Lila was in the air when the gun went off, and her shadow sprang after her, for the sun had risen. She crumpled down across a couple of dead Pekes. Their blood dabbled her breasts and her pale throat.

Mrs. Braun screamed like a lunch whistle. She knocked the superintendent into the street and sprawled over Lila, hiding her completely from Farrell's sight. "Lila, Lila," she keened to her daughter, "poor baby, you never had a chance. He killed you because you were different, the way they kill everything different." Farrell approached her and stooped down, but she pushed him against a wall without looking up. "Lila, Lila, poor baby, poor darling, maybe it's better, maybe you're happy now. You never had a chance, poor Lila."

The dog owners were edging slowly back and the surviving dogs were running to them. The superintendent squatted on the curb with his head in his arms. A wary, muffled voice said, "For God's sake, Bernice, would you get up off me? You don't have to stop yelling, just get off."

When she stood up, the cars began to stop in the street again. It made it very difficult for the police to get through. Nobody pressed charges, because there was no one to lodge them against. The killer dog—or wolf, as some insisted—was gone; and if she had an owner, he could not be found. As for the people who had actually seen the wolf turn into a young girl when the sunlight touched her, most of them managed not to have seen it, though they never really forgot. There were a few who knew quite well what they had seen, and never forgot it either, but they never said anything. They did, however, chip in to pay the superintendent's fine for possessing an unlicensed handgun. Farrell gave what he could.

Lila vanished out of Farrell's life before sunset. She did not go uptown with her mother, but packed her things and went to stay with friends in the Village. Later he heard that she was living on Christopher Street, and later still, that she had moved to Berkeley and gone back to school. He never saw her again.

"It had to be like that," he told Ben once. "We got to know too much about each other. See, there's another side to knowing. She couldn't look at me."

"You mean because you saw her with all those dogs? Or because she knew you'd have let that little nut shoot her?" Farrell shook his head.

"It was that, I guess, but it was more something else, something I know. When she sprang, just as he shot at her that last time, she wasn't leaping at him. She was going straight for her mother. She'd have got her too, if it hadn't been sunrise."

Ben whistled softly. "I wonder if her old lady knows."

"Bernice knows everything about Lila," Farrell said.

Mrs. Braun called him nearly two years later to tell him that Lila was getting married. It must have cost her a good deal of money and ingenuity to find him (where Farrell was living then, the telephone line was open for four hours a day), but he knew by the spitefulness in the static that she considered it money well spent.

"He's at Stanford," she crackled. "A research psychologist. They're going to Japan for their honeymoon."

"That's fine," Farrell said. "I'm really happy for her, Bernice." He hesitated before he asked, "Does he know about Lila? I mean, about what happens—?"

"Does he know?" she cried. "He's proud of it—he thinks it's wonderful! It's his field!"

"That's great. That's fine. Goodbye, Bernice. I really am glad."

And he was glad, and a little wistful, thinking about it. The girl he was living with here had a really strange hang-up.

GORDON, THE SELF-MADE CAT

The first draft of "Gordon, The Self-Made Cat" was written more than forty years ago, when I was living on nine wild acres in the hills north of Santa Cruz, California, with my young family. We had an unguessable number of cats in those days, if you count not only the indoor and outdoor residents, but also the visitors who treated our peeling red shack as a sort of bed-and-breakfast establishment. What we definitely *didn't* have was a mouse problem (gophers were another matter). I made up the valiant Gordon to amuse the children, sent his story off to an animation company that had requested ideas for a feature film, shrugged at their almost immediate rejection, then buried the piece in my battered filing cabinet and completely forgot about it. It didn't surface again until 2001, when some friends stumbled across it while helping me move.

I'm currently working on expanding it, adding new characters and more adventures, for eventual book publication. I've always loved *Charlotte's Web* and *Stuart Little*; the longer version of *Gordon* will be my own small nod in that very challenging direction.

ONCE UPON A TIME to a family of house mice there was born a son named Gordon. He looked very much like his father and mother and all his brothers and sisters, who were gray and had bright, twitchy, black eyes, but what went on inside Gordon was very different from what went on inside the rest of his family. He was forever asking why everything had to be the way it was, and never satisfied with the answer. Why did mice eat cheese? Why did they live in the dark and only go out when it was dark? Where did mice come from, anyway? *What were people?* Why did people smell so funny? Suppose mice were big and people were tiny? Suppose mice could fly? Most mice don't ask many questions, but Gordon never stopped.

One evening, when Gordon was only a few weeks old, his next-to-eldest sister was sent out to see if anything interesting had been left open in the pantry. She never returned. Gordon's father shrugged sadly and spread his front paws, and said, "The cat."

"What's a cat?" Gordon asked.

His mother and father looked at one another and sighed. "They have to know sometime," his father said. "Better he learns it at home than on the streets."

His mother sniffled a little and said, "But he's so young," and his father answered, "Cats don't care." So they told Gordon about cats right then, expecting him to start crying and saying that there weren't any such things. It's a hard idea to get used to. But Gordon only asked, "Why do cats eat mice?"

"I guess we taste very good," his father said.

Gordon said, "But cats don't have to eat mice. They get plenty of other food that probably tastes as good. Why should anybody eat anybody if he doesn't have to?"

"Gordon," said his father. "Listen to me. There are two kinds of creatures in the world. There are animals that hunt, and animals that are hunted. We mice just happen to be the kind of animal that gets hunted, and it doesn't really matter if the cat *is* hungry or not. It's the way life is. It's really a great honor to be the hunted, if you just look at it the right way."

"Phooey on that," said Gordon. "Where do I go to learn to be a cat?"

They thought he was joking, but as soon as Gordon was old enough to go places by himself, he packed a clean shirt and some peanut butter, and started off for cat school. "I love you very much," he said to his parents before he left, "but this business of being hunted for the rest of my life just because I happened to be born a mouse is not for me." And off he went, all by himself.

All cats go to school, you know, whether you ever see them going or not. Dogs don't, but cats always have and always will. There are a great many cat schools, so Gordon found one easily enough, and he walked bravely up the front steps and knocked at the door. He said that he wanted to speak to the Principal.

He almost expected to be eaten right there, but the cats—students and teachers alike—were so astonished that they let him pass through, and one of the teachers took him to the Principal's office. Gordon could feel the cats looking at him, and hear the sounds their noses made as they smelled how good he was, but he held on tight to the suitcase with his shirt and the peanut butter, and he never looked back.

The Principal was a fat old tiger cat who chewed on his tail all the time he was talking to Gordon. "You must be out of your mind," he said when Gordon told him he wanted to be a cat. "I'd smack you up this minute, but it's bad luck to eat crazies. Get out of here! The day mice go to cat school . . ."

"Why not?" said Gordon. "Is it in writing? Where does it say that I can't go to school here if I want?"

Well, of course there's nothing in the rules of cat schools that says mice can't enroll. Nobody ever thought of putting it in.

The Principal folded his paws and said, "Gordon, look at it this way—"

"You look at it *my* way," said Gordon. "I want to be a cat, and I bet I'd make a better one than the dopey-looking animals I've seen in this school. Most of them look as if they wouldn't even make good mice! So let's make a deal. You let me come to school here and study for one term, and if at the end of that time I'm not doing better than any cat in the school—if even one cat has better grades than I have—then you can eat me and that'll be the end of it. Is that fair?"

No cat can resist a challenge like that. But before agreeing, the Principal insisted on one small change: at the end of the term, if Gordon didn't have the very best marks in the school, then the privilege of eating him would go to the cat that did.

"Ought to encourage some of those louts to work harder," the Principal said to himself, as Gordon left his office. "He's crazy, but he's right—most of them wouldn't even make good mice. I almost hope he does it."

So Gordon went to cat school. Every day he sat at his special little desk, surrounded by a hundred kittens and half-grown cats who would have liked nothing better than to leap on him and play games with him for a while before they gobbled him. He learned how to wash himself, and what to do to keep his claws sharp, and how to watch everything in the room while pretending to be asleep. There was a class on Dealing with Dogs, and another on Getting Down from Trees, which is much harder than climbing up, and also a particularly scholarly seminar on the various meanings of "Bad Kitty!" Gordon's personal favorite was the Visions class, which had to do with the enchanting things all cats can see that no one else ever does—the great, gliding ancestors, and faraway castles, and mysterious forests full of monsters to chase. The Professor of Visions told his colleagues that he had never had such a brilliant student. "It would be a crime to eat such a mouse!" he proclaimed everywhere. "An absolute, shameful, yummy crime."

The class in Mouse-Hunting was a bit awkward at first, because usually the teacher asks one of the students to be the mouse, and in Gordon's case the Principal felt that would be too risky. But Gordon insisted on being chased like everyone else, and not only was he never caught (well, *almost* never; there was one blue Persian who could turn on a dime), but when he took his own turn at chasing, he proved to be a natural expert. In fact his instant mastery of the Flying Pounce caused his teacher and the entire class to sit up and applaud. Gordon took three bows and an encore.

There was also a class where the cats learned the necessities of getting along with people: how to lie in laps, how to keep from scratching furniture even when you feel you have to, what to do when children pick you up, and how to ask for food or affection in such a sweet manner that people call other people to look at you. These classes always made Gordon a little sad. He didn't suppose that he would ever be a real "people" cat, for who would want to hold a mouse on his lap, or scratch it behind the ears while it purred? Still, he paid strict attention in People Class, as he did in all the others, for all the cats knew that whoever did

best in school that term would be the one who ate him, and they worked harder than they ever had in their lives. The Principal said that they were becoming the best students in the school's history, and he talked openly about making this a regular thing, one mouse to a term.

When all the marks were in, and all the grades added up, two students led the rankings: Gordon and the blue Persian. Their scores weren't even a whisker's thickness apart. In the really important classes, like Running and Pouncing, Climbing, Stalking, and Waiting for the Prey to Forget You're Still There; and in matters of feline manners such as Washing, Tail Etiquette, The Elegant Yawn, Sleeping in Undignified Positions, and Making Sure You Get Enough Food Without Looking Greedy (101 *and* 102)—in all of these Gordon and the blue Persian were first, and the rest nowhere. Besides that, both could meow in five different dialects: Persian, Abyssinian, Siamese, Burmese (which almost no cat who isn't Burmese ever learns), and basic tiger.

But there can only be one Top Cat to a term; no ties allowed. In order to decide the matter once and for all between them, the Principal announced that Gordon and the blue Persian would have to face one another in a competitive mouse roundup.

The Persian and Gordon got along quite well, all things considered, so they shook paws—carefully—and the Persian purred, "No hard feelings."

"None at all," Gordon answered. "If anyone here got to eat me, I'd much rather it was you."

"Very sporting of you," the Persian said. "I hope so too."

"But it won't happen," Gordon said.

The blue Persian never had a chance. Once he and Gordon were set on their marks in a populous mouse neighborhood, Gordon ambushed and outsmarted and cornered all but a handful of the very quickest mice, and did it in a style so smooth, so effortlessly elegant—so *catlike*—that the Persian finally threw up his paws and surrendered. In front of the entire faculty and student body of the cat school, he announced, "I yield to Gordon. He's a better cat than I am, and I'm not ashamed to admit it. If all mice were like him, we cats would be vegetarians." (Persians are *very* dramatic.)

The cheering was so wild and thunderous that no one objected in the least when Gordon freed all the mice he had captured. Cats can appreciate a grand gesture, and everyone had already had lunch.

Gordon had won his bet, and, like the blue Persian, the Principal was cat enough to accept it graciously. He scheduled a celebration, which the whole school attended, and at the end of the party he announced that Gordon was now to be considered as much a cat as any student in the school, if not more so. He gave Gordon a little card to show that he was a cat in good standing, and all the students cheered, and Gordon made another speech that began, "Fellow cats . . ." As he spoke, he wished very much that his parents could be there to see what he had accomplished, and just how different things could be if you just asked questions and weren't afraid of new ideas.

Being acknowledged the best cat in the school didn't make Gordon let up in his studies. Instead, he worked even harder, and did so well that he graduated with the special degree of *felis maximus*, which is Latin for *some cat!* He stayed on at the school to teach a seminar in Evasive Maneuvers, which proved very popular, and a course in the Standing Jump (for a bird that comes flying over when you weren't looking).

The story of his new life spread everywhere among all mice, and grew very quickly into a myth more terrifying than any cat could have been. They whispered of "Gordon the Terrible," "Gordon, the Self-Made Cat," and, simply, "The Unspeakable," and told midnight tales of a gigantic mouse who lashed his tail and sprang at them with his razor claws out and his savage yellow eyes blazing; a mouse without pity who hunted them out in their deepest hiding places, walking without a sound. They believed unquestioningly that he ate mice like gingersnaps, and laughingly handed over to his cat friends those he was too full to devour. There was even a dreadful legend that Gordon had eaten his own family, and that he frequently took kittens from the school on field trips in order to teach them personally the secret mouse ways that no mere cat could ever have known.

These stories made Gordon deeply unhappy when he heard them, because he believed with absolute conviction that what he had achieved was for the good of all mice everywhere. Whether he trapped a lone mouse or cornered a dozen trembling in an attic or behind a refrigerator, he would say the same thing to them: "Look at me. *Look at me!* I am a mouse like you—nothing more, nothing less—and yet I walk with cats every day, and I am not eaten! I am respected, I am admired, I am even powerful among cats—and every one of you could be like me! Do not believe that we mice are born only to be hunted, humiliated, tormented, and finally gobbled up. It is not true! Instead of huddling in the shadows, in constant lifelong terror, pitiful little balls of fur, we too can be sleek, fierce hunters, fearing nothing and no one. Run now and spread the word! You must spread the word!"

Saying that, he would step back and let the mice scatter, hoping each time that they would finally understand what he was trying to show them. But it simply never happened. The mice always scurried away, convinced that they had escaped only by great good fortune, and myths and legends of the terrible Self-Made Cat were all that spread among them, growing ever more horrifying, ever more chilling. It didn't matter that not one mouse had ever actually seen Gordon doing any of the frightful things he was supposed to have done. That's the way it is with legends.

Now it happened that Gordon was walking down the street one day, on his way to a faculty meeting, padding along like a leopard, twitching his tail like a lion, and making the eager little noises in his throat that a tiger makes when he smells food. Quite suddenly an enormous shadow fell across his path, so big that he looked up to see if he were going through a tunnel. What he saw was a dog. What he actually saw was a leg, for this dog was huge, too big for even a full-grown cat to have understood his real size without looking twice. The dog rumbled, "Oh, goody! I love mice. Lots of phosphorus in mice. Yummy."

Gordon crouched, tail lashing, and lifted the fur along his spine. "Watch it, dog," he said warningly. "Don't mess with me, I'm telling you."

"Oh, how cute," the dog said. "He's playing he's a cat. I'm a cat too. Meow."

"I *am* a cat!" Gordon arched his back until it ached, hissing and spitting and growling in his throat, all more or less at the same time. "I *am!* You want to see my card? Look, right here."

"A crazy," the dog said wonderingly. "They say it's bad luck to eat a crazy. Good thing I'm not superstitious."

Having given the proper First Warning, exactly as he'd been taught, Gordon moved quickly to the Second—the lightning-swift slash of the right paw across the nose. Gordon had to leap straight up to reach the dog's big wet nose, but even with that handicap, he executed the Second Warning in superb style.

Instead of yelping and retreating in a properly humbled state, however, the dog only sneezed.

This, Gordon thought, is the difference between theory and practice.

But there was a reason that Gordon's seminar in Evasive Maneuvers was always so well attended. With astonishing daring, he went directly from the Second Warning right into the Fourth Avoidance, which involves a double feint—head looking *this* way, tail jerking *that* way—followed by a quick, threatening charge directly at the attacker, and *then* a leap to the side, which, done correctly, leaves one perfectly poised either for escape or the Flying Pounce, depending on the situation.

But the big dog had no idea that a classic Evasive Maneuver had just been performed upon him, leaving him looking like an idiot. He was used to looking like an idiot. He gave a delighted bounce, wuffed, "*Tag*—you're it!" and went straight for Gordon, who responded by going up a tree with the polished grace that always left his students too breathless to cheer. He found a comfortable branch and rested there, thinking ruefully that a real cat wouldn't have been so proud of being a cat as to waste time arguing about it.

The dog sat down too, grinning. "Be a bird now," he called to Gordon. "Let's see you be a bird and fly away."

Normally, Gordon could easily have stayed up in the tree longer than the dog felt like waiting below, but he was tired and rather thirsty, not to mention annoyed at the thought of being late for the faculty meeting. Something had to be done. But what?

He was bravely considering an original plan of leaping straight down at the dog, when three young mice happened along. They had been out shopping for their mother.

They were really very young, and as they had never seen Gordon the Terrible—though they had heard about him since they were blind babies—they didn't know who it was in the tree. All they saw was a fellow mouse in danger, and, being at the age when they didn't know any better than to do things like that, they carefully put down their packages and began luring the dog away from the tree. First one mouse would rush in at him and make the dog chase him a little way, and then another would come scampering from somewhere else, so that the dog would leave off chasing the first mouse and go after him.

The dog, who was actually quite good-natured, and not very hungry, had a fine time running after them all. He followed them farther and farther away from the tree, and had probably forgotten all about Gordon by the time the Unspeakable was able to spring down from the tree and vanish into the bushes.

Gordon would have waited to thank the three mice, but they had disappeared, along with the dog. Anxious not to miss his meeting, he dashed back to the school, slowing down before he got there to catch his breath and smooth his whiskers. "It could happen to anyone," he told himself. "There's nothing to be ashamed of." Yet there was something fundamentally troubling to Gordon about having run away. Feeling uncertain for the first time since he had marched up the front steps, he washed himself all over and stalked on into the school, outwardly calm and proud, the best cat anyone there would ever see, Gordon the Terrible, the Unspeakable—yes, the Self-Made Cat.

But another cat—the Assistant Professor of Tailchasing, in fact—had seen the whole incident, and had already interrupted the faculty meeting with the shocking tale.

The Principal tried to brush the news aside. "When it's time to climb a tree, you climb a tree," he said. "Any cat knows that." (He had become quite fond of Gordon, in his way.)

It wasn't enough. The Assistant Professor of Tailchasing (a chocolate-point Siamese who dreamed of one day heading the school himself) led the opposition. As the Assistant Professor saw it, Gordon was plainly a fraud, a pretender, a cat in card only, so friendly with his fellow mice that they had rushed to help him when he was in danger. In light of that, who could say what Gordon's *real* plans might be? Why had he come to the school in the first place? What if more like him followed? What if the mice were plotting to attack the cat school, all cat schools?

This thought rattled everyone at the table. With a mouse like Gordon in their midst, a mouse who knew far more about being a cat than the cats themselves, was any feline safe?

Just that quickly, fear replaced reason. Within minutes everyone but the Principal forgot how much they had liked and admired Gordon. Admitting him to the school had been a catastrophic mistake, one that must be set right without a moment's delay!

The Principal groaned and covered his eyes and sent for Gordon. He was almost crying as he took Gordon's cat card away.

Gordon protested like mad, of course. He spoke of Will and Choice, and Freedom, and the transforming power of Questioning Assumptions. But the Principal said sadly, "We just can't trust you, Gordon. Go away now, before I eat you myself. I always wondered what you'd taste like." Then he put his head down on his desk and really did begin to cry.

So Gordon packed his clean shirt and his leftover peanut butter and left the cat school. All the cats formed a double line to let him pass, their faces turned away, and nobody said a word. The Assistant Professor of Tailchasing was poised to pounce at the very last, but the Principal stepped on his tail.

Nobody ever heard of Gordon again. There were stories that he'd gone right on being a cat, even without his card; and there were other tales that said he had been driven out of the country by the mice themselves. But only the Principal knew for sure, because only the Principal had heard the words that Gordon was muttering to himself as he walked away from the cat school with his head held high.

"Woof," Gordon was murmuring thoughtfully. "Woof. Bow-wow. Shouldn't be too hard."

Four Fables

My father introduced me early on to George Ade's *Fables in Slang*; later, I discovered James Thurber's two books of *Fables for Our Time* on my own, and quite loved them.

"The Fable of the Moth" was first published in the 1960s, in Al Young's legendary little magazine *Love*, and owes something to Don Marquis' tales of archy and mehitabel. The other three fables in this set were written specifically for the collection *The Line Between*. They tend to suggest a dark—even cynical—view of the human condition, but then it has always seemed to me that fables and fabulists mostly do that. Aesop was lynched, after all, according to Herodotus.

The Fable of the Moth

Once there was a young moth who did not believe that the proper end for all mothkind was a zish and a frizzle. Whenever he saw a friend or a cousin or a total stranger rushing to a rendezvous with a menorah or a Coleman stove, he could feel a bit of his heart blacken and crumble. One evening, he called all the moths of the world together and preached to them. "Consider the sweetness of the world," he cried passionately. "Consider the moon, consider wet grass, consider company. Consider glove linings, camel's hair coats, fur stoles, feather boas, consider the heartbreaking, lost-innocence flavor of cashmere. Life is good, and love is all that matters. Why will we seek death, why do we truly hunger for nothing but the hateful hug of the candle, the bitter kiss of the filament? Accidents of the universe we may be, but we are beautiful accidents and we must not live as though we were ugly. The flame is a cheat, and love is the only."

All the other moths wept. They pressed around him by the billions, calling him a saint and vowing to change their lives. "What the world needs now is love," they cried as one bug. But then the lights began to come on all over the world, for it was nearing dinnertime. Fires were kindled, gas rings burned blue, electric coils glowed red, floodlights and searchlights and flashlights and porch lights blinked and creaked and blazed their mystery. And as one bug, as though nothing had been said, every moth at that historic assembly flew off on their nightly quest for cremation. The air sang with their eagerness.

"Come back! Come back!" called the poor moth, feeling his whole heart sizzle up this time. "What have I been telling you? I said that this was no way to live, that you must keep yourselves for love—and you knew the truth when you heard it. Why do you continue to embrace death when you know the truth?"

An old gypsy moth, her beauty ruined by a lifetime of singeing herself against nothing but arc lights at night games, paused by him for a moment. "Sonny, we couldn't agree with you more," she said. "Love is all that matters, and all that other stuff is as shadow. But there's just something about a good fire."

MORAL: Everybody knows better. That's the problem, not the answer.

The Fable of the Tyrannosaurus Rex

Once upon a very long ago, in a hot and steamy jungle, on an Earth that was mostly hot and steamy jungle, there lived a youngish *Tyrannosaurus rex*. (Actually, we should probably refer to her as a *Tyrannosaurus regina*, since she was a female, but never mind.) Not quite fully grown, she measured almost forty feet from nose to tail tip, weighed more than six tons, and had teeth the size of bananas. Although no intellectual, she was of a generally good-humored disposition, accepting with equanimity the fact that being as huge as she was meant that she was always hungry, except in her sleep. This, fortunately, she had been constructed to deal with.

Thanks to her size this Tyrannosaurus was, without a doubt, the queen of her late-Cretaceous world, which, in addition to great predators like herself, included the pack-hunting Velociraptor, the three-horned Triceratops, the Iguanodon, with its horse/duck face, and the long-necked, whiptailed Alamosaurus. But the world was populated also by assorted smaller animals—*much* smaller, most of them—distinguished from one another, as far as she was concerned, largely by their degree of quickness and crunchiness, and the amount of fur that was likely to get caught between her fangs. In fact, she rarely bothered to pursue them, since it generally cost her more in effort than the caloric intake was worth. She did eat them now and then, as we snap up potato chips or M&M's, but never considered them anything like a real meal, or even so much as *hors d'oeuvres*. It was just a reflex, something to do.

One afternoon, however, almost absent-mindedly, she pinned a tiny creature to earth under her left foot. It saved itself from being crushed only by wriggling frantically into the space between two of her toes, while simultaneously avoiding the rending claws in which they ended. As the Tyrannosaurus bent her head daintily to snatch it up, she heard a minuscule cry, "Wait! Wait! I have a very important message for you!"

The Tyrannosaurus—an innocent in many ways—had never had a personal message in her life, and the notion was an exciting one. Her forearms were small and weak, compared to her immense hind legs, but she was able to grip the nondescript little animal and lift him fifteen feet up, where she held him nose to nose, his beady red-brown eyes meeting her huge yellow ones with their long slit pupils. "Be quick," she advised him, "for I am hungry, and where there's one of you, there's usually a whole lot, like zucchini. What was the message you wanted to give me?"

The creature, if somewhat slow of action, atoned for this failing by thinking far faster than any dinosaur. "A large asteroid is about to crash into the Earth," it chirped brightly back at the Tyrannosaurus. "So if you happen to be nursing any unacted desires, now would be the time. To act them out, I mean," it added, realizing that the Tyrannosaurus was blinking in puzzlement at him. "It'll happen next Thursday."

"Asteroid," the Tyrannosaurus pondered. "What is an asteroid?" Before the little creature she held could answer, she asked, "Come to think of it, what's Thursday?"

"An asteroid is a rock," the animal informed her. "A big rock up in the sky, drifting through space. This one is about half the size of that mountain on the horizon, the one visible over the trees, and it's heading straight for us, and nothing can stop it. You and most other life on Earth are doomed."

"My goodness," said the Tyrannosaurus. "I'm certainly glad you told me about this." After a thoughtful moment, she inquired, "What does it all mean?"

"For you and most of your kind, absolute annihilation," the animal piped cheerfully. "For mine—evolution."

"I'm not very good with big words," the Tyrannosaurus said apologetically. "If you could . . ."

"You'll all be gone," the little creature said. "When the asteroid crashes into the Earth, it will raise a vast cloud of dust and debris that will circle the planet for years, cutting off all sunlight. You dinosaurs won't be able to survive the drastic change in the climate—you'll mostly vanish within a couple of generations. Then—just as when the fall of great trees makes room at last for the small ones struggling in their shadow—then we mammals will take our rightful place in the returning sun." Observing what it took to be a stricken expression on the Tyrannosaurus's yard-wide face, it added, "I'm really sorry. I just thought you should know."

"And your sort," the Tyrannosaurus ventured, "you will . . . evolute?"

"*Evolve*," the creature corrected her. "That means to change over time into something quite different in size or shape, or in your very nature, from what you were originally. My friend Max, for instance—smaller than I am right now—Max is going to evolve into a horse, if you'll believe it. And Louise, who came out of the sea with the rest of us, in the beginning—Louise is planning to go back there and become a whale. A blue whale, I think she said. It'll take millions of years, of course, but she's never in a hurry, Louise. And me—" here it preened itself as grandly as anyone possibly can in the grasp of a Tyrannosaurus Rex, fifteen feet in the air. "Me, I'm a sort of shrew or something right now, but I'm on my way to being a mammal with just two legs that will write books and fight wars, and won't believe in evolution. How cool is that?"

"And me?" the Tyrannosaurus asked, rather wistfully. "Everything will be changing—everyone will be turning into something else. Don't my relatives and I get to evolve at all?"

"You won't. But there's a bigger picture," the shrew reassured her. "It will take a good while, but some of your kind are going to fly, my dear. Those of your descendants who survive will find their scales turning gradually to feathers; their mighty jaws will in time become a highly adaptable beak, and they'll learn to build nests and sing songs. And hunt bugs."

"Well," said the Tyrannosaurus. "I can't say I follow all of this, but I guess it's better than being anni . . . annihil . . . what you said. But where does this Thursday come into it? What exactly *is* a Thursday?"

"Thursday—" began the shrew, but found itself at a disadvantage in trying to explain the arbitrary concept of days, weeks, months, and years to a beast who understood nothing beyond sunrise and sunset, light and dark, sun and moon. He said finally, "Thursday will happen three sleeps from now."

"Oh, *three* sleeps!" the Tyrannosaurus cried in great relief. "You should have said—I thought it was *two*! Well, there's plenty of time, then," and she promptly gulped down the shrew in one bite.

Savory, she thought. Nice crunch, too. But then again, there's that hair. They'd be better without the hair.

Turning away, she caught the scent of a nearby Triceratops on the wind, and was about to start in that new and tempting direction when she was hit squarely on the back of the neck by the asteroid, blazing from its descent through the atmosphere. As advertised, its impact killed her and wiped out most of the dinosaurs in a very short while, at least by geological standards. The shrew had simply miscalculated the asteroid's arrival time—which is hardly a surprise, as he didn't really have a good grasp on Thursdays, either.

MORAL: Gemini, Virgo, Aries, or Taurus,
knowing our future tends to bore us,
just like that poor Tyrannosaurus.

The Fable of the Ostrich

Once upon a time, in a remote corner of Africa, there was a young ostrich who refused to put his head in the sand at the slightest sign of danger. He strolled around unafraid, even when lions were near, cheerfully mocking his parents, his relations, and all his friends, every one of whom believed absolutely that their only safety lay in blind immobility. "It makes you invisible, foolish boy!" his father was forever shouting at him in vain. "You can't see the lion—the lion can't see you! What part of Q.E.D. don't you understand?"

"But the lion *always* sees us!" the ostrich would retort, equally exasperated. "What do you think happened to Uncle Julius? Cousin Hilda? Cousin Wilbraham? What good did hiding their stupid heads do them?"

"Oh," his father said. "Them. Well." He looked slightly embarrassed, which is hard for an ostrich. "Yes," he said. "Well, it's obvious, they moved. You mustn't *move,* not so much as a tail feather, that's half of it right there. *Head out of sight* and *hold still,* it's foolproof. Do you think your mother and I would still be here if it weren't foolproof?"

"The only thing foolproof," the young ostrich replied disdainfully, "is the fact that we can outrun lions—if we see them in time, which we can't do with our heads in the sand. That, and the fact that we can kick a lion into another time zone—which we also can't do—"

"Enough!" His father swatted at him with a wing, but missed. "We are ostriches, not eagles, and we have a heritage to maintain. Head out of sight and hold still—that's our legacy to you, and one day you'll thank me for it. Go away now. You're upsetting your mother."

So the young ostrich went away, angry and unconvinced. He attempted to enlist others to his cause, but not one disciple joined him in challenging this first and deepest-rooted of ostrich traditions. "You may very well be right," his friends told him, "we wouldn't be a bit surprised to see you vindicated one day. But right now there's a big, hungry-looking lion prowling over there, and if you'll excuse us . . ."

And they would hurry off to shove their heads deep into the coolest, softest patch of sand they could find, leaving their feathered rumps to cope with the consequences. Which suited lions well enough, on the whole, but deeply distressed the young ostrich. He continued doing everything he could to persuade other birds to change their behavior, but consistently met with such failure that he was cast down into utter despair.

It was then that he went to the Eldest Lion.

The pilgrimage across the wide savannas was a hard and perilous one, taking the young ostrich several days, even on his powerful naked legs. He would never have dared such a thing, of course, if the Eldest Lion had not long since grown toothless, mangy, and cripplingly arthritic. His heavy claws were blunt and useless, more of his once-black mane fell out every time he shook his head, and he survived entirely on the loyalty of two lionesses who hunted for him, and who snarled away all challengers to his feeble rule. But he was known for a wisdom most lions rarely live long enough to achieve, and the young ostrich felt that his counsel was worth the risk of approaching him in his den. Being very young, he also felt quick enough on his feet to take the chance.

Standing within a conversational distance of the Eldest Lion's lair, he called to him politely, until the great, shaggy—and distinctly smelly—beast shambled to the cave entrance to demand, "What does my lunch want of me? I must ask you, of your kindness, lunch, to come just a little closer. My hearing is not what it was—alas, what is? A little closer, only."

The young ostrich replied courteously, without taking a further step, "I thank you for the invitation, mightiest of lords, but I am only a humble and rather unsightly fowl, unworthy even to set foot on your royal shadow. Sir, Eldest, I have come a far journey to ask you a single simple question, after which I promise to retire to the midden-heap my folk call home and presume no more upon your grace." His mother had always placed much stress on the importance of manners.

The Eldest Lion squinted at him through cataract-fogged eyes, mumbling to himself. "Talks nicely, for a lunch. Nobody speaks properly anymore." Raising his deep, ragged voice, he inquired, "I will grant your request, civilized lunch. What wisdom will you have of me?"

For a moment the words he had come such a distance to say stuck in the young ostrich's throat (it is not true that ostriches can swallow and digest anything); but then they came tumbling out of him in one frantic burst. "Can you lions see us when we bury our heads in the sand? Are we really invisible? Because I don't think we are."

It seemed to the young ostrich that the Eldest Lion—most likely due to senility—had not understood the question at all. He blinked and sneezed and snorted, and the ostrich thought he even drooled, just a trifle. Only after some time did the ostrich realize that the Eldest Lion was, after his fashion, laughing.

"Invisible?" the ancient feline rumbled. "*Invisible?* Your stupidity is a legend among my people. We tell each other ostrich jokes as we sprawl in the sun after a kill, drowsily blowing away the feathers. Even the tiniest cub—even an ancestor like myself, half-blind and three-quarters dead—even we marvel at the existence of a creature so idiotic as to believe that hiding its head could keep it safe. We regard you as the gods' gift to our own idiots, the ones who can't learn to hunt anything else, and would surely starve but for you."

His laughter turned into a fusillade of spluttering coughs, and the young ostrich began to move cautiously away, because a lion's cough does not always signify illness, no matter how old he is. But the Eldest Lion called him back, grunting, "Wait a bit, my good lunch, I enjoy chatting with you. It's certainly a change from trying to make conversation with people whose jaws are occupied chewing my food for me. If you have other questions for me—though I dare not hope that a second could possibly be as foolish as that first—then, by all means, ask away." He lay down heavily, with his paws crossed in front of him, so as to appear less threatening.

"I have only one further question, great lord," the young ostrich ventured, "but I ask it with all my heart. If you were an ostrich—" here he had to pause for a time, because the Eldest Lion had gone into an even more tumultuous coughing spasm, waving him silent until he could control himself. "Tell me, if you were an ostrich, how would *you* conceal yourself from such as yourself? Lions, leopards, packs of hyenas and wild dogs . . . what would be *your* tactic?" He held his breath, waiting for the answer.

"It is extremely difficult for me to conceive of such an eventuality," the Eldest Lion replied grandly, "but one thing seems obvious, even to someone at the very top of the food chain. To bury your head while continuing to expose your entire body strikes me as the height of absurdity—"

"Exactly what I've been telling them and telling them!" the young ostrich broke in excitedly.

The Eldest Lion gave him a look no less imperious and menacing for being rheumy. "I ate the last person who interrupted me," he remarked to the air.

The ostrich apologized humbly, and the Eldest Lion continued, "As I was saying, the truly creative approach would be to reverse the policy, to keep the *body* hidden, leaving only the head visible—and thus, I might add, much better able to survey the situation." He paused for a moment, and then added thoughtfully, "I will confide to you, naïve lunch, that we lions are not nearly as crafty as you plainly suppose. We are creatures of habit, of routine, as indeed are most animals. Faced with an ostrich head sticking out of the sand, any lion would blink, shake his own head, and seek a meal somewhere else. I can assure you of this."

"Bury the *body, not* the head! Yes . . . yes . . . oh, *yes*!" The young ostrich was actually dancing with delight, which is a rare thing to see, and even the Eldest Lion's wise, weary, wicked eyes widened at the sight. "*Thank* you, sir—sir, thank you! What a wonder, imagine—you, a lion, have changed the course of ostrich history!" About to race off, he hesitated briefly, saying, "Sir, I would gladly let you devour me, out of gratitude for this revelation, but then there would be no one to carry the word back to my people, and that would be unforgivable of me. I trust you understand my dilemma?"

"Yes, yes, oh, *yes*," the Eldest Lion replied in grumbling mimicry. "Go away now. I see my lionesses coming home, bringing me a much tastier meal than gristly shanks and dusty feathers. Go away, silly lunch."

The two lionesses were indeed returning, and the young ostrich evaded their interest, not by burying any part of himself in the sand or elsewhere, but by taking to his heels and striding away at his best speed. He ran nearly all the way home, so excited and exalted he was by the inspiration he carried. Nor did he stop to rest, once he arrived, but immediately began spreading the words of wisdom that he had received from the Eldest Lion. "The *body*, not the head! All these generations, and we've been doing it all wrong! It's the *body* we bury, not the head!" He became an evangel of the new strategy, traveling tirelessly to proclaim his message to any and every ostrich who would listen. "It's the *body,* not the head!"

Some time afterward, one of the Eldest Lion's lionesses, who had been away visiting family, reported noticing a number of ostriches who, upon sighting her, promptly dug themselves down into the sand until only their heads, perched atop mounds of earth, remained visible, gazing down at her out of round, solemn eyes. "You've never seen anything like it," she told him. "They looked like fuzzy cabbages with beaks."

The Eldest Lion stared at her, wide-eyed as one of the ostriches. "They bought it?" he growled in disbelief. "Oh, you're kidding. They really . . . with their heads *really* sticking up? All of them?"

"Every one that *I* saw," the lioness replied. "I never laughed so much in my life."

"They bought it," the Eldest Lion repeated dazedly. "Well, I certainly hope you ate a couple at least, to teach them . . . well, to teach them *something.*" He was seriously confused.

But the lioness shook her head. "I told you, I was laughing too hard even to think about eating." The Eldest Lion retired to the darkest corner of his cave and lay down. He said nothing further then, but the two lionesses heard him muttering in the night, over and over, "Who knew? Who knew?"

And from that day to this, unique to that region of Africa, all ostriches respond to peril by burying themselves instantly, leaving only their heads in view. No trick works every time; but considering that predators are almost invariably reduced to helpless, hysterical laughter at the ridiculous sight—lions have a tendency to ruptures, leopards to actual heart attacks—the record of survival is truly remarkable.

MORAL: Stupidity always wins, as long as it's stupid enough.

The Fable of the Octopus

Once, deep down under the sea, down with the starfish and the sting rays and the conger eels, there lived an octopus who wanted to see God.

Octopi are among the most intelligent creatures in the sea, and shyly thoughtful as well, and this particular octopus spent a great deal of time in profound pondering and wondering. Often, curled on the deck of the sunken ship where he laired, he would allow perfectly edible prey to swim or scuttle by, while he silently questioned the here and the now, the if and the then, and—most especially—the may and the might and the why. Even among his family and friends, such rumination was considered somewhat excessive, but it was his way, and it suited him. He planned eventually to write a book of some sort, employing his own ink for the purpose. It was to be called *Concerns of a Cephalopod*, or possibly *Mollusc Meditations*.

Being as reflective as he was, the octopus had never envisioned God in his own image. He had met a number of his legendary giant cousins, and found them vulgar, insensitive sorts, totally—and perhaps understandably—preoccupied with nourishing their vast bodies; utterly uninterested in speculation or abstract thought. As for his many natural predators—the hammerhead and tiger shark, the barracuda, the orca, the sea lion, the moray eel—he dismissed them all in turn as equally shallow, equally lacking in the least suggestion of the celestial, however competent they might be at winkling his kind out of their rocky lairs and devouring them. The octopus was no romantic, but it seemed to him that God must of necessity have a deeper appreciation than this of the eternal mystery of everything, and surely other interests besides mating and lunch. The orca offered to debate the point with him, from a safe distance, before an invited audience, but the octopus was also not a fool.

For a while he did consider the possibility that the wandering albatross might conceivably be God. This was an easy notion for an octopus to entertain, since he glimpsed the albatross only when he occasionally slithered ashore in the twilight, to hunt the small crabs that scurried over the sand at that hour. He would look up then—difficult for an octopus—and sometimes catch sight of the great white wings, still as the clouds through which they slanted down the darkening sky. "So alone," he would think then. "So splendid, and so alone. What other words would suit the nature of divinity?"

But even the beauty and majesty of the albatross could never quite satisfy the octopus's spiritual hunger. It seemed to him that something else was essential to fulfilling his vision of God, and yet he had no word, no image, for what it should be. In time this came to trouble him to the point where he hardly ate or slept, but only brooded in his shipwreck den, concerning himself with no other question. His eight muscular arms themselves took sides in the matter, for each had its own opinion, and they often quarreled and wrestled with each other, which he hardly noticed. When anxious relatives came to visit, he most often hid from them, changing color to match wood or stone or shadow, as octopi will do. They were strangers to him; he no longer recognized any of them anymore.

Then, as suddenly as he himself might once have pounced out of darkness to seize a flatfish or a whelk, a grand new thought took hold of him. What if the old fisherman—the white-bearded one who sometimes rowed out to poke around his ship with a rusty trident when low tide exposed its barnacled hull and splintered masts—what if *he* might perhaps be God? He was poorly clad, beyond doubt, and permanently dirty, but there was a certain dignity about him all the same, and a bright imagination in his salt-reddened eyes that even the orca's eyes somehow lacked. More, he moved as easily on the waters as on land, both by day and night, seemingly not bound to prescribed sleeping and feeding hours like all other creatures. What if, after all the octopus's weary time of searching and wondering, God should have been searching for *him*?

Like every sea creature, the octopus knew that any human being holding any sharp object is a danger to everyone within reach, never to be trusted with body or soul. Nevertheless, he was helpless before his own curiosity; and the next time the fisherman came prowling out with the dawn tide, the octopus could not keep from climbing warily from the ship's keel . . . to the rudder . . . then to the broken, dangling taffrail, and clinging there to watch the old man prying and scraping under the hull, filling the rough-sewn waterproof bag at his belt with muddy mussels and the occasional long-necked clam. He was muddy to the waist himself, and smelled bad, but he hummed and grunted cheerfully as he toiled, and the octopus stared at him in great awe.

At last it became impossible for the octopus to hold his yearning at bay any longer. Taking his courage in all eight arms, he crawled all the way up onto the deck, fully exposed to the astonished gaze of the old fisherman. Haltingly, but clearly, he asked aloud, "Are you God?"

The fisherman's expression changed very slowly, passing from hard, patient resignation through dawning disbelief on the way to a kind of worn radiance. "No, my friend," he responded finally. "I am not God, no more than you. But I think you and I are equally part of God as we stand here," and he swept his arm wide to take in all the slow, dark shiver of the sea as it breathed under the blue and silver morning. "Surely we two are not merely surrounded by this divine splendor—we both belong to it, we are *of* it, now and for always. How else should it be?"

"The sea," the octopus said slowly. "The sea . . ."

"And the land," said the fisherman. "And the sky. And the firelights glittering beyond the sky. All things taken together form the whole, including things like an octopus and an old man, who play their tiny parts and wonder."

"My thoughts and questions were too small . . . I have lived in God all my life, and never known. Is this truly what you tell me?"

"Just so," the old man beamed. "Just so."

The octopus was speechless with joy. He stretched forth a tentative tentacle, and the fisherman took firm hold of it in his own rough hand.

As they stood together, both of them equally enraptured by their newfound accord, the octopus asked shyly, "Do you suppose that God is aware that we are here, within It—part of It?"

"I have no idea," the fisherman replied placidly. "What matters is that *we* know."

There was a rough *thump* as the boat tilted suddenly starboard and nose down, its gentle rocking halted. The sea lowered, falling away from the boat in a great rush, exposing faded paint and barnacles to the air. Shifting gravel and rock clawed at the hull and rudder. The octopus, automatically exerting his suckers against the deck, was unmoved, but the fisherman went tumbling, and above and below and around them the world itself seemed to open a great mouth and draw breath ever more steadily toward the west.

"And that?" the octopus inquired. He pointed with a second tentacle toward the naked expanse of ocean floor over which the tide had withdrawn almost to the horizon—surest sign of an approaching tsunami. "Is that also part of God, like us?"

"I am afraid so," replied the old fisherman, braced now against the slanting rail. "Along with typhoons, stinging jellyfish, my wife's parents, and really bad oysters. In such a case, I regard it as no sin to head for the high ground. The shore is far, true, but I was fast on my feet as a young man and this life has kept me fit. I will live, and buy another boat, and fish again."

"I wish you well," said the octopus, "but I am afraid my own options are somewhat more constrained. For escape I require the freedom of the deep sea, which is now entirely out of reach. No. God's great shrug will be here soon enough. I will watch it come, and when it arrives I will give it both our greetings."

"You'll be killed," said the fisherman.

The octopus was hardly equipped to smile, but the fisherman could hear one in his voice all the same. "I shall still be with God."

"That particular form of deep metaphysical appreciation will come to you soon enough without the help of fatalism or fifty-foot waves," said the fisherman, pulling the half-filled canvas bag from his belt. "Besides, *our* conversation has just begun."

Quick as the eels he was so good at catching, the fisherman slid over the rail and dropped to the exposed seabed. Once there he knelt down and pulled the open canvas bag back and forth through the silty, cross-cut shallows, losing his catch, but harvesting a full crop of seawater.

"Well? Are you coming?" the fisherman shouted up to the octopus. He held out the brimming bag exactly like the promise it was. "Time and tide, my many-armed friend. Time and tide!"

In the years that followed—and these were many, for the fisherman and the octopus did survive the tsunami, *just*—these two unlikely philosophers spent a great deal of time together. The fisherman found in the octopus a companion who shared all his interests, including Schopenhauer, Kierkegaard (whom the octopus found "a trifle nervous"), current events both above and below the water, and favorite kinds of fish. The octopus, in turn, learned more than he had ever imagined learning about the worlds of space and thought, and in time he even wrote his book. After suffering rejections from all the major publishing houses, it finally caught the attention of an editor at a Midwestern university press. That worthy, favoring the poetic over the literal, tacked *Eight Arms to Hold You* above the manuscript's original title—*Octopoidal Observations*—advertised the book as allegory, and watched it enjoy two and a half years on the New Age bestseller lists. Every three months he dutifully sent a royalty check and a forwarded packet of fan letters to a certain coastal post office box; and if the checks were never cashed, well, what business was it of his? Authors were eccentric—no one knew *that* better than he, as he said often.

The octopus's book found no underwater readership, of course, since in the ocean, just as on land, reviewers tend to be sharks. But the one-sidedness and anonymity of his fame never troubled him. When not visiting the fisherman, he was content to nibble on passing hermit crabs and drowse among the rocks in a favorite tide pool (his own sunken hulk having been smashed to as many flinders as the fisherman's old boat), thinking deeply, storing up questions and debating points to spring on his patient and honorable friend.

And he never asked if anyone or anything was God, not ever again. He didn't have to.

MORAL: The best answer to any question? It's always a surprise.

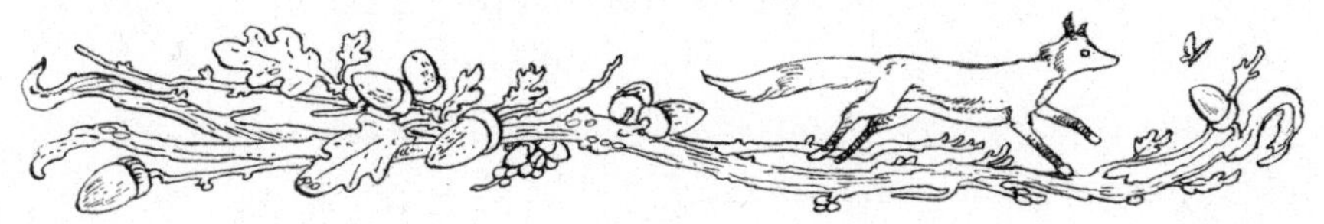

El Regalo

Sometimes a story interests me too much, for one reason or another, simply to let it go: I need to know what happens later. This doesn't happen often, and when it does I hate it, but there you are.

And so it is with this one. I *need* to know what comes next for Angie and Marvyn (not to mention *El Viejo*). That's why somewhere up ahead there will be a full novel detailing the further adventures of these two Korean-American siblings. I plan on giving it the title which inspired this story in the first place: *My Stupid Brother Marvyn the Witch.*

"You can't kill him," Mr. Luke said. "Your mother wouldn't like it." After some consideration, he added, "I'd be rather annoyed myself."

"But wait," Angie said, in the dramatic tones of a television commercial for some miraculous mop. "There's more. I didn't tell you about the brandied cupcakes—"

"Yes, you did."

"And about him telling Jennifer Williams what I got her for her birthday, and she pitched a fit, because she had two of them already—"

"He meant well," her father said cautiously. "I'm pretty sure."

"And then when he finked to Mom about me and Orlando Cruz, and we weren't doing *anything*—"

"Nevertheless. No killing."

Angie brushed sweaty mouse-brown hair off her forehead and regrouped. "Can I at least maim him a little? Trust me, he's earned it."

"I don't doubt you," Mr. Luke agreed. "But you're twelve, and Marvyn's eight. Eight and a half. You're bigger than he is, so beating him up isn't fair. When you're . . . oh, say, twenty, and he's sixteen and a half—okay, you can try it then. Not until."

Angie's wordless grunt might or might not have been assent. She started out of the room, but her father called her back, holding out his right hand. "Pinky-swear, kid." Angie eyed him warily, but hooked her little finger around his without hesitation, which was a mistake. "You did that much too easily," her father said, frowning. "Swear by Buffy."

"What? You can't swear by a television show!"

"Where is that written? Repeat after me—'I swear by *Buffy the Vampire Slayer*—'"

"You really *don't* trust me!"

"'I swear by *Buffy the Vampire Slayer* that I will keep my hands off my baby brother—'"

"My baby brother, the monster! He's gotten worse since he started sticking that y in his name—"

"'—and I will stop calling him Ex-Lax—'"

"Come on, I only do that when he makes me really mad—"

"'—until he shall have attained the age of sixteen years and six months, after which time—'"

"After which time I get to pound him into marmalade. Deal. I can wait." She grinned; then turned self-conscious, making a performance of pulling down her upper lip to cover the shiny new braces. At the door, she looked over her shoulder and said lightly, "You are way too smart to be a father."

From behind his book, Mr. Luke answered, "I've often thought so myself."

Angie spent the rest of the evening in her room, doing homework on the phone with Melissa Feldman, her best friend. Finished, feeling virtuously entitled to some low-fat chocolate reward, she wandered down the hall toward the kitchen, passing her brother's room on the way. Looking in—not because of any special interest, but because Marvyn invariably hung around her own doorway, gazing in aimless fascination at whatever she was doing, until shooed away—she saw him on the floor, playing with Milady, the gray, ancient family cat. Nothing unusual about that: Marvyn and Milady had been an item since he was old enough to realize that the cat wasn't something to eat. What halted Angie as though she had walked into a wall was that they were playing Monopoly, and that Milady appeared to be winning.

Angie leaned in the doorway, entranced and alarmed at the same time. Marvyn had to throw the dice for both Milady and himself, and the old cat was too riddled with arthritis to handle the pastel Monopoly money easily. But she waited her turn, and moved her piece—she had the silver top hat—very carefully, as though considering possible options. And she already had a hotel on Park Place.

Marvyn jumped up and slammed the door as soon as he noticed his sister watching the game, and Angie went on to liberate a larger-than-planned remnant of sorbet. Somewhere near the bottom of the container she finally managed to stuff what she'd just glimpsed deep in the part of her mind she called her "forgettery." As she'd once said to her friend Melissa, "There's such a thing as too much information, and it is not going to get me. I am never going to know more than I want to know about stuff. Look at the President."

For the next week or so Marvyn made a point of staying out of Angie's way, which was all by itself enough to put her mildly on edge. If she knew one thing about her brother, it was that the time to worry was when you didn't see him. All the same, on the surface things were peaceful enough, and continued so until the evening when Marvyn went dancing with the garbage.

The next day being pickup day, Mrs. Luke had handed him two big green plastic bags of trash for the rolling bins down the driveway. Marvyn had made enough of a fuss about the task that Angie stayed by the open front window to make sure that he didn't simply drop the bags in the grass, and vanish into one of his mysterious hideouts. Mrs. Luke was back in the living room with the news on, but Angie was still at the window when Marvyn looked around quickly, mumbled a few words she couldn't catch, and then did a thing with his left hand, so fast she saw no more than a blurry twitch. And the two garbage bags went dancing.

Angie's buckling knees dropped her to the couch under the window, though she never noticed it. Marvyn let go of the bags altogether, and they rocked alongside him—backwards, forwards, sideways, in perfect timing, with perfect steps, turning with him as though he were the star and they his backup singers. To Angie's astonishment, he was snapping his fingers and moonwalking, as she had never imagined he could do—and the bags were pushing out green arms and legs as the three of them danced down the driveway. When they reached the cans, Marvyn's partners promptly went limp and were nothing but plastic garbage bags again. Marvyn plopped them in, dusted his hands, and turned to walk back to the house.

When he saw Angie watching, neither of them spoke. Angie beckoned. They met at the door and stared at each other. Angie said only, "My room."

Marvyn dragged in behind her, looking everywhere and nowhere at once, and definitely not at his sister. Angie sat down on the bed and studied him: chubby and messy-looking, with an unmanageable sprawl of rusty-brown hair and an eyepatch meant to tame a wandering left eye. She said, "Talk to me."

"About what?" Marvyn had a deep, foggy voice for eight and a half—Mr. Luke always insisted that it had changed before Marvyn was born. "I didn't break your CD case."

"Yes, you did," Angie said. "But forget that. Let's talk about garbage bags. Let's talk about Monopoly."

Marvyn was utterly businesslike about lies: in a crisis he always told the truth, until he thought of something better. He said, "I'm warning you right now, you won't believe me."

"I never do. Make it a good one."

"Okay," Marvyn said. "I'm a witch."

When Angie could speak, she said the first thing that came into her head, which embarrassed her forever after. "You can't be a witch. You're a wizard, or a warlock or something." Like we're having a sane conversation, she thought.

Marvyn shook his head so hard that his eyepatch almost came loose. "Uh-uh! That's all books and movies and stuff. You're a man witch or you're a woman witch, that's it. I'm a man witch."

"You'll be a dead witch if you don't quit shitting me," Angie told him. But her brother knew he had her, and he grinned like a pirate (at home he often tied a bandanna around his head, and he was constantly after Mrs. Luke to buy him a parrot). He said, "You can ask Lidia. She was the one who knew."

Lidia del Carmen de Madero y Gomez had been the Lukes' housekeeper since well before Angie's birth. She was from Ciego de Avila in Cuba, and claimed to have changed Fidel Castro's diapers as a girl working for his family. For all her years—no one seemed to know her age; certainly not the Lukes—Lidia's eyes remained as clear as a child's, and Angie had on occasion nearly wept with envy of her beautiful wrinkled deep-dark skin. For her part, Lidia got on well with Angie, spoke Spanish with her mother, and was teaching Mr. Luke to cook Cuban food. But Marvyn had been hers since his infancy, beyond question or interference. They went to Spanish-language movies on Saturdays, and shopped together in the Bowen Street *barrio*.

"The one who knew," Angie said. "Knew what? Is Lidia a witch too?"

Marvyn's look suggested that he was wondering where their parents had actually found their daughter. "No, of course she's not a witch. She's a *santera*."

Angie stared. She knew as much about Santeria as anyone growing up in a big city with a growing population of Africans and South Americans—which wasn't much. Newspaper articles and television specials had informed her that *santeros* sacrificed chickens and goats and did . . . things with the blood. She tried to imagine Marvyn with a chicken, doing things, and couldn't. Not even Marvyn.

"So Lidia got you into it?" she finally asked. "Now you're a *santero* too?"

"Nah, I'm a witch, I told you." Marvyn's disgusted impatience was approaching critical mass.

Angie said, "Wicca? You're into the Goddess thing? There's a girl in my homeroom, Devlin Margulies, and she's a Wiccan, and that's all she talks about. Sabbats and esbats, and drawing down the moon, and the rest of it. She's got skin like a cheese-grater."

Marvyn blinked at her. "What's a Wiccan?" He sprawled suddenly on her bed, grabbing Milady as she hobbled in and pooting loudly on her furry stomach. "I already knew I could sort of mess with things—you remember the rubber duck, and that time at the baseball game?" Angie remembered. Especially the rubber duck. "Anyway, Lidia took me to meet this real old lady, in the farmers' market, she's even older than her, her name's Yemaya, something like that, she smokes this funny little pipe all the time. Anyway, she took hold of me, my face, and she looked in my eyes, and then she closed her eyes, and she just sat like that for so long!" He giggled. "I thought she'd fallen asleep, and I started to pull away, but Lidia wouldn't let me. So she sat like that, and she sat, and then she opened her eyes and she told me I was a witch, a *brujo*. And Lidia bought me a two-scoop ice-cream cone. Coffee and chocolate, with M&M's."

"You won't have a tooth in your head by the time you're fifteen." Angie didn't know what to say, what questions to ask. "So that's it? The old lady, she gives you witch lessons or something?"

"Nah—I told you, she's a big *santera*, that's different. I only saw her that one time. She kept telling Lidia that I had *el regalo*—I think that means the gift, she said that a lot—and I should keep practicing. Like you with the clarinet."

Angie winced. Her hands were small and stubby-fingered, and music slipped through them like rain. Her parents, sympathizing, had offered to cancel the clarinet lessons, but Angie refused. As she confessed to her friend Melissa, she had no skill at accepting defeat.

Now she asked, "So how do you practice? Boogieing with garbage bags?"

Marvyn shook his head. "That's getting old—so's playing board games with Milady. I was thinking maybe I could make the dishes wash themselves, like in *Beauty and the Beast*. I bet I could do that."

"You could enchant my homework," Angie suggested. "My algebra, for starters."

Her brother snorted. "Hey, I'm just a kid, I've got my limits! I mean, your homework?"

"Right," Angie said. "Right. Look, what about laying a major spell on Tim Hubley, the next time he's over here with Melissa? Like making his feet go flat so he can't play basketball—that's the only reason she likes him, anyway. Or—" her voice became slower and more hesitant "—what about getting Jake Petrakis to fall madly, wildly, totally in love with me? That'd be . . . funny."

Marvyn was occupied with Milady. "Girl stuff, who cares about all that? I want to be so good at soccer everybody'll want to be on my team—I want fat Josh Wilson to have patches over both eyes, so he'll leave me alone. I want Mom to order thin-crust pepperoni pizza every night, and I want Dad to—"

"No spells on Mom and Dad, not ever!" Angie was on her feet, leaning menacingly over him. "You got that, Ex-Lax? You mess with them even once, believe me, you'd better be one hella witch to keep me from strangling you. Understood?"

Marvyn nodded. Angie said, "Okay, I tell you what. How about practicing on Aunt Caroline when she comes next weekend?"

Marvyn's pudgy pirate face lit up at the suggestion. Aunt Caroline was their mother's older sister, celebrated in the Luke family for knowing everything about everything. A pleasant, perfectly decent person, her perpetual air of placid expertise would have turned a saint into a serial killer. Name a country, and Aunt Caroline had spent enough time there to know more about the place than a native; bring up a newspaper story, and without fail Aunt Caroline could tell you something about it that hadn't been in the paper; catch a cold, and Aunt Caroline could recite the maiden name of the top medical researcher in rhinoviruses' mother. (Mr. Luke said often that Aunt Caroline's motto was, "Say something, and I'll bet you're wrong.")

"Nothing dangerous," Angie commanded, "nothing scary. And nothing embarrassing or anything."

Marvyn looked sulky. "It's not going to be any fun that way."

"If it's too gross, they'll know you did it," his sister pointed out. "I would." Marvyn, who loved secrets and hidden identities, yielded.

During the week before Aunt Caroline's arrival, Marvyn kept so quietly to himself that Mrs. Luke worried about his health. Angie kept as close an eye on him as possible, but couldn't be at all sure what he might be planning—no more than he, she suspected. Once she caught him changing the TV channels without the remote; and once, left alone in the kitchen to peel potatoes and carrots for a stew, he had the peeler do it while he read the Sunday funnies. The apparent smallness of his ambitions relieved Angie's vague unease, lulling her into complacency about the big family dinner that was traditional on the first night of a visit from Aunt Caroline.

Aunt Caroline was, among other things, the sort of woman incapable of going anywhere without attempting to buy it. Her own house was jammed to the attic with sightseer souvenirs from all over the world: children's toys from Slovenia, sculptures from Afghanistan, napkin rings from Kenya shaped like lions and giraffes, legions of brass bangles, boxes and statues of gods from India, and so many Russian *matryoshka* dolls fitting inside each other that she gave them away as stocking-stuffers every Christmas. She never came to the table at the Lukes without bringing some new acquisition for approval; so dinner with Aunt Caroline, in Mr. Luke's words, was always Show and Tell time.

Her most recent hegira had brought her back to West Africa for the third or fourth time, and provided her with the most evil-looking doll Angie had ever seen. Standing beside Aunt Caroline's plate, it was about two feet high, with bat ears, too many fingers, and eyes like bright green marbles streaked with scarlet threads. Aunt Caroline explained rapturously that it was a fertility doll unique to a single Benin tribe, which Angie found impossible to credit. "No way!" she announced loudly. "Not for one minute am I even thinking about having babies with that thing staring at me! It doesn't even look pregnant, the way they do. No way in the world!"

Aunt Caroline had already had two of Mr. Luke's margaritas, and was working on a third. She replied with some heat that not all fertility figures came equipped with cannonball breasts, globular bellies and callipygous rumps—"Some of them are remarkably slender, even by Western standards!" Aunt Caroline herself, by anyone's standards, was built along the general lines of a chopstick.

Angie was drawing breath for a response when she heard her father say behind her, "Well, Jesus Harrison Christ," and then her mother's soft gasp, "Caroline." But Aunt Caroline was busy explaining to her niece that she knew absolutely nothing about fertility. Mrs. Luke said, considerably louder, "Caroline, shut up, your doll!"

Aunt Caroline said, "What, what?" and then turned, along with Angie. They both screamed.

The doll was growing all the things Aunt Caroline had been insisting it didn't need to qualify as a fertility figure. It was carved from ebony, or from something even harder, but it was pushing out breasts and belly and hips much as Marvyn's two garbage bags had suddenly developed arms and legs. Even its expression had changed, from hungry slyness to a downright silly grin, as though it were about to kiss someone, anyone. It took a few shaky steps forward on the table and put its foot in the salsa.

Then the babies started coming.

They came pattering down on the dinner table, fast and hard, like wooden rain, one after another, after another, after another . . . perfect little copies, miniatures, of the madly smiling doll-thing, plopping out of it—*just like Milady used to drop kittens in my lap,* Angie thought absurdly. One of them fell into her plate, and one bounced into the soup, and a couple rolled into Mr. Luke's lap, making him knock his chair over trying to get out of the way. Mrs. Luke was trying to grab them all up at once, which wasn't possible, and Aunt Caroline sat where she was and shrieked. And the doll kept grinning and having babies.

Marvyn was standing against the wall, looking both as terrified as Aunt Caroline and as stupidly pleased as the doll-thing. Angie caught his eye and made a fierce signal, *enough, quit, turn it off,* but either her brother was having too good a time, or else had no idea how to undo whatever spell he had raised. One of the miniatures hit her in the head, and she had a vision of her whole family being drowned in wooden doll-babies, everyone gurgling and reaching up pathetically toward the surface before they all went under for the third time. Another baby caromed off the soup tureen into her left ear, one sharp ebony fingertip drawing blood.

It stopped, finally—Angie never learned how Marvyn regained control—and things almost quieted down, except for Aunt Caroline. The fertility doll got the look of glazed joy off its face and went back to being a skinny, ugly, duty-free airport souvenir, while the doll-babies seemed to melt away exactly as though they had been made of ice instead of wood. Angie was quick enough to see one of them actually dissolving into nothingness directly in front of Aunt Caroline, who at this point stopped screaming and began hiccuping and beating the table with her palms. Mr. Luke pounded her on the back, and Angie volunteered to practice her Heimlich maneuver, but was overruled. Aunt Caroline went to bed early.

Later, in Marvyn's room, he kept his own bed between himself and Angie, indignantly demanding, "What? You said not scary—what's scary about a doll having babies? I thought it was cute."

"Cute," Angie said. "Uh-huh." She was wondering, in a distant sort of way, how much prison time she might get if she actually murdered her brother. *Ten years? Five, with good behavior and a lot of psychiatrists? I could manage it.* "And what did I tell you about not embarrassing Aunt Caroline?"

"How did I embarrass her?" Marvyn's visible eye was wide with outraged innocence. "She shouldn't drink so much, that's her problem. She embarrassed me."

"They're going to figure it out, you know," Angie warned him. "Maybe not Aunt Caroline, but Mom for sure. She's a witch herself that way. Your cover is blown, buddy."

But to her own astonishment, not a word was ever said about the episode, the next day or any other—not by her observant mother, not by her dryly perceptive father, nor even by Aunt Caroline, who might reasonably have been expected at least to comment at breakfast. A baffled Angie remarked to Milady, drowsing on her pillow, "I guess if a thing's weird enough, somehow nobody saw it." This explanation didn't satisfy her, not by a long shot, but lacking anything better she was stuck with it. The old cat blinked in squeezy-eyed agreement, wriggled herself into a more comfortable position, and fell asleep still purring.

Angie kept Marvyn more closely under her eye after that than she had done since he was quite small, and first showing a penchant for playing in traffic. Whether this observation was the cause or not, he did remain more or less on his best behavior, barring the time he turned the air in the bicycle tires of a boy who had stolen his superhero comic book to cement. There was also the affair of the enchanted soccer ball, which kept rolling back to him as though it couldn't bear to be with anyone else. And Angie learned to be extremely careful when making herself a sandwich, because if she lost track of her brother for too long, the sandwich was liable to acquire an extra ingredient. Paprika was one, tabasco another; and Scotch Bonnet peppers were a special favorite. But there were others less hot and even more objectionable. As she snarled to a sympathetic Melissa Feldman, who had two brothers of her own, "They ought to be able to jail kids just for being eight and a half."

Then there was the matter of Marvyn's attitude toward Angie's attitude about Jake Petrakis.

Jake Petrakis was a year ahead of Angie at school. He was half-Greek and half-Irish, and his blue eyes and thick poppy-colored hair contrasted so richly with his olive skin that she had not been able to look directly at him since the fourth grade. He was on the swim team, and he was the president of the Chess Club, and he went with Ashleigh Sutton, queen of the junior class, rechristened "Ghastly Ashleigh" by the loyal Melissa. But he spoke kindly and cheerfully to Angie without fail, always saying *Hey, Angie,* and *How's it going, Angie?* and *See you in the fall, Angie, have a good summer.* She clutched such things to herself, every one of them, and at the same time could not bear them.

Marvyn was as merciless as a mosquito when it came to Jake Petrakis. He made swooning, kissing noises whenever he spied Angie looking at Jake's picture in her yearbook, and drove her wild by holding invented conversations between them, just loudly enough for her to hear. His increasing ability at witchcraft meant that scented, decorated, and misspelled love notes were likely to flutter down onto her bed at any moment, as were long-stemmed roses, imitation jewelry (Marvyn had limited experience and poor taste), and small, smudgy photos of Jake and Ashleigh together. Mr. Luke had to invoke Angie's oath more than once, and to sweeten it with a promise of a new bicycle if Marvyn made it through the year undamaged. Angie held out for a mountain bike, and her father sighed. "That was always a myth, about the gypsies stealing children," he said, rather wistfully. "It was surely the other way around. Deal."

Yet there were intermittent peaceful moments between Marvyn and Angie, several occurring in Marvyn's room. It was a far tidier place than Angie's room, for all the clothes on the floor and battered board game boxes sticking out from under the bed. Marvyn had mounted *National Geographic* foldout maps all around the walls, lining them up so perfectly that the creases were invisible; and on one special wall were prints and photos of a lot of people with strange staring eyes. Angie recognized Rasputin, and knew a few of the other names—Aleister Crowley, for one, and a man in Renaissance dress called Dr. John Dee. There were two women, as well: the young witch Willow, from *Buffy the Vampire Slayer,* and a daguerreotype of a Black woman wearing a kind of turban folded into points. No Harry Potter, however. Marvyn had never taken to Harry Potter.

There was also, one day after school, a very young kitten wobbling among the books littering Marvyn's bed. A surprised Angie picked it up and held it over her face, feeling its purring between her hands. It was a dark, dusty gray, rather like Milady—indeed, Angie had never seen another cat of that exact color. She nuzzled its tummy happily, asking it, "Who are you, huh? Who could you ever be?"

Marvyn was feeding his angelfish, and didn't look up. He said, "She's Milady."

Angie dropped the kitten on the bed. Marvyn said, "I mean, she's Milady when she was young. I went back and got her."

When he did turn around, he was grinning the maddening pirate grin Angie could never stand, savoring her shock. It took her a minute to find words, and more time to make them come out. She said, "You went back. You went back in time?"

"It was easy," Marvyn said. "Forward's *hard*—I don't think I could ever get really forward. Maybe Dr. Dee could do it." He picked up the kitten and handed her back to his sister. It was Milady, down to the crooked left ear and the funny short tail with the darker bit on the end. He said, "She was hurting all the time, she was so old. I thought, if she could—you know—start over, before she got the arthritis . . . ."

He didn't finish. Angie said slowly, "So where's Milady? The other one? I mean, if you brought this one . . . I mean, how can they be in the same world?"

"They can't," Marvyn said. "The old Milady's gone."

Angie's throat closed up. Her eyes filled, and so did her nose, and she had to blow it before she could speak again. Looking at the kitten, she knew it was Milady, and made herself think about how good it would be to have her once again bouncing around the house, no longer limping grotesquely and meowing with the pain. But she had loved the old cat all her life, and never known her as a kitten, and when the new Milady started to climb into her lap, Angie pushed her away.

"All right," she said to Marvyn. "All right. How did you get . . . back, or whatever?"

Marvyn shrugged and went back to his fish. "No big deal. You just have to concentrate the right way."

Angie bounced a plastic Wiffle ball off the back of his neck, and he turned around, annoyed. "Leave me alone! Okay, you want to know—there's a spell, words you have to say over and over and over, until you're sick of them, and there's herbs in it too. You have to light them, and hang over them, and you shut your eyes and keep breathing them in and saying the words—"

"I knew I'd been smelling something weird in your room lately. I thought you were sneaking takeout curry to bed with you again."

"And then you open your eyes, and there you are," Marvyn said. "I told you, no big deal."

"There you are where? How do you know where you'll come out? When you'll come out? Click your heels together three times and say there's no place like home?"

"No, dork, you just *know*." And that was all Angie could get out of him—not, as she came to realize, because he wouldn't tell her, but because he couldn't. Witch or no witch, he was still a small boy, with almost no real idea of what he was doing. He was winging it all, playing it all by ear.

Arguing with Marvyn always gave her a headache, and her history homework—the rise of the English merchant class—was starting to look good in comparison. She went back to her own bedroom and read two whole chapters, and when the kitten Milady came stumbling and squeaking in, Angie let her sleep on the desk. "What the hell," she told it, "it's not your fault."

That evening, when Mr. and Mrs. Luke got home, Angie told them that Milady had died peacefully of illness and old age while they were at work, and was now buried in the back garden. (Marvyn had wanted to make it a horrible hit-and-run accident, complete with a black SUV and half-glimpsed license plate starting with the letter Q, but Angie vetoed this.) Marvyn's contribution to her solemn explanation was to explain that he had seen the new kitten in a petshop window, "and she just looked so much like Milady, and I used my whole allowance, and I'll take care of her, I promise!" Their mother, not being a true cat person, accepted the story easily enough, but Angie was never sure about Mr. Luke. She found him too often sitting with the kitten on his lap, the two of them staring solemnly at each other.

But she saw very little evidence of Marvyn fooling any further with time. Nor, for that matter, was he showing the interest she would have expected in turning himself into the world's best second-grade soccer player, ratcheting up his test scores high enough to be in college by the age of eleven, or simply getting even with people (since Marvyn forgot nothing and had a hit list going back to day-care). She could almost always tell when he'd been making his bed by magic, or making the window plants grow too fast, but he seemed content to remain on that level. Angie let it go.

Once she did catch him crawling on the ceiling, like Spider-Man, but she yelled at him and he fell on the bed and threw up. And there was, of course, the time—two times, actually—when, with Mrs. Luke away, Marvyn organized all the shoes in her closet into a chorus line, and had them tapping and kicking together like the Rockettes. It was fun for Angie to watch, but she made him stop because they were her mother's shoes. What if her clothes joined in? The notion was more than she wanted to deal with.

As it was, there was already plenty to deal with just then. Besides her schoolwork, there was band practice, and Melissa's problems with her boyfriend; not to mention the endless hours spent at the dentist, correcting a slight overbite. Melissa insisted that it made her look sexy, but the suggestion had the wrong effect on Angie's mother. In any case, as far as Angie could see, all Marvyn was doing was playing with a new box of toys, like an elaborate electric train layout, or a top-of-the-line Erector set. She was even able to imagine him getting bored with magic itself after a while. Marvyn had a low threshold for boredom.

Angie was in the orchestra, as well as the band, because of a chronic shortage of woodwinds, but she liked the marching band better. You were out of doors, performing at parades and football games, part of the joyful noise, and it was always more exciting than standing up in a dark, hushed auditorium playing for people you could hardly see. "Besides," as she confided to her mother, "in marching band nobody really notices how you sound. They just want you to keep in step."

On a bright spring afternoon, rehearsing "The Washington Post March" with the full band, Angie's clarinet abruptly went mad. No "licorice stick" now, but a stick of rapturous dynamite, it took off on flights of rowdy improvisation, doing outrageous somersaults, backflips, and cartwheels with the melody—things that Angie knew she could never have conceived of, even if her skill had been equal to the inspiration. Her bandmates, up and down the line, were turning to stare at her, and she wanted urgently to wail, "Hey, I'm not the one, it's my stupid brother, you know I can't play like that." But the music kept spilling out, excessive, absurd, unstoppable—unlike the march, which finally lurched to a disorderly halt. Angie had never been so embarrassed in her life.

Mr. Bishow, the bandmaster, came bumbling through the milling musicians to tell her, "Angie, that was fantastic—that was dazzling! I never knew you had such spirit, such freedom, such wit in your music!" He patted her—hugged her even, quickly and cautiously—then stepped back almost immediately and said, "Don't ever do it again."

"Like I'd have a choice," Angie mumbled, but Mr. Bishow was already shepherding the band back into formation for "Semper Fidelis" and "High Society," which Angie fumbled her way through as always, two bars behind the rest of the woodwinds. She was slouching disconsolately off the field when Jake Petrakis, his dark-gold hair still glinting damply from swimming practice, ran over to her to say, "Hey, Angie, cool," then punched her on the shoulder, as he would have done another boy, and dashed off again to meet one of his relay-team partners. And Angie went on home, and waited for Marvyn behind the door of his room.

She seized him by the hair the moment he walked in, and he squalled, "All right, let go, all right! I thought you'd like it!"

"Like it?" Angie shook him, hard. "*Like* it? You evil little ogre, you almost got me kicked out of the band! What else are you lining up for me that you think I'll *like?*"

"Nothing, I swear!" But he was giggling even while she was shaking him. "Okay, I was going to make you so beautiful, even Mom and Dad wouldn't recognize you, but I quit on that. Too much work." Angie grabbed for his hair again, but Marvyn ducked. "So what I thought, maybe I really could get Jake what's-his-face to go crazy about you. There's all kinds of spells and things for that—"

"Don't you dare," Angie said. She repeated the warning calmly and quietly. "Don't. You. Dare."

Marvyn was still giggling. "Nah, I didn't think you'd go for it. Would have been fun, though." Suddenly he was all earnestness, staring up at his sister out of one visible eye, strangely serious, even with his nose running. He said, "It is fun, Angie. It's the most fun I've ever had."

"Yeah, I'll bet," she said grimly. "Just leave me out of it from now on, if you've got any plans for the third grade." She stalked into the kitchen, looking for apple juice.

Marvyn tagged after her, chattering nervously about school, soccer games, the Milady-kitten's rapid growth, and a possible romance in his angelfish tank. "I'm sorry about the band thing, I won't do it again. I just thought it'd be nice if you could play really well, just one time. Did you like the music part, anyway?"

Angie did not trust herself to answer him. She was reaching for the apple juice bottle when the top flew off by itself, bouncing straight up at her face. As she flinched back, a glass came skidding down the counter toward her. She grabbed it before it crashed into the refrigerator, then turned and screamed at Marvyn, "Damn it, Ex-Lax, you quit that! You're going to hurt somebody, trying to do every damn thing by magic!"

"You said the D-word twice!" Marvyn shouted back at her. "I'm telling Mom!" But he made no move to leave the kitchen, and after a moment a small, grubby tear came sliding down from under the eyepatch. "I'm not using magic for everything! I just use it for the boring stuff, mostly. Like the garbage, and vacuuming up, and like putting my clothes away. And Milady's litter box, when it's my turn. That kind of stuff, okay?"

Angie studied him, marveling as always at his capacity for looking heartwrenchingly innocent. She said, "No point to it when I'm cleaning her box, right? Never mind—just stay out of my way, I've got a French midterm tomorrow." She poured the apple juice, put it back, snatched a raisin cookie, and headed for her room. But she paused in the doorway, for no reason she could ever name, except perhaps the way Marvyn had moved to follow her and then stopped himself. "What? Wipe your nose, it's gross. What's the matter now?"

"Nothing," Marvyn mumbled. He wiped his nose on his sleeve, which didn't help. He said, "Only I get scared, Angie. It's scary, doing the stuff I can do."

"What scary? Scary how? A minute ago it was more fun than you've ever had in your life."

"It is!" He moved closer, strangely hesitant: neither witch, nor pirate nor seraph, but an anxious, burdened small boy. "Only sometimes it's like too much fun. Sometimes, right in the middle, I think maybe I should stop, but I can't. Like one time, I was by myself, and I was just fooling around . . . and I sort of made this *thing*, which was really interesting, only it came out funny and then I couldn't unmake it for the longest time, and I was scared Mom and Dad would come home—"

Angie, grimly weighing her past French grades in her mind, reached back for another raisin cookie. "I told you before, you're going to get yourself into real trouble doing crazy stuff like that. Just quit, before something happens by magic that you can't fix by magic. You want advice, I just gave you advice. See you around."

Marvyn wandered forlornly after her to the door of her room. When she turned to close it, he mumbled, "I wish I were as old as you. So I'd know what to do."

"Ha," Angie said, and shut the door.

Whereupon, heedless of French irregular verbs, she sat down at her desk and began writing a letter to Jake Petrakis.

Neither then nor even much later was Angie ever able to explain to anyone why she had written that letter at precisely that time. Because he had slapped her shoulder and told her she—or at least her music—was cool? Because she had seen him, that same afternoon, totally tangled up with Ghastly Ashleigh in a shadowy corner of the library stacks? Because of Marvyn's relentless teasing? Or simply because she was twelve years old, and it was time for her to write such a letter to someone? Whatever the cause, she wrote what she wrote, and then she folded it up and put it away in her desk drawer.

Then she took it out, and put it back in, and then she finally put it into her backpack. And there the letter stayed for nearly three months, well past midterms, finals, and football, until the fateful Friday night when Angie was out with Melissa, walking and window-shopping in downtown Avicenna, placidly drifting in and out of every coffeeshop along Parnell Street. She told Melissa about the letter then, and Melissa promptly went into a fit of the giggles, which turned into hiccups and required another cappuccino to pacify them. When she could speak coherently, she said, "You ought to send it to him. You've got to send it to him."

Angie was outraged, at first. "No way! I wrote it for me, not for a test or a class, and damn sure not for Jake Petrakis. What kind of a dipshit do you think I am?"

Melissa grinned at her out of mocking green eyes. "The kind of dipshit who's got that letter in your backpack right now, and I bet it's in an envelope with an address and a stamp on it."

"It doesn't have a stamp! And the envelope's just to protect it! I just like having it with me, that's all—"

"And the address?"

"Just for practice, okay? But I didn't sign it, and there's no return address, so that shows you!"

"Right." Melissa nodded. "Right. That definitely shows me."

"Drop it," Angie told her, and Melissa dropped it then. But it was a Friday night, and both of them were allowed to stay out late, as long as they were together, and Avicenna has a lot of coffeeshops. Enough lattes and cappuccinos, with double shots of espresso, brought them to a state of cheerfully jittery abandon in which everything in the world was supremely, ridiculously funny. Melissa never left the subject of Angie's letter alone for very long—"Come on, what's the worst that could happen? Him reading it and maybe figuring out you wrote it? Listen, the really worst thing would be you being an old, old lady still wishing you'd told Jake Petrakis how you felt when you were young. And now he's married, and he's a grandfather, and probably dead, for all you know—"

"Quit it!" But Angie was giggling almost as much as Melissa now, and somehow they were walking down quiet Lovisi Street, past the gas station and the boarded-up health-food store, to find the darkened Petrakis house and tiptoe up the steps to the porch. Facing the front door, Angie dithered for a moment, but Melissa said, "An old lady, in a home, for God's sake, and he'll never know," and Angie took a quick breath and pushed the letter under the door. They ran all the way back to Parnell Street, laughing so wildly that they could barely breathe . . . .

. . . and Angie woke up in the morning whispering *omigod, omigod, omigod,* over and over, even before she was fully awake. She lay in bed for a good hour, praying silently and desperately that the night before had been some crazy, awful dream, and that when she dug into her backpack the letter would still be there. But she knew dreadfully better, and she never bothered to look for it on her frantic way to the telephone. Melissa said soothingly, "Well, at least you didn't sign the thing. There's that, anyway."

"I sort of lied about that," Angie said. Her friend did not answer. Angie said, "Please, you have to come with me. Please."

"Get over there," Melissa said finally. "Go, now—I'll meet you."

Living closer, Angie reached the Petrakis house first, but had no intention of ringing the bell until Melissa got there. She was pacing back and forth on the porch, cursing herself, banging her fists against her legs, and wondering whether she could go to live with her father's sister Peggy in Grand Rapids, when the woman next door called over to tell her that the Petrakises were all out of town at a family gathering. "Left yesterday afternoon. Asked me to keep an eye on the place, cause they won't be back till sometime Sunday night. That's how come I'm kind of watching out." She smiled warningly at Angie before she went back indoors.

The very large dog standing behind her stayed outside. He looked about the size of a Winnebago, and plainly had already made up his mind about Angie. She said, "Nice doggie," and he growled. When she tried out "Hey, sweet thing," which was what her father said to all animals, the dog showed his front teeth, and the hair stood up around his shoulders, and he lay down to keep an eye on things himself. Angie said sadly, "I'm usually really good with dogs."

When Melissa arrived, she said, "Well, you shoved it under the door, so it can't be that far inside. Maybe if we got something like a stick or a wire clotheshanger to hook it back with." But whenever they looked toward the neighboring house, they saw a curtain swaying, and finally they walked away, trying to decide what else to do. But there was nothing; and after a while Angie's throat was too swollen with not crying for her to talk without pain. She walked Melissa back to the bus stop, and they hugged goodbye as though they might never meet again.

Melissa said, "You know, my mother says nothing's ever as bad as you thought it was going to be. I mean, it can't be, because nothing beats all the horrible stuff you can imagine. So maybe . . . you know . . ." but she broke down before she could finish. She hugged Angie again and went home.

Alone in her own house, Angie sat quite still in the kitchen and went on not crying. Her entire face hurt with it, and her eyes felt unbearably heavy. Her mind was not moving at all, and she was vaguely grateful for that. She sat there until Marvyn walked in from playing basketball with his friends. Shorter than everyone else, he generally got stepped on a lot, and always came home scraped and bruised. Angie had rather expected him to try making himself taller, or able to jump higher, but he hadn't done anything of the sort so far. He looked at her now, bounced and shot an invisible basketball, and asked quietly, "What's the matter?"

It may have been the unexpected froggy gentleness of his voice, or simply the sudden fact of his having asked the question at all. Whatever the reason, Angie abruptly burst into furious tears, the rage directed entirely at herself, both for writing the letter to Jake Petrakis in the first place, and for crying about it now. She gestured to Marvyn to go away, but—amazing her further—he stood stolidly waiting for her to grow quiet. When at last she did, he repeated the question. "Angie. What's wrong?"

Angie told him. She was about to add a disclaimer—"You laugh even once, Ex-Lax—" when she realized that it wouldn't be necessary. Marvyn was scratching his head, scrunching up his brow until the eyepatch danced; then abruptly jamming both hands in his pockets and tilting his head back: the poster boy for careless insouciance. He said, almost absently, "I could get it back."

"Oh, right." Angie did not even look up. "Right."

"I could so!" Marvyn was instantly his normal self again: so much for casualness and dispassion. "There's all kinds of things I could do."

Angie dampened a paper towel and tried to do something with her hot, tear-streaked face. "Name two."

"Okay, I will! You remember which mailbox you put it in?"

"Under the door," Angie mumbled. "I put it under the door."

Marvyn snickered then. "*Aww,* like a Valentine." Angie hadn't the energy to hit him, but she made a grab at him anyway, for appearance's sake. "Well, I could make it walk right back out the door, that's one way. Or I bet I could just open the door, if nobody's home. Easiest trick in the world, for us witches."

"They're gone till Sunday night," Angie said. "But there's this lady next door, she's watching the place like a hawk. And even when she's not, she's got this immense dog. I don't care if you're the hottest witch in the world, you do not want to mess with this werewolf."

Marvyn, who—as Angie knew—was wary of big dogs, went back to scratching his head. "Too easy, anyway. No fun, forget it." He sat down next to her, completely absorbed in the problem. "How about I . . . no, that's kid stuff, anybody could do it. But there's a spell . . . I could make the letter self-destruct, right there in the house, like in that old TV show. It'd just be a little fluffy pile of ashes—they'd vacuum it up and never know. How about that?" Before Angie could express an opinion, he was already shaking his head. "Still too easy. A baby spell, for beginners. I hate those."

"Easy is good," Angie told him earnestly. "I like easy. And you are a beginner."

Marvyn was immediately outraged, his normal bass-baritone rumble going up to a wounded squeak. "I am not! No way in the world I'm a beginner!" He was up and stamping his feet, as he had not done since he was two. "I tell you what—just for that, I'm going to get your letter back for you, but I'm not going to tell you how. You'll see, that's all. You just wait and see."

He was stalking away toward his room when Angie called after him, with the first glimmer both of hope and of humor that she had felt in approximately a century, "All right, you're a big bad witch king. What do you want?"

Marvyn turned and stared, uncomprehending.

Angie said, "Nothing for nothing, that's my bro. So let's hear it—what's your price for saving my life?"

If Marvyn's voice had gone up any higher, only bats could have heard it. "I'm rescuing you, and you think I want something for it? Julius Christmas!" which was the only swearword he was ever allowed to get away with. "You don't have anything I want, anyway. Except maybe. . . ."

He let the thought hang in space, uncompleted. Angie said, "Except maybe what?"

Marvyn swung on the doorframe one-handed, grinning his pirate grin at her. "I hate you calling me Ex-Lax. You know I hate it, and you keep doing it."

"Okay, I won't do it anymore, ever again. I promise."

"Mmm. Not good enough." The grin had grown distinctly evil. "I think you ought to call me O Mighty One for two weeks."

"What?" Now Angie was on her feet, misery briefly forgotten. "Give it up, Ex-Lax—two weeks? No chance!" They glared at each other in silence for a long moment before she finally said, "A week. Don't push it. One week, no more. And not in front of people!"

"Ten days." Marvyn folded his arms. "Starting right now." Angie went on glowering. Marvyn said, "You want that letter?"

"Yes."

Marvyn waited.

"Yes, O Mighty One." Triumphant, Marvyn held out his hand and Angie slapped it. She said, "When?"

"Tonight. No, tomorrow—going to the movies with Sunil and his family tonight. Tomorrow." He wandered off, and Angie took her first deep breath in what felt like a year and a half. She wished she could tell Melissa that things were going to be all right, but she didn't dare; so she spent the day trying to appear normal—just the usual Angie, aimlessly content on a Saturday afternoon. When Marvyn came home from the movies, he spent the rest of the evening reading *Hellboy* comics in his room, with the Milady-kitten on his stomach. He was still doing it when Angie gave up peeking in at him and went to bed.

But he was gone on Sunday morning. Angie knew it the moment she woke up.

She had no idea where he could be, or why. She had rather expected him to work whatever spell he settled on in his bedroom, under the stern gaze of his wizard mentors. But he wasn't there, and he didn't come to breakfast. Angie told their mother that they'd been up late watching television together, and that she should probably let Marvyn sleep in. And when Mrs. Luke grew worried after breakfast, Angie went to his room herself, returning with word that Marvyn was working intensely on a project for his art class, and wasn't feeling sociable. Normally she would never have gotten away with it, but her parents were on their way to brunch and a concert, leaving her with the usual instructions to feed and water the cat, use the twenty on the cabinet for something moderately healthy, and to check on Marvyn "now and then," which actually meant frequently. ("The day we don't tell you that," Mr. Luke said once, when she objected to the regular duty, "will be the very day the kid steals a kayak and heads for Tahiti." Angie found it hard to argue the point.)

Alone in the empty house—more alone than she felt she had ever been—Angie turned constantly in circles, wandering from room to room with no least notion of what to do. As the hours passed and her brother failed to return, she found herself calling out to him aloud. "Marvyn? Marvyn, I swear, if you're doing this to drive me crazy . . . O Mighty One, where are you? You get back here, never mind the damn letter, just get back!" She stopped doing this after a time, because the cracks and tremors in her voice embarrassed her, and made her even more afraid.

Strangely, she seemed to feel him in the house all that time. She kept whirling to look over her shoulder, thinking that he might be sneaking up on her to scare her, a favorite game since his infancy. But he was never there.

Somewhere around noon the doorbell rang, and Angie tripped over herself scrambling to answer it, even though she had no hope—almost no hope—of its being Marvyn. But it was Lidia at the door—Angie had forgotten that she usually came to clean on Sunday afternoons. She stood there, old and smiling, and Angie hugged her wildly and wailed, "Lidia, Lidia, *socorro,* help me, *ayúdame,* Lidia." She had learned Spanish from the housekeeper when she was too little to know she was learning it.

Lidia put her hands on Angie's shoulders. She put her back a little and looked into her face, saying, "*Chuchi, dime qué pasa contigo?*" She had called Angie *Chuchi* since childhood, never explaining the origin or meaning of the word.

"It's Marvyn," Angie whispered. "It's Marvyn." She started to explain about the letter, and Marvyn's promise, but Lidia only nodded and asked no questions. She said firmly, *"El Viejo puede ayudar."*

Too frantic to pay attention to gender, Angie took her to mean Yemaya, the old woman in the farmer's market who had told Marvyn that he was a *brujo*. She said, "You mean *la santera*," but Lidia shook her head hard. "No, no, *El Viejo*. You go out there, you ask to see *El Viejo. Solamente El Viejo. Los otros no pueden ayudarte.*"

The others can't help you. Only the old man. Angie asked where she could find El Viejo, and Lidia directed her to a *Santeria* shop on Bowen Street. She drew a crude map, made sure Angie had money with her, kissed her on the cheek and made a blessing sign on her forehead. *"Cuidado, Chuchi,"* she said with a kind of cheerful solemnity, and Angie was out and running for the Gonzales Avenue bus, the same one she took to school. This time she stayed on a good deal farther.

The shop had no sign, and no street number, and it was so small that Angie kept walking past it for some while. Her attention was finally caught by the objects in the one dim window, and on the shelves to right and left. There was an astonishing variety of incense, and of candles encased in glass with pictures of Black saints, as well as boxes marked Fast Money Ritual Kit, and bottles of Elegua Floor Wash, whose label read "Keeps Trouble from Crossing Your Threshold." When Angie entered, the musky scent of the place made her feel dizzy and heavy and out of herself, as she always felt when she had a cold coming on. She heard a rooster crowing, somewhere in back.

She didn't see the old woman until her chair creaked slightly, because she was sitting in a corner, halfway hidden by long hanging garments like church choir robes, but with symbols and patterns on them that Angie had never seen before. The woman was very old, much older even than Lidia, and she had an absurdly small pipe in her toothless mouth. Angie said, "Yemaya?" The old woman looked at her with eyes like dead planets.

Angie's Spanish dried up completely, followed almost immediately by her English. She said, "My brother . . . my little brother . . . I'm supposed to ask for *El Viejo*. The old one, *viejo santero*? Lidia said." She ran out of words in either language at that point. A puff of smoke crawled from the little pipe, but the old woman made no other response.

Then, behind her, she heard a curtain being pulled aside. A hoarse, slow voice said, "*Quieres El Viejo?* Me."

Angie turned and saw him, coming toward her out of a long hallway whose end she could not see. He moved deliberately, and it seemed to take him forever to reach her, as though he were returning from another world. He was Black, dressed all in black, and he wore dark glasses, even in the dark, tiny shop. His hair was so white that it hurt her eyes when she stared. He said, "Your brother."

"Yes," Angie said. "Yes. He's doing magic for me—he's getting something I need—and I don't know where he is, but I know he's in trouble, and I want him back!" She did not cry or break down—Marvyn would never be able to say that she cried over him—but it was a near thing.

El Viejo pushed the dark glasses up on his forehead, and Angie saw that he was younger than she had first thought—certainly younger than Lidia—and that there were thick white half-circles under his eyes. She never knew whether they were somehow natural, or the result of heavy makeup; what she did see was that they made his eyes look bigger and brighter—all pupil, nothing more. They should have made him look at least slightly comical, like a reverse-image raccoon, but they didn't.

"I know you brother," *El Viejo* said. Angie fought to hold herself still as he came closer, smiling at her with the tips of his teeth. "A *brujito*—little, little witch, we know. Mama and me, we been watching." He nodded toward the old woman in the chair, who hadn't moved an inch or said a word since Angie's arrival. Angie smelled a damp, musty aroma, like potatoes going bad.

"Tell me where he is. Lidia said you could help." Close to, she could see blue highlights in El Viejo's skin, and a kind of V-shaped scar on each cheek. He was wearing a narrow black tie, which she had not noticed at first; for some reason, the vision of him tying it in the morning, in front of a mirror, was more chilling to her than anything else about him. He grinned fully at her now, showing teeth that she had expected to be yellow and stinking, but which were all white and square and a little too large. He said, "*Tu hermano está perdido.* Lost in Thursday."

"Thursday?" It took her a dazed moment to comprehend, and longer to get the words out. "Oh, God, he went back! Like with Milady—he went back to before I . . . when the letter was still in my backpack. The little showoff—he said forward was hard, coming forward—he wanted to show me he could do it. And he got stuck. Idiot, idiot, idiot!" *El Viejo* chuckled softly, nodding, saying nothing.

"You have to go find him, get him out of there, right now—I've got money." She began digging frantically in her coat pockets.

"No, no money." *El Viejo* waved her offering aside, studying her out of eyes the color of almost-ripened plums. The white markings under them looked real; the eyes didn't. He said, "I take you. We find you brother together."

Angie's legs were trembling so much that they hurt. She wanted to assent, but it was simply not possible. "No. I can't. I can't. You go back there and get him."

El Viejo laughed then: an enormous, astonishing Santa Claus *ho-ho-HO,* so rich and reassuring that it made Angie smile even as he was snatching her up and stuffing her under one arm. By the time she had recovered from her bewilderment enough to start kicking and fighting, he was walking away with her down the long hall he had come out of a moment before. Angie screamed until her voice splintered in her throat, but she could not hear herself: from the moment *El Viejo* stepped back into the darkness of the hallway, all sound had ended. She could hear neither his footsteps nor his laughter—though she could feel him laughing against her—and certainly not her own panicky racket. They could be in outer space. They could be anywhere.

Dazed and disoriented as she was, the hallway seemed to go soundlessly on and on, until wherever they truly were, it could never have been the tiny *Santeria* shop she had entered only—when?—minutes before. It was a cold place, smelling like an old basement; and for all its darkness, Angie had a sense of things happening far too fast on all sides, just out of range of her smothered vision. She could distinguish none of them clearly, but there was a sparkle to them all the same.

And then she was in Marvyn's room.

And it was unquestionably Marvyn's room: there were the bearded and beaded occultists on the walls; there were the flannel winter sheets that he slept on all year because they had pictures of the New York Mets ballplayers; there was the complete set of *Star Trek* action figures that Angie had given him at Christmas, posed just so on his bookcase. And there, sitting on the edge of his bed, was Marvyn, looking lonelier than anyone Angie had ever seen in her life.

He didn't move or look up until *El Viejo* abruptly dumped her down in front of him and stood back, grinning like a beartrap. Then he jumped to his feet, burst into tears, and started frenziedly climbing her, snuffling, "Angie, Angie, Angie," all the way up. Angie held him, trying somehow to preserve her neck and hair and back all at once, while mumbling, "It's all right, it's okay, I'm here. It's okay, Marvyn."

Behind her, *El Viejo* chuckled, "Crybaby witch—little, little *brujito* crybaby." Angie hefted her blubbering baby brother like a shopping bag, holding him on her hip as she had done when he was little, and turned to face the old man. She said, "Thank you. You can take us home now."

El Viejo smiled—not a grin this time, but a long, slow shutmouth smile like a paper cut. He said, "Maybe we let *him* do it, yes?" and then he turned and walked away and was gone, as though he had simply slipped between the molecules of the air. Angie stood with Marvyn in her arms, trying to peel him off like a Band-Aid, while he clung to her with his chin digging hard into the top of her head. She finally managed to dump him down on the bed and stood over him, demanding, "What happened? What were you thinking?" Marvyn was still crying too hard to answer her. Angie said, "You just had to do it this way, didn't you? No silly little beginner spells—you're playing with the big guys now, right, O Mighty One? So what happened? How come you couldn't get back?"

"I don't know!" Marvyn's face was red and puffy with tears, and the tears kept coming while Angie tried to straighten his eyepatch. It was impossible for him to get much out without breaking down again, but he kept wailing, "I don't know what went wrong! I did everything you're supposed to, but I couldn't make it work! I don't know . . . maybe I forgot . . ." He could not finish.

"Herbs," Angie said, as gently and calmly as she could. "You left your magic herbs back—" she had been going to say "back home," but she stopped, because they *were* back home, sitting on Marvyn's bed in Marvyn's room, and the confusion was too much for her to deal with just then. She said, "Just tell me. You left the stupid herbs."

Marvyn shook his head until the tears flew, protesting, "No, I didn't, I didn't—look!" He pointed to a handful of grubby dried weeds scattered on the bed—Lidia would have thrown them out in a minute. Marvyn gulped and wiped his nose and tried to stop crying. He said, "They're really hard to find, maybe they're not fresh anymore, I don't know—they've always looked like that. But now they don't work," and he was wailing afresh. Angie told him that Dr. John Dee and Willow would both have been ashamed of him, but it didn't help.

But she also sat with him and put her arm around him, and smoothed his messy hair, and said, "Come on, let's think this out. Maybe it's the herbs losing their juice, maybe it's something else. You did everything the way you did the other time, with Milady?"

"I thought I did." Marvyn's voice was small and shy, not his usual deep croak. "But I don't know anymore, Angie—the more I think about it, the more I don't know. It's all messed up, I can't remember anything now."

"Okay," Angie said. "Okay. So how about we just run through it all again? We'll do it together. You try everything you do remember about—you know—moving around in time, and I'll copy you. I'll do whatever you say."

Marvyn wiped his nose again and nodded. They sat down cross-legged on the floor, and Marvyn produced the grimy book of paper matches that he always carried with him, in case of firecrackers. Following his directions Angie placed all the crumbly herbs into Milady's dish, and her brother lit them. Or tried to: they didn't blaze up, but smoked and smoldered and smelled like old dust, setting both Angie and Marvyn sneezing almost immediately. Angie coughed and asked, "Did that happen the other time?" Marvyn did not answer.

There was a moment when she thought the charm might actually be going to work. The room around them grew blurry—slightly blurry, granted—and Angie heard indistinct faraway sounds that might have been themselves hurtling forward to sheltering Sunday. But when the fumes of Marvyn's herbs cleared away, they were still sitting in Thursday—they both knew it without saying a word. Angie said, "Okay, so much for that. What about all that special concentration you were telling me about? You think maybe your mind wandered? You pronounce any spells the wrong way? Think, Marvyn!"

"I am thinking! I told you forward was hard!" Marvyn looked ready to start crying again, but he didn't. He said slowly, "Something's wrong, but it's not me. I don't think it's me. Something's *pushing* . . . ." He brightened suddenly. "Maybe we should hold hands or something. Because of there being two of us this time. We could try that."

So they tried the spell that way, and then they tried working it inside a pentagram they made with masking tape on the floor, as Angie had seen such things done on *Buffy the Vampire Slayer*, even though Marvyn said that didn't really mean anything, and they tried the herbs again, in a special order that Marvyn thought he remembered. They even tried it with Angie saying the spell, after Marvyn had coached her, just on the chance that his voice itself might have been throwing off the pitch or the pronunciation. Nothing helped.

Marvyn gave up before Angie did. Suddenly, while she was trying the spell over herself, one more time—some of the words seemed to heat up in her mouth as she spoke them—he collapsed into a wretched ball of desolation on the floor, moaning over and over, "We're finished, it's finished, we'll never get out of Thursday!" Angie understood that he was only a terrified little boy, but she was frightened too, and it would have relieved her to slap him and scream at him. Instead, she tried as best she could to reassure him, saying, "He'll come back for us. He has to."

Her brother sat up, knuckles to his eyes. "No, he doesn't have to! Don't you understand? He knows I'm a witch like him, and he's just going to leave me here, out of his way. I'm sorry, Angie, I'm really sorry!" Angie had almost never heard that word from Marvyn, and never twice in the same sentence.

"Later for all that," she said. "I was just wondering—do you think we could get Mom and Dad's attention when they get home? You think they'd realize what's happened to us?"

Marvyn shook his head. "You haven't seen me all the time I've been gone. I saw you, and I screamed and hollered and everything, but you

never knew. They won't either. We're not really in our house—we're just here. We'll always be here."

Angie meant to laugh confidently, to give them both courage, but it came out more of a hiccupy snort. "Oh, no. No way. There is no way I'm spending the rest of my life trapped in your stupid bedroom. We're going to try this useless mess one more time, and then . . . then I'll do something else." Marvyn seemed about to ask her what else she could try, but he checked himself, which was good.

They attempted the spell more than one more time. They tried it in every style they could think of except standing on their heads and reciting the words backward, and they might just as well have done that, for all the effect it had. Whether Marvyn's herbs had truly lost all potency, or whether Marvyn had simply forgotten some vital phrase, they could not even recapture the fragile awareness of something almost happening that they had both felt on the first trial. Again and again they opened their eyes to last Thursday.

"Okay," Angie said at last. She stood up, to stretch cramped legs, and began to wander around the room, twisting a couple of the useless herbs between her fingers. "Okay," she said again, coming to a halt midway between the bedroom door and the window, facing Marvyn's small bureau. A leg of his red Dr. Seuss pajamas was hanging out of one of the drawers.

"Okay," she said a third time. "Let's go home."

Marvyn had fallen into a kind of fetal position, sitting up but with his arms tight around his knees and his head down hard on them. He did not look up at her words. Angie raised her voice. "Let's go, Marvyn. That hallway—tunnel-thing, whatever it is—it comes out right about where I'm standing. That's where *El Viejo* brought me, and that's the way he left when he . . . left. That's the way back to Sunday."

"It doesn't matter," Marvyn whimpered. "*El Viejo* . . . he's him! He's him!"

Angie promptly lost what little remained of her patience. She stalked over to Marvyn and shook him to his feet, dragging him to a spot in the air as though she were pointing out a painting in a gallery. "And you're Marvyn Luke, and you're the big bad new witch in town! You said it yourself—if you weren't, he'd never have bothered sticking you away here. Not even nine, and you can eat his lunch, and he knows it! Straighten your patch and take us home, bro." She nudged him playfully. "Oh, forgive me—I meant to say, O Mighty One."

"You don't have to call me that anymore." Marvyn's legs could barely hold him up, and he sagged against her, a dead weight of despair. "I can't, Angie. I can't get us home. I'm sorry . . . ."

The good thing—and Angie knew it then—would have been to turn and comfort him: to take his cold, wet face between her hands and tell him that all would yet be well, that they would soon be eating popcorn with far too much butter on it in his real room in their real house. But she was near her own limit, and pretending calm courage for his sake was prodding her, in spite of herself, closer to the edge. Without looking at Marvyn, she snapped, "Well, I'm not about to die in last Thursday! I'm walking out of here the same way he did, and you can come with me or not, that's up to you. But I'll tell you one thing, Ex-Lax—I won't be looking back."

And she stepped forward, walking briskly toward the dangling Dr. Seuss pajamas . . .

. . . and into a thick, sweet-smelling grayness that instantly filled her eyes and mouth, her nose and her ears, disorienting her so completely that she flailed her arms madly, all sense of direction lost, with no idea of which way she might be headed; drowning in syrup like a trapped bee or butterfly. Once she thought she heard Marvyn's voice, and called out for him—"I'm here, I'm here!" But she did not hear him again.

Then, between one lunge for air and another, the grayness was gone, leaving not so much as a dampness on her skin, nor even a sickly aftertaste of sugar in her mouth. She was back in the time-tunnel, as she had come to think of it, recognizing the uniquely dank odor: a little like the ashes of a long-dead fire, and a little like what she imagined moonlight might smell like, if it had a smell. The image was an ironic one, for she could see no more than she had when *El Viejo* was lugging her the other way under his arm. She could not even distinguish the ground under her feet; she knew only that it felt more like slippery stone than anything else, and she was careful to keep her footing as she plodded steadily forward.

The darkness was absolute—strange solace, in a way, since she could imagine Marvyn walking close behind her, even though he never answered her, no matter how often or how frantically she called his name. She moved along slowly, forcing her way through the clinging murk, vaguely conscious, as before, of a distant, flickering sense of sound and motion on every side of her. If there were walls to the time-tunnel, she could not touch them; if it had a roof, no air currents betrayed it; if there were any living creature in it besides herself, she felt no sign. And if time actually passed there, Angie could never have said. She moved along, her eyes closed, her mind empty, except for the formless fear that she was not moving at all, but merely raising and setting down her feet in the same place, endlessly. She wondered if she was hungry.

Not until she opened her eyes in a different darkness to the crowing of a rooster and a familiar heavy aroma did she realize that she was walking down the hallway leading from the *Santeria* shop to . . . wherever she had really been—and where Marvyn still must be, for he plainly had not followed her. She promptly turned and started back toward last Thursday, but halted at the deep, slightly grating chuckle behind her. She did not turn again, but stood very still.

El Viejo walked a slow full circle around her before he faced her, grinning down at her like the man in the moon. The dark glasses were off, and the twin scars on his cheeks were blazing up as though they had been slashed into him a moment before. He said, "I know. Before even I see you, I know."

Angie hit him in the stomach as hard as she could. It was like punching a frozen slab of beef, and she gasped in pain, instantly certain that she had broken her hand. But she hit him again, and again, screaming at the top of her voice, "Bring my brother back! If you don't bring him right back here, right now, I'll kill you! I will!"

El Viejo caught her hands, surprisingly gently, still laughing to himself. "Little girl, listen, listen now. *Niñita,* nobody else—nobody—ever do what you do. You understand? Nobody but me ever walk that road back from where I leave you, understand?" The big white half-circles under his eyes were stretching and curling like live things.

Angie pulled away from him with all her strength, as she had hit him. She said, "No. That's Marvyn. Marvyn's the witch, the brujo—don't go telling people it's me. Marvyn's the one with the power."

"Him?" Angie had never heard such monumental scorn packed into one syllable. *El Viejo* said, "Your brother nothing, nobody, we no bother with him. Forget him—you the one got the regalo, you just don't know." The big white teeth filled her vision; she saw nothing else. "I show you—me, *El Viejo.* I show you what you are."

It was beyond praise, beyond flattery. For all her dread and dislike of *El Viejo,* to have someone of his wicked wisdom tell her that she was like him in some awful, splendid way made Angie shiver in her heart. She wanted to turn away more than she had ever wanted anything—even Jake Petrakis—but the long walk home to Sunday was easier than breaking the clench of the white-haired man's malevolent presence would have been. Having often felt (and almost as often dismissed the notion) that Marvyn was special in the family by virtue of being the baby, and a boy—and now a potent witch—she let herself revel in the thought that the real gift was hers, not his, and that if she chose she had only to stretch out her hand to have her command settle home in it. It was at once the most frightening and the most purely, completely gratifying feeling she had ever known.

But it was not tempting. Angie knew the difference.

"Forget it," she said. "Forget it, buster. You've got nothing to show me."

El Viejo did not answer her. The old, old eyes that were all pupil continued slipping over her like hands, and Angie went on glaring back with the blue eyes she despaired of because they could never be as deep-set and deep green as her mother's eyes. They stood so—for how long, she never knew—until *El Viejo* turned and opened his mouth as though to speak to the silent old lady whose own stone eyes seemed not to have blinked since Angie had first entered the Santeria shop, a childhood ago. Whatever he meant to say, he never got the words out, because Marvyn came back then.

He came down the dark hall from a long way off, as *El Viejo* had done the first time she saw him—as she herself had trudged forever, only moments ago. But Marvyn had come a further journey: Angie could see that beyond doubt in the way he stumbled along, looking like a shadow casting a person. He was struggling to carry something in his arms, but she could not make out what it was. As long as she watched him approaching, he seemed hardly to draw any nearer.

Whatever he held looked too heavy for a small boy: it threatened constantly to slip from his hands, and he kept shifting it from one shoulder to the other, and back again. Before Angie could see it clearly, El Viejo screamed, and she knew on the instant that she would never hear a more terrible sound in her life. He might have been being skinned alive, or having his soul torn out of his body—she never even tried to tell herself what it was like, because there were no words. Nor did she tell anyone that she fell down at the sound, fell flat down on her hands and knees, and rocked and whimpered until the scream stopped. It went on for a long time.

When it finally stopped, El Viejo was gone, and Marvyn was standing beside her with a baby in his arms. The baby was Black and immediately endearing, with big, bright, strikingly watchful eyes. Angie looked into them once, and looked quickly away.

Marvyn looked worn and exhausted. His eyepatch was gone, and the left eye that Angie had not seen for months was as bloodshot as though he had just come off a three-day drunk—though she noticed that it was not wandering at all. He said in a small, dazed voice, "I had to go back a really long way, Angie. Really long."

Angie wanted to hold him, but she was afraid of the baby. Marvyn looked toward the old woman in the corner and sighed; then hitched up his burden one more time and clumped over to her. He said, "Ma'am, I think this is yours?" Adults always commented on Marvyn's excellent manners.

The old woman moved then, for the first time. She moved like a wave, Angie thought: a wave seen from a cliff or an airplane, crawling along so slowly that it seemed impossible for it ever to break, ever to reach the shore. But the sea was in that motion, all of it caught up in that one wave; and when she set down her pipe, took the baby from Marvyn and smiled, that was the wave too. She looked down at the baby, and said one word, which Angie did not catch. Then Angie had her brother by the arm, and they were out of the shop. Marvyn never looked back, but Angie did, in time to see the old woman baring blue gums in soundless laughter.

All the way home in a taxi, Angie prayed silently that her parents hadn't returned yet. Lidia was waiting, and together they whisked Marvyn into bed without any serious protest. Lidia washed his face with a rough cloth, and then slapped him and shouted at him in Spanish—Angie learned a few words she couldn't wait to use—and then she kissed him and left, and Angie brought him a pitcher of orange juice and a whole plate of gingersnaps, and sat on the bed and said, "What happened?"

Marvyn was already working on the cookies as though he hadn't eaten in days—which, in a sense, was quite true. He asked, with his mouth full, "What's *malcriado* mean?"

"What? Oh. Like badly raised, badly brought up—troublemaking kid. About the only thing Lidia didn't call you. Why?"

"Well, that's what that lady called . . . him. The baby."

"Right," Angie said. "Leave me a couple of those, and tell me how he got to be a baby. You did like with Milady?"

"Uh-huh. Only I had to go way, way, way back, like I told you." Marvyn's voice took on the faraway sound it had had in the Santeria shop. "Angie, he's so old."

Angie said nothing. Marvyn said in a whisper, "I couldn't follow you, Angie. I was scared."

"Forget it," she answered. She had meant to be soothing, but the words burst out of her. "If you just hadn't had to show off, if you'd gotten that letter back some simple, ordinary way—" Her entire chest froze solid at the word. "The letter! We forgot all about my stupid letter!" She leaned forward and snatched the plate of cookies away from Marvyn. "Did you forget? You forgot, didn't you?" She was shaking as had not happened even when *El Viejo* had hold of her. "Oh, God, after all that!"

But Marvyn was smiling for the first time in a very long while. "Calm down, be cool—I've got it here." He dug her letter to Jake Petrakis—more than a little grimy by now—out of his back pocket and held it out to Angie. "There. Don't say I never did nuttin' for you." It was a favorite phrase of his, gleaned from a television show, and most often employed when he had fed Milady, washed his breakfast dish, or folded his clothes. "Take it, open it up," he said now. "Make sure it's the right one."

"I don't need to," Angie protested irritably. "It's my letter—believe me, I know it when I see it." But she opened the envelope anyway and withdrew a single folded sheet of paper, which she glanced at . . . then *stared* at, in absolute disbelief.

She handed the sheet to Marvyn. It was empty on both sides.

"Well, you did your job all right," she said, mildly enough, to her stunned, slack-jawed brother. "No question about that. I'm just trying to figure out why we had to go through this whole incredible hoo-ha for a blank sheet of paper."

Marvyn actually shrank away from her in the bed.

"I didn't do it, Angie! I swear!" Marvyn scrambled to his feet, standing up on the bed with his hands raised, as though to ward her off in case she attacked him. "I just grabbed it out of your backpack—I never even looked at it."

"And what, I wrote the whole thing in grapefruit juice, so nobody could read it unless you held it over a lamp or something? Come on, it doesn't matter now. Get your feet off your damn pillow and sit down."

Marvyn obeyed warily, crouching rather than sitting next to her on the edge of the bed. They were silent together for a little while before he said, "You did that. With the letter. You wanted it not written so much, it just *wasn't*. That's what happened."

"Oh, right," she said. "Me being the dynamite witch around here. I told you, it doesn't matter."

"It matters." She had grown so unused to seeing a two-eyed Marvyn that his expression seemed more than doubly earnest to her just then. He said, quite quietly, "You are the dynamite witch, Angie. He was after you, not me."

This time she did not answer him. Marvyn said, "I was the bait. I do garbage bags and clarinets—okay, and I make ugly dolls walk around. What's he care about that? But he knew you'd come after me, so he held me there—back there in Thursday—until he could grab you. Only he didn't figure you could walk all the way home on your own, without any spells or anything. I know that's how it happened, Angie! That's how I know you're the real witch."

"No," she said, raising her voice now. "No, I was just pissed-off, that's different. Never underestimate the power of a pissed-off woman, O Mighty One. But you . . . you went all the way back, on *your* own, and you grabbed *him*. You're going to be way stronger and better than he is, and he knows it. He just figured he'd get rid of the competition early on, while he had the chance. Not a generous guy, *El Viejo*."

Marvyn's chubby face turned gray. "But I'm *not* like him! I don't want to be like him!" Both eyes suddenly filled with tears, and he clung to his sister as he had not done since his return. "It was horrible, Angie, it was so horrible. You were gone, and I was all alone, and I didn't know what to do, only I had to do *something*. And I remembered Milady, and I figured if he wasn't letting me come forward I'd go the other way, and I was so scared and mad I just walked and walked and walked in the dark, until I . . ." He was crying so hard that Angie could hardly make the words out. "I don't want to be a witch anymore, Angie, I don't *want* to! And I don't want *you* being a witch either . . . ."

Angie held him and rocked him, as she had loved doing when he was three or four years old, and the cookies got scattered all over the bed. "It's all right," she told him, with one ear listening for their parents' car pulling into the garage. "*Shh, shh,* it's all right, it's over, we're safe, it's okay, *shh*. It's okay, we're not going to be witches, neither one of us." She laid him down and pulled the covers back over him. "You go to sleep now."

Marvyn looked up at her, and then at the wizards' wall beyond her shoulder. "I might take some of those down," he mumbled. "Maybe put some soccer players up for a while. The Brazilian team's really good." He was just beginning to doze off in her arms, when suddenly he sat up again and said, "Angie? The baby?"

"What about the baby? I thought he made a beautiful baby, *El Viejo*. Mad as hell; but lovable."

"It was bigger when we left," Marvyn said. Angie stared at him. "I looked back at it in that lady's lap, and it was already bigger than when I was carrying it. He's starting over, Angie, like Milady."

"Better him than me," Angie said. "I hope he gets a kid brother this time, he's got it coming." She heard the car, and then the sound of a key in the lock. She said, "Go to sleep, don't worry about it. After what we've been through, we can handle anything. The two of us. And without witchcraft. Whichever one of us it is—no witch stuff."

Marvyn smiled drowsily. "Unless we really, *really* need it." Angie held out her hand and they slapped palms in formal agreement. She looked down at her fingers and said, "*Ick*! Blow your *nose*!"

But Marvyn was asleep.

Uncle Chaim and Aunt Rifke and The Angel

This was the first story since my novel *A Fine and Private Place* that I drew specifically from my New York Jewish childhood. ("My Daughter's Name Is Sarah," based on a story from my mother's childhood, was published later than *A Fine and Private Place*, but written a few years earlier.) It is also powerfully influenced by three of my mother's four brothers, Raphael, Moses, and Isaac Soyer, who all became well-known painters in the New York realist style. As a child I spent a lot of time in my uncles' studios, whether visiting or actually posing for them, and Uncle Chaim's Greenwich Village *atelier* is based on my memory of Uncle Moses' workplace. Uncle Moses wasn't at all like my fictional Uncle Chaim in his speech and his mannerisms; but in terms of their attitudes toward their work, I do believe the real uncle and the imagined one would have understood each other.

My Uncle Chaim, who was a painter, was working in his studio—as he did on every day except Shabbos—when the blue angel showed up. I was there.

I was usually there most afternoons, dropping in on my way home from Fiorello LaGuardia Elementary School. I was what they call a "latchkey kid," these days. My parents both worked and traveled full-time, and Uncle Chaim's studio had been my home base and my real playground since I was small. I was shy and uncomfortable with other children. Uncle Chaim didn't have any kids, and didn't know much about them, so he talked to me like an adult when he talked at all, which suited me perfectly. I looked through his paintings and drawings, tried some of my own, and ate Chinese food with him in silent companionship, when he remembered that we should probably eat. Sometimes I fell asleep on the cot. And when his friends—who were mostly painters like himself—dropped in to visit, I withdrew into my favorite corner and listened to their talk, and understood what I understood. Until the blue angel came.

It was very sudden: one moment I was looking through a couple of the comic books Uncle Chaim kept around for me, while he was trying to catch the highlight on the tendons under his model's chin, and the next moment there was this angel standing before him, actually *posing*, with her arms spread out and her great wings taking up almost half the studio. She was not blue herself—a light beige would be closer—but she wore a blue robe that managed to look at once graceful and grand, with a white undergarment glimmering beneath. Her face, half-shadowed by a loose hood, looked disapproving.

I dropped the comic book and stared. No, I *gaped*, there's a difference. Uncle Chaim said to her, "I can't see my model. If you wouldn't mind moving just a bit?" He was grumpy when he was working, but never rude.

"*I* am your model," the angel said. "From this day forth, you will paint no one but me."

"I don't work on commission," Uncle Chaim answered. "I used to, but you have to put up with too many aggravating rich people. Now I just paint what I paint, take it to the gallery. Easier on my stomach, you know?"

His model, the wife of a fellow painter, said, "Chaim, who are you talking to?"

"Nobody, nobody, Ruthie. Just myself, same way your Jules does when he's working. Old guys get like that." To the angel, in a lower voice, he said, "Also, whatever you're doing to the light, could you not? I got some great shadows going right now." For a celestial brightness was swelling in the grubby little warehouse district studio, illuminating the warped floor boards, the wrinkled tubes of colors scattered everywhere, the canvases stacked and propped in the corners, along with several ancient rickety easels. It scared me, but not Uncle Chaim. He said, "So you're an angel, fine, that's terrific. Now give me back my shadows."

The room darkened obediently. "*Thank* you. Now about *moving* . . ." He made a brushing-away gesture with the hand holding the little glass of Scotch.

The model said, "Chaim, you're worrying me."

"What, I'm seventy-six years old, I'm not entitled to a hallucination now and then? I'm seeing an angel, you're not—this is no big deal. I just want it should move out of the way, let me work." The angel, in response, spread her wings even wider, and Uncle Chaim snapped, "Oh, for God's sake, shoo!"

"It is for God's sake that I am here," the angel announced majestically. "The Lord—Yahweh—I Am That I Am—has sent me down to be your muse." She inclined her head a trifle, by way of accepting the worship and wonder she expected.

From Uncle Chaim, she didn't get it, unless very nearly dropping his glass of Scotch counts as a compliment. "A muse?" he snorted. "I don't need a muse—I got models!"

"That's it," Ruthie said. "I'm calling Jules, I'll make him come over and sit with you." She put on her coat, picked up her purse, and headed for the door, saying over her shoulder, "Same time Thursday? If you're still here?"

"I got more models than I know what to do with," Uncle Chaim told the blue angel. "Men, women, old, young—even a cat, there's one lady always brings her cat, what am I going to do?" He heard the door slam, realized that Ruthie was gone, and sighed irritably, taking a larger swallow of whiskey than he usually allowed himself. "Now she's upset, she thinks she's my mother anyway, she'll send Jules with chicken soup and an enema." He narrowed his eyes at the angel. "And what's this, how I'm only going to be painting you from now on? Like Velazquez stuck painting royal Hapsburg imbeciles over and over? Some hope you've got! Listen, you go back and tell,"—he hesitated just a trifle—"tell whoever sent you that Chaim Malakoff is too old not to paint what he likes, when he likes, and for who he likes. You got all that? We're clear?"

It was surely no way to speak to an angel; but as Uncle Chaim used to warn me about everyone from neighborhood bullies to my fourth-grade teacher, who hit people, "You give the bastards an inch, they'll walk all over you. From me they get *bupkes, nichevo,* nothing. Not an inch." I got beaten up more than once in those days, saying that to the wrong people.

And the blue angel was definitely one of them. The entire room suddenly filled with her: with the wings spreading higher than the ceiling, wider than the walls, yet somehow not touching so much as a stick of charcoal; with the aroma almost too impossibly haunting to be borne; with the vast, unutterable beauty that a thousand medieval and Renaissance artists had somehow not gone mad (for the most part) trying to ambush on canvas or trap in stone. In that moment, Uncle Chaim confided later, he didn't know whether to pity or envy Muslims their ancient ban on depictions of the human body.

"I thought maybe I should kneel, what would it hurt? But then I thought, *what would it hurt?* It'd hurt my left knee, the one had the arthritis twenty years, that's what it would hurt." So he only shrugged a little and told her, "I could manage a sitting on Monday. Somebody cancelled, I got the whole morning free."

"Now," the angel said. Her air of distinct disapproval had become one of authority. The difference was slight but notable.

"*Now,*" Uncle Chaim mimicked her. "All right, already—Ruthie left early, so why not?" He moved the unfinished portrait over to another easel, and carefully selected a blank canvas from several propped against a wall. "I got to clean off a couple of brushes here, we'll start. You want to take off that thing, whatever, on your head?" Even I knew perfectly well that it was a halo, but Uncle Chaim always told me that you had to start with people as you meant to go on.

"You will require a larger surface," the angel instructed him. "I am not to be represented in miniature."

Uncle Chaim raised one eyebrow (an ability I envied him to the point of practicing—futilely—in the bathroom mirror for hours, until my parents banged on the door, certain I was up to the worst kind of no good). "No, huh? Good enough for the Persians, good enough for Holbein and Hilliard and Sam Cooper, but not for you? So okay, so we'll try this one. . ." Rummaging in a corner, he fetched out his biggest canvas, dusted it off, eyed it critically—"Don't even remember what I'm doing with anything this size, must have been saving it for you"—and finally set it up on the empty easel, turning it away from the angel. "Okay, Malakoff's rules. Nobody—*nobody*—looks at my painting till I'm done. Not angels, not Adonai, not my nephew over there in the corner, that's David, Duvidl—not even my wife. Nobody. Understood?"

The angel nodded, almost imperceptibly. With surprising meekness, she asked, "Where shall I sit?"

"Not a lot of choices," Uncle Chaim grunted, lifting a brush from a jar of turpentine. "Over there's okay, where Ruthie was sitting—or maybe by the big window. The window would be good, we've lost the shadows already. Take the red chair, I'll fix the color later."

But sitting down is not a natural act for an angel: they stand or they fly; check any Renaissance painting. The great wings inevitably get crumpled, the halo always winds up distinctly askew; and there is simply no way, even for Uncle Chaim, to ask an angel to cross her legs or to hook one over the arm of the chair. In the end they compromised, and the blue angel rose up to pose in the window, holding herself there effortlessly, with her wings not stirring at all. Uncle Chaim, settling in to work—brushes cleaned and Scotch replenished—could not refrain from remarking, "I always imagined you guys sort of hovered. Like hummingbirds."

"We fly only by the Will of God," the angel replied. "If Yahweh, praised be His name,"—I could actually *hear* the capital letters—"withdrew that mighty Will from us, we would fall from the sky on the instant, every single one."

"Doesn't bear thinking about," Uncle Chaim muttered. "Raining angels all over everywhere—falling on people's heads, tying up traffic—"

The angel looked, first startled, and then notably shocked. "I was speaking of our sky," she explained haughtily, "the sky of Paradise, which compares to yours as gold to lead, tapestry to tissue, heavenly choirs to the bellowing of feeding hogs—"

"All *right* already, I get the picture." Uncle Chaim cocked an eye at her, poised up there in the window with no visible means of support, and then back at his canvas. "I was going to ask you about being an angel, what it's like, but if you're going to talk about us like that—badmouthing the *sky*, for God's sake, the whole *planet*."

The angel did not answer him immediately, and when she did, she appeared considerably abashed and spoke very quietly, almost like a scolded schoolgirl. "You are right. It is His sky, His world, and I shame my Lord, my fellows, and my breeding by speaking slightingly of any part of it." In a lower voice, she added, as though speaking only to herself, "Perhaps that is why I am here."

Uncle Chaim was covering the canvas with a thin layer of very light blue, to give the painting an undertone. Without looking up, he said, "What, you got sent down here like a punishment? You talked back, you didn't take out the garbage? I could believe it. Your boy Yahweh, he always did have a short fuse."

"I was told only that I was to come to you and be your model and your muse," the angel answered. She pushed her hood back from her face, revealing hair that was not bright gold, as so often painted, but of a color resembling the night sky when it pales into dawn. "Angels do not ask questions."

"Mmm." Uncle Chaim sipped thoughtfully at his Scotch. "Well, one did, anyway, you believe the story."

The angel did not reply, but she looked at him as though he had uttered some unimaginable obscenity. Uncle Chaim shrugged and continued preparing the ground for the portrait. Neither one said anything for some time, and it was the angel who spoke first. She said, a trifle hesitantly, "I have never been a muse before."

"Never had one," Uncle Chaim replied sourly. "Did just fine."

"I do not know what the duties of a muse would be," the angel confessed. "You will need to advise me."

"What?" Uncle Chaim put down his brush. "Okay now, wait a minute. I got to tell you how to get into my hair, order me around, probably tell me how I'm not painting you right? Forget it, lady—you figure it out for yourself, I'm working here."

But the blue angel looked confused and unhappy, which is no more natural for an angel than sitting down. Uncle Chaim scratched his head and said, more gently, "What do I know? I guess you're supposed to stimulate my creativity, something like that. Give me ideas, visions, make me see things, think about things I've never thought about." After a pause, he added, "Frankly, Goya pretty much has that effect on me already. Goya and Matisse. So that's covered, the stimulation—maybe you could just tell them, *him*, about that . . ."

Seeing the expression on the angel's marble-smooth face, he let the sentence trail away. Rabbi Shulevitz, who cut his blond hair close and wore shorts when he watered his lawn, once told me that angels are supposed to express God's emotions and desires, without being troubled by any of their own. "Like a number of other heavenly dictates," he murmured when my mother was out of the room, "that one has never quite functioned as I'm sure it was intended."

They were still working in the studio when my mother called and ordered me home. The angel had required no rest or food at all, while Uncle Chaim had actually been drinking his Scotch instead of sipping it (I never once saw him drunk, but I'm not sure that I ever saw him entirely sober), and needed more bathroom breaks than usual. Daylight gone, and his precarious array of 60-watt bulbs proving increasingly unsatisfactory, he looked briefly at the portrait, covered it, and said to the angel, "Well, *that* stinks, but we'll do better tomorrow. What time you want to start?"

The angel floated down from the window to stand before him. Uncle Chaim was a small man, dark and balding, but he already knew that the angel altered her height when they faced each other, so as not to overwhelm him completely. She said, "I will be here when you are."

Uncle Chaim misunderstood. He assured her that if she had no other place to sleep but the studio, it wouldn't be the first time a model or a friend had spent the night on that trundle bed in the far corner. "Only no peeking at the picture, okay? On your honor as a muse."

The blue angel looked for a moment as though she were going to smile, but she didn't. "I will not sleep here, or anywhere on this earth," she said. "But you will find me waiting when you come."

"Oh," Uncle Chaim said. "Right. Of course. Fine. But don't change your clothes, okay? Absolutely no changing." The angel nodded.

When Uncle Chaim got home that night, my Aunt Rifke told my mother on the phone at some length, he was in a state that simply did not register on her long-practiced seismograph of her husband's moods. "He comes in, he's telling jokes, he eats up everything on the table, we snuggle up, watch a little TV, I can figure the work went well today. He doesn't talk, he's not hungry, he goes to bed early, tosses and tumbles around all night . . . okay, not so good. Thirty-seven years with a person, wait, you'll find out." Aunt Rifke had been Uncle Chaim's model until they married, and his agent, accountant, and road manager ever since.

But the night he returned from beginning his portrait of the angel brought Aunt Rifke a husband she barely recognized. "Not up, not down, not happy, not *not* happy, just . . . *dazed,* I guess that's the best word. He'd start to eat something, then he'd forget about it, wander around the apartment—couldn't sit still, couldn't keep his mind on anything, had trouble even finishing a sentence. One sentence. I tell you, it scared me. I couldn't keep from wondering, *is this how it begins?* A man starts acting strange, one day to the next, you think about things like that, you know?" Talking about it, even long past the moment's terror, tears still started in her eyes.

Uncle Chaim did tell her that he had been visited by an angel who demanded that he paint her portrait. *That* Aunt Rifke had no trouble believing, thirty-seven years of marriage to an artist having inured her to certain revelations. Her main concern was how painting an angel might affect Uncle Chaim's working hours, and his daily conduct.

"Like actors, you know, Duvidl? They *become* the people they're doing, I've seen it over and over." Also, blasphemous as it might sound, she wondered how much the angel would be paying, and in what currency. "And saying we'll get a big credit in the next world is not funny, Chaim. *Not* funny."

Uncle Chaim urged Rifke to come to the studio the very next day to meet his new model for herself. Strangely, that lady, whom I'd known all my life as a legendary repository of other people's lives, stories, and secrets, flatly refused to take him up on the offer. "I got nothing to wear, not for meeting an angel in. Besides, what would we talk about? No, you just give her my best, I'll make some *rugelach*." And she never wavered from that position, except once.

The blue angel was indeed waiting when Uncle Chaim arrived in the studio early the next morning. She had even made coffee in his ancient glass percolator, and was offended when he informed her that it was as thin as rain and tasted like used dishwater. "Where I come from, no one ever *makes* coffee," she returned fire. "We command it."

"That's what's wrong with this crap," Uncle Chaim answered her. "Coffee's like art, you don't order coffee around." He waved the angel aside, and set about a second pot, which came out strong enough to widen the angel's eyes when she sipped it. Uncle Chaim teased her—"Don't get stuff like *that* in the Green Pastures, huh?"—and confided that he made much better coffee than Aunt Rifke. "Not her fault. Woman was raised on decaf, what can you expect? Cooks like an angel, though."

The angel either missed the joke or ignored it. She began to resume her pose in the window, but Uncle Chaim stopped her. "Later, later, the sun's not right. Just stand where you are, I want to do some work on the head." As I remember, he never used the personal possessive in referring to his models' bodies: it was invariably "turn the face a little," "relax the shoulder," "move the foot to the left." Amateurs often resented it; professionals tended to find it liberating. Uncle Chaim didn't much care either way.

For himself, he was grateful that the angel proved capable of holding a pose indefinitely, without complaining, asking for a break, or needing the toilet. What he found distracting was her steadily emerging interest in talking and asking questions. As requested, her expression never changed and her lips hardly moved; indeed, there were times when he would have sworn he was hearing her only in his mind. Enough of her queries had to do with his work, with how he did what he was doing, that he finally demanded point-blank, "All those angels, seraphs, cherubim, centuries of them—all those Virgins and Assumptions and whatnot—and you've never once been painted? Not one time?"

"I have never set foot on earth before," the angel confessed. "Not until I was sent to you."

"Sent to me. Directly. Special Delivery, Chaim Shlomovitch Malakoff—one angel, totally inexperienced at modeling. Or anything else, got anything to do with human life." The angel nodded, somewhat shyly. Uncle Chaim spoke only one word. "*Why?*"

"I am only eleven thousand, seven hundred and twenty-two years old," the angel said, with a slight but distinct suggestion of resentment in her voice. "No one tells me a *thing*."

Uncle Chaim was silent for some time, squinting at her face from different angles and distances, even closing one eye from time to time. Finally he grumbled, more than half to himself, "I got a very bad feeling that we're both supposed to learn something from this. Bad, bad feeling." He filled the little glass for the first time that day, and went back to work.

But if there was to be any learning involved in their near-daily meetings in the studio, it appeared to be entirely on her part. She was ravenously curious about human life on the blue-green ball of damp dirt that she had observed so distantly for so long, and her constant questioning reminded a weary Uncle Chaim—as he informed me more than once—of me at the age of four. Except that an angel cannot be bought off, even temporarily, with strawberry ice cream, or threatened with loss of a bedtime story if she can't learn to take "I don't *know*!" for an answer. At times he pretended not to hear her; on other occasions, he would make up some patently ridiculous explanation that a grandchild would have laughed to scorn, but that the angel took so seriously that he was guiltily certain he was bound to be struck by lightning. Only the lightning never came, and the tactic usually did buy him a few moments' peace—until the next question.

Once he said to her, in some desperation, "You're an angel, you're supposed to know everything about human beings. Listen, I'll take you out to Bleecker, MacDougal, Washington Square, you can look at the books, magazines, TV, the classes, the beads and crystals . . . it's all about how to get in touch with angels. Real ones, real angels, never mind that stuff about the angel inside you. Everybody wants some of that angel wisdom, and they want it bad, and they want it right now. We'll take an afternoon off, I'll show you."

The blue angel said simply, "The streets and the shops have nothing to show me, nothing to teach. You do."

"No," Uncle Chaim said. "No, no, no, no *no*. I'm a painter—that's all, that's it, that's what I know. Painting. But you, you sit at the right hand of God—"

"He doesn't have hands," the angel interrupted. "And nobody exactly *sits*—"

"The point I'm making, you're the one who ought to be answering questions. About the universe, and about Darwin, and how everything really happened, and what is it with God and shellfish, and the whole business with the milk and the meat—*those* kinds of questions. I mean, I should be asking them, I know that, only I'm working right now."

It was almost impossible to judge the angel's emotions from the expressions of her chillingly beautiful porcelain face; but as far as Uncle Chaim could tell, she looked sad. She said, "I also am what I am. We angels—as you call us—we are messengers, minions, lackeys, knowing only what we are told, what we are ordered to do. A few of the Oldest, the ones who were there at the Beginning—Michael, Gabriel, Raphael—they have names, thoughts, histories, choices, powers. The rest of us, we tremble, we hide when we see them passing by. We think, *if those are angels, we must be something else altogether,* but we can never find a better word for ourselves."

She looked straight at Uncle Chaim—he noticed in some surprise that in a certain light her eyes were not nearly as blue as he had been painting them, but closer to a dark sea-green—and he looked away from an anguish that he had never seen before, and did not know how to paint. He said, "So okay, you're a low-class angel, a heavenly grunt, like they say now. So how come they picked you to be my muse? Got to mean *something,* no? Right?"

The angel did not answer his question, nor did she speak much for the rest of the day. Uncle Chaim posed her in several positions, but the unwonted sadness in her eyes depressed him past even Laphroaig's ability to ameliorate. He quit work early, allowing the angel—as he would never have permitted Aunt Rifke or me—to potter around the studio, putting it to rights according to her inexpert notions, organizing brushes, oils, watercolors, pastels and pencils, fixatives, rolls of canvas, bottles of tempera and turpentine, even dusty chunks of rabbit skin glue, according to size. As he told his friend Jules Sidelsky, meeting for their traditional weekly lunch at a Ukrainian restaurant on Second Avenue, where the two of them spoke only Russian, "maybe God could figure where things are anymore. Me, I just shut my eyes and pray."

Jules was large and fat, like Diego Rivera, and I thought of him as a sort of uncle too, because he and Ruthie always remembered my birthday, just like Uncle Chaim and Aunt Rifke. Jules did not believe in angels, but he knew that Uncle Chaim didn't necessarily believe in them either, just because he had one in his studio every day. He asked seriously, "That helps? The praying?" Uncle Chaim gave him a look, and Jules dropped the subject. "So what's she like? I mean, as a model? You like painting her?"

Uncle Chaim held his hand out, palm down, and wobbled it gently from side to side. "What's not to like? She'll hold any pose absolutely forever—you could leave her all night, morning I guarantee she wouldn't have moved a muscle. No whining, no bellyaching—listen, she'd make Cinderella look like the witch in that movie, the green one. In my life I never worked with anybody gave me less *tsuris*."

"So what's with—?" and Jules mimicked his fluttering hand. "I'm waiting for the but, Chaim."

Uncle Chaim was still for a while, neither answering nor appearing to notice the steaming *varyniki* that the waitress had just set down before him. Finally he grumbled, "She's an angel, what can I tell you? Go reason with an angel." He found himself vaguely angry with Jules, for no reason that made any sense. He went on, "She's got it in her head she's supposed to be my muse. It's not the most comfortable thing sometimes, all right?"

Perhaps due to their shared childhood on Tenth Avenue, Jules did not laugh, but it was plainly a near thing. He said, mildly enough, "Matisse had muses. Rodin, up to here with muses. Picasso about had to give them serial numbers—I think he married them just to keep them straight in his head. You, me . . . I don't see it, Chaim. We're not muse types, you know? Never were, not in all our lives. Also, Rifke would kill you dead. Deader."

"What, I don't know that? Anyway, it's not what you're thinking." He grinned suddenly, in spite of himself. "She's not that kind of girl, you ought to be ashamed. It's just she wants to help, to inspire, that's what muses do. I don't mind her messing around with *my* mess in the studio—I mean, yeah, I mind it, but I can live with it. But the other day,"—he paused briefly, taking a long breath—"the other day she wanted to give me a haircut. A haircut. It's all right, go ahead."

For Jules was definitely laughing this time, spluttering tea through his nose, so that he turned a bright cerise as other diners stared at them. "A haircut," he managed to get out, when he could speak at all clearly. "An angel gave you a haircut."

"No, she didn't give me a haircut," Uncle Chaim snapped back crossly. "She wanted to, she offered—and then, when I said *no, thanks,* after awhile she said she could play music for me while I worked. I usually have the news on, and she doesn't like it, I can tell. Well, it wouldn't make much sense to her, would it? Hardly does to me anymore."

"So she's going to be posing *and* playing music? What, on her harp? That's true, the harp business?"

"No, she just said she could command the music. The way they do with coffee." Jules stared at him. "Well, I don't know—I guess it's like some heavenly Muzak or something. Anyway, I told her no, and I'm sorry I told you anything. Eat, forget it, okay?"

But Jules was not to be put off so easily. He dug down into his *galushki poltavski* for a little time, and then looked up and said with his mouth full, "Tell me one thing, then I'll drop it. Would you say she was beautiful?"

"She's an angel," Uncle Chaim said.

"That's not what I asked. Angels are all supposed to be beautiful, right? Beyond words, beyond description, the works. So?" He smiled serenely at Uncle Chaim over his folded hands.

Uncle Chaim took so long to answer him that Jules actually waved a hand directly in front of his eyes. "Hello? Earth to Malakoff—this is your wakeup call. You in there, Chaim?"

"I'm there, I'm there, stop with the kid stuff." Uncle Chaim flicked his own fingers dismissively at his friend's hand. "Jules, all I can tell you, I never saw anyone looked like her before. Maybe that's beauty all by itself, maybe it's just novelty. Some days she looks eleven thousand years old, like she says—some days . . . some days she could be younger than Duvidl, she could be the first child in the world, first one ever." He shook his head helplessly. "I don't *know*, Jules. I wish I could ask Rembrandt or somebody. Vermeer. Vermeer would know."

Strangely, of the small corps of visitors to the studio—old painters like himself and Jules, gallery owners, art brokers, friends from the neighborhood—I seemed to be the only one who ever saw the blue angel as anything other than one of his unsought acolytes, perfectly happy to stretch canvases, make sandwiches, and occasionally pose, all for the gift of a growled thanks and the privilege of covertly studying him at work. My memory is that I regarded her as a nice-looking older lady with wings, but not my type at all, I having just discovered Alice Faye. Lauren Bacall, Lizabeth Scott, and Lena Horne came a bit later in my development.

I knew she was an angel. I also knew better than to tell any of my own friends about her: we were a cynical lot, who regularly got thrown out of movie theaters for cheering on the Wolfman and booing Shirley Temple and Bobby Breen. But I was shy with the angel, and—I guess—she with me, so I can't honestly say I remember much either in the way of conversation or revelation. Though I am still haunted by one particular moment when I asked her, straight out, "Up there, in heaven—do you ever see Jesus? Jesus Christ, I mean." We were hardly an observant family, any of us, but it still felt strange and a bit dangerous to say the name.

The blue angel turned from cleaning off a palette knife and looked directly at me, really for the first time since we had been introduced. I noticed that the color of her wings seemed to change from moment to moment, rippling constantly through a supple spectrum different from any I knew; and that I had no words either for her hair color, or for her smell. She said, "No, I have never seen him."

"Oh," I said, vaguely disappointed, Jewish or not. "Well—uh—what about his mother? The—the Virgin?" Funny, I remember that *that* seemed more daringly wicked than saying the other name out loud. I wonder why that should have been.

"No," the angel answered. "Nor,"—heading me off—"have I ever seen God. You are closer to God now, as you stand there, than I have ever been."

"That doesn't make any sense," I said. She kept looking at me, but did not reply. I said, "I mean, you're an angel. Angels live with God, don't they?"

She shook her head. In that moment—and just for that moment—her richly empty face showed me a sadness that I don't think a human face could ever have contained. "Angels live alone. If we were with God, we would not be angels." She turned away, and I thought she had finished speaking. But then she looked back quite suddenly to say, in a voice that did not sound like her voice at all, being lower than the sound I knew, and almost masculine in texture, *"Dark and dark and dark . . . so empty . . . so dark . . ."*

It frightened me deeply, that one broken sentence, though I couldn't have said why: it was just so dislocating, so completely out of place—even the rhythm of those few words sounded more like the hesitant English of our old Latvian rabbi than that of Uncle Chaim's muse. He didn't hear it, and I didn't tell him about it, because I thought it must be me, that I was making it up, or I'd heard it wrong. I was accustomed to thinking like that when I was a boy.

"She's got like a dimmer switch," Uncle Chaim explained to Aunt Rifke; they were putting freshly washed sheets on the guest bed at the time, because I was staying the night to interview them for my Immigrant Experience class project. "Dial it one way, you wouldn't notice her if she were running naked down Madison Avenue at high noon, flapping her wings and waving a gun. Two guns. Turn that dial back the other way, all the way . . . well, thank God she wouldn't ever do that, because she'd likely set the studio on fire. You think I'm joking. I'm not joking."

"No, Chaim, I know you're not joking." Rifke silently undid and remade both of his attempts at hospital corners, as she always did. She said, "What I want to know is, just where's that dial set when you're painting her? And I'd think a bit about that answer, if I were you." Rifke's favorite cousin Harvey, a career social worker, had recently abandoned wife and children to run off with a beautiful young dope dealer, and Rifke was feeling more than slightly edgy.

Uncle Chaim did think about it, and replied, "About a third, I'd say. Maybe half, once or twice, no more. I remember, I had to ask her a couple times, turn it down, please—go work when somebody's *glowing* six feet away from you. I mean, the moon takes up a lot of space, a little studio like mine. Bad enough with the wings."

Rifke tucked in the last corner, smoothed the sheet tight, faced him across the bed and said, "You're never going to finish this one, are you? Thirty-seven years, I know all the signs. You'll do it over and over, you'll frame it, you'll hang it, you'll say, *okay, that's it, I'm done*—but you won't be done, you'll just start the whole thing again, only maybe a different style, a brighter palette, a bigger canvas, a smaller canvas. But you'll never get it the way it's in your head, not for you." She smacked the pillows fluffy and tossed them back on the bed. "Don't even bother arguing with me, Malakoff. Not when I'm right."

"So am I arguing? Does it look like I'm arguing?" Uncle Chaim rarely drank at home, but on this occasion he walked into the kitchen, filled a glass from the dusty bottle of *grappa*, and turned back to his wife. He said very quietly, "Crazy to think I could get an angel right. Who could paint an angel?"

Aunt Rifke came to him then and put her hands on his shoulders. "My crazy old man, that's who," she answered him. "Nobody else. God would know."

And my Uncle Chaim blushed for the first time in many years. I didn't see this, but Aunt Rifke told me.

Of course, she was quite right about that painting, or any of the many, many others he made of the blue angel. He was never satisfied with any of them, not a one. There was always *something* wrong, something missing, something there but *not* there, glimpsed but gone. "Like that Chinese monkey trying to grab the moon in the water," Uncle Chaim said to me once. "That's me, a Chinese monkey."

Not that you could say he suffered financially from working with only one model, as the angel had commanded. The failed portraits that he lugged down to the gallery handling his paintings sold almost instantly to museums, private collectors and corporations decorating their lobbies and meeting rooms, under such generic titles as *Angel in the Window, Blue Wings, Angel with Wineglass,* and *Midnight Angel.* Aunt Rifke banked the money, and Uncle Chaim endured the unveilings and the receptions as best he could—without ever looking at the paintings themselves—and then shuffled back to his studio to start over. The angel was always waiting.

I was doing my homework in the studio when Jules Sidelsky visited at last, lured there by other reasons than art, beauty, or deity. The blue angel hadn't given up the notion of acting as Uncle Chaim's muse, but never seemed able to take it much beyond making a tuna salad sandwich, or a pot of coffee (at which, to be fair, she had become quite skilled), summoning music, or reciting the lost works of legendary or forgotten poets while he worked. He tried to discourage this habit; but he did learn a number of Shakespeare's unpublished sonnets, and was able to write down for Jules three poems that drowned with Shelley off the Livorno coast. "Also, your boy Pushkin, his wife destroyed a mess of his stuff right after his death. My girl's got it all by heart, you believe that?"

Pushkin did it. If the great Russian had been declared a saint, Jules would have reported for instruction to the Patriarch of Moscow on the following day. As it was, he came down to Uncle Chaim's studio instead, and was at last introduced to the blue angel, who was as gracious as Jules did his bewildered best to be. She spent the afternoon declaiming Pushkin's vanished verse to him in the original, while hovering tirelessly upside down, just above the crossbar of a second easel. Uncle Chaim thought he might be entering a surrealist phase.

Leaving, Jules caught Uncle Chaim's arm and dragged him out his door into the hot, bustling Village streets, once his dearest subject before the coming of the blue angel. Uncle Chaim, knowing his purpose, said, "So now you see? Now you see?"

"I see." Jules's voice was dark and flat, and almost without expression. "I see you got an angel there, all right. No question in the world about that." The grip on Uncle Chaim's arm tightened. Jules said, "You have to get rid of her."

"*What?* What are you *talking* about? Just finally doing the most important work of my life, and you want me . . . ?" Uncle Chaim's eyes narrowed, and he pulled forcefully away from his friend. "What is it with you and my models? You got like this once before, when I was painting that Puerto Rican guy, the teacher, with the big nose, and you just couldn't stand it, you remember? Said I'd stolen him, wouldn't speak to me for weeks, *weeks*, you remember?"

"Chaim, that's not true—"

"And so now I've got this angel, it's the same thing—worse, with the Pushkin and all—"

"Chaim, damn it, I wouldn't care if she were Pushkin's sister, they played Monopoly together—"

Uncle Chaim's voice abruptly grew calmer; the top of his head stopped sweating and lost its crimson tinge. "I'm sorry, I'm sorry, Jules. It's not I don't understand, I've been the same way about other people's models." He patted the other's shoulder awkwardly. "Look, I tell you what, anytime you want, you come on over, we'll work together. How about that?"

Poor Jules must have been completely staggered by all this. On the one hand he knew—I mean, even *I* knew—that Uncle Chaim never invited other artists to share space with him, let alone a model; on the other, the sudden change can only have sharpened his anxiety about his old friend's state of mind. He said, "Chaim, I'm just trying to tell you, whatever's going on, it isn't good for you. Not her fault, not your fault. People and angels aren't supposed to hang out together—we aren't built for it, and neither are they. She really needs to go back where she belongs."

"She can't. Absolutely not." Uncle Chaim was shaking his head, and kept on shaking it. "She got *sent* here, Jules, she got sent to *me*—"

"By whom? You ever ask yourself that?" They stared at each other. Jules said, very carefully, "No, not by the Devil. I don't believe in the Devil any more than I believe in God, although he always gets the good lines. But it's a free country, and I *can* believe in angels without swallowing all the rest of it, if I want to." He paused, and took a gentler hold on Uncle Chaim's arm. "And I can also imagine that angels might not be exactly what we think they are. That an angel might lie, and still be an angel. That an angel might be selfish—jealous, even. That an angel might just be a little bit out of her head."

In a very pale and quiet voice, Uncle Chaim said, "You're talking about a fallen angel, aren't you?"

"I don't know what I'm talking about," Jules answered. "That's the God's truth." Both of them smiled wearily, but neither one laughed. Jules said, "I'm dead serious, Chaim. For your sake, your sanity, she needs to go."

"And for my sake, she can't." Uncle Chaim was plainly too exhausted for either pretense or bluster, but there was no give in him. He said, "*Landsmann*, it doesn't matter. You could be right, you could be wrong, I'm telling you, it doesn't matter. There's no one else I want to paint anymore—there's no one else I *can* paint, Jules, that's just how it is. Go home now." He refused to say another word.

In the months that followed, Uncle Chaim became steadily more silent, more reclusive, more closed-off from everything that did not directly involve the current portrait of the blue angel. By autumn, he was no longer meeting Jules for lunch at the Ukrainian restaurant; he could rarely be induced to appear at his own openings, or anyone else's; he frequently spent the night at his studio, sleeping briefly in his chair, when he slept at all. It had been understood between Uncle Chaim and me since I was three that I had the run of the place at any time; and while it was still true, I felt far less comfortable there than I was accustomed, and left it more and more to him and the strange lady with the wings.

When an exasperated—and increasingly frightened—Aunt Rifke would challenge him, "You've turned into Red Skelton, painting nothing but clowns on velvet—Margaret Keane, all those big-eyed war orphans," he only shrugged and replied, when he even bothered to respond, "You were the one who told me I could paint an angel. Change your mind?"

Whatever she truly thought, it was not in Aunt Rifke to say such a thing to him directly. Her only recourse was to mumble something like, "Even Leonardo gave up on drawing cats," or "You've done the best anybody could ever do—let it go now, let *her* go." Her own theory, differing somewhat from Jules's, was that it was as much Uncle Chaim's obsession as his model's possible madness that was holding the angel to earth. "Like Ella and Sam," she said to me, referring to the perpetually quarrelling parents of my favorite cousin Arthur. "Locked together, like some kind of punishment machine. Thirty years they hate each other, cats and dogs, but they're so scared of being alone, if one of them died,"—she snapped her fingers—"the other one would be gone in a week. Like that. Okay, so not exactly like that, but like that." Aunt Rifke wasn't getting a lot of sleep either just then.

She confessed to me—it astonishes me to this day—that she prayed more than once herself, during the worst times. Even in my family, which still runs to atheists, agnostics, and cranky anarchists, Aunt Rifke's unbelief was regarded as the standard by which all other blasphemy had to be judged, and set against which it invariably paled. The idea of a prayer from her lips was, on the one hand, fascinating—how would Aunt Rifke conceivably address a Supreme Being?—and more than a little alarming as well. Supplication was not in her vocabulary, let alone her repertoire. Command was.

I didn't ask her what she had prayed for. I did ask, trying to make her laugh, if she had commenced by saying, "To Whom it may concern . . ." She slapped my hand lightly. "Don't talk fresh, just because you're in fifth grade, sixth grade, whatever. Of course I didn't say that, an old Socialist Worker like me. I started off like you'd talk to some kid's mother on the phone, I said, 'It's time for your little girl to go home, we're going to be having dinner. You better call her in now, it's getting dark.' Like that, polite. But not fancy."

"And you got an answer?" Her face clouded, but she made no reply. "You didn't get an answer? Bad connection?" I honestly wasn't being fresh: this was my story too, somehow, all the way back, from the beginning, and I had to know where we were in it. "Come *on*, Aunt Rifke."

"I got an answer." The words came slowly, and cut off abruptly, though she seemed to want to say something more. Instead, she got up and went to the stove, all my aunts' traditional *querencia* in times of emotional stress. Without turning her head, she said in a curiously dull tone, "You go home now. Your mother'll yell at me."

My mother worried about my grades and my taste in friends, not about me; but I had never seen Aunt Rifke quite like this, and I knew better than to push her any further. So I went on home.

From that day, however, I made a new point of stopping by the studio literally every day—except Shabbos, naturally—even if only for a few minutes, just to let Uncle Chaim know that someone besides Aunt Rifke was concerned about him. Of course, obviously, a whole lot of other people would have been, from family to gallery owners to friends like Jules and Ruthie; but I was ten years old, and feeling like my uncle's only guardian, and a private detective to boot. A guardian against *what?* An angel? Detecting *what?* A portrait? I couldn't have said for a minute, but a ten-year-old boy with a sense of mission definitely qualifies as a dangerous flying object.

Uncle Chaim didn't talk to me anymore while he was working, and I really missed that. To this day, almost everything I know about painting—about *being* a painter, every day, all day—I learned from him, grumbled out of the side of his mouth as he sized a canvas, touched up a troublesome corner, or stood back, scratching his head, to reconsider a composition or a subject's expression, or simply to study the stoop of a shadow. Now he worked in bleak near-total silence; and since the blue angel never spoke unless addressed directly, the studio had become a far less inviting place than my three-year-old self had found it. Yet I felt that Uncle Chaim still liked having me there, even if he didn't say anything, so I kept going, but it was an effort some days, mission or no mission.

His only conversation was with the angel—Uncle Chaim always chatted with his models; paradoxically, he felt that it helped them to concentrate—and while I honestly wasn't trying to eavesdrop (except sometimes), I couldn't help overhearing their talk. Uncle Chaim would ask the angel to lift a wing slightly, or to alter her stance somewhat: as

I've said, sitting remained uncomfortable and unnatural for her, but she had finally been able to manage a sort of semi-recumbent posture, which made her look curiously vulnerable, almost like a tired child after an adult party, playing at being her mother, with the grownups all asleep upstairs. I can close my eyes today and see her so.

One winter afternoon, having come tired, and stayed late, I was half-asleep on a padded rocker in a far corner when I heard Uncle Chaim saying, "You ever think that maybe we might both be dead, you and me?"

"We angels do not die," the blue angel responded. "It is not in us to die."

"I told you, lift your chin," Uncle Chaim grunted. "Well, it's built into *us*, believe me, it's mostly what we do from day one." He looked up at her from the easel. "But I'm trying to get you into a painting, and I'll never be able to do it, but it doesn't matter, got to keep trying. The head a *little* bit to the left—no, that's too much, I said a *little*." He put down his brush and walked over to the angel, taking her chin in his hand. He said, "And you . . . whatever you're after, you're not going to get that right, either, are you? So it's like we're stuck here together—and if we were dead, maybe this is hell. Would we know? You ever think about things like that?"

"No." The angel said nothing further for a long time, and I was dozing off again when I heard her speak. "You would not speak so lightly of hell if you had seen it. I have seen it. It is not what you think."

"*Nu?*" Uncle Chaim's voice could raise an eyebrow itself. "So what's it like?"

"*Cold.*" The words were almost inaudible. "So cold . . . so lonely . . . so *empty*. God is not there . . . no one is there. No one, no one, no one . . . no one . . ."

It was that voice, that other voice that I had heard once before, and I have never again been as frightened as I was by the murmuring terror in her words. I actually grabbed my books and got up to leave, already framing some sort of gotta-go to Uncle Chaim, but just then Aunt

Rifke walked into the studio for the first time, with Rabbi Shulevitz trailing behind her, so I stayed where I was. I don't know a thing about ten-year-olds today; but in those times one of the major functions of adults was to supply drama and mystery to our lives, and we took such things where we found them.

Rabbi Stuart Shulevitz was the nearest thing my family had to an actual regular rabbi. He was Reform, of course, which meant that he had no beard, played the guitar, performed Bat Mitzvahs and interfaith marriages, invited local priests and imams to lead the Passover ritual, and put up perpetually with all the jokes told, even by his own congregation, about young, beardless, terminally tolerant Reform rabbis. Uncle Chaim, who allowed Aunt Rifke to drag him to *shul* twice a year, on the High Holidays, regarded him as being somewhere between a mild head cold and mouse droppings in the pantry. But Aunt Rifke always defended Rabbi Shulevitz, saying, "He's smarter than he looks, and anyway he can't help being blond. Also, he smells good."

Uncle Chaim and I had to concede the point. Rabbi Shulevitz's immediate predecessor, a huge, hairy, bespectacled man from Riga, had smelled mainly of rancid hair oil and cheap peach *schnapps*. And he couldn't sing "Red River Valley," either.

Aunt Rifke was generally a placid-appearing, *hamishe* sort of woman, but now her plump face was set in lines that would have told even an angel that she meant business. The blue angel froze in position in a different way than she usually held still as required by the pose. Her strange eyes seemed almost to change their shape, widening in the center and somehow *lifting* at the corners, as though to echo her wings. She stood at near-attention, silently regarding Aunt Rifke and the rabbi.

Uncle Chaim never stopped painting. Over his shoulder he said, "Rifke, what do you want? I'll be home when I'm home."

"So who's rushing you?" Aunt Rifke snapped back. "We didn't come about you. We came the rabbi should take a look at your *model* here." The word burst from her mouth trailing blue smoke.

"What look? I'm working, I'm going to lose the light in ten, fifteen minutes. Sorry, Rabbi, I got no time. Come back next week, you could say a *barucha* for the whole studio. Goodbye, Rifke."

But my eyes were on the rabbi, and on the angel, as he slowly approached her, paying no heed to the quarreling voices of Uncle Chaim and Aunt Rifke. Blond or not, "Red River Valley" or not, he was still magic in my sight, the official representative of a power as real as my disbelief. On the other hand, the angel could fly. The Chassidic wonder-*rebbes* of my parents' Eastern Europe could fly up to heaven and share the Shabbos meal with God, when they chose. Reform rabbis couldn't fly.

As Rabbi Shulevitz neared her, the blue angel became larger and more stately, and there was now a certain menacing aspect to her divine radiance, which set me shrinking into a corner, half-concealed by a dusty drape. But the rabbi came on.

"Come no closer," the angel warned him. Her voice sounded deeper, and slightly distorted, like a phonograph record when the Victrola hasn't been wound tight enough. "It is not for mortals to lay hands on the Lord's servant and messenger."

"I'm not touching you," Rabbi Shulevitz answered mildly. "I just want to look in your eyes. An angel can't object to that, surely."

"The full blaze of an angel's eyes would leave you ashes, impudent man." Even I could hear the undertone of anxiety in her voice.

"That is foolishness." The rabbi's tone continued gentle, almost playful. "My friend Chaim paints your eyes full of compassion, of sorrow for the world and all its creatures, every one. Only turn those eyes to me for a minute, for a very little minute, where's the harm?"

Obediently he stayed where he was, taking off his hat to reveal the black *yarmulke* underneath. Behind him, Aunt Rifke made as though to take Uncle Chaim's arm, but he shrugged her away, never taking his own eyes from Rabbi Shulevitz and the blue angel. His face was very pale. The glass of Scotch in his left hand, plainly as forgotten as the brush in his right, was beginning to slosh over the rim with his trembling, and I was distracted with fascination, waiting for him to drop it. So I wasn't quite present, you might say, when the rabbi's eyes looked into the eyes of the blue angel.

But I heard the rabbi gasp, and I saw him stagger backwards a couple of steps, with his arm up in front of his eyes. And I saw the angel turning away, instantly; the whole encounter can't have lasted more than five seconds, if that much. And if Rabbi Shulevitz looked stunned and frightened—which he did—there is no word that I know to describe the expression on the angel's face. No words.

Rabbi Shulevitz spoke to Aunt Rifke in Hebrew, which I didn't know, and she answered him in swift, fierce Yiddish, which I did, but only insofar as it pertained to things my parents felt were best kept hidden from me, such as money problems, family gossip, and sex. So I missed most of her words, but I caught anyway three of them. One was *shofar,* which is the ram's horn blown at sundown on the High Holidays, and about which I already knew two good dirty jokes. The second was *minyan,* the number of adult Jews needed to form a prayer circle on special occasions. Reform *minyanim* include women, which Aunt Rifke always told me I'd come to appreciate in a couple of years. She was right.

The third word was *dybbuk.*

I knew the word, and I didn't know it. If you'd asked me its meaning, I would have answered that it meant some kind of bogey, like the Invisible Man, or just maybe the Mummy. But I learned the real meaning fast, because Rabbi Shulevitz had taken off his glasses and was wiping his forehead, and whispering, "*No. No. Ich vershtaye nicht . . .*"

Uncle Chaim was complaining, "What the hell is this? See now, we've lost the light already, I *told* you." No one—me included—was paying any attention.

Aunt Rifke—who was never entirely sure that Rabbi Shulevitz really understood Yiddish—burst into English. "It's a *dybbuk,* what's not to understand? There's a *dybbuk* in that woman, you've got to get rid of it! You get a *minyan* together, right now, you get rid of it! Exorcise!"

Why on earth did she want the rabbi to start doing push-ups or jumping-jacks in this moment? I was still puzzling over that when he said, "That woman, as you call her, is an angel. You cannot . . . Rifke, you do not exorcise an angel." He was trembling—I could see that—but his voice was steady and firm.

"You do when it's possessed!" Aunt Rifke looked utterly exasperated with everybody. "I don't know how it could happen, but Chaim's angel's got a *dybbuk* in her—" she whirled on her husband—"which is why she makes you just keep painting her and painting her, day and night. You finish—really finish, it's done, over—she might have to go back out where it's not so nice for a *dybbuk*, you know about that? Look at her!" and she pointed an orange-nailed finger straight in the blue angel's face. "She hears me, *she* knows what I'm talking about. You know what I'm talking, don't you, Miss Angel? Or I should say, Mister *Dybbuk*? You tell me, okay?"

I had never seen Aunt Rifke like this; she might have been possessed herself. Rabbi Shulevitz was trying to calm her, while Uncle Chaim fumed at the intruders disturbing his model. To my eyes, the angel looked more than disturbed—she looked as terrified as a cat I'd seen backed against a railing by a couple of dogs, strays, with no one to call them away from tearing her to pieces. I was anxious for her, but much more so for my aunt and uncle, truly expecting them to be struck by lightning, or turned to salt, or something on that order. I was scared for the rabbi as well, but I figured he could take care of himself. Maybe even with Aunt Rifke.

"A *dybbuk* cannot possibly possess an angel," the rabbi was saying. "Believe me, I majored in Ashkenazic folklore—wrote my thesis on Lilith, as a matter of fact—and there are no accounts, no legends, not so much as a single *bubbemeise* of such a thing. *Dybbuks* are wandering spirits, some of them good, some malicious, but all houseless in the universe. They cannot enter heaven, and Gehenna won't have them, so they take refuge within the first human being they can reach, like any parasite. But an angel? Inconceivable, take my word. Inconceivable."

"In the mind of God," the blue angel said, "nothing is inconceivable."

Strangely, we hardly heard her; she had almost been forgotten in the dispute over her possession. But her voice was that other voice—I could see Uncle Chaim's eyes widen as he caught the difference. That voice said now, "She is right. I am a *dybbuk*."

In the sudden absolute silence, Aunt Rifke, serenely complacent, said, "Told you."

I heard myself say, "Is she bad? I thought she was an angel."

Uncle Chaim said impatiently, "What? She's a model."

Rabbi Shulevitz put his glasses back on, his eyes soft with pity behind the heavy lenses. I expected him to point at the angel, like Aunt Rifke, and thunder out stern and stately Hebrew maledictions, but he only said, "Poor thing, poor thing. Poor creature."

Through the angel's mouth, the *dybbuk* said, "Rabbi, go away. Let me alone, let me be. I am warning you."

I could not take my eyes off her. I don't know whether I was more fascinated by what she was saying, and the adults' having to deal with its mystery, or by the fact that all the time I had known her as Uncle Chaim's winged and haloed model, someone else was using her the way I played with my little puppet theater at home—moving her, making up things for her to say, perhaps even putting her away at night when the studio was empty. Already it was as though I had never heard her strange, shy voice asking a child's endless questions about the world, but only this grownup voice, speaking to Rabbi Shulevitz. "You cannot force me to leave her."

"I don't want to force you to do anything," the rabbi said gently. "I want to help you."

I wish I had never heard the laughter that answered him. I was too young to hear something like that, if anyone could ever be old enough. I cried out and doubled up around myself, hugging my stomach, although what I felt was worse than the worst bellyache I had ever wakened with in the night. Aunt Rifke came and put her arms around me, trying to soothe me, murmuring, half in English, half in Yiddish, "Shh, shh, it's all right, *der rebbe* will make it all right. He's helping the angel, he's getting rid of that thing inside her, like a doctor. Wait, wait, you'll see, it'll be all right." But I went on crying, because I had been visited by a monstrous grief not my own, and I was only ten.

The *dybbuk* said, "If you wish to help me, rabbi, leave me alone. I will not go into the dark again."

Rabbi Shulevitz wiped his forehead. He asked, his tone still gentle and wondering, "What did you do to become . . . what you are? Do you remember?"

The *dybbuk* did not answer him for a long time. Nobody spoke, except for Uncle Chaim muttering unhappily to himself, "Who needs this? Try to get your work done, it turns into a *ferkockte* party. Who needs it?" Aunt Rifke shushed him, but she reached for his arm, and this time he let her take it.

The rabbi said, "You are a Jew."

"I was. Now I am nothing."

"No, you are still a Jew. You must know that we do not practice exorcism, not as others do. We heal, we try to heal both the person possessed and the one possessing. But you must tell me what you have done. Why you cannot find peace."

The change in Rabbi Shulevitz astonished me as much as the difference between Uncle Chaim's blue angel and the spirit that inhabited her and spoke through her. He didn't even look like the crewcut, blue-eyed, guitar-playing, basketball-playing (well, he tried) college-student-dressing young man whose idea of a good time was getting people to sit in a circle and sing "So Long, It's Been Good to Know You" or "Dreidel, Dreidel, Dreidel" together. There was a power of his own inhabiting him, and clearly the *dybbuk* recognized it. It said slowly, "You cannot help me. You cannot heal."

"Well, we don't know that, do we?" Rabbi Shulevitz said brightly. "So, a bargain. You tell me what holds you here, and I will tell you, honestly, what I can do for you. Honestly."

Again the *dybbuk* was slow to reply. Aunt Rifke said hotly, "What is this? What *help*? We're here to expel, to get rid of a demon that's taken over one of God's angels, if that's what she really is, and enchanted my husband so it's all he can paint, all he can think about painting. Who's talking about *helping* a demon?"

"The rabbi is," I said, and they all turned as though they'd forgotten I was there. I gulped and stumbled along, feeling like I might throw up. I said, "I don't think it's a demon, but even if it is, it's given Uncle Chaim a chance to paint a real angel, and everybody loves the paintings, and they buy them, which we wouldn't have had them to sell if the—the *thing*—hadn't made her stay in Uncle Chaim's studio." I ran out of breath, gas, and show-business ambitions all at pretty much the same time, and sat down, grateful that I had neither puked nor started to cry. I was still grandly capable of both back then.

Aunt Rifke looked at me in a way I didn't recall her ever doing before. She didn't say anything, but her arm tightened around me. Rabbi Shulevitz said quietly, "Thank you, David." He turned back to face the angel. In the same voice, he said, "Please. Tell me."

When the *dybbuk* spoke again, the words came one by one—two by two, at most. "A girl . . . There was a girl . . . a young woman . . ."

"*Ai*, how not?" Aunt Rifke's sigh was resigned, but not angry or mocking, just as Uncle Chaim's "*Shah*, Rifkela" was neither a dismissal nor an order. The rabbi, in turn, gestured them to silence.

"She wanted us to marry," the *dybbuk* said. "I did too. But there was time. There was a world . . . there was my work . . . there were things to see . . . to taste and smell and do and be . . . It could wait a little. She could wait . . ."

"Uh-huh. Of course. You could *die* waiting around for some damn man!"

"*Shah*, Rifkela!"

"But this one did not wait around," Rabbi Shulevitz said to the *dybbuk*. "She did not wait for you, am I right?"

"She married another man," came the reply, and it seemed to my ten-year-old imagination that every tortured syllable came away tinged with blood. "They had been married for two years when he beat her to death."

It was my Uncle Chaim who gasped in shock. I don't think anyone else made a sound.

The *dybbuk* said, "She sent me a message. I came as fast as I could. I *did* come," though no one had challenged his statement. "But it was too late."

This time we were the ones who did not speak for a long time. Rabbi Shulevitz finally asked, "What did you do?"

"I looked for him. I meant to kill him, but he killed himself before I found him. So I was too late again."

"What happened then?" That was me, once more to my own surprise. "When you didn't get to kill him?"

"I lived. I wanted to die, but I lived."

From Aunt Rifke—how not? "You ever got married?"

"No. I lived alone, and I grew old and died. That is all."

"Excuse me, but that is *not* all." The rabbi's voice had suddenly, startlingly, turned probing, almost harsh. "That is only the beginning." Everyone looked at him. The rabbi said, "So, after you died, what did happen? Where did you go?"

There was no answer. Rabbi Shulevitz repeated the question. The *dybbuk* responded finally, "You have said it yourself. Houseless in the universe I am, and how should it be otherwise? The woman I loved died because I did not love her enough—what greater sin is there than that? Even her murderer had the courage to atone, but I dared not offer my own life in payment for hers. I chose to live, and living on has been my punishment, in death as well as in life. To wander back and forth in a cold you cannot know, shunned by heaven, scorned by purgatory . . . do you wonder that I sought shelter where I could, even in an angel? God himself would have to come and cast me out again, Rabbi—you never can."

I became aware that my aunt and uncle had drawn close around me, as though expecting something dangerous and possibly explosive to happen. Rabbi Shulevitz took off his glasses again, ran his hand through his crewcut, stared at the glasses as though he had never seen them before, and put them back on.

"You are right," he said to the *dybbuk*. "I'm a rabbi, not a *rebbe*—no Solomonic wisdom, no magical powers, just a degree from a second-class seminary in Metuchen, New Jersey. You wouldn't know it." He drew a deep breath and moved a few steps closer to the blue angel. He said, "But this *gornisht* rabbi knows anyway that you would never have been allowed this refuge if God had not taken pity on you. You must know this, surely?" The *dybbuk* did not answer. Rabbi Shulevitz said, "And if God pities you, might you not have a little pity on yourself? A little forgiveness?"

"Forgiveness . . ." Now it was the *dybbuk* who whispered. "Forgiveness may be God's business. It is not mine."

"Forgiveness is everyone's business. Even the dead. On this earth or under it, there is no peace without forgiveness." The rabbi reached out then, to touch the blue angel comfortingly. She did not react, but he winced and drew his hand back instantly, blowing hard on his fingers, hitting them against his leg. Even I could see that they had turned white with cold.

"You need not fear for her," the *dybbuk* said. "Angels feel neither cold nor heat. You have touched where I have been."

Rabbi Shulevitz shook his head. He said, "I touched you. I touched your shame and your grief—as raw today, I know, as on the day your love died. But the cold . . . the cold is yours. The loneliness, the endless guilt over what you should have done, the endless turning to and fro in empty darkness . . . none of that comes from God. You must believe me, my friend." He paused, still flexing his frozen fingers. "And you must come forth from God's angel now. For her sake and your own."

The *dybbuk* did not respond. Aunt Rifke said, far more sympathetically than she had before, "You need a *minyan*, I could make some calls. We'd be careful, we wouldn't hurt it."

Uncle Chaim looked from her to the rabbi, then back to the blue angel. He opened his mouth to say something, but didn't.

The rabbi said, "You have suffered enough at your own hands. It is time for you to surrender your pain." When there was still no reply, he asked, "Are you afraid to be without it? Is that your real fear?"

"It has been my only friend!" the *dybbuk* answered at last. "Even God cannot understand what I have done so well as my pain does. Without the pain, there is only me."

"There is heaven," Rabbi Shulevitz said. "Heaven is waiting for you. Heaven has been waiting a long, long time."

"I am waiting for me!" It burst out of the *dybbuk* in a long wail of purest terror, the kind you only hear from small children trapped in a nightmare. "You want me to abandon the one sanctuary I have ever found, where I can huddle warm in the consciousness of an angel and sometimes—for a little—even forget the thing I am. You want me to be naked to myself again, and I am telling you *no, not ever, not ever, not ever.* Do what you must, Rabbi, and I will do the only thing I can." It paused, and then added, somewhat stiffly, "Thank you for your efforts. You are a good man."

Rabbi Shulevitz looked genuinely embarrassed. He also looked weary, frustrated, and older than he had been when he first recognized the possession of Uncle Chaim's angel. Looking vaguely around at us, he said, "I don't know—maybe it *will* take a *minyan*. I don't want to, but we can't just . . ." His voice trailed away sadly, too defeated even to finish the sentence.

Or maybe he didn't finish because that was when I stepped forward, pulling away from my aunt and uncle, and said, "He can come with me, if he wants. He can come and live in me. Like with the angel."

Uncle Chaim said, *"What?"* and Aunt Rifke said, *"No!"* and Rabbi Shulevitz said, *"David!"* He turned and grabbed me by the shoulders, and I could feel him wanting to shake me, but he didn't. He seemed to be having trouble breathing. He said, "David, you don't know what you're saying."

"Yes, I do," I said. "He's scared, he's so scared. I know about scared."

Aunt Rifke crouched down beside me, peering hard into my face. "David, you're ten years old, you're a little boy. This one, he could be a thousand years, he's been hiding from God in an angel's body. How could you know what he's feeling?"

I said, "Aunt Rifke, I go to school. I wake up every morning, and right away I think about the boys waiting to beat me up because I'm small, or because I'm Jewish, or because they just don't like my face, the way I look at them. Every day I want to stay home and read, and listen to the radio, and play my All-Star Baseball game, but I get dressed and I eat breakfast, and I walk to school. And every day I have to think how I'm going to get through recess, get through gym class, get home without running into Jay Taffer, George DiLucca. Billy Kronish. I know all about not wanting to go outside."

Nobody said anything. The rabbi tried several times, but it was Uncle Chaim who finally said loudly, "I got to teach you to box. A little Archie Moore, a little Willie Pep, we'll take care of those *mamzers*." He looked ready to give me my first lesson right there.

When the *dybbuk* spoke again, its voice was somehow different: quiet, slow, wondering. It said, "Boy, you would do that?" I didn't speak, but I nodded.

Aunt Rifke said, "Your mother would kill me! She's hated me since I married Chaim."

The dybbuk said, "Boy, if I come . . . outside, I cannot go back. Do you understand that?"

"Yes," I said. "I understand."

But I was shaking. I tried to imagine what it would be like to have someone living inside me, like a baby, or a tapeworm. I was fascinated by tapeworms that year. Only this would be a spirit, not an actual physical thing—that wouldn't be so bad, would it? It might even be company, in a way, almost like being a comic-book superhero and having a secret identity. I wondered whether the angel had even known the *dybbuk* was in her, as quiet as he had been until he spoke to Rabbi Shulevitz. Who, at the moment, was repeating over and over, "No, I can't permit this. This is wrong, this can't be allowed. No." He began to mutter prayers in Hebrew.

Aunt Rifke was saying, "I don't care, I'm calling some people from the *shul*, I'm getting some people down here right away!" Uncle Chaim was gripping my shoulder so hard it hurt, but he didn't say anything. But there was really no one in the room except the *dybbuk* and me. When I think about it, when I remember, that's all I see.

I remember being thirsty, terribly thirsty, because my throat and my mouth were so dry. I pulled away from Uncle Chaim and Aunt Rifke, and I moved past Rabbi Shulevitz, and I croaked out to the *dybbuk*, "Come on, then. You can come out of the angel, it's safe, it's okay." I remember thinking that it was like trying to talk a cat down out of a tree, and I almost giggled.

I never saw him actually leave the blue angel. I don't think anyone did. He was simply standing right in front of me, tall enough that I had to look up to meet his eyes. Maybe he wasn't a thousand years old, but Aunt Rifke hadn't missed by much. It wasn't his clothes that told me—he wore a white turban that looked almost square, a dark-red vest sort of thing and white trousers, under a gray robe that came all the way to the ground—it was the eyes. If blackness is the absence of light, then those were the blackest eyes I'll ever see, because there was no light in those eyes, and no smallest possibility of light ever. You couldn't call them sad: *sad* at least knows what *joy* is, and grieves at being exiled from joy. However old he really was, those eyes were a thousand years past sad.

"Sephardi," Rabbi Shulevitz murmured. "Of course he'd be Sephardi."

Aunt Rifke said, "You can see through him. Right through."

In fact he seemed to come and go: near-solid one moment, cobweb and smoke the next. His face was lean and dark, and must have been a proud face once. Now it was just weary, unspeakably weary—even a ten-year-old could see that. The lines down his cheeks and around the eyes and mouth made me think of desert pictures I'd seen, where the earth gets so dry that it pulls apart, cracks and pulls away from itself. He looked like that.

But he smiled at me. No, he smiled *into* me, and just as I've never seen eyes like his again, I've never seen a smile as beautiful. Maybe it couldn't reach his eyes, but it must have reached mine, because I can still see it. He said softly, "Thank you. You are a kind boy. I promise you, I will not take up much room."

I braced myself. The only invasive procedures I'd had any experience with then were my twice-monthly allergy shots and the time our doctor had to lance an infected finger that had swollen to twice its size. Would possession be anything like that? Would it make a difference if you were sort of inviting the possession, not being ambushed and taken over, like in *Invasion of the Body Snatchers*? I didn't mean to close my eyes, but I did.

Then I heard the voice of the blue angel.

"There is no need." It sounded like the voice I knew, but the *breath* in it was different—I don't know how else to put it. I could say it sounded stronger, or clearer, or maybe more musical; but it was the breath, the free breath. Or maybe that isn't right either, I can't tell you—I'm not even certain whether angels breathe, and I knew an angel once. There it is.

"Manassa, there is no need," she said again. I turned to look at her then, when she called the *dybbuk* by his name, and she was smiling herself, for the first time. It wasn't like his; it was a faraway smile at something I couldn't see, but it was real, and I heard Uncle Chaim catch his breath. To no one in particular, he said, "*Now* she smiles. Never once, I could never once get her to smile."

"Listen," the blue angel said. I didn't hear anything but my uncle grumbling, and Rabbi Shulevitz's continued Hebrew prayers. But the *dybbuk*—Manassa—lifted his head, and the endlessly black eyes widened, just a little.

The angel said again, "Listen," and this time I did hear something, and so did everyone else. It was music, definitely music, but too faint with distance for me to make anything out of it. But Aunt Rifke, who loved more kinds of music than you'd think, put her hand to her mouth and whispered, "*Oh.*"

"Manassa, listen," the angel said for the third time, and the two of them looked at each other as the music grew stronger and clearer. I can't describe it properly: it wasn't harps and psalteries—whatever a psaltery is, maybe you use it singing psalms—and it wasn't a choir of soaring heavenly voices, either. It was almost a little scary, the way you feel when you hear the wild geese passing over in the autumn night. It made me think of that poem of Tennyson's, with that line about *the horns of Elfland faintly blowing*. We'd been studying it in school.

"It is your welcome, Manassa," the blue angel said. "The gates are open for you. They were always open."

But the *dybbuk* backed away, suddenly whimpering. "I cannot! I am afraid! They will see!"

The angel took his hand. "They see now, as they saw you then. Come with me, I will take you there."

The *dybbuk* looked around, just this side of panicking. He even tugged a bit at the blue angel's hand, but she would not let him go. Finally he sighed very deeply—lord, you could feel the dust of the tombs in that sigh, and the wind between the stars—and nodded to her. He said, "I will go with you."

The blue angel turned to look at all of us, but mostly at Uncle Chaim. She said to him, "You are a better painter than I was a muse. And you taught me a great deal about other things than painting. I will tell Rembrandt."

Aunt Rifke said, a little hesitantly, "I was maybe rude. I'm sorry." The angel smiled at her.

Rabbi Shulevitz said, "Only when I saw you did I realize that I had never believed in angels."

"Continue not to," the angel replied. "We rather prefer it, to tell you the truth. We work better that way."

Then she and the *dybbuk* both looked at me, and I didn't feel even ten years old; more like four or so. I threw my arms around Aunt Rifke and buried my face in her skirt. She patted my head—at least I guess it was her, I didn't actually see her. I heard the blue angel say in Yiddish, "*Sei gesund*, Chaim's Duvidl. You were always courteous to me. Be well."

I looked up in time to meet the old, old eyes of the *dybbuk*. He said, "In a thousand years, no one has ever offered me freely what you did." He said something else, too, but it wasn't in either Hebrew or Yiddish, and I didn't understand.

The blue angel spread her splendid, shimmering wings one last time, filling the studio—as, for a moment, the mean winter sky outside seemed to flare with a sunset hope that could not have been. Then she and Manassa, the *dybbuk*, were gone, vanished instantly, which makes me think that the wings aren't really for flying. I don't know what other purpose they could serve, except they did seem somehow to enfold us all and hold us close. But maybe they're just really decorative. I'll never know now.

Uncle Chaim blew out his breath in one long, exasperated sigh. He said to Aunt Rifke, "I never did get her right. You know that."

I was trying to hear the music, but Aunt Rifke was busy hugging me, and kissing me all over my face, and telling me not ever, *ever* to do such a thing again, what was I thinking? But she smiled up at Uncle Chaim and answered him, "Well, she got *you* right, that's what matters." Uncle Chaim blinked at her. Aunt Rifke said, "She's probably telling Rembrandt about you right now. Maybe Vermeer, too."

"You think so?" Uncle Chaim looked doubtful at first, but then he shrugged and began to smile himself. "Could be."

I asked Rabbi Shulevitz, "He said something to me, the *dybbuk*, just at the end. I didn't understand."

The rabbi put his arm around me. "He was speaking in old Ladino, the language of the Sephardim. He said, '*I will not forget you*.'" His smile was a little shaky, and I could feel him trembling himself, with everything over. "I think you have a friend in heaven, David. Extraordinary Duvidl."

The music was gone. We stood together in the studio, and although there were four of us, it felt as empty as the winter street beyond the window where the blue angel had posed so often. A taxi took the corner too fast, and almost hit a truck; a cloud bank was pearly with the moon's muffled light. A group of young women crossed the street, singing. I could feel everyone wanting to move away, but nobody did, and nobody spoke, until Uncle Chaim finally said, "Rabbi, you got time for a sitting tomorrow? Don't wear that suit."

We Never Talk About My Brother

The great songwriter Johnny Mercer insisted on sharing the royalties from "I Wanna Be Around To Pick Up The Pieces When Somebody Breaks Your Heart" with the Cincinnati department-store clerk who suggested the title to him, because he believed that the right title was at least half of a successful song.

Titles really are that valuable, and good ones rarely come to me at all, let alone easily: so I pay attention when they do. The title for this story popped into my head while I was headed out from a hotel room in Austin, Texas, so I mentioned it to the fellow driving me to the World Fantasy Convention that was my reason for being there. He asked me what it was about, and I said "I *think* it might be about a satyr."

Turns out I was wrong.

Therefore, since the world has still
Much good, but much less good than ill,
And while the sun and moon endure
Luck's a chance, but trouble's sure,
I'd face it as a wise man would,
And train for ill and not for good.
—A. E. Housman

Nobody does anymore, haven't for years—well, that's why you're here, ain't it, one of those "Where Are They Now" pieces of yours?—but it's funny, when you think about it. I mean, even after what happened, and all this time, you'd think Willa and I—Willa's my sister—you'd think we'd say at least Word One about him now and then. To each other, maybe not to anyone else. But we don't, not ever, even now. Hell, my wife won't talk about Esau, and she'd have more reason than most. Lucky you found me first—she'd have run you right on out of the house, and she could do it, too. Tell the truth, shame the devil, the only reason I'm sitting here talking to you at all is you having the mother wit to bring along that bottle of Blanton's Single Barrel. Lord, I swear I can*not* remember the last time I had any of that in the house.

Mind if you record me? No, no, you go ahead on, get your little tape thing going, okay by me. Doesn't make a bit of difference. You're like to think I'm pretty crazy before we're through, one way or another, but that don't make any difference either.

Well, okay then. Let's get started.

Last of the great TV anchormen, my brother, just as big as newsmen ever used to get. Not like today—too many of them in the game, too much competition, all sort of, I don't know, interchangeable. More and more folks getting the news on their computers, those little earphone gadgets, I don't know what-all. It's just different than it was. Way different. Confess I kind of like it.

But back then, back then, Esau was just a little way south of a movie star. Couldn't walk down the street, go out grocery shopping, he'd get jumped by a whole mob of his fans, his groupies. Couldn't turn on the TV and not see him on half a dozen channels, broadcasting, or being interviewed, or being a special guest on some show or other. I mean everything from big political stuff to cooking shows, for heaven's sake. My friend Buddy Andreason, we go fishing weekends, us and Kirby Rich, Buddy used to always tease me about it. Point to those little girls on the news, screaming and running after Esau for autographs, and he'd say, "Man, you could get yourself some of that so easy! Just tell them you're his brother, you'll introduce them—man, they'd be all over you! All over you!"

No, it's not a nickname, that was real. Esau Robbins. Right out of the Bible, the Old Testament, the guy who sold his birthright to his brother for a mess of pottage. Pottage is like soup or stew, something like that. Our Papa was a big Bible reader, and there was . . . I don't know, there was stuff that was funny to him that wasn't real funny to anyone else. Like naming me and Esau like he did.

A lot easier to live with Jacob than a funny name like Esau, I guess—you know, when you're a kid. But I wasn't all that crazy about my name either, tell you the truth, which is why I went with Jake first time anybody ever called me that in school, never looked back. I mean, you think about it now. The Bible Esau's the hunter, the fisherman, the outdoor guy—okay, maybe not the brightest fellow, not the most mannerly, maybe he cusses too much and spits his tobacco where he shouldn't, but still. And Jacob's the sneaky one, you know? Esau's come home beat and hungry and thirsty, and Jacob tricks him—face it, Jacob tricks him right out of his inheritance, his whole future, and their mama helps him do it, and God thinks that's righteous, a righteous act. Makes you wonder about some things, don't it?

Did he have a bad time of it growing up, account of his name? 'Bout like you'd expect. I had to fight his battles time to time, if some big fellow was bullyragging him, and my sister Willa did the same, because we were the older ones, and that's just what you do, right? But we didn't see him, you know what I mean? Didn't have any idea who he was, except a nuisance we had to take care of, watch after, keep out of traffic. He's seven years younger than Willa, five years younger than me. Doesn't sound like much now, but when you're a kid it's a lot. He might have been growing up in China, for all we knew about him.

I'm embarrassed to say it flat out, but there's not a lot I really recall about him as a kid, before the whole thing with Donnie Schmidt. I remember Esau loved tomatoes ripe off the vine—got into trouble every summer, stealing them out of the neighbors' yards—and he was scared of squirrels, can you believe that? Squirrels, for God's sake. Said they chased him. Oh, and he used to hurt himself a lot, jumping down from higher and higher places—ladders, trees, sheds and all such. Practicing landing, that was the idea. Practicing landing.

But I surely remember the first time I ever really looked at Esau and thought, wow, what's going on here? Not at school—in the old Pott Street playground, it was. Donnie Schmidt—mean kid with red hair and a squinty eye—Donnie had Esau down on his back, and was just beating him like a rug. Bloody nose, big purple shiner already coming up . . . I came running all the way across the playground, Willa too, and I got Donnie by the neck and hauled him right off my brother. Whopped him a couple of times too, I don't mind telling you. He was a nasty one, Donnie Schmidt.

Esau had quit fighting, but he didn't bounce up right away, and I wouldn't have neither, the whupping he'd taken. He was just staring at Donnie, and his eyes had gone really pale, both of them, and he pointed straight at Donnie—looked funny, I'm bound to say, with him still lying flat down in that red-clay mud—and he kind of whispered, "You got run over." Hadn't been as close as I was, I'd never have heard him.

"You got run over." Like that—like it had already happened, you see? Exactly—like he was reading the news. You got it.

Okay. Now. This is what's important. This is where you're going to start wondering whether you should have maybe sat just a little closer to the door. See, what happened to Donnie, didn't happen then—it had already happened a week before. Seriously. Donnie, he didn't disappear, blink out of sight, right when Esau said those words. He just shrugged and walked away, and Willa took Esau home to clean him up, and I got into a one-a-cat game—what you probably call "horse" or "catcher-flies-up"—with a couple of my pals until dinnertime. And Ma yelled some at Esau for getting into a fight, but nobody else thought anything more about it, then or ever. Nobody except me.

Because when I woke up next morning, everybody in town knew Donnie Schmidt had been dead for a week. Hell, we'd all been to the funeral.

I didn't see it happen, but Willa did—or that's what she thought, anyway. Donnie'd been walking to school, and old Mack Moffett's car went out of control somehow, crossed three lanes in two, three seconds, and pinned him against the wall of a house. Poor kid never knew what hit him, and neither did anyone who ever went over the car or gave poor Mack a sobriety test. The old man died a couple of months later, by the way. Call it shock, call it a broken heart, if you like—I don't know.

But the point is. The point is that Donnie Schmidt was alive as could be the day before, beating up on Esau on the playground. I remembered that. But I'd also swear on a stack of Bibles that he'd been killed in an accident the week before, and Willa would swear on the Day of Judgment that she was there. And we'd both pass any and every lie-detector test you want to put us through. Because we *know,* we know we're telling the truth, so it's not a lie. Right?

It's just not true.

Told you. Told you you'd be looking at me like that about now . . . no, don't say nothing, just *listen,* okay? There's more.

Now I got no idea if that was the first time he did it—made something happen by saying it already had. No idea. Like I said before, it was just the first time I ever really saw my brother.

Nor it didn't change a lot between us, him and Willa and me. Willa was all books and choir rehearsals, and I was all cars and trucks and hunting with my Uncle Rick, and Esau pretty much got along on his own, same as he'd always done. He was just Esau, bony as a clothes rack, all elbows and knees—Papa used to say that he was so thin you could shave with him—but if you looked closely, I guess you could have seen how he might yet turn out good-looking. Only we weren't looking closely, none of us were, not even me. Not even after Donnie. One of anything is still just one of anything, even if it's strange. You can put it out of your mind. So across the dinner table was about it for Willa and me. If we were home.

But while I wasn't really looking, I can't say I didn't pay a little more attention in the looking I did, if you know what I mean.

One time I do recall, when Esau was maybe twelve, maybe thirteen, in there somewhere. Must have been thirteen, because I was already out of high school and working five days a week to help with the rent.

Anyway I'm up on the roof of the house on a Saturday, replacing a few shingles got blown off in the last windstorm. Hammering and humming, not thinking about much of anything, and suddenly I turn my head and there's Esau, a few feet away, squatting on his heels and watching me. Never heard him climbing up, no idea how long he's been there, but I know I don't like that look—sets me to thinking about the one he gave Donnie. What if he says to me, "*You* fell off the roof," and it turns out I'm dead, and been dead some while? So I say "Hey, you want to hand me those nails over there?" friendly and peaceable as you like. Probably the most I've said to him in a week, more.

So he hands me the nails, and I say thanks, and I go back to work, and Esau sits watching me a few minutes more, and then he asks, right out of nowhere, "Jake, you believe in God?"

Like that. I didn't even look up, just grunted, "Guess I do."

"You think God's nice?"

His voice was still breaking, I recall—went up and down like a seesaw, made me laugh. I said, "Minister says so."

He wouldn't quit on it, wouldn't let up. "But do *you* think God's nice?"

I dropped a couple of shingles, and made him go down and bring them back up to the roof for me. When he'd done that, I said, "You look around at this world, you think God's nice?"

He didn't answer for a while, just sat there watching me work. By and by he said, "If I was God, I'd be nice."

I set my eye on him then, and I don't know what made me do it, but I said, "You would, huh? Tell it to Donnie Schmidt."

I'd never said anything like that to him before. I'd never mentioned Donnie Schmidt since the funeral, because I knew in my mind—like Willa, like everyone else—that Donnie was dead and buried a week before him and Esau had that fight. Anyway, Esau's eyes filled up, which hardly ever happened, he wasn't ever a crier, and his face got all red, and he stood up, and for a minute I thought he actually was about to come at me. But he didn't—he just screamed, with that funny breaking voice, "I *would* be a nice God! I *would*!"

And he was off and gone, I guess down the ladder, though maybe he jumped, the way he was doing then, because he was limping a bit at dinnertime. Anyway, we never talked about God no more, nor about Donnie Schmidt neither, at least while Esau still lived here.

I never talked about any of this with Papa. He was pretty much taken up with his Bible and his notions and his work at the tannery, before he passed. But Ma saw more than she let on. One time . . . there was this one time she was still up when I come home from little Sadie Morrison's place, she as later married that Canuck fellow, Rene Arceneaux, and she said—that's Ma, not Sadie—she said to me, "Jacob, Esau's bad."

I said, "Ma, goodness' sake, don't say that. There's nothing wrong with the kid except he's kind of a pain in the ass. Otherwise I got no quarrel with him." Which was true enough then, and maybe still is, depending how you measure.

Ma shook her head. I remember, she was sitting right where you are, by the fireplace—this was their house, you know—just rocking and shelling peas—and she said, "Jacob, I ain't nearly as silly as everybody always thinks I am. I know when somebody's bad. Esau, he makes people into ghosts."

I looked at her. I said, "Ma. Ma, don't you never go round saying stuff like that, they'll put you away for sure. You're saying Esau kills people, and he never killed nobody!" And I believed it, you see, absolutely, even though I also knew better.

And Ma . . . Ma, whatever she knew, maybe she knew it because she was just as silly as folks thought she was. Hard to say about Ma. She said, "That girl last year, the one he was so gone on, who wanted to go off to New York to be an actress. You remember her?"

"Susie Harkin," I said. "Sure I remember. Plane crashed, killed everybody on board. It was real sad."

Ma didn't say nothing for a long time. Rocked and shelled, rocked and shelled. I stood and watched her, snatching myself a pea now and then, and thinking on how wearied she was getting to look. Then she said, almost mumbling-like, "I don't think so, Jacob. I'm *persuaded* she got killed in that crash, but I don't *think* so."

That's exactly how she put it—exactly. I didn't say anything myself, because what could I say—Ma, you're right, I remember it both ways too? I remember you telling me she gave him the mitten—that's the way Ma talks; she meant the girl broke up with him—and left, and I remember Susie doing just fine up there in the city, she even sent me a letter . . . but I also remember her and Esau talking about getting married someday, only then she stepped on that flight and never got to New York at all . . . I'm going to tell Ma that, and get her going, when the city health people already thought she ought to be off in some facility somewhere? Not hardly.

Things wandered along, way they do, just happening and not happening. Willa went all the way on to state college and become a teacher, and then she got married and moved all that way to Florida, Jacksonville Beach. Got two nice kids, my niece Carol-Ann and my nephew Ben. Ma finally did have to go away, and soon enough she passed too. Me, I kept on at the same hardware store where you found me, only after a while I came to own it—me and the bank. Married Middy Jo Staines, but she died. No children.

And Esau . . . well, he graduated the town high school like me and Willa—unless maybe we just think he did—and then the University of Colorado gave him a scholarship, unless they just think so, and he was gone out of here quicker than scat. Never really came home after that, except the once, which I'll get to in a bit. Got through college, got the job with that station in Baltimore, and the next time we saw him he was on the air, feeding stories to the network, the way they do—like, "And here's Esau Robbins, our Baltimore correspondent, to tell you more about today's tragic explosion," or whatever. And pretty soon it was D.C. and the national news, every night, and you look up and your baby brother's famous. Couldn't have been over thirty.

And looking good, too, no question about it. Grew up taller than me, taller than Papa, with Ma's dark hair and dark blue eyes, and that look—like he belonged right where he was, telling you things he knows that you don't, and telling them in that deep, warm, friendly voice he had. Lord, I don't know where he rented that voice—he sure didn't have it when he lived in this town. Voice like that, he could have been reciting Mother Goose or something, wouldn't have mattered. When you heard it you just wanted to listen.

I used to watch him on the TV, my brother Esau, telling us what's really doing in Afghanistan, in Somalia, in France, in D.C., and I'd look at his eyes, and I'd wonder if he ever even thought about poor nasty Donnie Schmidt. And I'd wonder how he found out he could do it, how'd he discover his talent, his knack, whatever you want to call it. I mean, how does a little boy, schoolyard-age boy—how does he deal with a thing like that? How does he even practice it, predicting something he wants to happen—and then, like that, it's true, and it's always been true, it's just a plain fact, like gravity or something, with nobody knowing any better for sure but me? Town like this, there's not a lot of people you can talk to about that kind of thing. Must of made him feel even more alone, you know?

The visit. Whoo. Yeah, well—all right. All right.

It wasn't hardly a real visit, first off. See, he'd already been the anchorman on that big news program for at least ten, twelve years when they got the notion to do a show on his return to the old home town. So they sent a whole crowd along with him—a camera crew, and a couple of producers, the way they do, and there was a writer, and some publicity people, and some other folks I can't recall. Anyway, I'll tell you, it was for sure the biggest thing to hit this place since Ruth and Gehrig barnstormed through here back in the twenties. They were here a whole week, that gang, and they spent a lot of money, and made all the businesses happy. Can't beat that with a stick, can you?

And Esau walked through it all like a king—just like a king, no other word for it. They filmed him greeting old friends, talking with his old teachers, stopping in at all his old hangouts, even reading to kids at the library. Mind you, I don't remember him ever having any hangouts, and the teachers didn't seem to remember him much at all. As for the old friends . . . look, if Esau had any friends when we were all kids, I swear I don't recall them. I mean, there they were in this documentary thing, shaking his hand, slapping his back, having a beer with him in Henry's—been there fifty, sixty years, that place—but I'd never seen any of them with him as a kid, 'ceptin maybe a few of them were pounding on him, back before Donnie. Thing is, I don't imagine Esau was trying very hard to get the details right. Wouldn't have hardly thought we was worth the trouble. Willa thought she recognized one or two, and remembered this and that, but even she wasn't sure.

Oh, yeah, her and me, we were both in it. They paid for Willa to come from Florida—flew little Ben and Carol-Ann, too, but not her husband Jerry, cause they just wanted to show Esau being an uncle. They'd have put her and the kids up at the Laurel Inn with the crew, but she wanted to stay here at the old house, which was fine with me. Don't get to be around children much.

We didn't see much of Esau even after Willa got here, but a day or two before they wrapped up the film, he dropped over to the house for dinner, which meant that the whole crew dropped over too. We were the only ones eating, and it was the strangest meal I've ever had in my life, what with all those electricians setting up lights, and the sound people running cables every which way, and a director, for God's sake, a director telling us when to start eating—they sent out to Horshach's for prime rib—and where to look when the camera was on us, and what Willa should say to the kids when they asked for seconds. Carol-Ann got so nervous, she actually threw up her creamed corn. And Willa got so mad at the lighting guy, because Ben's got eye trouble, and the lights were so bright and hot . . . well, it was a real mess, that's all. Just a real mess.

But Esau, he just sat through it all like it was just another broadcast, which I guess to him it was. Never got upset about all the retakes—lord, that dinner must have taken three hours, one thing another—never looked sweaty or tired, always found something new and funny to say to the camera when it started rolling again. But that's who he was talking to, all through that show—not us, for sure. He never once looked straight at any of us, Willa or the kids or me, if the camera wasn't on him.

He was a stranger in this house, the house where we'd all grown up—more of a stranger than all those cameramen, those producers. He could just as well have been from another country, where everybody's great-looking, but they don't speak any language you ever heard of. With all the craziness and confusion, the lights and the reflectors, and the microphones swinging around on pole-things, I probably studied on my brother longer and harder than I'd ever done in my life before. There at that table, having that fake dinner, I studied on him, and I thought a few new things.

See, I couldn't believe it was just Esau. What I *could* believe is there's no such thing as history, not the way they teach it to you in school. Wars, revolutions, all those big inventions, all those big discoveries . . . if there's been a bunch of people like Esau right through time—or even a few, a handful—then the history books don't signify, you understand what I'm saying? Then it's all just been what any one of them wanted, decided on, right at this moment or that, and no great, you know, patterns to the way things happen. Just Esau, and whatever Others, and *you got run over.* Like that. That's what I came to think.

And I know I'm right. Because Susie Harkin was in that film.

Yeah, yeah, I know what I told you about the plane crash, the rest of it, I'm telling you this now. She walked in by herself, bright as you please, just before they finally got around to putting real food on the table, and sat right down across from Esau, between me and little Ben. The TV people looked at the director for orders, and I guess he figured she was family, no point fussing about it, and let her stay. He was too busy yelling at the crew about the lights, anyway.

Esau was good. I am here to tell you, Esau was *good.* There was just that one moment when he saw her . . . and even then, you might have had to be me or Willa, and watching close, before you noticed the twist of blank panic in his eyes. After that he never looked straight at her, and he sure never said her name, but you couldn't have told one thing from his expression. Susie didn't waste no time on him, neither; she was busy helping little Ben with his food, cutting his meat up small for him, and making faces to make him laugh. Ma had said "Esau makes people into ghosts," but I don't guess you'd find a ghost cutting up a boy's prime rib for him, do you? Not any kind of ghost I ever heard about.

When she'd finished helping Ben, she looked right up at me, and she winked.

As long as she'd been gone, Susie Harkin didn't look a day different. I don't suppose you'd ever have called her a beauty, best day she ever saw. Face too thin, forehead a shade low, nose maybe a bit beaky—but she had real nice brown eyes, and when she smiled you didn't see a thing but that smile. I'd liked her a good bit when she was going out with Esau, and I was real sorry when she died in that plane crash. So was Willa. And now here Susie was again, sitting at our old dinner table with all these people around, winking at me like the two of us had a secret together. And we did, because I knew she'd been dead, and now she wasn't, and *she* knew I knew, and she knew *why* I knew besides. So, yeah, you could say we had our secret.

Esau didn't do much more looking at me during the dinner than he did at Susie, but that was the one time he did. I saw him when I turned to say something to Willa. It wasn't any special kind of a look he gave me, not in particular; it was maybe more like the first time I really looked at him, when he did what he did to Donnie Schmidt. As though he hadn't ever seen me either, until that glance, that wink, passed between Susie Harkin and me.

Anyway, by and by the little ones fell asleep, and Willa took them off to bed, and the crew packed up and went back to the Laurel Inn, and Susie right away vanished into the kitchen with all the dirty dishes—"No, I insist, you boys just stay and talk." You don't hear women say that much anymore.

So there we were, me and Esau, everything gotten quiet now—always more quiet after a lot of noise, you notice?—and him still not really looking at me, and me too tired and fussed and befuddled not to come straight at him. But the first thing I asked was about as dumb as it could be. "Squirrels still chasing you?"

Whatever he was or wasn't expecting from me, that sure as hell wasn't it. He practically laughed, or maybe it was more like he grunted in a laugh sort of way, and he said, "Not so much these days." Close to, he looked exactly like he looked on the TV—exactly, right down to the one curl off to the left on his forehead, and the inlaid belt buckle, and that steepling thing he did with his fingers. Really was like talking to the screen.

"Susie's looking fine, don't you think?" I asked him. "I mean, for having been dead and all."

Oh, that reached him. That got his attention. He looked at me then, all right, and he answered, real slow and cold and careful, "I don't know what you're talking about. What *are* you talking about?"

"Come on, Esau," I said. "Tomorrow I might wake up remembering mostly whatever you want me to remember, the way you do people, but right now, tonight, I'm afraid you're just going to have to sit here and talk to me—"

"Or *what*?" Those two words cracked out of him just like a whip does—there's the forward throw, almost gentle, like you're fly-fishing, and then the way you bring it back, that's what makes that sound. He didn't say anything more, but the color had drained right out of his eyes, same way it happened with Donnie Schmidt. Didn't look much like the TV now.

I asked him, "You planning to make me a ghost too? Kill me off in a plane crash a few weeks ago? I ought to tell you, I hate flying, and everybody knows it, so you might want to try something different. Me, I always wanted to get shot by a jealous husband at ninety-five or so, but it's your business, I wouldn't presume." I don't know, something just took me over and I didn't care what I said right then.

He didn't answer. We could hear Susie rattling things in the kitchen, and Willa singing softly to her kids upstairs. Got a pretty voice, Willa does. Wanted to do something with it, but what with school, and then there was Jerry, and then there was the trouble starting with Ma . . . well, nothing ever came of it somehow. But I could see Esau listening, and just for a minute or so he looked like somebody who really might have had a sister, and maybe a brother too, and was just visiting with them for the evening, like always. I took the moment to say, "Papa was funny, wasn't he, Esau? Getting us backwards like that, with the naming?"

He stared at me. I shrugged a little bit. I said, "Well, you think about it some. Here's Jacob, which I'm named for, cheating Esau out of his inheritance, tricks him into swapping everything due him for a mess of chicken soup or some such. But with us . . . with us, it kind of worked out t'other way round, wouldn't you say? I mean, when you think about it."

"I don't know what you're talking about." He said it in the TV voice, but his eyes still weren't his TV eyes, reassuring everyone that the world hadn't ended just yet. "Papa was as crazy as Ma, only different, and our names don't signify a thing except he was likely drunk at the time." He slammed his hand on the table, setting all the dishes Susie hadn't cleared off yet to rattling. Esau lowered his voice some. "I never stole anything from you, Jake Robbins. I wouldn't have lowered myself to it, any more than I'd have lowered myself to take along a lump of sand-covered catshit from this litterbox of a town, the day I finally got out of here. The one thing I ever took away was me, do you understand that, brother? Nothing more. Not one damn thing more."

His face was so cramped up with anger and plain contempt that I couldn't help putting a finger out toward him, like I was aiming to smooth away a bunch of rumples. "You want to watch out," I said. "Crack your makeup." Esau came to his feet then, and I really thought he was bound to clock me a good one. I said, "Sit down. There's ladies in the house."

He went on glaring in my face, but by and by he kind of stood down—didn't quite sit, you understand, but more leaned on the table, staring at me. He'd cracked his makeup, all right, and I don't mean the stuff they'd put on his skin for the filming. You wouldn't want that face telling you any kind of news right then.

"I bet Papa knew," I said. "Ma just had like a glimmer of the truth, but Papa . . . likely it's how come he drank so much, and read the Bible so crazy. It's his side of the family, after all."

Esau said it again. "I don't know what you're talking about," but there wasn't much what you might call conviction in the words. It's an odd thing, but he was always a real bad liar—embarrassing bad. I'd guess it's because he's never had to lie in his life: he could always make the lie be true, if he cared to. Handy.

I said, "I'm talking about genetics. Now there's a word I hadn't had much use for until recently—knew what it meant, more or less, and let it go at that. But there's a deal *to* genetics when you look close, you know?" No answer; nothing but that bad-guy stare, with something under it that maybe might be fear, and maybe not. I kept going. "Papa and his Bible. There's a lot in the Bible makes a lot more sense that way, genetics. What if . . . let's say all those miracles didn't have a thing to do with God, nor Moses, nor Jesus, nor Adam's left ball, whatever. What if it was all people like you? Two, three, four, five thousand years of people like you? The Bible zigs and zags and contradicts itself, tells the same story forty ways from Sunday, and don't connect up to nothing half the time, even to a preacher. But now you back off and suppose for one moment that the Bible's actually trying to record a world that keeps shifting this way and that, because people keep messing with it. What would you say about that, Esau?"

Nothing. Not a word, not a flicker of an eyelid, nothing for the longest time—and then, of all things, my brother began to smile. "Declare to goodness," he said, and it wasn't the smooth TV voice at all, but more like the way his mouth was born, as we say around here. "Even a blind hog finds an acorn once in a while. Continue, please. You have all my attention."

"No, I don't yet," I said back to him, "but I will. Because with genetics, it's a family thing. Somebody in a family has a gift, a talent, there's likely to be somebody else who has it too. Oh, maybe not the same size or shape of a gift, but close enough. Close enough."

I surely had his attention now, let me tell you. His hands were opening and closing like leaves starting to stir when a storm's coming. "Willa doesn't have that thing you have," I said, "none of it, not at all. She's the lucky one. But *I* do. Wouldn't have guessed it before, not even seeing what you'd done, but now I know better. That same power to mess with things, only I guess I never needed to. Not like you."

Esau started to say something, but then he didn't. I said, "I turned out pretty lucky myself. I had Middy Jo—for a while, anyway. I got a job suited me down to the ground. Didn't have nearly so many people to get even with as you had, and the ones I did I have I mostly forgot over time. I was always forgetful that way. Forget my head, it wasn't screwed on." Papa always used to say that about me, the same way he used to say Willa'd make some woman a great husband, because she could get the car started when he couldn't. Never yet heard old Jerry Flores complain.

"What you did to Donnie Schmidt," I said. "What you did to Susie. What I know you did to a few other folks, even though you made sure the rest of everybody didn't remember. It all scared me so bad, I would never gone anywhere *near* power like that, if I'd known I had it."

Esau's voice was sort of thickish now, like he was trying not to cry, which surely wasn't the case. He said, "You can't do what I do."

"You know better than that, Esau. Same way I know you've never bent reality towards even one good thing. I watch you on the TV, every night, just about, and everything you report on—it's death, it's all death, nothing but death, one way or another. A million baby girls left out on the street in China, a raft full of people capsizes off Haiti, some kid wipes out a whole schoolyard in Iowa, there's more people starving in Africa, getting massacred, there's suicide bombers and serial killers all over the place—it's you, it's your half of the genetics. It's what you are, Esau, and I'm sorry for you."

"Don't be." It was only a whisper, but it came at me like a little sideways swipe from one of those old-time straight razors, the kind Papa had. Esau said, "You're the good one." It wasn't a question. "Well, who'd have thought it? My loud-mouthed, clumsy, stupid big brother turns out to be the superhero in the closet, the champion with a secret identity. Amazing. Just shows you something or other. Truly amazing."

"No," I said. "No, I don't care about that. I just wanted you to know I know. About the genetics and so forth." And then I said it—because he's right, I am stupid. I said, "You're trying to be the Angel of Death, Esau, and I'm just so sorry for you, that's all."

He'd been looking toward the kitchen, like he expected something—or maybe didn't expect it—but now he turned around on me, and I'm not ever about to forget what I saw then. It was like we were kids again, and he was screaming at me, "I *would* be a nice God! I *would*!" Except now the scream was all in his eyes: they were stretched wide as wide, like howling jaws, and the whites had gone too white, so they made the pupils look, not black, but a kind of musty, crumbly gray, like his eyes were rotting, nothing left in there but gray anger, gray pain, gray brick-lined schoolyards, where my brother Esau learned what he was. I'd been halfway joking when I'd said that about the Angel of Death. Not any more.

"Sorry for me, Jake?" It wasn't the razor-whisper, but it wasn't any voice you'd have recognized, either. Esau said, "Sorry for me? I'm on television, asshole. I'm a *star*. Have you the slightest notion of what that means? It means millions—*millions*—of people inviting me into their homes, listening to me, believing in me, *trusting* me. Hell, I'm a family member—a wise old uncle, a mysteriously well-traveled cousin, dropping by to tell them tales of the monsters and fools who run their lives, of the innocents who died horribly today, the people murdered to please somebody's god, the soldiers being sent to die in some place they never heard of, the catastrophes waiting to happen tomorrow, unless somebody does something right away. Which they won't, but that isn't my work. I can't claim credit there."

He smiled at me then, and it was a real smile, young and joyous as you like. He said, "Don't you understand? They *love* death, all those people, they love what I do—they *need* it, no matter how awful they say it is. It's built into the whole species, from the beginning, and you know it as well as I do. You may be the Good Angel, but I'm the one they hang out with in the kitchen and the living room, I'm the one they have their coffee with, or a beer, while I smile and lay on some more horror for them. Meaning no offense, but who wants what *you're* selling?"

"Those people who watch you don't know what they're buying," I said back. "Your stories aren't just stories, you aren't just reporting. You're making real things happen in the real world. I see you on the TV and I can feel all those things you talk about, and explain about, and tell folks to be afraid of, I can feel them coming true, every night. It's like Ma said, your stories kill people." He didn't turn a hair, or look away, and I didn't expect him to. I said, "And I keep wondering, how many like us might be doing the same right now, all over everywhere. Messing with people, messing with the world so nothing makes no sense, one day to the next, so most everybody gets run over in the end, like Donnie Schmidt. You suppose that's all we can do? That's all it's for, this gift we've got? This heritage?"

Esau shrugged. "No idea. It suits me." He gave me that smile again, made him look like a happier little kid than he ever was. "But why should it concern you, Jake? Are you planning to devote the rest of your life to writing letters to my sponsors, telling them I'm the source of all the pain and misery in the world? I'll be very interested in watching your efforts. Fascinated, you could say."

"No," I told him. "I've got a store to run, and I meet Earl Howser and Buddy Andreason for breakfast at Buttercup on Tuesdays, and it's not my place to chase around after you, fixing stuff. What I know's what I know, and it don't include putting the world back the way it ought to be. It's too late for that. Way too late for heroes, champions, miracles. Don't matter what our heritage was maybe meant for—your side got hold of it first, and you won long ago. No undoing that, Esau, I ain't fool enough to think otherwise. I'm still sorry for you, but I know your side's won, this side the grave."

He wasn't listening to me, not really. Just about all his attention was focusing on the kitchen right then, because Susie'd begun whistling while she was clattering pots in the sink. She could always whistle like a man, Susie could. Esau took a step toward the sound.

"I wouldn't," I advised him. "Best leave her be for a bit. What with one thing another, she's not real partial to you just now. You know how it is."

He stopped where he was, but he didn't answer. Halfway crouched, halfway plain puzzled—I've seen dogs look like that, when they couldn't figure what to do about that big new dog on the block. He said, real low, "I didn't bring her back."

"No," I said. "You couldn't have."

He didn't hear that right off; then he did, and he was just starting to turn when Susie came out of the kitchen, drying her hands on a dishtowel and asking, "Jake, would you like me to wash that old black roasting pan while I'm at it?" Then she saw Esau standing there, and she stood real still, and he did too. Lord, if I closed my eyes, I'd see them like that right now.

I stood up from the table, so that made three of us on our feet, saying nothing. Esau was breathing hard, and I couldn't hardly tell if Susie was breathing at all. That made me anxious—you know, considering—so I said, "Esau was just leaving. Wanted to say goodbye."

Neither of them paid the least bit of attention to me. Susie finally managed to say, "You're looking well, Esau. That's a really nice tie."

Esau's voice sounded like a cold wind in an empty place. He said, "You're rotting in the ground. You're bones."

"No." Susie's own voice was shaky, but stronger than his, some way. "No, Esau, I'm not. I refuse."

She sort of peeked past him at me as she said that, and Esau caught it. He turned.

"Susie stays," I said. I was madder than I ever remembered being, and I was wound up, ready to go at whoever, let's do it, just pick your weapons. And I was heavily spooked, too, because pretty much the only mixups I've been in my whole life, they were always about hauling some guy off my baby brother one more time. Heritage or not, I'm no fighter, never wanted to be one. It's just I always liked Susie.

As for the way Esau stared at me, it did clear up a few things, and that's about all I'm going to tell you. I looked back into those TV eyes, and I saw what lived in there, and I thought, well, anyway, I've still got a sister. If you can get through the rest of your life without ever having that feeling, I'd recommend it.

Esau said, "She goes back where she belongs. Now."

"She didn't belong there in the first place," I said to him. "Leave her be, Esau. She's got no business being dead."

"You don't know what you're doing," he said. His lips were twitching like they didn't belong to his face. "Stay out of it, Jake."

"Not a chance," I said. "I can't fix up all the things you do, what you've already done. Might be Superman, Spider-Man, Batman could, but it's not in me, I'm no hero. I'm just a stubborn man who runs a hardware store. But I always liked Susie. Nice girl. Terrific whistler. Susie's not going back nowhere."

Even a little bit younger, I'm sure I'd have been showing off for her, backed away against the wall as she was, looking like a lady tied up for the dragon. But I wasn't showing off for anybody right then, being almost as scared as I was angry. Esau sighed—very dramatic, very heavy. He said, "I did warn you. Nobody can say I didn't warn you. You're my brother, after all."

I started to answer him, but I can't remember what I meant to say, because that was when Esau hit me. Not with his fists, but with such a blast of—I still don't know what to call it . . . hatred? Contempt? Plain meanness?—that it knocked me off my feet and right over my chair. For a moment I swear I thought I'd caught on fire. My head wouldn't work; *nothing* worked; it was like every single string in my body had been cut—I couldn't even flop around on the floor. I didn't know who I was. I didn't know *what* I was.

Susie screamed, and Esau hit me again. That time I did flop around, after I slid across the floor and fetched up against the wall. To this day I can't honestly explain how it felt—been trying to describe it to myself for years. Best I can do is that it wasn't like an electric shock, and it wasn't really like being burned, or beaten up either, although I was all over bruises next day. It was more . . . it was more like he was *unmaking* me, like he was starting to take me apart, atom by atom, molecule by molecule, so I wouldn't exist anymore—I wouldn't ever *have* existed, he'd never have *had* a brother. I could feel it happening, and I tell you, I'll never be scared of anything again.

But I didn't die. I mean, I didn't get *lost,* the way he wanted me to. Susie ran to me, but I managed to wave her off, because I didn't want her getting caught between us. Esau went on hammering me with whatever it was he had that let him smash planes out of the sky, trains off the tracks, set mudslides boiling down on little mud villages. But it wasn't hurting me any more, not like it had been. I was still me. He hadn't been able to make me not *be,* you understand?

I got my back against the wall and pushed myself up till I was on my feet. Took more time than you might think—I work, I don't work *out*—and anyway Esau just kept at me, like point-blank, coming close up to me now and knocking me this way and that, one belt of crazy rage after another. I couldn't do much about it yet, but he couldn't quite put me down again, either.

I did tell him to stop it. Same way he warned me, I told him to stop. But he wouldn't.

So I stopped him. Or the thing stopped him, the thing that had been rousing up in me all this time, while he was whupping the daylights out of me. It burst out of me like from a flamethrower, searing me—mouth, throat, chest, guts—way worse than anything Esau'd done to me, and slamming me back against the wall harder than he had. I couldn't see, and I couldn't hear a thing, and right that moment, that's when I did think I was going to die. Looked forward to it, too, just then.

When my eyes cleared some—ears took a lot longer—I saw Esau lying on the floor. He wasn't moving.

If it was just me, the way I was feeling, I'd likely have left him lying there till the neighbors started complaining. But . . . see, I already told you how Willa and me, we were always supposed to watch over our baby brother—protect him in those schoolyard fights, make sure he did his homework, all that—and I guess old habits die hard. I said, "Esau? Esau?" and when he didn't answer, I tried to get to him, but he seemed an awful long way off. Susie helped me. She'd been crying, but she stopped, and she got me to Esau.

He was trying to sit up by the time we reached him, and we helped him onto his feet in a while. He looked like pounded shit, excuse my French, what with his nice shirt in rags, and that tie Susie liked gone, and an arm of his suit jacket dangling by a few threads. I'd seen him wear that same jacket on the TV, I don't know how many times. His face was gray. I don't mean pale, or white—it was gray like old cement, old grout, and it was like the gray went all the way through. Susie and me, we might be the only people in the world ever saw him like that.

He actually tried to smile. He said, "I should have made you check your guns at the door. Where on earth did you pick up *that* trick?"

"Just got pissed off," I said. "And I'll do worse if you're not out of here in two minutes by Papa's watch. Susie stays."

Esau shrugged, or he tried to. "Got to catch a plane tomorrow, anyway. Back to the old grindstone." He looked at Susie. She kind of edged behind my shoulder some, and Esau's smile widened. He said, "Don't worry, my dear. You really should have stayed dead, you know, but it's not your fault." He turned back toward me. "Your doing, of course."

"Watching those folks pile in," I told him. My head was still ringing. "That whole crew, all those people come to paint up your homecoming for the world to see. Couldn't help thinking there ought to be someone like Susie there too. Like Donnie Schmidt. I swear, I was just thinking on it."

"Glad it wasn't Donnie who showed up," Esau murmured. He tugged on the loose arm of his ruined jacket; it came free, and he dropped it on the floor. "Sneaky old Brother Jake," he said. "You've likely got more of the family inheritance than I do. Just like in Papa's Bible, after all."

I was still feeling hollowed-out, burned-out, not by anything he'd done, but by whatever it was I'd had to do. I said, "I can't let you go on, Esau."

He smiled. "You can't kill me, Jake. We both know you better than that."

"You might not know me well enough," I said. "Gone as long as you've been. There's worse things than killing you. Maybe way worse."

And he saw. He looked into my eyes, for a change, and he saw what I had it in mind to do. "You wouldn't dare," he said in a whisper. "You wouldn't dare."

"I wouldn't dare *not* do it," I answered him straight. "You're a time bomb, Esau, you're a loaded gun. Didn't matter before, when I could pretend I didn't really know—but now, if I don't take the bullets out of you, I'm as bad you are. Can't see that I've got a choice."

He's Esau. He didn't beg, and he didn't bother with threatening. All he said was, "It won't be easy for you. It's my life you're talking about. I'll fight you for it."

"I know you will," I said. "And you'll have a better chance than Donnie Schmidt."

"Or me," Susie said, standing right next to me. "Goodbye, Esau."

He gave her a different kind of smile than he'd given me—practically kind, practically real. It looked nice on him. He said, "Goodbye, Susie. See you on the six o'clock." And he was away, that fast, vanished into the dark. I looked after him for some while, then said what I had to say, and closed the door.

Susie had heard me, of course. "He always meant to be a good God," I told her. "A good God, a good angel, whatever. Don't know how he got to be . . . what he was."

Susie picked up Esau's torn-off sleeve and turned it around and around in her hands, not looking at it, not looking at anything much. She said finally, "I read once, in India they've got gods that are also demons. Depends on their mood, I guess, or the time of year. Or maybe just their lunch."

"Well, I wasn't planning to go into the god business myself," I told her. "Really wasn't looking to set up in competition with any Angel of Death. Piss-poor job, you ask me. No benefits, no paid vacations. And damn sure no union."

Susie shook her head and laughed a little bit, but after that she got quiet again, and sort of broody. By and by, she said, "There's a union. There's always been others like you, Jake. The ones who mend the world."

"The world's no torn shirt," I said. My insides felt like they'd been scooped out, dragged over gravel, and put back. "I got a store to run." Susie looked at me, didn't say anything. I said, "There's others like him out there, I don't know how many. Can't stop them all." I put my hand on Susie's shoulder to steady myself.

Willa came in behind us in her bathrobe, looked around at the dining room, and demanded, "What was all that tarryhooting around in here after we went to bed? Did you and Esau get to wrestling or something?"

"Kind of," I mumbled. "Boys with beers. I'll clean up, I promise."

Willa shrugged. "Your house. I was just afraid you'd wake up the kids. Esau already gone?" I nodded, and she peered at me in that older-sister way of hers. "You sure nothing happened between you two?" She wasn't expecting an answer, so I didn't have to fix one up. She studied Susie a lot more closely and carefully than she'd done during dinner, and there wasn't any question what she was thinking. But what Willa thinks and what Willa says never did spend a lot of time together. This time she just said, "Good of you to take the time with Ben, Susie. I was just frazzled out, dealing with those crazy TV people and Carol-Ann."

"It's been some time since I've been around children," Susie said. "I like yours."

Willa said, "Stay the night, why don't you? It's late, and there's a spare bedroom downstairs." As she left, she said over her shoulder, "And I make great Mexican eggs. My husband loves them, and *he's* Mexican."

Susie looked at me. I said, "If you aren't worried about compromising your reputation, that is, staying over in the house of a widower man. There's still folks in this town would raise their eyebrows."

Susie laughed full-out then, for the first time. That was nice. She said, "I'm older than I look."

Well.

What else? The network never ran that show, of course, what with one thing another. Didn't get the chance. Seems like it all started turning bad for Esau, just about then, slow but steady. That stock-option business. Those people who sued the whole network about his fouled-up dirty-bomb story. The sexual harassment charges. *Those* got settled out of court, like a bunch of other stuff, but there was a mountain landing on his head and he couldn't duck it all. Still, he hung on like a bullrider. He's almost as stubborn as I am. Almost.

Tell the truth, he might have ridden that bull all the way home, if he'd still been selling the same kind of stories. But the things that had made him who he was, the big disasters and the common-man nightmares, somehow there just weren't as many of them as there had been. The news got smaller, and so did he.

Did I feel bad? Interesting, you asking me that. Yeah, I did feel bad for him, I couldn't help it. I still wonder how he felt when he woke up—the morning *after* the night he told the country all about those Kansas cult-murders, with the ritual mutilating and all—only it turned out they hadn't ever happened, even though he'd made them up just as pretty and scary as all the other lies he'd always made real. How's the Angel of Death supposed to do his job with clipped wings?

I got a call in the store that day. Picked up on the second ring, but when I said hello there wasn't anybody on the line.

The guns were the last straw. The automatics and the Uzis and whatever in his office, in the dressing-room, those were bad enough, the tabloids had a field day with those. But trying to go through Los Angeles airport security with a pistol butt just sticking out of his coat pocket . . . lord, that did him in. Network hustled him out of there so fast, his desk was smoking behind him. That wasn't me, by the way, all those guns. That was just the state he was in by then. Poor Esau. All those years jumping off things, he still never did learn how to land.

Or maybe I should have chosen my words better as he walked away that night. Probably would have, if I'd had more time. All I knew then was I had to speak up before he did. Jam my foot in the door.

"My brother thinks he's an angel," I'd said. "He thinks he can change anything in the world just by saying so. But that's crazy. He can't do that."

Didn't know what else to say. Might have had a little too much what we used to call *English* on it, but I done what I could.

Lord, don't I wish I had a movie of you for the last half-hour or so, the way you've been looking at me. You'd get to keep that, anyway, even though there won't be nothing on your tape tomorrow, nor nothing in your memory. Couple of hours, you couldn't even find this house again, same as your editor won't ever remember giving out this assignment. Because nobody talks about my brother anymore. Nobody's talked about him in years. And it's a sad thing, some ways, because being Esau Robbins every night, everywhere, six o'clock . . . that *mattered* to him. Being the Angel of Death, that *mattered* to him. They were the only things that ever filled him, you understand me? That's all he ever could do in his life, my poor damn brother—get even with us, with people, for being alive. And I took all that away. Stole his birthright and shut down the life he built with it. That don't balance the scales, nor make up for all he did, but it's going to have to do.

Esau Robbins no longer exists. He's not dead. He's just . . . gone. Maybe someday I'll go and look for him, like an older brother should, but right now gone is how it stays. Price of the pottage.

Thanks for the Blanton's, young man. Puts a smile on my face, and even though it isn't her drink Susie will certainly applaud your thoughtfulness.

You'll likely be finding a bonus in your next paycheck. Nobody in accounting will be able to explain why—and you sure as hell won't, either—but just you roll with it.

KING PELLES THE SURE

My old friend, the novelist Darryl Brock, has described this as the best anti-war story he has ever read. My vote would probably go to William March's *Company K,* which I read at seventeen, and have never since gotten out of my head, though I wish I could.

Whatever the comparative ranking, I'm proud of this one.

ONCE THERE WAS A KING who dreamed of war. His name was Pelles.

He was a gentle and kindly monarch, who ruled over a small but wealthy and completely tranquil kingdom, beloved alike by noble and peasant, despite the fact that he had no queen, and so no heir except a brother to ensure an orderly succession. Even so, he was the envy of mightier kings, whose days were so full of putting down uprisings, fighting off one another's invasions, and wiping out rebellious villages that they never knew a single moment of comfort or security. King Pelles—and his people, and his land—knew nothing else.

But the king dreamed of war.

"Nobody is ever remembered for living out a dull, placid, uneventful life," he would say to his Grand Vizier, whom he daily compelled to play at toy soldiers with him on the parlor floor. "Peace is all very well—a fine thing, certainly—but do you ever hear ballads about King Herman the Peaceful? Do you ever listen to bards chanting the deeds of King Leslie the Calm, or read great national epics about King James the Docile, King William the Diplomatic? You do not!"

"There was Ethelred the Unready," suggested the Grand Vizier, whose back hurt from crouching over the carpet battlefield every afternoon. "Meaning unready for conflict or crusade, unwilling to slaughter needlessly. And King Charles the Good—"

"But it is Charles the Hammer who lives in legend," King Pelles retorted. "William the Conqueror—Erik Bloodaxe—Alfonso the Avenger—Selim the Valiant—Ivan the Terrible. Our own schoolchildren know *those* names . . . and why not," he added bitterly, "since we don't have any heroes of our own. How can we, when nobody ever even raids us, or bothers to challenge us over land or resources, or attempts to annex us, to swallow our little realm whole, as has happened to so many such lands in our time? Sometimes I feel as though I should send out a dozen heralds to proclaim our need of an enemy. I *do,* Vizier."

"No, sire," said the Grand Vizier earnestly. "No, truly, you don't want to do anything like that. I promise you, you don't." He straightened up, rubbing his back and smoothing out his robe of office. He said, "Sire, Majesty, if I may humbly suggest it, you would do well—as would every soul dwelling on this soil that we call home—to appreciate what you see as our insignificance. There is an old saying that there is no country as unhappy as one that needs heroes. Trust me when I say in my turn that our land's happiness is your greatest victory in this life, and that you will never know another to equal it. Nor should you try, for that would show you both greedy and ungrateful, and offend the gods. I urge you to leave well enough alone."

Having spoken so, the Grand Vizier braced himself for an angry response, or at least a petulant one, being a man in late middle age who had served other kings. He was both astonished and alarmed to realize that King Pelles had hardly heard him, so caught up was he in romantic visions of battle. "It would have to be in self-defense, of course," the king was saying dreamily. "We have no interest in others' treasure or territory—we're not that sort of nation. If someone would only try to invade us by crafty wiles, such as filling a wooden horse with armed soldiers and leaving it invitingly outside the gates of our capital city. Then we could set it afire and roast them all—"

He caught sight of the horrified expression on the Grand Vizier's face, and added hurriedly, "Not that we ever *would,* of course, certainly not, I was just speculating."

"Of course, sire," murmured the Grand Vizier. But his breath was turning increasingly short and painful, as King Pelles went on.

"Or if they should come by sea, slipping into our port on a foggy night, we would be ready with a corps of young men trained to swim out with braces and augurs and sink their ships. And if they struck by air, perhaps dropping silently from the sky in dark balloons, our archers could shoot all of them down with fire-arrows. Or if we could induce them to tunnel under the castle walls—oh, *that* would be good, if they tunneled—then we could . . ."

The Grand Vizier coughed, as delicately as he could manage it, given the panicky constriction of his throat. He said, "Your Highness, meaning absolutely no disrespect, you have never seen war—"

"Exactly, exactly!" King Pelles broke in. "How can one know the true meaning of peace, who has no experience of its undoubtedly horrid counterpart? Can you answer me that, Vizier?"

"Majesty, I have known that experience," the Grand Vizier replied quietly. "It was far from here, in a land I traveled to as a boy. I shared it with many brave and dear and young friends, who are all dead now—as I should have been, but for the courtesy of the gods, and the enemy's poor aim. You have missed nothing, my lord."

He seemed to have grown older as he spoke, and the king—who may have been foolish, but who was not a fool—saw, and answered him equally gently. "I understand what you are telling me, good Vizier. But this would be only a little war, truly—no more enduring or consuming than one of our delightful carpet clashes. A *manageable* war—a demonstration, one might say, just to let our rivals see that our people are not to be trifled with. In case they were thinking about trifling. Do you see the difference, Vizier? Between this war and yours?"

With another king, the Grand Vizier would have considered long and carefully before risking the truth. With King Pelles, he had no

such fears, but he also knew his man well enough to recognize when hearing the truth would make no smallest difference to what the king decided to do. So he said only, "Well, well, be sure to employ great precision in choosing your foe—"

"*Our* foe," King Pelles corrected him. "Our *nation's* foe."

"*Our* foe," the Grand Vizier agreed. "We must, whatever else we do, select the weakest enemy available—"

"But that would be dishonorable!" the king protested. "Ignoble! Unsporting!" He was decidedly upset.

The Grand Vizier was firm in this. "We are hardly a nation at all; we are more like a shire or a county with an army. A distinctly small army. A more powerful adversary would destroy us—that is simply a fact, my king. You cannot *manage* a war without attention to facts."

He was hoping that his sardonic emphasis on the notion of managing such a capricious thing as war might deter King Pelles from the whole fancy, but it did not. After a silence, the king finally sighed and said, "Well. If that is what a war is, so be it. Consider our choices, Vizier, and make your recommendation." He added then, rather quickly, "But do arrange for a *gracious* war, if you possibly can. Something . . . something a little *tidy*. With songs in it, you know."

The Grand Vizier said, "I will do what I can."

As it turned out, he did tragically better than he meant. Perhaps because King Pelles had never wanted to know it, he truly had no notion of how deeply his land was hated for its prosperity on the one hand and coveted on the other. The Grand Vizier had hoped to engineer a very brief war for the king, quickly over, with minimum damage, disruption, or inconvenience to everyone involved, and easily succeeded in tempting their little country's nearest neighbor to invade (in the traditional style, as it happens, by marching across borders). But his plan went completely out of control in a matter of hours. Wise enough to lure a weaker country into a foolish attack, he was as innocent, in his own way, as his king, never having considered that other lands might be utterly delighted to join with the lone aggressor he had bargained for. An alliance of territories which normally despised each other formed swiftly, and King Pelles's land came under siege from all sides.

Actually, it was no war at all, but a massacre, a butchery. There was a good deal of death, which was something else the king had never seen. He was still shaking and crying from the horror of it, and the pity, and his terrible shame, when the Grand Vizier disguised them both as peasant women and set them scurrying out the back way as the flaming castle came down, seeming to melt and dissolve like so much pink candy floss. King Pelles looked back and wept anew for his home, and for his country; and the Grand Vizier remembered the words of Boabdil's mother when the Moorish king looked back in tears from the mountain pass at lost Spain behind him. "*Weep not like a woman for the kingdom you could not defend like a man.*" But then he thought that defending things like men was what had gotten them into this catastrophe in the first place, and decided to say nothing.

The king and his Grand Vizier scrambled day on wretched day across the trampled, smoking land, handicapped somewhat by their long skirts and heavy muddy boots, but running like a pair of aging thieves all the same. No one stopped them, or even looked at them closely, although there were mighty rewards posted everywhere for their heads, and they really looked very little like peasant women, even on their best days. But the country was in such havoc, with so many others—displaced, homeless, penniless, mad with terror and loss—fleeing in every direction, that no one had the time or the inclination to concern themselves with the identities of their poor companions on the road. The soldiers of the alliance were too busy looting and burning, and those whose homes were being looted and burned were too busy not being in them. King Pelles and the Grand Vizier were never once recognized.

One evening, dazed as a child abruptly awakened from a happy dream, the king finally asked where they were bound.

"I have relatives in the south country beyond those hills you see," the Grand Vizier told him. "A cousin and her husband—they have a farm. It has been a long time since I last saw them, and I cannot entirely remember where they live. But they will take us in, I am sure of it."

King Pelles sighed like the great Moor. "Better your family than mine. *My* cousins—my own brother—would demand a bribe, and then turn us over to the conquerors anyway. They are bad people, the lot of them." He huddled deeper into his ragged blanket, shrugging himself closer to their tiny fire. "But I am the worst by far," he added, "the worst, there is no comparison. I deserve whatever becomes of me."

"You did not know, sire," the Grand Vizier offered in attempted solace. "That is the worst that can be said of you, that you did not know."

"But you did, you *did*, and you tried to warn me, and I refused to listen to you. And you obeyed my orders, and now you share my fate, and my people's innocent lives lie in ruins, and it is my doing, and there is no atoning for it." The king rocked back and forth, then stretched on the ground in his blanket, as though he were trying to bury himself where he lay, whimpering again and again, "No atoning, no atoning." He hurt himself doing this, for the ground was shingly and rock-strewn. The Grand Vizier knew he would see the bruises in the morning.

"You were a good king," the Vizier said. "You meant well."

"*No!*" The word came out as a scream of agony. "I *never* meant well! I meant glory for myself—nothing less or more than that. And I knew it, I *knew* it, I knew it at the time, and still I had to go ahead, had to play out my toy battle with soft, breakable human bodies, breakable human souls. *No atoning . . .*"

There was nothing for the Grand Vizier then, but to say, as to a child, "Go to sleep, Your Majesty. What's done is done, and one of us is as guilty as the other. And even so, we must sleep."

But he himself slept poorly—perhaps even worse than King Pelles—in the barns and the empty cattle byres and the caves; and the king's piteous murmurings as he dreamed were hardly of any help. There was always the smell of smoke, from one direction or another; at times there would come noises in the night, which might as easily have been restless cows as pursuing spies or soldiers, but there was never any way for the Vizier to make certain of either. All he allowed himself to think about was the need to guide the king safely to shelter from one night to the next—further than that, his imagining dared not go, if he meant to sleep at all. *And even if we find my cousin—what was her husband's name again?—even if we do find their farm, what then?*

By great good fortune, they did find the Grand Vizier's cousin, whose name was Nerissa—her husband's name was Antonio—and were welcomed as though they had last visited only days ago, or a week at most. The little farm was a crowded place, since Nerissa and Antonio, with no children of their own, had gladly taken in their widowed friend Clara and her four, who ranged in age from six to seventeen years. Nevertheless, they received King Pelles and the Grand Vizier unhesitatingly: as Antonio said, "No farm was ever the worse for more hands in the fields, nor more faces around the dinner table. And whoever noticed the smudged and sunburned face of a farmworker who wasn't one himself? Have no fear—you are safe with us. In these times, there is no safety but family."

So it was that he who had been the king of all the land and he who had been its most powerful dignitary became nothing more than hands in the fields, and were grateful. Neither was young, but they worked hard and long all the same, and proudly kept even with Antonio and the others when it came time to bring the harvest home. And every evening, King Pelles told stories about wise animals and clever magicians to Clara's children, and later the Grand Vizier conducted an informal history lesson for the older ones, in which their mother often joined. Still an attractive woman, she had clear brown skin and dark, amused eyes which were increasingly attentive, as time passed, to whatever the Vizier said or did. Antonio and Nerissa saw this, and were glad of it, as was the king. "Your cousin has wasted his life on my foolishness," he said to Nerissa. "I am so happy that she will give it back to him."

When the Grand Vizier could do it without feeling intrusive, he listened—with the back of his head, perhaps, or the back of his mind—to the king's fairytales. They were not like any he had ever heard, and they fascinated and alarmed him at the same time. Few had what he would have considered happy endings, especially as a child—the gallant prince frequently failed to arrive in time to rescue the princess from the dragon, more often than not the poison was not counteracted, the talking cat could not always preserve his master from his own stupidity. Endings changed, as well, with each telling, and characters wandered from one story into a different one, often changing their natures as they did so. On occasion grief flowed into overwhelming joy, though that outcome was never something you might want to bet on. The Grand Vizier constantly expected the children to become frightened or upset, but they listened in obvious absorption, the younger ones crowding each other on the king's lap, and all four nodding silently from time to time, as children do to express trust in the tale.

Maybe it is the way he tells them, the Grand Vizier thought more than once, for King Pelles always had a special voice at those times, different than the way he spoke in the fields or at evening table. It was a low voice, with a calmness in it that—as the Vizier knew—had grown directly from suffering and remorse, and seemed to draw the children's confidence whether or not the words were understood.

Yet content as King Pelles was in his new life, fond of Clara's children as he was, warmed far deeper than his bones by being a true part of a family for the first time . . . even so, he still wept in his sleep, whispering brokenly, "*No atoning* . . ." The Grand Vizier heard him every night.

Winter was always hard in that kingdom, even in the south country, but the Grand Vizier was profoundly glad of it. The snow and mud closed the roads, for one thing: there would be no further pursuit of the king for a time, and who knew what might happen, or have happened, by spring? What news reached the farm suggested that a group of the king's former advisors had banded together to install a ruler of their choosing, and thus restore at least their notion of order to the kingdom, but the Vizier could not discover his name, nor learn any further details of the story. But he allowed himself to be somewhat hopeful, to imagine that perhaps—just *perhaps*—the hunt might have dwindled away, and that the king's existence might have become completely unimportant to the new regime. For the first time in his long career of service, the Grand Vizier dreamed a small dream for himself.

But with the thawing of the roads, with the tinkling dissolution of the icicles that had fringed the farmhouse's gables for many months, with the first tentative sounds of the frogs who had slept in the deep beds of the frozen streams all winter . . . the soldiers came marching. With the first storks, they came.

Martine, Clara's younger daughter, was playing by the awakening pond one afternoon, and heard their boots and the rattle of their mail before they had rounded the bend in the road. She, like all the others, had been told over and over that if she ever saw even one soldier she must run straight to the house and warn her mother's special friend, and the other one as well, the storyteller. She never waited to see these, but was up and away at the first sound, and through the front door in a muddy flash, crying, "They're here! They're here!"

Antonio had long since prepared a hiding place for King Pelles and the Grand Vizier in case of just such an emergency. It lay under the floor of his own bedroom, so cunningly made and so close-fit that it was impossible to tell which boards might turn on hinges, or how to make them open, even if you knew. The two men were down there, motionless in the dark, well before the soldiers had reached the farmhouse; until the first fist hammered on the front door, the only sound they heard was the beating of each other's hearts.

The soldiers were polite, as soldiers go. They trampled no chickens, broke nothing in the house, and kept their hands off Antonio's fresh stock of winter ale, last of the season. Filling the kitchen with their size and the noise of their bodies, they treated Nerissa and Clara with truly remarkable courtesy; and their captain offered boiled sweets to the children clustered behind them, even responding with a good-humored chuckle when little Martine kicked his shin. Nor did they ask a single question concerning guests, or visitors, or new-hired laborers. Indeed, they were so amiable and considerate, by contrast with what the family had expected, that it took Nerissa a moment longer than it should have to realize that they had not been sent for the king and the Grand Vizier at all.

They had come for her husband.

"You see, ma'am," the Captain explained, as three of his men laid hold of Antonio, who had bolted too late for the back door, "the war just keeps going *on*. Wars, I mean. It's chaos, madness, really it is, ever since that idiot Pelles started the whole thing. Everyone turning against everyone else—whole regiments changing sides, generals selling out their own troops—mutiny over *there*, rebellion *here*, betrayal *that* way, corruption *this* way . . . and what's a poor soldier to do but follow his orders, no matter who's giving them today? And my orders all winter have been to round up every single warm body, which means every able, breathing male with both legs under him, and ship them straightaway to the front. And so that's what I do."

"The front," Nerissa said numbly. "Which front? Where is the battle?"

The Captain spread his arms in dramatic frustration. "Well, I don't know *which* front, do I? As many of them as there are these days? Somebody else tells me that when we get there. Very sorry to be snatching away your breadwinner, ma'am—'pon my soul, I am—but there it is, you see, and I put it to you, what's a poor soldier to do?" He turned irritably toward the soldiers struggling with Antonio. "*Hold* him, blast you! What's the bloody matter with you?"

In the moment that his gaze was not on her, Nerissa reached for her favorite butchering knife. Behind her, Clara's hand closed silently on a cleaver. Only Martine saw, and drew breath to scream more loudly than she ever had in her short life. But the Captain was never to know how close he was to death in that moment, because just then King Pelles walked alone into the kitchen.

He wore his royal robes, and his crown as well, which the children had never seen in all the time he had lived with them. Nodding pleasantly at the soldiers, he said to the Captain, "Let the man go. You will have a much richer prize to show your general than some poor farmer."

The Captain was dumb with amazement, turning all sorts of colors as he gaped at the king. His men, thoroughly astounded themselves, eased their grip on Antonio, who promptly burst free and headed for the door a second time. Some would have given chase, but King Pelles snapped out again, "Let him go!" and it was a king's order, prisoner or no. The men fell back.

"We weren't looking for you, sir," the Captain said, almost meekly. "We thought you were dead."

"Well, how much better for you that I'm not," the king replied briskly. "There will be a bonus involved, surely, and you certainly should be able to trade me to one side or another—possibly all of them, if you manage it right. I know all about managing," he added, in a somewhat different voice.

A young officer just behind the captain demanded, "Where is the Grand Vizier? He was seen with you on the road."

King Pelles shrugged lightly and sighed. "And that was where he died, on the way here, poor chap. I buried him myself." He turned back to the Captain. "Where are you supposed to take me, if I may ask?"

"To the new king," the Captain muttered in answer. "To King Phoebus."

"To my brother?" It was the king's turn to be astonished. "My brother is king now?"

"As of three days ago, anyway. When I left headquarters, he was." The Captain spread his arms wide again. "What do *I* know, these days?"

Even in his happiest moments on Nerissa and Antonio's farm, the king had never laughed as he laughed now, with a kind of delight no less rich for being ironic. "Well," he said finally. "Well, by all means, let us go to my brother. Let us go to King Phoebus, then—and on the way, perhaps we might talk about managing." He removed his crown, smiling as he handed it to the Captain. "There you are. Can't be king if you don't have a crown, you know."

Nerissa and Clara stood equally as stunned as the men who cautiously laid hands on the unresisting King Pelles; but the two youngest children set up a wail of angry protest when they began leading him away. They clung to his legs and wept, and neither the Captain nor their mother could part them from him. That took the king himself, who finally turned to put his arms around them, calling each by name, and saying, "Remember the stories. My stories will always be with you." He embraced the two women, saying to Clara in a low voice, "Take care of him, as he took care of me." Then he went away with the soldiers, eyes clear and a smile on his face.

If the Captain had looked back, he might well have seen the Grand Vizier, who came wandering into the kitchen a moment later, nursing a large bruise on his cheekbone, and another already forming on his jaw. Clara flew to him, as he said dazedly, "He hit me. I wouldn't let him surrender himself alone, so then he . . . Call them back—I'm his Vizier, he can't go without me. Call them back."

"Hush," Clara said, holding him. "Hush."

In time the long night of wars, rebellions, and retaliations of every sort slowly gave way at least to truces born of simple exhaustion, and reliable news became easier to come by, even for wary hillfolk like themselves. Thus the Grand Vizier was able to discover that the king's brother Phoebus had quite quickly been overthrown, very likely while the soldiers were still on the road with their captive. But further he could not go. He never found out what had become of King Pelles, and after some time he came to realize that he did not really want to.

"As long as we don't know anything certainly," he said to his family, "it is always possible that he might still be alive. Somewhere. I cannot speak for anyone else, but that is the only way I can live with his sacrifice."

"Perhaps sacrifice was the only way he could live," suggested his wife. The Grand Vizier turned to her in some surprise, and Clara smiled at him. "I heard him in the night too," she said.

"*I* hear his stories," young Martine said importantly. "I close my eyes when I get into bed, and he tells me a story."

"Yes," said the Grand Vizier softly. "Yes, he tells me stories too."

The Last and Only; or, Mr. Moscowitz Becomes French

I started writing this in the late 1960s, when my family and I had settled into our first house with real central heating, which was located in farming country just outside Watsonville, California. I sent an early version off to my agent, Elizabeth Otis, in New York, and in so doing initiated a sputtering cycle of rewrites and rejections that went on quietly in the background for a couple of years. By that time I'd stumbled into screenwriting, and for the next decade I largely abandoned prose fiction while in hot pursuit of the first serious money I'd ever seen. "The Last and Only" languished in my battered, dangerous filing cabinet until well past the turn of the new century, when Connor Cochran—once more exploring the dark continent of that cabinet with gun and camera—came across it and asked me to try again from a slightly different angle. What happened next was the oddest collaboration I've ever experienced, in which one of the two writers at the table was a younger, hairier me whom I didn't always recognize and only barely remembered.

It often happens that stories have to wait a very long time for the author to catch up with what they already know. But usually not *this* long.

Once upon a time, there lived in California a Frenchman named George Moscowitz. His name is of no importance—there are old families in France named Wilson and Holmes, and the first president of the Third Republic was named MacMahon—but what was interesting about Mr. Moscowitz was that he had not always been French. Nor was he entirely French at the time we meet him, but he was becoming perceptibly more so every day. His wife, whose name was Miriam, drew his silhouette on a child's blackboard and filled him in from the feet up with tricolor chalk, adding a little more color daily. She was at mid-thigh when we begin our story.

Most of the doctors who examined Mr. Moscowitz agreed that his affliction was due to some sort of bug that he must have picked up in France when he and Mrs. Moscowitz were honeymooning there, fifteen years before. In its dormant stage, the bug had manifested itself only as a kind of pleasant Francophilia: on their return from France Mr. Moscowitz had begun to buy Linguaphone CDs, and to get up at six in the morning to watch a cable television show on beginner's French. He took to collecting French books and magazines, French music and painting and sculpture, French recipes, French folklore, French attitudes, and, inevitably, French people. As a librarian in a large university, he came in contact with a good many French exchange students and visiting professors, and he went far out of his way to make friends with them—Mr. Moscowitz, shy as a badger. The students had a saying among themselves that if you wanted to be French in that town, you had to clear it with Monsieur Moscowitz, who issued licenses and *cartes de séjour*. The joke was not especially unkind, because Mr. Moscowitz often had them to dinner at his home, and in his quiet delight in the very sound of their voices they found themselves curiously less bored with themselves, and with one another. Their companions at dinner were quite likely to be the ignorant Marseillais tailor who got all of Mr. Moscowitz's custom, or the Canuck coach of the soccer team, but there was something so touching in Mr. Moscowitz's assumption that all French-speaking people must be naturally at home together that professors and proletariat generally managed to find each other charming and valuable. And Mr. Moscowitz himself, speaking rarely, but sometimes smiling uncontrollably, like an exhalation of joy—he was a snob in that he preferred the culture and manners of another country to his own, and certainly a fool in that he could find wisdom in every foolishness uttered in French—he was marvelously happy then, and it was impossible for those around him to escape his happiness. Now and then he would address a compliment or a witticism to his wife, who would smile and answer softly, "*Merci,*" or "*La-la,*" for she knew that at such moments he believed without thinking about it that she too spoke French.

Mrs. Moscowitz herself was, as must be obvious, a patient woman of a tolerant humor, who greatly enjoyed her husband's enjoyment of all things French, and who believed, firmly and serenely, that this curious obsession would fade with time, to be replaced by bridge or chess, or—though she prayed not—golf. "At least he's dressing much better these days," she told her sister Dina, who lived in Scottsdale, Arizona. "Thank God you don't have to wear plaid pants to be French."

Then, after fifteen years, whatever it was that he had contracted in France, if that was what he had done, came fully out of hiding; and here stood Mr. Moscowitz in one doctor's office after another, French from his soles to his ankles, to his shins, to his knees, and still heading north for a second spring. (Mrs. Moscowitz's little drawing is, of course, only a convenient metaphor—if anything her husband was becoming French from his bones out.) He was treated with drugs as common as candy and as rare as turtle tears by doctors ranging from Johns Hopkins specialists to a New Guinea shaman; he was examined by herbalists and honey-doctors, and by committees of medical men so reputable as to make illness in their presence seem almost criminal; and he was dragged to a crossroads one howling midnight to meet with a half-naked, foamy-chinned old man who claimed to be the son of Merlin's affair with Nimue, and a colonel in the Marine Reserves besides. This fellow's diagnosis was supernatural possession; his prescribed remedy would cost Mr. Moscowitz a black pig (and the pig its liver), and was impractical, but the idea left Mr. Moscowitz thoughtful for a long time.

In bed that night, he said to his wife, "Perhaps it is possession. It's frightening, yes, but it's exciting too, if you want the truth. I feel something growing inside me, taking shape as it crowds me out, and the closer I get to disappearing, the clearer it becomes. And yet, it is me too, if you understand—I wish I could explain to you how it feels—it is like, 'ow you say . . ."

"Don't say that," Mrs. Moscowitz interrupted with tears in her voice. She had begun to whimper quietly when he spoke of disappearing. "Only TV Frenchmen talk like that."

"*Excuse-moi, ma vieille.* The more it crowds me, the more it makes me feel like *me*. I feel a whole country growing inside me, thousands of years, millions of people, stupid, crazy, shrewd people, and all of them me. I never felt like that before, I never felt that there was anything inside me, even myself. Now I'm pregnant with a whole country, and I'm growing fat with it, and one day—" He began to cry himself then, and the two of them huddled small in their bed, holding hands all night long. He dreamed in French that night, as he had been doing for weeks, but he woke up still speaking it, and he did not regain his English until he had had his first cup of coffee. It took him longer each morning thereafter.

A psychiatrist whom they visited when Mr. Moscowitz's silhouette was French to the waist commented that his theory of possession by himself was a way of sidling up to the truth that Mr. Moscowitz was actually willing his transformation. "The unconscious is ingenious at devising methods of withdrawal," he explained, pulling at his fingertips as though milking a cow, "and national character is certainly no barrier to a mind so determined to get out from under the weight of being an American. It's not as uncommon as you might think, these days."

"*Qu'est-ce qu'il dit?*" whispered Mr. Moscowitz to his wife.

"I have a patient," mused the psychiatrist, "who believes that he is gradually being metamorphosed into a roc, such a giant bird as carried off Sindbad the Sailor to lands unimaginable and riches beyond comprehension. He has asked me to come with him to the very same lands when his change is complete."

"*Qu'est-ce qu'il dit? Qu'est-ce que c'est, roc?*" Mrs. Moscowitz shushed her husband nervously and said, "Yes, yes, but what about George? Do you think you can cure him?"

"I won't be around," said the psychiatrist. There came a stoop of great wings outside the window, and the Moscowitzes fled.

"Well, there it is," Mrs. Moscowitz said when they were home, "and I must confess I thought as much. You could stop this stupid change yourself if you really wanted to, but you don't want to stop it. You're withdrawing, just the way he said, you're escaping from the responsibility of being plain old George Moscowitz in the plain old United States. You're quitting, and I'm ashamed of you—you're copping out." She hadn't used the phrase since her own college days, at Vassar, and it made her feel old and even less in control of this disturbing situation.

"Cop-out, cop-out," said Mr. Moscowitz thoughtfully. "What charm! I love it very much, the American slang. Cop-out, copping out. I cop out, *tu* cop out, they all cop out . . ."

Then Mrs. Moscowitz burst into tears, and picking up her colored chalks, she scribbled up and down and across the neat silhouette of her husband until the chalk screamed and broke, and the whole blackboard was plastered red, white, and blue; and as she did this, she cried "I don't care, I don't care if you're escaping or not, or what you change into. I wouldn't care if you turned into a cockroach, if I could be a cockroach too." Her eyes were so blurred with tears that Mr. Moscowitz seemed to be sliding away from her like a cloud. He took her in his arms then, but all the comfort he offered her was in French, and she cried even harder.

It was the only time she ever allowed herself to break down. The next day she set about learning French. It was difficult for her, for she had no natural ear for language, but she enrolled in three schools at once—one for group study, one for private lessons, and the other online—and she worked very hard. She even dug out her husband's abandoned language CDs and listened to them constantly. And during her days and evenings, if she found herself near a mirror, she would peer at the plump, tired face she saw there and say carefully to it, "*Je suis la professeur. Vous êtes l'étudiante. Je suis française. Vous n'êtes pas française.*" These were the first four sentences that the recordings spoke to her every day. It had occurred to her—though she never voiced the idea—that she might be able to will the same change that had befallen her husband on herself.

She told herself often, especially after triumphing over her reflection, that she felt more French daily; and when she finally gave up the pretense of being transformed, she said to herself, "It's my fault. I want to change for him, not for myself. It's not enough." She kept up with her French lessons, all the same.

Mr. Moscowitz, on his part, was finding it necessary to take English lessons. His work in the library was growing more harassing every day: he could no longer read the requests filed by the students—let alone the forms and instructions on his own computer screen—and he had to resort to desperate guessing games and mnemonic systems to find anything in the stacks or on the shelves. His condition was obvious to his friends on the library staff, and they covered up for him as best they could, doing most of his work while a graduate student from the French department sat with him in a carrel, teaching him English as elementary as though he had never spoken it. But he did not learn it quickly, and he never learned it well, and his friends could not keep him hidden all the time. Inevitably, the Chancellor of the university interested himself in the matter, and after a series of interviews with Mr. Moscowitz—conducted in French, for the Chancellor was a traveled man who had studied at the Sorbonne—announced regretfully that he saw no way but to let Mr. Moscowitz go. "You understand my position, Georges, my old one," he said, shrugging slightly and twitching his mouth. "It is a damage, of course, well understood, but there will be much severance pay and a pension of the fullest." The presence of a Frenchman always made the Chancellor a little giddy.

"You speak French like a Spanish cow," observed Mr. Moscowitz, who had been expecting this decision and was quite calm. He then pointed out to the Chancellor that he had tenure and to spare, and that he was not about to be gotten rid of so easily. Even in this imbecile country, a teacher had his rights, and it was on the Chancellor's shoulders to find a reason for discharging him. He requested the Chancellor to show him a single university code, past or present, that listed change of nationality as sufficient grounds for terminating a contract; and he added that he was older than the Chancellor and had given him no encouragement to call him *tu*.

"But you're not the same man we hired!" cried the Chancellor in English.

"No?" asked Mr. Moscowitz when the remark had been explained to him. "Then who am I, please?"

The university would have been glad to settle the case out of court, and Mrs. Moscowitz pleaded with her husband to accept their offered terms, which were liberal enough; but he refused, for no reason that she could see but delight at the confusion and embarrassment he was about to cause, and a positive hunger for the tumult of a court battle. The man she had married, she remembered, had always found it hard to show anger even to his worst enemy, for fear of hurting his feelings; but she stopped thinking about it at that point, not wanting to make the Chancellor's case for him. "You are quite right, George," she told him, and then, carefully, "*Tu as raison, mon chou.*" He told her—as nearly as she could understand—that if she ever learned to speak French properly she would sound like a Basque, so she might as well not try. He was very rude to the Marseillais tailor these days.

The ACLU appointed a lawyer for Mr. Moscowitz, and, for all purposes but the practical, he won his case as decisively as Darrow defending Darwin. The lawyer laid great and tearful stress on the calamity (hisses from the gallery, where a sizeable French contingent grew larger every day) that had befallen a simple, ordinary man, leaving him dumb and defenseless in the midst of academic piranhas who would strip him of position, tenure, reputation, even statehood, in one pitiless bite. (This last was in reference to a foolish statement by the university counsel that Mr. Moscowitz would have some difficulty passing a citizenship test now, let alone a librarian's examination.) But his main defense was the same as Mr. Moscowitz's before the Chancellor: there was no precedent for such a situation as his client's, nor was this case likely to set one. If the universities wanted to write it into their common code that any man proved to be changing his nationality should summarily be discharged, then the universities could do that, and very silly they would look, too. ("What would constitute proof?" he wondered aloud, and what degree of change would it be necessary to prove? "Fifty percent? Thirty-three and one-third? Or just, as the French say, a *soupçon?*") But as matters stood, the university had no more right to fire Mr. Moscowitz for becoming a Frenchman than they would have if he became fat, or gray-haired, or two inches taller. The lawyer ended his plea by bowing deeply to his client and crying "*Vive* Moscowitz!" And the whole courthouse rang and thundered then as Americans and French, judge and jury, counsels and bailiffs and the whole audience rose and roared, "*Vive* Moscowitz! *Vive* Moscowitz!" The Chancellor thought of the Sorbonne, and wept.

There were newspapermen in the courtroom, and by that last day there were television cameras. Mr. Moscowitz sat at home that night and leaned forward to stare at his face whenever it came on the screen. His wife, thinking he was criticizing his appearance, remarked, "You look nice. A little like Jean Gabin." Mr. Moscowitz grunted. "*Le camera t'aime,*" she said carefully. She answered the phone when it rang, which was often. Many of the callers had television shows of their own. The others wanted Mr. Moscowitz to write books.

Within a week of the trial, Mr. Moscowitz was a national celebrity, which meant that as many people knew his name as knew the name of the actor who played the dashing Gilles de Rais in a new television serial, and not quite as many as recognized the eleven-year-old Racine girl with a forty-inch bust, who sang Christian techno-rap. Mrs. Moscowitz saw him more often on television than she did at home—at seven on a Sunday morning he was invited to discuss post-existential film or France's relations with her former African colonies; at two o'clock he might be awarding a ticket to Paris to the winner of the daily *My Ex Will Hate This* contest; and at 11:00 p.m., on one of the late-night shows, she could watch him speaking the lyrics to the internationally popular French song, *Je M'en Fous De Tout Ça,* while a covey of teenage dancers yipped and jiggled around him. Mrs. Moscowitz would sigh, switch off the set, and sit down at the computer to study her assigned installment of the adventures of the family Vincent, who spoke basic French to one another and were always having breakfast, visiting aunts, or making lists. "Regard Helene," said Mrs. Moscowitz bitterly. "She is in train of falling into the quicksand again. Yes, she falls. Naughty, naughty Helene. She talks too much."

There was a good deal of scientific and political interest taken in Mr. Moscowitz as well. He spent several weekends in Washington, being examined and interviewed, and he met the President, briefly. The President shook his hand, and gave him a souvenir fountain pen and a flag lapel, and said that he regarded Mr. Moscowitz's transformation as the ultimate expression of the American dream, for it surely proved to the world that any American could become whatever he wanted enough to be, even if what he wanted to be was a snail-eating French wimp.

The scientists, whose lingering fear had been that the metamorphosis of Mr. Moscowitz had been somehow accomplished by the Russians or the Iranians, as a practice run before they turned everybody into Russians or Iranians, found nothing in Mr. Moscowitz either to enlighten or alert them. He was a small, suspicious man who spoke often of his rights, and might, as far as they could tell, have been born French. They sent him home at last, to his business manager, to his television commitments, to his endorsements, to his ghostwritten autobiography, and to his wife; and they told the President, "Go figure. Maybe this is the way the world ends, we wouldn't know. And it might not hurt to avoid crêpes for a while."

Mr. Moscowitz's celebrity lasted for almost two months—quite a long time, considering that it was autumn and there were a lot of other public novas flaring and dying on prime time. His high-water mark was certainly reached on the weekend that the officials of at least one cable network were watching one another's eyes to see how they might react to the idea of a George Moscowitz Show. His fortunes began to ebb on Monday morning—public interest is a matter of momentum, and there just wasn't anything Mr. Moscowitz could do for an encore.

"If he were only a *nice* Frenchman, or a *sexy* Frenchman!" the producers and the publishers and the ghostwriters and the A&R executives and the sponsors sighed separately and in conference. "Someone like Jean Reno or Charles Boyer, or Chevalier, or Jacques Pépin, or even Louis Jourdan—somebody charming, somebody with style, with manners, with maybe a little ho-*ho*, Mimi, you good-for-nothing little Mimi . . ." But what they had, as far as they could see, was one of those surly frogs in a cloth cap who rioted in front of the American Embassy and trashed the Paris McDonald's. Once, on a talk show, he said, taking great care with his English grammar, "The United States is like a very large dog which has not been—*qu'est-ce que c'est le mot?*—housebroken. It is well enough in its place, but its place is not on the couch. Or in the Mideast, or in Africa, or in a restaurant kitchen." The television station began to get letters. They suggested that Mr. Moscowitz go back where he came from.

So Mr. Moscowitz was whisked out of the public consciousness as deftly as an unpleasant report on what else gives mice cancer or makes eating fish as hazardous as bullfighting. His television bookings were cancelled; he was replaced by reruns, motivational speakers, old John Payne musicals, or one of the less distressing rappers. The contracts for his books and columns and articles remained unsigned, or turned out to conceal escape clauses, elusive and elliptical, but enforceable. Within a week of his last public utterance—"American women smell bad, they smell of fear and vomit and *l'ennui*"—George Moscowitz was no longer a celebrity. He wasn't even a Special Guest.

Nor was he a librarian anymore, in spite of the court's decision. He could not be discharged, but he certainly couldn't be kept on in the library. The obvious solution would have been to find him a position in the French department, but he was no teacher, no translator, no scholar; he was unqualified to teach the language in a junior high school. The Chancellor graciously offered him a departmental scholarship to get a degree in French, but he turned it down as an insult. "At least, a couple of education courses—" said the Chancellor. "Take them yourself," said Mr. Moscowitz, and he resigned.

"What will we do now, George?" asked his wife. *"Que ferons-nous?"* She was glad to have her husband back from the land of magic, even though he was as much a stranger to her now as he sometimes seemed to be to himself. ("What does a butterfly think of its chrysalis?" she wondered modestly, "Or of milkweed?") His fall from grace seemed to have made him kind again. They spent their days together now, walking, or reading Chateaubriand aloud; often silent, for it was hard for Mrs. Moscowitz to speak truly in French, and her husband could not mutter along in English for long without becoming angry. "Will we go to France?" she asked, knowing his answer.

"Yes," Mr. Moscowitz said. He showed her a letter. "The French government will pay our passage. We are going home." He said it many times, now with joy, now with a certain desperation. "We are going home."

The French of course insisted on making the news of Mr. Moscowitz's departure public in America, and the general American attitude was a curious mix of relief and chagrin. They were glad to have Mr. Moscowitz safely out of the way, but it was "doubtless unpleasant," as a French newspaper suggested, "to see a recognizable human shape insist on emerging from the great melting pot, instead of eagerly dissolving away." Various influences in the United States warned that Mr. Moscowitz was obviously a spy for some international conspiracy, but the President, who had vaguely liked him, said, "Well, good for him, great. Enjoy, baby." The government made up a special loose-leaf passport for Mr. Moscowitz, with room for other changes of nationality, just in case.

Mrs. Moscowitz, who made few demands on her husband, or anyone else, insisted on going to visit her sister Dina in Scottsdale before the move to France. She spent several days being taught to play video games by her nephew and enjoying countless tea parties with her two nieces, and sitting up late with Dina and her sympathetic husband, talking over all the ramifications of her coming exile. "Because that's the way I know I see it," she said, "in my heart. I try to feel excited—I really do try, for George's sake—but inside, inside . . ." She never wept or broke down at such points, but would pause for a few moments, while her sister fussed with the coffee cups and her brother-in-law looked away. "It's not that I'll miss that many people," she would go on, "or our life—well, George's life—around the university. Or the apartment, or all the things we can't take with us—that doesn't really matter, all that. Maybe if we had children, like you . . ." and she would fall silent again, but not for long, before she burst out, "But *me*, I'll miss *me!* I don't know who I'll be, living in France, but it'll be someone else, it won't ever be *me* again. And I did . . . I *did* like me the way I was, and so did George, no matter what he says now." But in time, as they knew she would, she would recover her familiar reliable calmness and decide, "Oh, it will be all right, I'm sure. I'm just being an old stick-in-the-mud. It *will* be an adventure, after all."

The French government sent a specially-chartered jet to summon the Moscowitzes; it was very grand treatment, Mrs. Moscowitz thought, but she had hoped they would sail. "On a boat, we would be nowhere for a few days," she said to herself, "and I do need to be nowhere first, just a little while." She took her books and CDs about the Vincent family along with her, and she drew a long breath and held onto Mr. Moscowitz's sleeve when the plane doors opened onto the black and glowing airfield, and they were invited to step down among the roaring people who had been waiting for two days to welcome them. "Here we go," she said softly. "*Allons-y.* We are home."

France greeted them with great pride and great delight, in which there was mixed not the smallest drop of humor. To the overwhelming majority of the French press, to the poets and politicians, and certainly to the mass of the people—who read the papers and the poems, and waited at the airport—it seemed both utterly logical and magnificently just that a man's soul should discover itself to be French. Was it not possible that all the souls in the world might be French, born in exile but beginning to find their way home from the cold countries, one by one? Think of all the tourists, the wonderful middle-aged tourists—where will we put them all? Anywhere, anywhere, it won't matter, for all the world will be France, as it should have been long ago, when our souls began to speak different languages. *Vive* Moscowitz then, *vive* Moscowitz! And see if you can get him to do a spread in *Paris-Match*, or on your television program, or book him for a few weeks at the Olympia. Got to make your money before Judgment Day.

But the government had not invited Mr. Moscowitz to France to abandon him to free enterprise—he was much too important for that. His television appearances were made on government time; his public speeches were staged and sponsored by the government; and he would never have been allowed, even had he wished, to endorse a soft drink that claimed that it made the imbiber 22 percent more French. He was not for rent. He traveled—or, rather, he was traveled—through the country, from Provence to Brittany, gently guarded, fenced round in a civilized manner; and throngs of people came out to see him. Then he was returned to Paris.

The government officials in charge of Mr. Moscowitz found a beautiful apartment in safe, quiet Passy for him and his wife, and let them understand that the rent would be paid for the rest of their lives. There was a maid and a cook, both paid for, and there was a garden that seemed as big as the Bois de Boulogne to the Moscowitzes, and there was a government chauffeur to take them wherever they wanted to go, whenever. And finally—for the government understood that many men will die without work—there was a job ready for Mr. Moscowitz when he chose to take it up, as the librarian of the Benjamin Franklin library, behind the Odeon. He had hoped for the Bibliothèque nationale, but he was satisfied with the lesser post. "We are home," he said to his wife. "Having one job or another—one thing or another—only makes a difference to those who are not truly at home. *Tu m'comprends?*

"Oui," said Mrs. Moscowitz. They were forever asking each other that, *Do you understand me?* and they both always said *yes*. He spoke often of home and of belonging, she noticed; perhaps he meant to reassure her. For herself, she had come to realize that all the lists and journeys of the family Vincent would never make her a moment more French than she was, which was not at all, regardless. Indeed, the more she studied

the language—the government had provided a series of tutors for her—the less she seemed to understand it, and she lived in anxiety that she and Mr. Moscowitz would lose this hold of one another, like children separated in a parade. Yet she was not as unhappy as she had feared, for her old capacity for making the best of things surfaced once again, and actually did make her new life as kind and rewarding as it could possibly have been, not only for her, but for those with whom she came in any sort of contact. She would have been very surprised to learn this last.

But Mr. Moscowitz himself was not happy for long in France. It was certainly no one's fault but his own. The government took the wisest care of him it knew—though it exhibited him, still it always remembered that he was a human being, which is hard for a government—and the people of France sent him silly, lovely gifts and letters of welcome from all across the country. In their neighborhood, the Moscowitzes were the reigning couple without really knowing it. Students gathered under their windows on the spring nights to sing to them, and the students' fathers, the butchers and grocers and druggists and booksellers of Passy, would never let Mrs. Moscowitz pay for anything when she went shopping. They made friends, good, intelligent, government-approved friends—and yet Mr. Moscowitz brooded more and more visibly, until his wife finally asked him, "What is it, George? What's the matter?"

"They are not French," he said. "All these people. They don't know what it *is* to be French."

"Because they live like Americans?" she asked gently. "George,"—she had learned to pronounce it *Jhorj,* in the soft French manner—"everyone does that, or everyone will. To be anything but American is very hard these days. I think they do very well."

"They are not French," Mr. Moscowitz repeated. "I am French, but they are not French. I wonder if they ever were." She looked at him in some alarm. It was her first intimation that the process was not complete.

His dissatisfaction with the people who thought they were French grew more apparent every day. Friends, neighbors, fellow employees, and a wide spectrum of official persons passed in turn before his eyes; and he studied each one and plainly discarded them. Once he had been the kind of man who said nothing, rather than lie; but now he said everything he thought, which is not necessarily more honest. He stalked through the streets of Paris, muttering, "You are not French, none of you are—you are imposters! What have you done with my own people, where have they gone?" It was impossible for such a search to go unnoticed for long. Children as well as grown men began to run up to him on the street, begging, *"Monsieur Moscowitz, regardez-moi, je suis vraiment français!"* He would look at them once, speak or say nothing, and stride on. The rejected quite often wept as they looked after him.

There were some Frenchmen, of both high and low estate, who became furious with Mr. Moscowitz—who was *he*, a first-generation American, French only by extremely dubious mutation, to claim that they, whose ancestors had either laid the foundations of European culture, or died, ignorant, in its defense, were not French? But in the main, a deep sadness shadowed the country. An inquisitor had come among them, an apostle, and they had been found wanting. France mourned herself, and began wondering if she had ever existed at all; for Mr. Moscowitz hunted hungrily through all recorded French history, searching for his lost kindred, and cried at last that from the days of the first paintings in the Dordogne caves, there was no evidence that a single true Frenchman had ever fought a battle, or written a poem, or built a city, or comprehended a law of the universe. "Dear France," he said with a kind of cold sorrow, "for all the Frenchmen who have ever turned your soil, you might have remained virgin and empty all these centuries. As far back in time as I can see, there has never been one, until now."

The President of France, a great man, his own monument in his own time, a man who had never wavered in the certainty that he himself was France, wrote Mr. Moscowitz a letter in which he stated: "We have always been French. We have been Gauls and Goths, Celts and Franks, but we have always been French. We, and no one else, have made France live. What else should we be but French?"

Mr. Moscowitz wrote him a letter in answer, saying, "You have inhabited France, you have occupied it, you have held it in trust if you like, and you have served it varyingly well—but that has not made you French, nor will it, any more than generations of monkeys breeding in a lion's empty cage will become lions. As for what else you may truly be, that you will have to find out for yourselves, as I had to find out."

The President, who was a religious man, thought of Belshazzar's Feast. He called on Mr. Moscowitz at his home in Passy, to the awe of Mrs. Moscowitz, who knew that ambassadors had lived out their terms in Paris without ever meeting the President face-to-face. The President said, "M. Moscowitz, you are denying us the right to believe in ourselves as a continuity, as part of the process of history. No nation can exist without that belief."

"Monsieur le Président, je suis désolée," answered Mr. Moscowitz. He had grown blue-gray and thin, bones hinting more and more under the once-genial flesh.

"We have done you honor," mused the President, "though I admit before you say it that we believed we were honoring ourselves. But you turn us into ghosts, *Monsieur* Moscowitz, homeless figments, and our grip on the earth is too precarious at the best of times for me to allow you to do this. You must be silent, or I will make you so. I do not want to, but I will."

Mr. Moscowitz smiled, almost wistfully, and the President grew afraid. He had a sudden vision of Mr. Moscowitz banishing him and every other soul in France with a single word, a single gesture; and in that moment's vision it seemed to him that they all went away like clouds, leaving Mr. Moscowitz to dance by himself in cobwebbed Paris on Bastille Day. The President shivered and cried out, "What is it that you want of us? What should we be? What is it, to be French, what does the stupid word mean?"

Mr. Moscowitz answered him. "I do not know, any more than you do. But I do not need to ask." His eyes were full of tears and his nose was running. "The French are inside me," he said, "singing and stamping to be let out, all of them, the wonderful children that I will never see. I am like Moses, who led his people to the Promised Land, but never set his own foot down there. All fathers are a little like Moses."

The next day, Mr. Moscowitz put on his good clothes and asked his wife to pack him a lunch. "With an apple, please," he said, "and the good Camembert, and a whole onion. Two apples." His new hat, cocked at a youthful angle, scraped coldly beside her eye when he kissed her. She did not hold him a moment longer than she ever had when he kissed her goodbye. Then Mr. Moscowitz walked away from her, and into legend.

No one ever saw him again. There were stories about him, as there still are; rumors out of Concarneau, and Sète, and Lille, from misty cities and yellow villages. Most of the tales concerned strange, magic infants, as marvelous in the families that bore them as merchildren in herring nets. The President sent out his messengers, but quite often there were no such children at all, and when there were they were the usual cases of cross-eyes and extra fingers, webbed feet and cauls. The President was relieved, and said so frankly to Mrs. Moscowitz. "With all respectful sympathy, Madame," he told her, "the happiest place for your husband now is a fairy story. It is warm inside a myth, and safe, quite safe, and the company is of the best. I envy him, for I will never know such companions. I will get politicians and generals."

"And I will get his pension and his belongings," Mrs. Moscowitz said to herself. "And I will know solitude."

The President went on, "He was mad, of course, your husband, but what a mission he set himself! It was worthy of one of Charlemagne's paladins, or of your—" he fumbled through his limited stock of non-partisan American heroes—"your Johnny Appleseed. Yes."

The President died in the country, an old man, and Mrs. Moscowitz in time died alone in Passy. She never returned to America, even to visit, partly out of loyalty to Mr. Moscowitz's dream, and partly because if there is one thing besides cheese that the French do better than any other people, it is the careful and assiduous tending of a great man's widow. She wanted for nothing to the end of her days, except her husband—and, in a very real sense, France was all she had left of him.

That was a long time ago, but the legends go on quietly, not only of the seafoam children who will create France, but of Mr. Moscowitz as well. In Paris and the provinces, anyone who listens long enough can hear stories of the American who became French. He wanders through the warm nights and the cold, under stars and streetlamps, walking with the bright purpose of a child who has slipped out of his parents' sight and is now free to do as he pleases. In the country, they say that he is on his way to see how his children are growing up, and perhaps there are mothers who lull their own children with that story, or warn them with it when they behave badly. But Parisians like to dress things up, and as they tell it, Mr. Moscowitz is never alone. Cyrano is with him, and St. Joan, Roland, D'Artagnan, and Villon—and there are others. The light of them brightens the road for Mr. Moscowitz to see his way.

But even in Paris there are people, especially women, who say that Mr. Moscowitz's only companion on his journey is Mrs. Moscowitz herself, holding his arm or running to catch up. And she deserves to be there, they will tell you, for she would have been glad of any child at all; and if he was the one who dreamed and loved France so much, still and all, she suffered.

Spook

To describe this story in any detail would, I think, spoil the fun. I'll just say that it's one of my Joe Farrell adventures (Julie Tanikawa definitely figures in it, if only *in absentia*); that it takes place in Avicenna, the shadow-Berkeley that lives in the California of my imagination; and that it was inspired—as were both "King Pelles the Sure" and "Uncle Chaim and Aunt Rifke and the Angel"—by a long spell of staring at the paintings and collages of the splendid artist Lisa Snellings-Clark. I had a *very* nice time writing it, and can't wait to record the audiobook version. I think you'll be able to tell that.

When they came out of the consultation with the santero, Farrell said, "Seventy-five bucks. For seventy-five bucks I can get an Eskimo and make my own ice." It was his favorite Marx Brothers line, employed often.

Ben said, "Come on, we learned *something.* At least we know it's bound to the house, can't even go round the block. You and Julie can find another place easy, it's a buyers' market right now. I'm sure you could get the deposit back."

"Julie loves that dump," Farrell said sourly. "Says she's finally got the north light exactly the way she wants it, and she'll never move again, ever. And she means it, I know her." He kicked a bottle into the gutter, and then felt guilty and went back and picked it up. "Buddies, lovers, partners—whatever the hell it is we are after twenty-five years—listen, if the Spook isn't gone when she gets back, I'll be sleeping at the restaurant with my clothes in a plastic bag. Live with an artist, you take your chances."

Ben grunted, not seeing much difference between the huge old loft and any of the studios Julie had always chosen since she settled for good in Avicenna. Cashing in a handful of sick-leave days from his job in Los Angeles, he had come up to help the two of them move in, finishing only a week before. There had been odd small occurrences from the first day—flickers of almost-movement in the rafters, and noises that were finally pronounced to be squirrel fights on the roof and in the vines outside the windows—but the thing he and Farrell were calling the Spook hadn't fully presented itself until the evening after Julie left to visit relatives in Seattle.

Farrell said, "Julie's grandmother. Grandma would know how to handle this."

"Her grandmother's dead," Ben said. After a moment he added, "Isn't she?" because one never quite knew with the Tanikawa family.

"Oh, yeah, long gone. But that doesn't mean a whole lot to those two." Farrell sighed. "No help for it. Not a thing to do but look up Andy Mac."

"Andy Mac." Ben stopped walking. Farrell turned, and they stood on the sidewalk, looking at each other. Ben said, "Couldn't we just have our tonsils out or something? Or go in for prostate surgery? I'll bet there's a two-for-one sale at Sisters of Mercy."

"Come on, it won't be *that* bad. Okay, Andy Mac's incredibly aggravating, and he smells sort of—"

"Dead."

"Dead, yes, granted. But he's the only man for the job, and we both know it. And one thing about him—he keeps his word."

"This is true. Which reminds me that he hates your guts. He despises me, but it's not nearly the same thing. Why on earth would he even consider helping you?"

"On the chance of getting even. Andy Mac likes getting even."

"Even for *what?* Now would be a really fine time to tell me."

"Long story. Long and unbelievably unedifying."

Ben said, "Then you find him. I don't care if you're being haunted by Hannibal Lecter, Truman Capote, and the Bride of Frankenstein. You want him, you go find him."

So Farrell tracked down Andy Mac by himself, eventually finding him in a dubious Herrera Street bathhouse, and got him to agree to come over that evening. Andy Mac, as always, flatly refused any suggestion of payment for his services; but it was just as flatly understood—again, as always—that there would be much care and feeding involved, so as to avoid any mysterious power outage in the spirit world. Farrell had worked with Andy Mac before.

"You just have to know how to handle him. It's not an art—it's more like reading the simple instructions that came with the package. *Insert Tab A into Slot B . . . fold flap over . . . insert two C batteries, this way up* . . . Amazing how many people never read the instructions."

"The print's too small. And Andy Mac doesn't come from Office Depot. You're worrying me, Farrell. Again."

The new loft was in North Avicenna, right across from a community theater given to staging poetry slams on Fridays. The location could hardly have been improved upon: apart from Julie's perfect north light, it lay within walking distance of the area hospital and her job as a part-time medical illustrator, and a short bicycle ride to the Gourmet Ghetto restaurant where Farrell worked as a *sous*-chef. Ben stayed with them whenever he came to town, in spite of the inevitable long flights of stairs—two, this time—and things occasionally falling down or off the walls. Like most houses in that part of Avicenna, it was very old. Farrell simply picked the things up, fixed them, and Krazy Glued them more or less back where they belonged.

"No way Andy Mac makes it up those stairs," Ben said with absolute certainty. "Twelve to seven against."

"I laid in a ton of smoked salmon. You know he'll trample babies and puppies for smoked salmon."

"Even so. Five to two."

Andy Mac made it, though he could be heard wheezing for a good five minutes before he knocked on the door. Farrell met him with a glass and a plate, and he grabbed both and sank into Julie's favorite overstuffed chair with a sound like a whalespout. For the next five minutes all he could say was "Jesus, Farrell . . . *Jesus* . . ."

Andy Mac was fifty-something: the size and general texture of the chair, only damper and stickier. His orange-freckled face always looked to Ben like a huge prizewinning Half-Moon Bay pumpkin just beginning to collapse of its own weight. His arms were disproportionally short, he sweated a good deal, and he had breath like a Chicago stockyard and little, flicky eyes the color of baby shit. He made his official living as a translator from the Finno-Ugric languages—there are more Hungarians and Estonians in Avicenna than one might think—and rumor credited him with a small sideline in blackmail, smuggling, and gentlemanly extortion. But he was also as learned a man as Farrell had ever known, who had more than once called him "the only medium worth a damn in the entire Bay Area—the only one who can really deliver, every time, on contact with that Other Place, whatever it actually is. In a pinch, that's worth a lot of lox and armpits."

"Sorry, Andy," Farrell said meekly. "I'm getting a little old for those stairs myself."

"Always been a liar," Andy Mac mumbled through a whiskey-soaked mouthful of salmon. "You *said* there'd be teacakes."

Farrell said, "Teacakes, bloody *hell*," and looked at Ben with what could only have been described as mute appeal. Ben said, "Olga's might still be open. I'll go see."

By the time he got back with the pastries (the local Russian bakery, two blocks away, really was called Olga From The Volga), Ben could hear the Spook through the door. It was zooming around the apartment like a mad parakeet, dive-bombing Farrell and howling in that thin, tinny voice, which was scarier for being so distant. The Spook looked like a cross between an airport windsock and a very weary broom. It was scarlet, and it had floppy, empty scarlet sleeves, and no face. Ben it only strafed now and then; Andy Mac it left strictly alone. But it went viciously, purposefully after Farrell, not simply swooping and stooping at him, but chittering wildly—and it was *words*, not just noise, Ben could tell that much. The thing was *after* Farrell, no question about it.

Farrell himself was in the closet, literally, scrunched back among the winter coats, yelling to Andy Mac, "What *is* it? What the hell *is* it?" From time to time he cautiously opened the closet door to peer out, and the Spook would immediately go for him like a cat after a chipmunk. Ben fully expected it either to slam into the door and knock itself out, or to pass right through it, but it merely veered away and waited around for another shot at Farrell. Andy Mac sat where he was, looking as bored as though he were watching TV or a kids' Thanksgiving Day pageant, even yawning once or twice. But his small eyes were stretched wider than Ben had ever seen them, and even his orange freckles looked pale.

"Well," he finally said. "There's a new one on me."

Ben asked, "Is it a ghost?" Andy Mac nodded slightly, and Farrell stuck his head out of the coat closet and said, "A ghost of *what?* A lampshade?"

"A man," Andy Mac said. "Ghosts don't always come back looking the way they did in life. Sometimes they just don't remember, they'll grab onto any shape that looks halfway familiar." On Andy Mac quiet and serious looked deeply impressive, in a sinister way. He said, "This one doesn't remember his own name, never mind what he looked like. But he knows how he died."

Dramatic pause. Andy Mac's voice dropped an octave. "He was murdered. Ambushed and strangled in his own house, in his own room. This room."

The Spook was obviously listening, bobbing up and down near the ceiling like a child's birthday balloon. Andy Mac went on, "A hundred and seventy years ago. Give or take."

Farrell called from the coat closet, "Not possible. This dump isn't *that* old—it just feels like it."

"Go argue with a ghost," Andy Mac said. "There was *some* house on this spot a hundred and seventy years ago, and he definitely died here, or he wouldn't be hanging around. Ghosts don't freelance."

"He's never bothered Julie." Farrell was edging halfway out of the closet for a second time. "Never showed up until she'd left for Seattle."

"Yes," Andy Mac purred. "That's because he doesn't think she murdered him."

The total silence that followed after Farrell's "*What?*" was broken at last by the Spook's yowl of vindication. Farrell yowled right back to match it. "For Christ's sake, I wasn't *born* a hundred-seventy years ago! Whoever murdered the thing—the guy, okay—it wasn't me. Tell it—*him*—tell him it wasn't me!"

Andy Mac took a huge bite of smoked salmon and washed it down with a slug of Johnnie Walker Black. "Go argue with a ghost. All they've got—all they *are*—are their memories, and they get them screwed up all the time. But once they lock into a thing the way they want to remember it—" he shrugged immensely—"that's it, game over. Not a lot to do about it."

"Nothing to do about it?" Spook or no Spook, Farrell was all the way out of the closet by then, practically shouting in Andy Mac's big face. "What are you talking about? There's got to be something we can do!"

Another vast, sweaty shrug, another mouthful of lox. "I don't do exorcisms. They're messy, and they only work on demons, anyway. This one's just an aggrieved householder with an obsession. Misguided, but one could sympathize. And after all, he can't really *hurt* you. In any significant way."

Farrell growled at him. Andy Mac considered, pulling at his lower lip, which made Ben feel slightly seasick. "Well, there's *one* thing . . ." Another dramatic pause, lasting so long that Ben put his hand on Farrell's shoulder, in case of accidents. He was confident that Farrell hadn't murdered the Spook, but he wasn't a bit sure about his intentions toward Andy Mac. But Farrell only said two words, both of them through his teeth. "What? Talk."

"What happened to those teacakes?" The phone rang as Ben was bringing them over, but no one even looked toward it. Andy Mac grabbed a fistful of the cookies and said, "Let's see what he wants. He knows he can't have the revenge he craves, but I'll bet he's got something in mind. Ghosts have agendas, like everybody else, and agendas go last."

The Spook dived at Farrell again, who shot back into the closet with a wail of despair, "Damn it, this shit has got to *stop!*" The ghost swerved away from the door once again and hung in the air, chittering like a pissed-off squirrel. Andy Mac heaved himself up and out of the armchair, cocking his head sideways, listening as intently as though the Spook were reciting Tonight's Seafood Specials. Then he started to laugh.

Andy Mac's laugh was rare, but legendary among his acquaintances. Julie had once compared it to a volcanic mud slide she had seen in the Philippines. He shook, and he coughed, and he rumbled and gurgled, and he twitched all over, and the corners of his mouth got wet. Even the Spook stopped carrying on to stare at him—eyeless and faceless as it was—and Andy Mac just kept laughing.

When he did stop, on an inhale that sounded like a moose pulling its feet out of a swamp, he yelled, "Farrell! Get out here!"

From the closet, Farrell answered, "Not a chance. I'm running cable in here and sending out for Chinese."

"Get out here," Andy Mac repeated. "Walter won't attack you." To the Spook, he added, "You don't mind me calling you Walter?"

The answer appeared to be in the affirmative. Farrell returned, slowly and cautiously, making sure to keep an escape route clear. The Spook's shrill snarl rose higher, but it stayed where it was. Andy Mac said, "Farrell, this is the late Walter Smith—at least, he *thinks* that might have been his name. Walter, meet Joe Farrell." He might have been introducing them at a faculty cocktail party.

"Tell him I didn't kill him," Farrell demanded. "I mean, I wouldn't mind killing him *now*, but I didn't do it *then*. Tell him!"

"Won't do any good. Doesn't even register." Andy Mac crunched down the last of the Russian teacakes and wiped his sugary hands on his pants. "Anyway. Walter is challenging you to a duel."

It was as though Farrell had been expecting something like this: Ben's memory afterward was that he himself was the one who protested "This is *crazy!*" while Farrell mostly looked back and forth between Andy

Mac and Walter the Spook, while the phone rang unanswered again, and Ben went on making loud noises. Finally he said the obvious. "But what's the point of it? Even if he could hold a weapon, he can't hurt me—so what's in it for him? What kind of a revenge is that?"

"There are other weapons than swords and pistols," Andy Mac replied, "and other stakes than life and death. You can't hurt him either, obviously, and you get to choose the armaments, because you're the challenged party. But *he* gets to set the terms." He smiled like an oil spill. "If you win, Walter will never bother you again. Period. No strings, no small print. He'll be here, because he lives here, but you'll never see him. Fair enough?"

Farrell nodded. "And if he wins?"

"Ah," Andy Mac said. "Well. It appears that our Walter has conceived something of a *tendresse* for the absent Ms. Tanikawa. He gets a bit incoherent here, but he certainly thinks that she's much too good for the man who murdered him."

"Damn it, I *didn't*—" Farrell began, but then he stopped himself and said only, "Julie's not part of the deal. That is not negotiable."

Andy Mac shrugged. "If you lose, you leave. Nothing to do with your lady. You make what excuse you like—you even tell her the truth, if that's your idea of a good time—and you're permanently off the premises by dinnertime tomorrow, before Ms. Tanikawa returns on the following day. That simple."

"Not really," Farrell said. "If I tell Julie why I'm having to move—and yes, I will—she'll walk right out with me, like a shot, I promise you. Julie rather hates being manipulated." He grinned tauntingly up at the Spook fluttering overhead. "Where's your *tendresse* then, Walter, old buddy?"

The oil spill smile spread, and Andy Mac answered him. "Walter has listened often to Ms. Tanikawa expressing her own *tendresse* for this loft. He's willing to chance it."

Ben glanced anxiously at Farrell, remembering their morning's conversation. Julie wouldn't ever leave this loft, not even for Farrell, nor would he have expected her to. He'd been bluffing, and it hadn't worked. But Ben saw him recouping, gathering his psychic feet under him, bracing himself for whatever came next. He took a long, slow breath.

"All right," Farrell said. "All right, then. The duel will take place precisely at dawn tomorrow. I'll choose the weapons then. Right now, it's late, and I'll require a peaceful night and morning to make my decision. I trust that won't be a problem?"

"No problem at all," Andy Mac answered for the Spook. "Just so the combat doesn't turn on manual dexterity."

"Me? Hardly." Farrell turned to Ben. "You'll be my second?"

"Like I've got a choice. What's a second expected to do?"

Farrell was brisk. "Oh, you check out the weapons, and you carry my body home if I lose, and you tell Julie I died bravely. The usual. You've seen the movie."

Andy Mac said that he'd second the Spook, out of fairness and necessity. "Like a public defender, backbone of our system." The phone rang once more, and this time Farrell picked it up. It was Julie, as the other two calls had been, letting Farrell know the time and number of her flight from Seattle. Andy Mac left, and Ben went to haul out the air mattress and sleeping bag he always used staying over with Farrell and Julie. When he came back, the phone call was finished, and Farrell was lying on his bed with his hands behind his head, staring at the ceiling. And where Walter the Spook spent the night, neither of them had the least idea.

Farrell didn't move or speak while Ben undressed and crawled into the sleeping bag; but then he murmured thoughtfully, more to himself, "I wonder who *did* kill old Walter Smith, all that time ago. Aggravating, never to know."

"Well, if he was anything like the way he is now, they could have sold tickets. Held a raffle." Farrell chuckled softly. Ben said, "About why Andy Mac hates you."

"I told you . . . long story."

"You also told me he went for the gig on the chance of getting even. What did you do to him, for God's sake?" Farrell did not answer. Ben said, "I really hate to call in old markers, but you remember that paper on *Moby Dick?* You remember your grade? I do."

"You're a very hard man," Farrell said after a further silence. "You were a very hard five-year-old." He sighed. "It's not as long a story as all that, I just don't come out of it looking very good. Andy Mac's a snob and a showoff, but he's not a monster, not even a bad guy, really. He's got a whole lot to show off, lord knows, but it's not enough, it's never enough. And he has to be right, *has* to—it's that important to him. Anyway, some time back, years, there was this party, and he was working on impressing Julie—"

"Julie? I never thought Andy Mac liked girls that way."

"I don't think he really likes anybody that way. But he dearly likes making an impression, subject doesn't matter. So he was lecturing her about James Joyce and *Finnegan's Wake*—and maybe I got jealous, maybe the devil made me do it, but I butted in and started talking about this Romanian linguistics professor, whom I made up on the spot, and how he had this big theory that Joyce was actually . . . what did I say, a Mason? No, I said the Romanian guy proved beyond doubt that Joyce was a Rosicrucian, and I quoted whole passages from his well-known book on Joyce—"

"Which, of course, Andy Mac knew by heart. Oh, lord, I see where this is going—"

"Right, he was great, really. Improvised better than I did—explained to Julie how *Finnegan's Wake* was absolutely transparent, once you understood the code. And she looked at him, and then she looked at me, and people were listening . . . and I sort of wandered off—"

"And by and by, the word got back to him. . . . Oh, you're bad, Farrell. That was a terrible thing to do. I'm ashamed of you."

"What can I tell you? I was younger then."

"And you think he's still carrying a grudge about that?"

"I know he is."

Ben slept fitfully, and Farrell not at all, so both were up well before dawn. The Spook was still invisible, and Andy Mac wasn't due till showtime, so Ben made Eggs Benjamin, as requested—notorious on two continents or not—plus a pot of equally notorious coffee, and went for a walk in the still-misty streets to keep himself from staring and pacing and offering helpful suggestions. They had seen each other through other dawns, and other duels.

He had left his cell phone on, which was a good thing, because Farrell called halfway through his fourth time around the block. "Come on back—I need you to look up some stuff for me! *Hurry!*"

Ben ran up the two flights, sounding exactly like Andy Mac when he lurched through the door, and sat down at Julie's computer to look up stuff. He printed it out as he came across it, and Farrell sat there reading and reading; and for a few hours it was like the old times of studying together, trying to write dates and formulas all over shirt cuffs, and even fingernails. Farrell had always had the better memory, and if Ben had envied it then, he was glad of it now. They spoke very little.

They stayed at it until they heard Andy Mac at the door, which Ben opened before he could knock. It seemed to annoy him. He was dressed for opening night at the opera: evening clothes, white tie, gorgeous red-and-gold cravat, lacking only the silk hat. He looked surprised to see Ben in everyday street clothes, and more than a bit contemptuous as well. He said, "I understood that proper seconds wore proper clothing to a duel of honor."

"Well, I'm an *im*proper second."

Farrell looked up for a moment and waved languidly before he went back to reading. Ben said, "Hey, this isn't the *Bois de Boulogne*. We'll be ready come sunrise."

Andy Mac had to leave it at that, and leave it with no snacks this time, no Johnnie Walker Black to occupy him until the hour of the duel. Ben could watch him getting more and more annoyed, and couldn't help sympathizing: here he'd gotten totally, uncharacteristically, involved in an affair that not only wouldn't feed him, but was most likely going to turn out too weird even to dine out on. He said finally, "You know, it wouldn't hurt you to see the man's point of view."

Farrell didn't bother to look up this time. "He has no point of view. What he has is a thing about my girlfriend, and he'll make our lives hell if I don't get out and give her up. I'm sorry, but that's not a point of view. That's a hissy fit."

"But he was murdered!" Andy Mac bellowed.

Farrell shrugged, long and slow, and very deliberate. "That's not a point of view either. I didn't do it, and I'm tired of him saying I did. In this century, in this country, that's considered slander. I may very well sue."

"After all, you've only got *his* word for it," Ben added. "And we already know about *him*." To his own surprise, he was actually starting to enjoy this—especially watching the dampness spreading under Andy Mac's tuxedoed armpits. "Old Walter might be amusing himself, attacking Farrell and spinning all this shit out for you, just because he's bored out of his mind. It's not exactly much of a life he's got, is it?"

He swept his arm up toward the ceiling in a dramatic gesture, and that was when he saw Walter the Spook perched up in the rafters. To be accurate, not having anything to perch *with*, he was hovering, as hummingbirds do, and definitely vibrating like a hummingbird, ready for the duel, ready for his close-up. *Probably the most exciting thing that's happened to him in the last hundred years.* Ben couldn't help wondering what weapon he might have chosen if Farrell had been the challenger. Maybe he did have hands—though there had been no sign of any—maybe he could be hiding a couple of Derringers up in those empty, floppy scarlet sleeves. *Is a ghost simply what you always were, inside? What does it tell us that he's this?*

Andy Mac looked at his watch and said, "Sunrise in five minutes. I think we might get started."

"Dawn," Farrell said firmly. So they waited out the last five minutes, with Walter the Spook plainly struggling with a profound and passionate need to start diving at Farrell again, and Farrell peacefully ignoring everybody, looking through papers and making a few notes, as though he were prepping for a final. Ben stood by, waiting for instructions, as previously agreed. Farrell unplugged the phone.

"Okay," he said. "Now."

He said nothing more, but only sat there, smiling a little bit at nothing in particular. What seemed like another five minutes went by before Andy Mac finally said, "Now *what?*"

"Now I name the weapons," Farrell said. "And the terms." The smile broadened, but this time it was aimed directly at the Spook above their heads. Farrell said, "Bad poetry at twenty paces. To the death."

In the silence that followed, he added, "*Really* bad poetry," just before Andy Mac went up in smoke.

"What the *hell* are you talking about? You can't fight a duel with poetry!"

"You can with these," Farrell replied happily. "Trust me, it'll be like dueling with cobras, crocodiles." He was as purry and sleepy-eyed as a kitten serenely attached to a nipple. "Wait till you hear a couple of sparkling stanzas from Julia A. Moore . . . Margaret Cavendish, the Duchess of Newcastle . . . J. B. Smiley. Oh, your boy is toast already, Andy, burned toast. Honestly, I'd tell him to hang it up now, in the first round."

Whether or not Walter the Spook was capable, at this point in his career, of fully comprehending human speech, Ben had no idea, but he never doubted that the ghost got the gist. He was squalling like a buggered banshee before Farrell was half through; but instead of going for him, he flew down straight to Andy Mac, looking a bit like an old-fashioned ear trumpet as he yammered to him. Andy Mac was all attention, listening so intently that the listening was *visible:* Ben felt he could actually see the translation going on in his head, the frontal lobes and cerebellum wringing meaning out of angry gibberish. He couldn't help wondering whether Walter the Spook had originally spoken Estonian.

"Well," Andy Mac finally announced. "Speaking as Mr. Smith's second, I must immediately register a formal protest. It's shameful and immoral to force a person to fight with a weapon with which he is completely unacquainted, and with which you—I'm quite certain—are an expert." Farrell inclined his head modestly. "And for my own curiosity, how can such a duel possibly be considered a combat to the death? It may be absurd, and even humiliating, but there's nothing lethal about even the worst poetry."

Farrell didn't answer immediately. When he did, his voice was quiet and reflective, and not at all mocking. He said, "You know, Andy, in a way I owe your little red buddy something very important. Something I might never have realized without his intervention. Tell him I'm really grateful."

Andy Mac very clearly did not want to ask the question, but there was just as clearly no way not to. "Grateful for what?"

"For teaching me that I want to stay where I am," Farrell said. "It never used to matter to me. One place, one job, one pleasant, convenient other . . . it's always been like any other place, any other person, you know? But not now, some way. Not now." He stood up, again addressing himself to Walter the Spook. "Even if I moved out tomorrow, you still wouldn't have a chance with Julie. I'd find a place of my own—there's a neat little two-bedroom right by the restaurant—and she'd likely be over there when she wasn't working here. That's the way we've always lived, all these years—except sometimes *over there* was in another time zone, or another country. Or maybe *here* was, depending. A lot of years like that."

Andy Mac started to say something, but Farrell cut him off. "But not now. It's a funny thing,"—he hesitated for a long moment—"but now I think that leaving this particular dump actually would mean some kind of death for me. So there's a certain lethal incentive, you could say, right?"

The Spook chattered furiously, but Andy Mac paid no heed. Farrell continued, "And as for what's at risk for the good Walter . . . well, I'm not just talking about sentimental Hallmark cards. I'm talking poetry so bad that a wise man would listen to it through smoked glass. Poetry that sets the blood cringing backwards in your veins—poetry from which one's very kidneys shrink, poetry that curdles the lymph glands and makes the teeth whine like dogs." His voice had acquired the half-taunting urgency of a carnival pitchman. "Poetry so horrid, the brain will simply refuse to recognize it as English, let alone verse. Be warned—oh, be warned—it's deadly stuff, toxic as the East River." He smacked his hands together, grinning a werewolf grin. "Let's *go!*"

He began stepping off twenty paces, while Walter the Spook dithered shrilly, and Andy Mac said, "You know I'm going to have to speak for him, translate for him. That's only fair."

"You're his second," Farrell said calmly, still counting, with his back to the others. "I want him to have every proper advantage." He turned at the far wall, where Julie habitually hung paintings and drawings she had doubts about and wanted to live with for awhile—she called it the "Parole Wall"—and said, "I'll even give him the first shot. Fair?"

"And the referee?" Andy Mac demanded. He glanced at Ben even more scornfully than usual. "Tonto here, your faithful, hairy sidekick? I don't think so."

"And risk your vengeance?" Ben answered. "You'd come to my house in the dead of night and steal my newspaper." Andy Mac didn't bother to respond. He was muttering to Walter the Spook, who was hovering at such an angle that—just for a moment—Ben thought he glimpsed a pair of tiny eyes as sharp as frost glittering further back than they should have been under the Little Red Riding Hood hood. But then they were gone, and Ben never caught sight of them again.

Farrell said, "A referee won't be necessary. Trust me, we'll know." He smiled cheerfully at Walter the Spook. "Go ahead, then. Hit me with the horror."

And to Ben's amazement, Walter reared back and did exactly that. The first volley caught both him and Farrell shockingly off guard, as Andy Mac listened carefully and then recited:

"Beautiful Railway Bridge of the Silv'ry Tay!

Alas! I am very sorry to say
That ninety lives have been taken away
On the last Sabbath day of 1879,
Which will be remember'd for a very long time."

"McGonagall the Magnificent," Farrell said softly. "Wow. Tell Walter I'm very impressed. I'd have led off with Dr. Fuller, or someone like that."

Walter went straight through the poem, with Andy Mac's aid: all the way through the storm, the bridge's collapse and the ensuing train wreck, and onward to the inescapable moral.

"Oh! Ill-fated Bridge of the Silv'ry Tay,
I must now conclude my lay
By telling the world fearlessly without least dismay,
That your central girders would not have given way,
At least many sensible men do say,
Had they been supported on each side with buttresses,
At least many sensible men confesses,
For the stronger we our houses do build,
The less chance we have of being killed."

Ben could feel the blood leaving his face, and Farrell himself looked, as he said, definitely impressed, and maybe a bit more. He said slowly, "McGonagall, is it? O-*kay*, McGonagall right back at'cha."

"Beautiful city of Glasgow, with your streets so neat and clean,
Your stately mansions, and beautiful Green!
Likewise your beautiful bridges across the river Clyde,
And on your bonnie banks I would like to reside . . ."

Neither Walter the Spook nor Andy Mac seemed much affected by this serve; nor, in all honesty, was Ben himself. It was bad, true, but not bad enough—it didn't belong in the same league with the first poem, and Farrell plainly knew it. He said, with some defiance, "It gets better," and continued:

"'Tis beautiful to see ships passing to and fro,
Laden with goods for the high and the low,
So let the beautiful city of Glasgow flourish,
And may the inhabitants always find food their bodies to nourish . . ."

But "The Tay Bridge Disaster" had plainly left Walter ahead on points, no question about it, and the Spook was strutting and squawking in the air like Tinker Bell on speed. Andy Mac was smiling all over his pumpkin face, as though he had just put through a successful 800 call to the spirit world. He listened attentively to the swaggering chatter, and announced "Nature's Cook."

"Cavendish," Farrell muttered. "Damn, *I* was going to come back with that one." He was actually looking somewhat alarmed. Walter recited:

"Death is the cook of Nature, and we find
Meat dressed several ways to please her mind.
Some meats she roasts with fevers, burning hot,
And some she boils with dropsies in a pot.
Some for jelly consuming by degrees,
And some with ulcers, gravy out to squeeze . . ."

Ben became aware of a sudden, desperate need to pee. He faced it for the cowardly reaction it was, whispered, "Right back" to Farrell and headed for the toilet while Walter went charging on through the Cavendish recipe book.

"In sweat sometimes she stews with savory smell
A hodge-podge of diseases tasteth well.
Brains dressed with apoplexy to Nature's wish,

Or swims with sauce of megrims in a dish.
And tongues she dries with smoke from stomachs ill . . ."

Given a choice, Ben would gladly have stayed in the john long enough to get his mail there, but friendship comes with obligations, even for cowards. He got back in time for the Duchess's grand finale.

"Then Death cuts throats, for blood puddings to make,
And puts them in the guts, which colics rack.
Some hunted are by Death, for deer that's red,
Or stall-fed oxen, knocked on the head.
Some for bacon by Death are singed, or scalt,
Then powdered up with phlegm, and rheum that's salt."

There fell a deadly silence in the room when the last horrendous syllable had thudded to the floor. Farrell had clearly not bargained for this: they had both underestimated Walter the Spook, and for all their preparations Ben was beginning to think that they might just be outgunned. He whispered, "Moore. No more fooling around—*Moore.*"

Farrell nodded grimly. "All right," he said. "All right. Because there is a season for casual mercy—there is a season for fooling around—and then there is a time for Julia A. Moore. The Bible tells us so." Raising his voice, he announced, "Lament on the Death of Willie."

Andy Mac looked like the manager of a team facing the Yankees who had just been told that Mariano Rivera was coming in to pitch. Farrell shook himself once, like a wet dog, and went to work.

"Willie had a purple monkey climbing on a yellow stick,
And when he sucked the paint all off it made him deathly sick;
And in his latest hours he clasped that monkey in his hand,
And bid goodbye to earth and went into a better land.
Oh! no more he'll shoot his sister with his little wooden gun
And no more he'll twist the pussy's tail and make her yowl, for fun.

> *The pussy's tail now stands out straight; the gun is laid aside*
> *The monkey doesn't jump around since little Willie died."*

Silence followed this one too; but it was more like a sort of holy hush, even from Walter the Spook. The presence of simple greatness has that effect. Ben heard Andy Mac mumble, more to himself, "A hit, a very palpable hit," and agreed silently that sometimes only Shakespeare will do when you're talking about Julia A. Moore.

Andy Mac cleared his throat. "You must be in trouble, calling on the Goddess so early in the game. You do know that Emmeline Grangerford's poetry is Twain's parody of Moore?"

Farrell grinned at him. "You're stalling. The Sweet Singer of Michigan is beyond parody, beyond imitation—beyond category, as Duke Ellington used to say. Come on, hotshot—I'm waiting."

But Farrell's playing the Moore option had thrown the Spook off balance in his turn. He fumbled through a couple of minor responses—another McGonagall, and a couple by Dr. William Fuller—which Farrell brushed aside with J. B. Smiley's perfectly charming poem about the Kalamazoo insane asylum ("*The folks are not all of them crazy / Who hail from Kalamazoo*") and Moore's poem about the death of Lord Byron, which ends with the magnificent and legendary rhyme:

> *"Lord Byron's age was 36 years,*
> *Then closed the sad career,*
> *Of the most celebrated 'Englishman'*
> *Of the nineteenth century."*

Farrell sighed as contentedly as though he had just finished making love. "Call me an elitist, but it doesn't *get* any better than that, I'm sorry."

Andy Mac faced the attack impassively; one would have had to know him and be looking for it to see Farrell's merciless grapeshot reaching him at all. But Walter the Spook was visibly wilting and paling under the bombardment, as escaped toy balloons always do, sooner or later. In a strange way, he did look like a fatally wounded duelist, stumbling in the air, lurching inevitably down toward stillness. It was over, obviously, and Ben—now that they could afford it—felt honestly sorry for him.

It was over . . . and then Walter the Spook played his ace.

Or maybe it was Andy Mac himself, getting even at last for an old humiliation. Whichever it was, Farrell and Ben were abruptly sandbagged, sideswiped by a great poet—no Sweet Singer of Michigan here, but Samuel Taylor Coleridge himself, celebrated author of *The Rime of the Ancient Mariner* and *Xanadu*—not to mention "To a Young Ass (Its Mother Being Tethered Near It)."

"Poor little foal of an oppressed race!
I love the languid patience of thy face:
And oft with gentle hand I give thee bread,
And clap thy ragged coat, and pat thy head . . ."

Ben had never read or heard the poem, but one look at his friend's stricken face told him that Farrell had.

"Or is thy sad heart filled with filial pain
To see thy wretched mother's shortened chain?
And truly, very piteous is her lot—
Chained to a log within a narrow spot,
Where the close-eaten grass is scarcely seen,
While sweet around her waves the tempting green!"

They looked at each other helplessly. Ben whispered, "Coleridge was a doper, wasn't he? Opium, hash, like that?" Farrell didn't answer.

Thoroughly revived, Walter the Spook rolled on, zooming above Andy Mac's head as the man recited, like a matador taking a victory lap. Farrell grunted slightly with each line, and seemed to roll with them, as though each were a blow slamming into him.

"Innocent foal! thou poor despised forlorn
I hail thee Brother—spite of the fool's scorn!
And fain would take thee with me, in the Dell
Of Peace and mild Equality to dwell,
Where Toil shall call the charmer Health his bride,
And Laughter tickle Plenty's ribless side!
How thou would toss thy heels in gamesome play,
And frisk about, as lamb or kitten gay!
Yea! and more musically sweet to me
Thy dissonant harsh bray of joy would be,
Than warbled melodies that soothe to rest
The aching of pale Fashion's vacant breast!"

Nobody said a word for a long while after he finished—nobody except Walter the Spook, who couldn't stop chattering in triumph, as though he were singing some kind of tribal conquest song over Farrell's body. Farrell neither moved nor spoke, unresponsive to anything or anyone. Ben could not read his eyes, as he usually could, out of the long old friendship. *Nothing now. No one there.*

Andy Mac said, "Well." Farrell didn't answer. Andy Mac said, "I think we can consider this duel dueled, don't you? Throw in the towel, call it a TKO?"

"Coleridge," Farrell said wearily. "I wrote a thing about Coleridge in college, I just never thought . . ." His voice trailed off tonelessly.

"Well, it's as *I've* always said." If the self-satisfaction in Andy Mac's voice could have been tapped, it would have powered a fair-sized suburb. "In the end, it's always a matter of who's got the best lawyer. *Everything* comes down to the best lawyer."

Ben took a couple of steps toward him, without realizing that he had done so. Later, he had no memory of what he'd had in mind, except that the defeat on Farrell's face, combined with that triumphant purr, was more than he could bear. Farrell said, "I'll start packing. It never takes me long."

"Oh, take your time, by all means," Andy Mac said grandly. The Spook was chittering in his ear, and he was nodding steadily. "Walter is quite content to have received justice, at long last. He doesn't wish any further inconvenience to anyone, even his murderer." The oil spill smile took a victory lap itself. "No, of course not—*I* know you didn't do it, and *you* and Tonto here know it, so what does it matter what *he* thinks? He's just a little red flying whiskbroom, after all."

Farrell was already trudging toward the bedroom. Ben turned away, unable to watch him. He said to Andy Mac, "I don't know who killed him, a hundred-and-whatever years ago, but if I ever get my hands on him anytime—"

"Oh, please," Andy Mac said. "It's life, Tonto. Stop making such a bloody tragedy of it—it's just life. Your leader knows that, don't you, Farrell?"

Ben's father, a would-be song-and-dance man born out of his time, had raised him on a good many old vaudeville songs and comedy sketches, including a classic routine built around the recurring line, "*Slowly I turned . . .*" Ben had never fully understood what was supposed to be funny about the sketch, but he used the line occasionally, without comprehension, as his father most likely had. He thought of it then, absurdly, because on the word *tragedy* Farrell turned back—very, very slowly—to face Andy Mac and Walter the Spook. At the expression on his face the Spook stopped yodeling and went for the rafters, zipping straight up, like a helicopter, and Andy Mac said "What?" Farrell didn't speak. Andy Mac said "*What?*" again.

"Theophilus Marzials," Farrell said. Ben wasn't entirely sure whether it was a name or a curse, an incantation of some kind. But Andy Mac knew. He opened his mouth, but nothing came out. Farrell said, "A Tragedy."

"You can't do that," Andy Mac whispered. "That's like . . . you can't *use* Marzials. That's . . . that's not *fair.*"

"Ah, it's just life, Andy," Farrell said. "And desperate times require desperate measures." He winked at Ben and announced again, "A

Tragedy. By Theophilus Julius Henry Marzials, lesser Pre-Raphaelite poet, born in England of Belgian and English parents. Second son, and youngest of five children. Remind me to tell you how I learned it—there was a Kiowa Indian involved." Andy Mac closed his eyes as Farrell began.

"Death!
Plop.
The barges down in the river flop.
Flop, plop.
Above, beneath.
From the slimy branches the grey drips drop,
As they scraggle black on the thin grey sky,
Where the black cloud rack-hackles drizzle and fly
To the oozy waters, that lounge and flop
On the black scrag piles, where the loose cords plop,
As the raw wind whines in the thin tree-top.
Plop, plop.
And scudding by
The boatmen call out hoy! and hey!
All is running water and sky,
And my head shrieks—'Stop,'
And my heart shrieks—'Die . . .'"

"The worst poem ever written in English," Andy Mac moaned softly. He had not opened his eyes. "Like bringing a nuclear weapon into a beach volleyball game."

Andy Mac played volleyball? On the beach? Ben decided not to think about that more than he absolutely had to. Farrell was giving the poem the serious works now, nodding with the rhythm, altering his tone to suit the line. Ben caught a glimpse of Walter the Spook, huddled in the shadows atop a huge old hutch that somehow managed to follow Julie everywhere she lived, despite Farrell's undying enmity. Even at that distance, with not a lot to go on, he looked sick and increasingly drained as Marzials rolled remorselessly on.

"And the shrill wind whines in the thin tree-top
Flop, plop.
A curse on him.
Ugh! yet I knew—I knew—
If a woman is false can a friend be true?
It was only a lie from beginning to end –
My Devil—My 'Friend'
I had trusted the whole of my living to!
Ugh; and I knew!"

"No more!" Andy Mac's eyes were open, and his hands were out in piteous supplication. "It's done, you win, we give—please, no more!"

"Shh, shh," Farrell soothed him. "There's only a little more." He might have been a nurse or a torturer in that moment. Ben expected to see the poor Spook go *flop, plop* then himself, but he managed to shuffle out of sight along a curtain rod as Farrell was building to a rolling climax.

"Ugh!
So what do I care,
And my head is as empty as air—
I can do,
I can dare,
(Plop, plop
The barges flop
Drip, drop.)
I can dare! I can dare!
And let myself all run away with my head
And stop.
Drop.
Dead.

Plop, flop.
Plop."

There wasn't a great deal for anyone to say after that last *plop,* and nobody tried. Farrell managed to dig up at least some leftovers for Andy Mac, out of compassion for that sweat-soaked tuxedo, which would surely never be the same, and then Ben drove him back to the Herrera Street bathhouse. He was silent on the way, but just before getting out of the car he said, "He'll keep his word. They won't see him again."

"But they'll know he's there," Ben said. "I'd have trouble with that, a ghost watching everything."

Andy Mac chuckled, so softly that it was almost a whisper. "Ghosts watch everything we do, everywhere, all the time. Get used to it, sidekick."

He walked away slowly, shaking his head, and Ben drove back to the loft and settled down to serious coffee drinking. Placid by nature, he only got the shakes *after* a crisis, not *during,* and coffee always calmed him. Farrell was asleep, snoring as peacefully as though he hadn't spent the morning involved in a genuine duel to the death. Ben saw no sign of Walter the Spook. He drank coffee, made more, read the newspaper, and tried to get all the lines of "A Tragedy" out of his head. He never quite did, not all of them, but came in time to regard them as honorable wounds, sustained in a noble cause.

When Farrell woke up ravenous they scrambled everything in the pantry, and celebrated the victory with Farrell's prized stash of Aventinus beer; but they also did their best to talk about ordinary matters, with reasonable success. Ben did finally ask, "You planning to tell Julie about the Gunfight at the Booga-Booga Corral when she gets home?"

Farrell nodded. "Right away. She always finds stuff like this out, anyway—I might as well get points for candor. I think she might even be flattered, a bit. Not *too* flattered, but still. And she'll feel sorry for him, sure as hell, I know the woman." He sighed. "It's as I said, Ben—the poor guy really did teach me something I didn't want to know, and I do owe him, some way. Believe me, I've gotten used to way weirder stuff in my time, and so has Julie. Just so he's *quiet*. Quiet, I can live with. *And* invisible. We'll deal."

Ben said, "I stay with you guys, I always hate to go home."

"Oh, you're much better off in Los Angeles. There've been times when it was all I could do not to go home with you. Julie too, probably. Things just keep *happening* here." Another sigh; and then that bent, warped, crookedy smile that he had in the first grade. "Besides, you must never forget the immortal words of our Julia—the Goddess herself."

"Which are?"

"'*Literary is a work very difficult to do.*'"

"Amen and amen," Ben said. He reached for the last bottle of Aventinus, but Farrell slapped his hand.

The Stickball Witch

Everything in this story is as real and true of my 1940s/1950s Bronx childhood as I can remember it. One of my two closest childhood friends has already assured his grown kids that it happened exactly as recounted; and the other one would cheerfully swear the same, if properly remunerated.

This was written to be read aloud as the first of four season-themed podcasts for a delightful online magazine called *The Green Man Review*. It was my nod to Spring, and appeared in print for the first time in *We Never Talk About My Brother.*

I was a boy, and it was spring in the Bronx. School would be out in less than two months. My friend Phil's folks had just gotten a television set, and he and I could watch Ralph Bellamy in *Man Against Crime* on Friday nights. There was a new war on in Korea, and red-haired Sandy Greenbaum was being even more insufferable than usual, because her big brother Sam was some kind of aide to General Mark Clark, whose name she always pronounced in full, like an incantation. Or perhaps a prayer, I wonder now: who knows how frightened for Sam her family actually was? Maybe saying the general's whole name was a way of not stepping on a crack, not breaking the charm that would bring her brother home whole himself? What did I know? I was eleven years old, and she was obnoxious and had freckles.

I was eleven, and it was spring. The dogwood was blossoming in the cemetery down the block; the park two blocks away in the other direction was bright with budding goldenrod, and would be brilliant with forsythia and ragweed in another week or so. My allergy shots had already begun; but so, one after another, also like wildflowers in their season, had rollerskates and bicycles, jacks and double-Dutch and hopscotch (which we called "potsy") for the girls, catch and one-o'cat and schoolyard fights for the pure hell of fighting for the boys. And stickball. Between one day and the next, stickball again.

Stickball is—*was,* I guess; who plays it now?—street baseball, played with broomsticks and a specific kind of ball. It was manufactured by the Spalding Company—though I never heard it called anything but a *Spaldeen*—and was made of a particular kind of pink rubber, which emitted a flaky whitish powder when fresh, and smelled indescribably of . . . of spring, finally, and of laundry drying on apartment-building roofs and on lines strung between apartment windows, and sunlight lasting a little longer every day. In the Bronx in 1950, spring smelled like Spaldeens.

There were never enough players to make up two full teams; it was quite common for boys to play for both sides, as necessary. (Although choosing up sides, arguing over the fairness of which team got stuck with which fat or slow or stone-fingered kid could easily take longer than the game itself.) As for the playing field, the ground rules literally varied with the parking along Tryon Avenue that afternoon. First and third bases were almost always cars, though we made do with bicycles or wagons when we had to; second and home were usually one manhole cover apart, though this might be affected by the spatial relationship of first and third. Since we were always short on fielders (if anyone actually had a glove, it usually wound up being a base), a hit that traveled as far as two manhole covers' distance was an automatic double; so, also, was a ball hit into traffic, wedged under a car, or carried away forever by Richie Williams' damn dog. A three-manhole shot was a triple. Home runs . . . well, fat Stewie Hauser hit one once, far down the block toward the cemetery, and mean Joey Gonsalves hit one that he *said* was a homer, go argue with Joey Gonsalves. He had brothers.

Of course, we could have walked two blocks to the park and played on a real baseball diamond, but that was just the point of stickball. It had to be played with *sticks*, not real bats, balls, and gloves; it *had* to be improvised, from equipment to the contours of the baselines, to the constantly evolving rules, which were quite likely to be significantly different over on Decatur Avenue, or DeKalb. You played baseball or softball in the park—stickball was for the street, only and always. Not all of life was that simple, even in 1950, even at the age of eleven, but stickball . . . oh, stickball, yes.

I wasn't good at stickball; let's have *that* clear. I wasn't one of those chosen last, or forced on one team or the other like a handicap, but I was a lot closer to that social class than to the stars like Stewie Hauser, Miltie Mellinger, or J.T. Jones. The only athletic gift I had was that I could run, which wasn't much use in our game, since we didn't have stolen bases, the way they played down on Rochambeau Avenue. If I actually connected, I'd make it home well before anybody ran the ball down, but it didn't happen often. To this day, I remember every time that it did.

Today Tryon's lined with condos on both sides, but back then there were still a lot of trees, and a lot of one-family houses: thirty, forty years old, older, most still occupied by the original owners, who had built and settled in when the Bronx was still largely farming country, and my mother would often meet a cow or a goat on her way to school. Fragments of those farms survived in my own school years: they were usually inhabited by half-mad hermits who threw stones at kids trying to cut through their overgrown fields and blighted orchards. All gone now, of course, all leveled and paved-over by the end of that decade. I'm not nostalgic. I just remember.

Tryon Avenue had a witch. Many streets did; it was almost a necessity to local tradition, back when a single block, a single apartment building, was an entire country for a child, complete with history, royalty, a peasant class, endless threats from outsiders, and a rich and varied folklore. The designated witch was always some old lady living alone, quite often foreign-born and oddly dressed (by our highly Puritanical standards for adults); and known to us, beyond any reasonable doubt, as implacably menacing, whether or not they'd done anything at all to merit the verdict. Whatever else they had in common, the universal factor—going all the way back to the Brothers Grimm, and surely beyond—was that any ball hit into their front yards, or their ragged little gardens, stayed there forever. We were often surprisingly daring—foolhardly, even, looking back—but we weren't crazy.

Mrs. Poliakov was *our* witch. She lived about halfway down the block, in a small gray house, which I keep seeing as stone, though I'm sure it wasn't, no more than it could have been gingerbread. Mrs. Poliakov almost never left the gray house; such deliveries as she needed came to her, as was more common in those days. Since we hardly kept exact track of just who went into the house and who came out, we were happy to spread—and, by and by, absolutely believe—a rumor that Mrs. Poliakov sometimes ate deliverymen, or turned them into . . . things. Which would certainly account for the absence of a Mr. Poliakov, after all. We thought hard about stuff like that. We had discussions. We *ruminated.*

She was a tiny woman, really, gray and nondescript as her house, but we equipped her with fangs (if you looked closely, which nobody was about to do), and with what the Italian kids called the *mal'occhio,* and the Puerto Ricans the *mal ojo*—the evil eye. My memory has her backing carefully down her front steps when she did come out, usually wrapped in an old tweed overcoat, no matter the weather. She always wore a man's battered felt hat, and she limped a bit on her right leg.

Spaldeens hit into Mrs. Poliakov's yard, as I've said, were lost balls, even though we could usually see them where they lay against her fence, often actually within reach through the wobbly, peeling slats. She never threw them back, of course, but she never got rid of them either, so there they lay like spoils of some mysterious war nobody but the participants remembered. We visualized her gloating over them, using them to cast spells, as we knew beyond question she did. For spite we threw other things into her yard at night—rotting garbage, dead animals, paper bags filled with patiently collected dog and cat shit—and then ran like hell. I felt bad sometimes, thinking about it . . . but that'd teach *her* to be sitting up midnights, casting spells.

What changed everything—especially for me—was the day Chuck Golden dared me to go get the ball that I'd just fouled off into Mrs. Poliakov's front yard. (Anything in the street, including parked cars and Schwartz's fruit truck, was fair territory; the curbs were our foul lines.) Chuck Golden was a sawed-off loudmouth, but that Spaldeen happened to be our last one, and it was just wrong to quit playing on a Saturday, with the sun still high. Junius Dinkins, who usually had more sense, said, "You hit it, you oughta get it," and Stewie Hauser—always the second guy to do or say anything, said he double-dared me. So there it was. You couldn't walk away from a double-dare, even from a dumbshit like Stewie. I mean, you *could*, but the rest of your life wouldn't ever be worth living after that. I knew that then. Not believed. Knew.

But I also knew absolutely that if I entered that yard, I'd never come back. Not as myself, anyway—maybe as some kind of monster, which

was almost tempting when I thought of Joey Gonsalves and all his brothers. What if Mrs. Poliakov grabbed me in her claws and dragged me into her house—that house we'd spent hours peopling with every horror we'd ever seen in a movie or a comic book? Oh, sure, my mom and dad would call the cops. But what good would the police be if I'd already been eaten, or fed into a meatgrinder, or turned into furniture? I wasn't aware of it until later, but it was in that moment that I woke up to the realization that you couldn't depend on your parents in a *real* crisis, any more than you could on the police. I never managed to unlearn that discovery, though I did try.

But when you're eleven years old, there's no such thing as a choice between being a witch's afternoon snack or being a fink and a chicken-shit. I made the best scene I could (having already seen *A Tale of Two Cities)* out of accepting my doom; and, rot them, the team played right back to me. They didn't exactly ask for any last messages to my nearest and dearest, but J.T. Jones shook my hand hard, and Miltie gave me back the immie he'd won off me two weeks before. And I handed my broomstick to Richie Williams—as formally as if it were a sword or a custom-made pool cue—and I made my legs walk me straight across the street and into Mrs. Poliakov's front yard.

I picked up the ball I'd hit, suddenly entertaining a mad notion of scooping up as many others as I could carry and racing back in triumph from behind enemy lines with an armload of trophies to flaunt, both at Chuck Golden and Mrs. Poliakov. That vision lasted until I heard her voice, deep and rough as a man's. "Boy! You!"

She was standing on her top step, beckoning to me with an appropriately clawlike forefinger. For once she wasn't wearing that weird tweed topcoat, but a long dark wool skirt and blouse that made her look like our idea of a gypsy. The old fedora covered her scanty white hair, giving substance to our belief that she wore it even in bed. She said it a second time. "You!"

I'd never heard her voice before. None of us had, as far as I ever knew. As long as she'd lived in that gray house, she must have yelled at two or three generations of children to stay out of her yard. By the time we came along, it wasn't necessary anymore: the fear had been passed down to us with the legend, and however much we might mock her in private, she didn't have to say a word to scatter us when she wanted to. Our parents, when they noticed, teased us for scaredy-cats, but we knew what we knew.

Now I walked slowly toward her, feeling my friends' terror behind me, but unable to turn my head. I stopped at the bottom of Mrs. Poliakov's front steps. She looked at me out of eyes so gray they were almost black, eyes younger than the drooping, wrinkled lids under which they studied me. The grating, heavily accented voice—Russian, I think now, but maybe Polish—said, "You ball, boy?"

"Uh," I said. "Uh, yes. My ball. Our ball."

"That game," Mrs. Poliakov said. "What game? *Lapta?*"

Oddly enough, I knew about *lapta,* because my mother was born in the Ukraine. *Lapta* involves a bat and ball, and a lot of running back and forth, but it's more like cricket than baseball. I said, "No, no *lapta.* Stickball. *Steeck-boll.*"

Mrs. Poliakov said, "*Steeck . . .*" and then "Sticks . . . ball," and about got it right. I nodded eagerly, "Stickball, that's it, we play it all the time. We don't mean to hit the balls into your yard, we're really sorry . . ." My own voice gradually dried up as I stared into those old, gray, relentlessly clear eyes. "Can we . . . could we have our ball back now? *Ball,* okay?" and I held the rescued Spaldeen up, so she'd understand what I was talking about. "Ball?"

Quicker than I can say this, she snatched that ball back from me, holding it over her head as though she expected me to jump for it. "No, *nyet,* no ball," and she pointed toward the street with her free hand. I thought she was telling me to get the hell out of her yard, but that wasn't it either, nor was she throwing me out when she grabbed my arm and started walking with me, saying, "Game, *hanh?* Show—show me *sticks*-ball. You show."

And here we came, the two of us, marching as to war, back into the street where my friends were standing gaping at us, some of them backing away from a scary old neighborhood witch, none of them with a word to say. *She* was enjoying herself—you could actually see it in the glint of her eyes, and in the way she limped over to J.T. Jones and slapped the Spaldeen into his hand. "Sticksball, okay, *hanh?* Show."

I wonder less about how she guessed that J.T. was our pitcher, than how she knew that we used a pitcher at all. Most teams didn't: no matter how much the rules vary, block to block, in the majority of stickball games the batter just tosses the ball up himself and times his swing to its descent. But we always had a real pitcher, even though that meant our taking turns at catcher; even if he had to pitch for both sides, as he mostly did. And J.T. was *good,* even throwing underhand, and he was honest as well; never took anything off his pitches when we were at bat, which pissed some guys off, but most of us were proud of him. He was a legend, at least in the North Bronx. At least on Tryon Avenue, and all the way to Jerome on one side, and down to Webster the other way. Down to White Plains Road, really.

We chose up sides again and started a new game; but who could keep his mind on playing, with that woman who'd terrified us all our lives standing there watching, with her hands behind her back and a very slight smile on her whiskery old lips? J.T.'s hands were so sweaty the ball kept getting away from him, and Miltie Mellinger kept losing the broomstick when he swung, for the same reason—almost nailed me one time, the stick flew straight at my head. We hit, all right, so much that keeping score quickly became pointless. J.T. wasn't up to anything but just laying it in there, and even the weakest hitters like Howie Stern and Marv Cooper were slamming it over the parked cars and the green trees for the rest of us to run down. Not me, though: I struck out three or four times and slunk off to lean against Howie's father's Packard, which was our dugout. For all the scoring, nobody talked or cheered much, I remember that.

Mrs. Poliakov said "*Hanh,*" again, loudly, like a whale coming up to blow. She said, "Sticksball. Give me. Give." She held out her hand.

J.T. looked around at everyone before he put the Spaldeen into her hand. Stewie Hauser said, "Okay, relief pitcher coming in, pop that glove, *bubbe*," and crouched down to catch. *Bubbe* is grandma, but nobody laughed. Mrs. Poliakov adjusted her fedora, and turned the rubber ball slowly between the swollen-knuckled fingers of both hands, studying the *Spalding* logo intently for minutes before she looked up and repeated, "Okay." She gestured to Marv to stand in, even though he wasn't due up yet. He didn't argue. Mrs. Poliakov gave an arthritic little hop, clumsily imitating J.T.'s motion, and she pitched.

Marv never saw it. I'm not sure Stewie did, either, until he was yelling "Jesus *Christ*, sonofa*bitch!*" and sucking his fingers as the ball bounced away from him toward the sidewalk. J.T.'s mouth was open, and Richie Williams was actually crossing himself. Junius Dinkins was just saying softly, "*Naww*, man," over and over. And Mrs. Poliakov beckoned, as she had beckoned to me in her front yard, and the Spaldeen came back to her.

It rolled meekly then; later on, it came bouncing jauntily as though it knew the way better. Mrs. Poliakov was an awkward fielder; anyone who even made contact would easily have been on base by the time she picked the ball up. But none of us ever did—J.T. managed a couple of trickling fouls, but that was it. The Spaldeen either came in so impossibly fast and hard that after a little we were bailing out before she released it; or else the thing simply zigzagged, dodged our bats, curved around us, dropped literally out of sight, or changed its pink-rubber mind and backed up in mid-flight. Satchel Paige messed with batters' heads by warning and half-convincing them that he could make a baseball do all those things. Mrs. Poliakov was *doing* it, and doing it with a toy you could get at Lapin's corner store for forty-nine cents, with tax; cheaper, you buy a dozen. I will always believe—and so, I promise you, will anyone else who was there—that she could have done exactly the same thing with a pair of rolled-up gym socks.

Stewie Hauser hadn't stopped saying "Jesus *Christ*!" from that first pitch, and Miltie Mellinger kept mumbling, "It's a trick, she *does* something to the ball, a *spin.*" Chuck Golden, who always had to know more than you did, was explaining learnedly, "She's throwing a spitball, that's illegal. My dad told me about spitballs." Some of the girls jumping rope and pushing doll-carriages had stopped playing, and were staring from the sidewalk; there were even one or two adult onlookers, who could tell that *something* was going on. We ourselves would have quit, if we could, but Mrs. Poliakov wouldn't let us, not until she was good and ready. We'd have to keep dragging our broomsticks up there all night, if she wanted; through all eternity, if she chose. That we knew without a word.

All the same, she gave me my one great moment in sports, there in the cobblestone street, at five o'clock on a spring afternoon, with mothers already starting to call from windows about dinner and homework. When I stepped in for one last hopeless at-bat against her, she gave me a gray, snaggly grin—the only real smile anyone ever had from her—and she called in to me, "For you, boy. For brave!"

And she grooved one. It floated in chest-high, not veering, not dropping or hopping, just minding its own business, timing itself to my swing, rather than the other way around. Shirley Temple couldn't have missed it. Miss Eschenberg, who taught fourth grade, couldn't have missed it. My seven-year-old brother couldn't have missed it.

And for once *I* didn't miss it. It vanished down the block, tearing through leaves, knocking down twigs, soaring high and far enough to clear the cemetery wall. I can't say whether it actually did or not, or would have, because it caught fire at the top of its arc—simply burst into flames as it flew on out of sight. We never found any charred fragments, though Stewie Hauser hunted for two days, determined to prove that it hadn't outdistanced his legendary home run. Nobody else cared, but I understood. Those things mattered then.

Mrs. Poliakov looked briefly after my shot, said "*Hanh,*" to herself, pushed her fedora down hard on her head, and turned back toward her house. We never moved, but stood watching her, sensing perhaps that the game—or whatever it really was—might be ended, but that *some-*

thing was not yet complete. Just before entering her yard, she turned again to face us, waiting there in the street. Her face was dark and warning under the old hat, and not at all friendly.

"Next ugly in my yard," she said clearly, "next nasty"—and she pointed to indicate the last flight of the Spaldeen—"same thing you, all you." Now she waved both arms as high as she could reach, and went, "*Whoooaww!* All heads, all heads, like you ball. *Whoooawww!*"

We must all have been at least halfway home when I heard her call after us, "You come get balls! Balls, okay!" I *think* she was laughing, but I've never been sure. In any case, it took me a week to get Junius Dinkins' nerve up, but then we went together and rescued all the abandoned Spaldeens littering her front yard. Mrs. Poliakov didn't put in an appearance, though Junius swore that he caught a glimpse of that felt hat slipping around a corner—not her, just the hat, keeping an eye on us—which could have been true. Witches' hats are magic too, as any eleven-year-old can tell you. Or they could have then.

A Dance for Emilia

First published as a small stand-alone gift book several years ago, I am pleased to see "A Dance for Emilia" in wider circulation at last. This is the story within these pages that means the most to me. It's fiction, certainly, and very much a fantasy in its nature; but it's also as autobiographical as anything I've ever written, and it was born out of mourning for my closest friend, who died in 1994. His name was Joe Mazo, and we did meet in a high-school drama class, as Jake, the narrator, and his friend Sam do. But Joe was a frustrated actor, not a dancer (just as I'm a writer who, like most writers, would love to be a performer), and who became in fact a well-known dance critic and the author of three highly respected and influential books on modern dance. Jake and Sam's daily lives are as different from Joe's and mine as they were meant to be; but the relationship between them is as close to the way things were as I could write it. As for the original of Emilia, I couldn't really do justice to her, and her love for Joe, but I tried my best.

For Nancy, Peter and Jessa,
And for Joe

The cat. The cat is doing what?

Believe me, it's no good to tell you. You have to see.

Emilia, she's old. Old cats get really weird sometimes.

Not like this. You have to see, that's all.

You're serious. You're going to put Millamant in a box, a case, and bring her all the way to California, just for me to . . . When are you coming?

I thought Tuesday. I'm due ten days' sick leave. . . .

⁂

No. This isn't how you do it. This isn't how you talk about Sam and Emilia and yourself. And Millamant. You've got hold of the wrong end, same as usual. Start from the beginning. For your own sake, tell it, just write it down the way it was, as far as you'll ever know. Start with the answering machine. That much you're sure about, anyway. . . .

The machine was twinkling at me when I came home from the Pacific Rep's last-but-one performance of *The Iceman Cometh*. I ignored it. You can live with things like computers, answering gadgets, fax machines, even email, but they have to know their place. I hung up my coat, checked the mail, made myself a drink, took it and the newspaper over to the one comfortable chair I've got, sank down in it, drank my usual toast to our lead—who is undoubtedly off playing Hickey in Alaska today, feeding wrong cues to a cast of polar bears—and finally hit the PLAY button.

"Jacob, it's Marianne. In New York." I only hear from Marianne Hooper at Christmas these days, but we've known each other a long time, in the odd, offhand way of theater people, and there's no mistaking that husky, incredibly world-weary sound—she's been making a fortune doing voice-overs for the last twenty years. There was a pause. Marianne could always get more mileage out of a well-timed pause than Jack Benny. I raised my glass to the answering machine.

"Jacob, I'm so sorry, I hate to be the one to tell you. Sam was found dead in his apartment last night. I'm so sorry."

It didn't mean anything. It bounced off me—*it didn't mean anything*. Marianne went on. "People at the magazine got worried when he didn't come in to work, didn't answer the phone for two days. They finally broke into the apartment." The famous anonymous voice was trembling now. "Jacob, I'm so terribly . . . Jacob, I can't do this anymore, on a machine. Please call me." She left her number and hung up.

I sat there. I put my drink down, but otherwise I didn't move. I sat very still where I was, and I thought, There's been a mistake. It's his turn to call me on Saturday, I called last week. Marianne's made a mistake. I thought, Oh, Christ, the cat, Millamant—who's feeding Millamant? Those two, back and forth, over and over.

I don't know how late it was when I finally got up and phoned Marianne, but I know I woke her. She said, "I called you last. I called his parents before I could make myself call you."

"He was just here," I said. "In July, for God's sake. He was fine." I had to heave the words up one at a time, like prying stones out of a wall. "We went for walks."

"It was his heart." Marianne's voice was so toneless and uninflected that she sounded like someone else. "He was in the bathroom—he must have just come home from Lincoln Center—"

"The Schönberg. He was going to review that concert *Moses and Aron*—"

"He was still wearing his gangster suit, the one he always wore to openings—"

I was with him when he bought that stupid, enviable suit. I said, "The Italian silk thing. I remember."

Marianne said, "As far as they—the police—as far as anyone can figure, he came home, fed the cat, kicked off his shoes, went into the bathroom and—and died." She was crying now, in a hiccupy, totally unprofessional way. "Jacob, they think it was instant. I mean, they don't think he suffered at all."

I heard myself say, "I never knew he had a heart condition. Secretive little fink, he never told me."

Marianne managed a kind of laugh. "I don't think he ever told anyone. Even his mother and father didn't know."

"The cigarettes," I said. "The goddamn cigarettes. He was here last summer, trying to cut down—he said his doctor had scared the hell out of him. I just thought, lung cancer, he's afraid of getting cancer. I never thought about his heart, I'm such an idiot. Oh, God, I have to call them, Mike and Sarah."

"Not tonight, don't call them tonight." She'd been getting the voice back under control, but now it went again. "They're in shock; I did it to them, don't you. Wait till morning. Call them in the morning."

My mouth and throat were so dry they hurt, but I couldn't pick up my drink again. I said, "What's being done? You have to notify people, the police. I don't even know if he had a will. Where's the—where is he now?"

"The police have the body, and the apartment's closed. Sealed—it's what they do when somebody dies without a witness. I don't know what happens next. Jacob, can you please come?"

"Thursday," I said. "Day after tomorrow. I'll catch the redeye right after the last performance."

"Come to my place. I've moved, there's a guest room." She managed to give me an East Eighties address before the tears came again. "I'm sorry, I'm sorry, I've been fine all day. I guess it's just caught up with me now."

"I'm not quite sure why," I said. I heard Marianne draw in her breath, and I went on, "Marianne, *I'm* sorry, I know how cold that sounds, but you and Sam haven't been an item for—what?—twelve years? Fifteen? I mean, this is me, Marianne. You can't be the grieving widow, it's just not your role."

I've always said things to Marianne that I'd never say to anyone else—it's the only way to get her full attention. Besides, it made her indignant, which beat the hell out of maudlin. She said, "We always stayed friends, you know that. We'd go out for dinner, he took me to plays—he must have told you. We were *always* friends, Jacob."

Sam cried over her. It was the only time that I ever saw Sam cry. "Thursday morning, then. It'll be good to see you." Words, thanks, sniffles. We hung up.

I couldn't stay sitting. I got up and walked around the room. "Oh, you little bastard," I said aloud. "Kagan, you miserable, miserable twit, who said you could just leave? We had *plans*, we were going to be old together, you forgot about that?" I was shouting, bumping into things. "We were going to be these terrible, totally irresponsible old men, so elegant and mannerly nobody would ever believe we just peed in the potted palm. We were going to learn karate, enter the Poker World Series, moon our fiftieth high school reunion, sit in the sun at spring-training baseball camps—we had stuff to *do*! What the hell were you *thinking* of, walking out in the middle of the movie? You think I'm about to do all that crap alone?"

I don't know how long I kept it up, but I know I was still yelling while I packed. I didn't have another show lined up after *Iceman* until the Rep's *Christmas Carol* went into rehearsal in two months, with Bob Cratchit paying my rent one more time. No pets to feed, no babies crying, no excuses to make to anyone . . . there's something to be said for being fifty-six, twice divorced and increasingly set in my ways. I'm a good actor, with a fairly wide range for someone who looks quite a bit like Mister Ed, but I've got no more ambition than I have star quality. Which may be a large part of the reason why Sam Kagan and I were so close for so long.

We met in high school, in a drama class. I already knew that I was going to be an actor—though of course it was Olivier back then, not Mister Ed. The teacher was choosing students at random to read various scenes, and we, sitting at neighboring desks, got picked for a dialogue from *Major Barbara*. I was Adolphus Cusins, Barbara's Salvation Army fiancé; Sam played Undershaft, the arms manufacturer. He wasn't familiar with the play, but I was, and with Rex Harrison, who'd played Cusins in the movie, and whose every vocal mannerism I had down cold. Yet when we faced off over Barbara's ultimate allegiance and Sam proclaimed, in an outrageously fragrant British accent, Undershaft's gospel of "money and gunpowder—freedom and power—command of life and command of death," there wasn't an eye in that classroom resting anywhere but on him. I may have known the play better than he, but he knew that it was a play. It was the first real acting lesson I ever had.

I told him so in the hall after class. He looked honestly surprised. "Oh, good *night*, Undershaft's easy, he's all one thing—in that scene, anyway." The astonishing accent was even riper than before. "Now Cusins is bloody tricky, Cusins is much harder to play." He grinned at me—God, were the cigarettes already starting to stain his teeth then?—and added, "You do a great early Harrison, though. Did you ever see *St. Martin's Lane?* They're running it at the Thalia all next week."

He was the first person I had ever met in my life who talked like me. What I mean by that is that both of us much preferred theatrical dialogue to ordinary Brooklyn conversation, theatrical structure and action to life as it had been laid out for us. It makes for an awkward childhood—I'm sure that's one reason I got into acting so young—and people like us learn about protective coloration earlier than most. And we tend to recognize each other.

Sam. He was short—notably shorter than I, and I'm not tall—with dark eyes and dark, wavy hair, the transparent skin and soft mouth of a child, and a perpetual look of being just about to laugh. Yet even that early on, he kept his deep places apart: when he did laugh or smile, it was always quick and mischievous and gone. The eyes were warm, but that child's mouth held fast—to what, I don't think I ever knew.

He was a much better student than I—if it hadn't been for his help in half my subjects, I'd still be in high school. Like me, he was completely uninterested in anything beyond literature and drama; quite unlike me, he accepted the existence of geometry, chemistry, and push-ups, where I never believed in their reality for a minute. "Think of it as a role," he used to tell me. "Right now you're playing a student, you're learning the periodic table like dialogue. Some day, good *night,* you might have to play a math teacher, a coach, a mad scientist. Everything has to come in useful to an actor, sooner or later."

He called me Jake, as only one other person ever has. He was a gracious loser at card and board games, but a terrible winner, who could gloat for two days over a gin rummy triumph. He was the only soul I ever told about my stillborn older brother, whose name was Elias. I knew where he was buried—though I had not been told—and I took Sam there once. He was outraged when he learned that we never spoke of Elias at home, and made me promise that I'd celebrate Elias's birthday every year. Because of Sam, I've been giving my brother a private birthday party for more than forty years. I've only missed twice.

Sam had surprisingly large hands, but his feet were so tiny that I used to tease him, referring to them as "ankles with toes." It was a sure way to rile him, as nothing else would do. Those small feet mattered terribly to Sam.

He was a dance student, most often going directly from last-period math to classes downtown. Wanting to dance wasn't something boys admitted to easily then—certainly not in our Brooklyn high school, where being interested in *anything* besides football, fighting, and very large breasts could get you called a faggot. I was the one person who knew about those classes; and we were seniors, with a lot of operas, Dodgers games, and old Universal horror movies behind us, before I actually saw him dance.

There was a program at the shabby East Village studio where he was taking classes three times a week by then. Two pianos, folding chairs, and a sequence of presentations by students doing solo bits or *pas de deux* from the classic ballets. Sam's parents were there, sitting quietly in the very last row. I knew them, of course, as well as any kid who comes over to visit a friend for an afternoon ever knows the grown-ups floating around in the background. Mike was a lawyer, fragile-looking Sarah an elementary school teacher; beyond that, all I could have said about them—or can say now—was that they so plainly thought their only child was the entire purpose of evolution that it touched even my hard adolescent heart. I can still see them on those splintery, rickety chairs: holding hands, except when they tolerantly applauded the fragments of Swan Lake and Giselle, waiting patiently for Sam to come onstage.

He was next to last on the program—the traditional starring slot in vaudeville—performing his own choreography to the music of Borodin's *In the Steppes of Central Asia*. And what his dance was like I cannot tell you now, and I couldn't have told you then, dumbly enthralled as I was by the sight of my lunchroom friend hurling himself about the stage with an explosive ferocity that I'd never seen or imagined in him. Some dancers cut their shapes in the air; some burn them; but Sam tore and clawed his, and seemed literally to leave the air bleeding behind him. I can't even say whether he was *good* or not, as the word is used—though he was unquestionably the best: in that school, and more people than his parents were on their feet when he finished. What I did somehow understand, bright and blind as I was, was that he was dancing for his life.

When I went backstage, he was sitting alone on a bench in his sweat-blackened leotard, head bowed into his hands. He didn't look up until I said, "Boy, that was something else. You are something else." The phrase was fairly new then, in our circles at least.

He looked old when he raised his head. I don't mean older; I mean old. The glass-clear skin was gray, pebbled with beard stubble—I hadn't thought he shaved—and the dark eyes appeared too heavy for his face to bear. He said slowly, "Sometimes I'm good, Jake. Sometimes I really think I might make it."

I said something I hadn't at all thought to say. "You have to make it. I don't think there's a damn thing else you're fit for."

Sam laughed. Really laughed, so that some color came back into his face and his eyes became his age again. "Good *night*, let's just hope I never have to find out." He got dressed and we went out front to meet Mike and Sarah.

He didn't have to find out for some time. We graduated, and I went off to Carnegie Tech in Pittsburgh on a genuine theater scholarship, while Sam stayed home, attending CCNY to please his parents, and literally spending all the rest of his time at Garrett-Klieman, a dance school whose top prospects seemed to be funneled directly into the New York City Ballet. I'd see him on holidays and over the summer, and we'd do everything we'd always done together: going to plays and baseball games, hitting the secondhand bookstores on Fourth Avenue, drinking beer and debating whether the internal rhymes in the songs we were always trying to write were as clever and crackling as Noël Coward's. On Friday nights, we usually played poker with a mixed bag of other would-be actors and dancers. As far as either of us was willing to acknowledge, nothing at all had changed.

But while I talked about plays I'd been in, about Artaud, Brecht, the Living Theatre, the Method, improv workshops and sense memories, Sam avoided almost all mention of his own career. If he danced in any of the Garrett-Klieman showcases, he never told me—it was all I could do to persuade him to let me sit in on a couple of his choreography classes. As before, I couldn't look away from him for a moment; but I was already beginning to learn that some dancers, actors, musicians simply have that. It doesn't have a thing to do with talent or craft—it just is, like blue eyes or being able to touch your nose with your tongue. I don't have it.

We were eating lunch at the Automat on Forty-second and Sixth the day he told me abruptly, "They haven't recommended me. Not to City Ballet, not to anybody. It's over."

I gaped at him over my crusty brown cup of baked beans. I said, "What over? This is crazy. You're the best dancer I ever knew."

"You don't know any dancers," Sam said. Which was perfectly true—I still don't know many; I'm not in a lot of musicals—but irritating under the circumstances. Sam went on, "They didn't tell me it was over. I knew. I'm not good enough."

I was properly outraged, not only at Garrett-Klieman, but also at him, for acceding so docilely to their decision. I said, "Well, the hell with them. What the hell do *they* know?"

Sam shook his head. "Jake, I'm not good enough. It's that simple."

"Nothing's that simple. You've been dancing all your life, you've been the best everywhere you've gone—"

"I was never the best!" The Noël Coward accent had dropped away for the first time in my memory, and Sam's voice was all aching Brooklyn. "You remember that story you told me about Queen Elizabeth—the real one—that thing she said when she was old. 'No, I was never beautiful, but I had the name for it.' It was like that with me. I can be dazzling—I worked on it, I about killed myself learning to be dazzling—but there isn't a move in me that I didn't copy from d'Amboise or Bruhn or Eddie Villella or someone. And these people aren't fools, Jake. They know the difference between dazzling and dancing. So do I."

I didn't know how to answer him; not because of what he had said, but because of the utter nakedness of his voice. He stared at me in silence for a long time, and then suddenly he looked away, the break so sharp that it felt physical, painful. He said, "Anyway, I'm too short."

I laughed. I remember that. "What are you talking about? Even I know ballet dancers can't be tall—Villella's practically a midget, for God's sake—"

"No, he's not. And he's strong as a horse; he can lift his partners all day and not break a sweat. I can't do that." All these years, and I can still see the absolute, unarguable shame in his face. "My upper body's never going to be strong enough to do what it has to do. And I look wrong onstage, Jake. My legs are stubby, they spoil the line. It is that bloody simple, and I'm very glad someone finally laid it out for me. Now all I have to do is figure out what exactly to do with the rest of my life."

He stood up and walked out of the Automat, and by the time I got outside, he was gone. We didn't see each other for the rest of the summer, although we talked on the phone a couple of times. By then, thanks to sending out ninety-four sets of résumés, I actually had a job waiting for me after graduation, building sets and doing walk-ons for a rep company in Seattle. Over the next five years I worked my way down to the Bay Area, by way of theaters in Eugene and Portland and stock jobs all over Northern California. I've been here in Avicenna ever since.

But we did stay in contact, Sam and I. I broke the ice, sending light postcards from the summer tours, and then a real letter from my first real address—South Parnell Street, that was. Two rooms and a ficus plant.

He didn't answer for some while, long enough that I began to believe he never would. But when it did come, the letter began with typical abruptness, asking whether I remembered *The Body Snatcher,* an old Val Lewton movie we'd loved and seen half a dozen times.

> *Remember that splendid, chilling moment when Karloff says through his teeth, "And I have done some things that I did not want to do . . ."? Me these last several years. I'll tell you the worst straight off, and leave the rest to your imagination. No, not the year spent teaching folk-dancing in Junior High School 80—much worse than that. I am become an Arts Cricket! Pray for me. . . .*

We'd been using Gully Jimson's term for a critic ever since reading *The Horse's Mouth* in high school. Sam's letter went on to say that he was writing regularly for a brand-new Manhattan arts magazine, now and then for a couple of upstate papers, and lately even filing occasional dispatches to Japan:

> *I mostly review music, sometimes theater, sometimes movies, if the first-stringer's off at Sundance or Cannes. No, Jake, I don't ever cover dance. I don't dare write about dance, because I couldn't possibly be fair to people who are up there doing what I want to do more than I want anything in the world. Music, yes. I can manage music. . . .*

We wrote, and sometimes called, for another three years before we met again. I hope my letters weren't as full of myself as I'm sure they were: entirely concerned with what plays I'd auditioned for, what roles I should have gotten, what actors I scorned or admired; what celebrated director had seemed very impressed but never called back. Sam, on the other hand, recounted the astonishing success of *Ceilidh,* the new magazine, described every editor and photographer he worked with; detailed, with solemn hilarity, the kind of performance he was most often sent to cover. "Most of them are so far *avant* that they lap the field and become the *derrière-garde*. Try to imagine the Three Stooges on downers."

But of his own feelings and dreams, of his world beyond work, of how he lived without dancing—nothing, not ever. And there we left it until I came to New York for a smallish part in a goodish play that survived barely a month. It was to be my Broadway break, that one—to be in it I turned down a TV movie, which later spun off into a syndicated series that's probably still running somewhere. I have an infallible gift for picking the losing side.

I never regretted the gamble, though, for I stayed with Sam during our brief run. He had found a studio apartment in the West Seventies, half a block off Columbus: one huge, high room, a vestigial kitchen nook, a bathroom, a deep and sinister coat closet that Sam called "The Dark Continent," a solid wall of books, the two biggest stereo speakers I'd ever seen, and a mattress in a far corner. I slept on the floor by the stereo that month, in a tangle of quilts from his Brooklyn bedroom. It was the first time we'd ever spent together as adults, with jobs to go to instead of classes. We kept completely different hours, what with me being at the theater six nights and two afternoons a week, while Sam put in five full days at the magazine, and was likely to be off covering a performance in the evenings. Yet we bumbled along so comfortably that I can't recall a cross word between us—only an evening when something changed.

At the time I was skidding into my first marriage, a head-on collision, born of mutual misunderstandings, with the woman who was lighting the play. On the windy, rainy evening that the closing notice was posted, she and I had a fight about nothing, and I sulked my way back to Sam's place to find him practicing a Bach sarabande on his classical guitar. He wasn't very good, and he wouldn't ever be good, no matter how dutifully he worked at it, and to my shame I said so that night. "Give it up, Sam. You haven't made a dent in that poor Bach in all the time I've been here. Guitar's just not your instrument—it's like me and directing. I can't even get three people lined up properly for a photograph. It's not the end of the world."

It helped a bit on the flight to New York, staring at the fold-down tray in front of me for five hours, to remember that Sam didn't pay the least bit of attention to me. When the sarabande had lurched to a close, he said, "Jake, I don't have any illusions about the way I play. But I don't think anyone should write about music who doesn't have at least some idea of what it takes to make your fingers pull one clear note out of an instrument. Out of yourself."

"The guitar you keep hacking at. The thing you could *do*, you quit. Right." I can still hear the pure damn meanness in my voice.

Sam put the guitar away and began rummaging in the refrigerator for a couple of beers. His back was to me when he said, "Yes, well, I did have some illusions about my dancing." He hadn't used the word all during my visit. "But that's what they were, Jake, illusions, and I'm glad I understood that when I did. I haven't lost any sleep over them in . . . what? Years."

"You were good," I said. "You were terrific." Sam didn't turn or answer. Completely out of character, out of control, I kept pushing. "Ever wish you hadn't quit?"

"I still dance." For the first time since that long-ago lunch in the Automat, the voice was raw Brooklyn again, but much lower, a harsh mumble. "I take classes, I keep in shape." He did turn to face me then, and now there was anger in his eyes. "And no, Jake, I don't wish a damn thing. I'm just grateful that I had the sense to know what to stop wishing for. I didn't quit, I let go. There's a difference."

"Is there?"

What possessed me? What made me bait him, invade him so? The failure of the play, premonitions about my Lady of the Follow Spots? I have no more idea now than I did then. I said, "I've envied you half my life, you know that? You were born to be a dancer—*born*—and I've had to work my butt off just to be the journeyman I am." The words chewed their way out of me. "Sam, see, by now I know I'm never going to be anything more than pretty good. Professional, I'll settle for that. But you . . . you walked away from it, from your gift. I was so furious at you for doing that. I guess I still am. I really still am."

"That's your business," Sam said. His voice had gotten very quiet. "My loss is my loss, you don't get to deal yourself in. Sorry." He said it carefully, word by word, each one a branding iron. "I have enough trouble with my own dreams without living yours."

"What dreams?" I asked. He should have hit me then—not for the two words, but for the way I said them. I can still hear myself today, now, as I write this, and I am still ashamed.

But Sam smiled at me. Whatever else I manage to forget about my behavior that night, I'll always remember that he smiled. He said, "Anyway, you're a bloody good actor. You're much better than a journeyman." And he handed me a bottle of beer, and suddenly we were talking about my career, about me again. We weren't to have another moment that intense, that intimate, for a very long time.

Over the years I came east more often than he came west, unless he had a Seattle Opera *Ring* to cover, or a Los Angeles symphony conductor to interview. He published three books: one on a year spent with the musicians of the Lincoln Center orchestra, one on Lou Harrison, and one—my favorite—about Verdi's last four operas. They got fine reviews and neither sold nor stayed in print. But the studio apartment was rent-controlled, and *Ceilidh* flourished, to its own considerable surprise. Occasionally they were even able to send Sam abroad, to cover music festivals in England or Italy. He visited his parents—long retired in Fort Lauderdale—four times a year, had another floor-to-ceiling bookcase installed, and got a cat.

About the cat. It was an Abyssinian female, almost maroon in color, and even as a kitten she had the slouchy preen of a high-fashion model. Sam named her Millamant, after Congreve's wicked heroine. Because both of the women I married had been cat-lovers, Sam appointed me his feline expert, and called me almost every day during the first weeks of Millamant's residency. "She just sits in her litter box and stares—is that normal?" "She keeps catching moths in The Dark Continent—should I make her stop?" "Jake, I took her for her shots, and now she's mad at me. How long do cats stay mad?" "Is it all right for her to eat pizza?" Millamant grew up to look like a miniature mountain lion, the reigning *grande horizontale* of the studio, and whenever I slept on the floor, she honored me with her favors. Usually at three in the morning.

As for myself, I peaked early. Right or wrong about Sam's talent, I was bang on the money about my own. I've never worked in New York again, unless you count summer stock in Utica, and there have been stretches when a voiceover, a TV cameo, or residuals from a soap-opera guest shot were all that kept a roof over my head. It's mostly theater, especially the Pacific Rep, that pays the bills; but the only long-running stage gig I have ever had was as a villain in a camp 1890s melodrama, which inexplicably ran for five years at a tiny San Francisco theater. It coincided almost exactly with my second marriage; they closed in the same week. That one's a director, and she's good. I think she's off doing *Sweet Bird of Youth* in China right now.

All the same, for good or ill, I'm still doing what I'm fit for and living as I always wanted to live—just not quite as well as I'd imagined—and Sam wasn't. That was a wider gap by far than the continent that separated us, but we never again talked about it. Everything else, yes, on weekends, when the rates were down—everything else from politics, literature, and the general nature of the universe to shortstops and whether Oscar Alemán could really have been as good a guitarist as Django. We went along like that until Marianne.

No, we went along like that until *after* Marianne. After she'd moved in with him, and after she'd left him two months and five days later for a playwright who'd written a one-woman show about Duse for her. I borrowed plane fare to New York because of the way he sounded on the phone. He was fine all the way through the nice dinner at the deli, and fine through the usual amble along Columbus, twenty blocks or so down, twenty blocks back. It wasn't until we were in the apartment, until I'd found a hairbrush of Marianne's and casually asked him where I should put it, that he came apart. I held him awkwardly while he cried, and Millamant came down from the bookshelf where she generally lived to sniff at his tears and butt her hard round head against his chin. It was a very long night, and I don't know whether I did or said anything right or anything wrong for him. I was just with him, that's all.

He came to Avicenna more often after that, always spending at least a weekend, sleeping on a futon, content with my books and record albums if I was in rehearsal; ready for a walk on balmy evenings—he never quite lost the unmistakable near-waddle of the ballet dancer—equally easy with silences long grown as comfortable as the lazily circular arguments that might go on until one of us dozed off. I recall asking one midnight, during his last visit, "Do you remember what your dad used to say, every time he heard us discussing something or other?"

Sam laughed in the darkness. "'Those two, they're a couple of *alte kockers* already! Old men sitting in the park, squabbling about Tennessee Williams and Mickey Mantle.' Fifteen, sixteen, and he had us pegged."

I remember everything about that visit, when he holed up in my house for a full week, trying so determinedly to quit smoking. The walks got longer, to keep his mind off cigarettes; he managed quite well during the daytime, but the nights were hard, as I could tell from the smell in the bathroom most mornings. Even so, he cut down steadily until, a couple of days before he left, he got by on two half-smoked cigarettes, and we went out to my favorite Caribbean restaurant to celebrate. He had the jerk chicken and I had the *ropa vieja*.

There's an unmarked alley not far from my house that leads to a freeway overpass, and from there into a children's park as dainty and miniature as a scene in one of those gilded Victorian eggs. We walked there after dinner, talking obliquely of Marianne, for the first time in a long while, and of my ex-wives. It was when we stopped to drink at a child-size fountain that Sam said, "You know, when you think about it, you and I have been involved with a remarkable number of highly improbable women. I mean, for just two people."

"We could start a museum," I suggested. "The Museum of Truly Weird Relationships." That set us off. We walked round and round for hours, opening up the one aspect of our lives kept almost entirely private for all the years of our friendship. The public defender, the bookstore owner, the poet, the set designer, the truck mechanic—it doesn't matter which of us was embrangled with whom; only that the romances almost invariably ended as comedies of errors, leaving us to lick our wounds and shrug, and present our debacles to each other like wry trophies. We laughed and snorted, and said, "*What?*" and "Oh, you're *kidding*" and "You never said a word about that—that's a whole wing of the museum just by itself," until the children and their parents were all gone home, and we were the only two voices in the little park. It was just then that Sam told me about Emilia.

"She's too young," he said. "She is twenty-six-and-a-half years younger than I am, and she's from Metuchen, New Jersey, and she's not Jewish, and if you say either *bimbo* or *bunnyrabbit*, Jake, I will punch you right in the eye. I shouldn't have mentioned her, anyway. I don't think this one belongs in the Museum at all."

"Hoo-ha," I said. He looked at me, and I said, "Sorry, sorry, hoo-ha withdrawn—it's just I've never heard you sound like that. So. Would you maybe marry this one?"

"You're the chap who marries people. If I were the sort who gets married, I'd *be* married by now." He fell silent, and we walked on until we came to the swings and the sliding pond and the monkey bars. We sat down on the swings, pushing ourselves idly in small circles, letting our shoes scrape the ground. Sam said, "Emilia covers New York for a paper in Bergen County—that's how I met her, about a year ago. She takes the bus in on weekends."

"A journalist, yet. Not a cricket?"

"Good *night*, no, a real writer. If there were any real newspapers left, she'd have a real career ahead of her. I keep telling her to get into TV, but she hates it—she won't even watch the *News Hour*." He pushed off harder, gripping the chains of the swing and leaning back. "The whole thing's crazy, Jake, but it's not weird. It's just crazy." He looked over his shoulder at me and grinned suddenly. "But Millamant likes her."

"I'm jealous," I said, and I actually was, a little. Millamant doesn't like a lot of people. "She stays the weekend? And it works out?"

He was a heavy sleeper, and you had to be really careful about waking him, because he always came up fighting. I never knew why that was. Sam laughed then. "On top of everything, she's an insomniac. Only person I ever gave full permission to wake me up at any time. It works out."

"Hoo-*ha*. So she'll be moving in?"

Sam didn't answer for a long time. We swung together in the darkness, with no sound but the slow creak of the chains. Finally he said, "I don't think so. I think maybe I lost my nerve with Marianne." I started to say something, and then I didn't. Chains, owls, a few fireflies, the distant mumbling of the freeway. Sam said, "I couldn't go through that again. And it will happen again, Jake. Not for the same reasons, but it will."

"You don't know that," I said. "It works out sometimes, living with somebody. Not for me—I mean, both my marriages were absolute train wrecks—but there were good times even so, and they really might have worked. If I'd been different, or Elly had, or Suzette had. Anyway, it was worth it, pretty much. I wouldn't have missed it, I don't think."

"That," Sam said, pausing as precisely as our old hero Noël Coward would have done, "is the most inspirational tribute to the married state I've ever heard. You ought to crochet it into a sampler." He dropped lightly off the swing, and we went on walking, angling back the way we had come. Neither of us spoke again until we were on the overpass, looking down at the lights plunging toward the East Bay hills. Sam said, "She's not moving in. Millamant doesn't like her *that* much. But I want you to meet her, next time you come to New York. This one I want you to meet." I said I'd love to, and we walked on home.

At the airport, two nights later, we hugged each other, and I said, "Catch you next time, Jake." I don't remember when we started doing that at goodbyes, trading names.

"Next time, Sam. I'll call when I get home." He picked up his garment bag and started for the gate; then turned to flash me that fleeting grin out of childhood once more. "Keep a pedestal vacant in the Museum. You never know." And he was gone.

Marianne had Millamant, as it turned out when I made my way from JFK to her East Side town house. The Abyssinian met me at the door and immediately sprang to my shoulder, as she had always done whenever I arrived. Arthritis had set its teeth in her right hind leg since we last met, and it took her three tries, equally painful for us both. I tried to remove her, but Millamant wasn't having any. She dug her claws in even deeper, making a curious shrill sound I'd never heard from her before, and constantly pushing her head against my face. Her eyes were wide and mad.

"He's not with me," I said. "I'm sorry, cat. I don't know where he's gone."

Marianne—still all flying red hair and opening night, down to her gilded toenails—informed me that Sam hadn't left a will, which surprised me. He was always far neater than I, not merely about the apartment or his dress, but about his life in general. Letters were answered as they came in; his filing cabinet held actual alphabetized files; he always knew where his book and magazine contracts were; and he had a regular doctor and a real lawyer as well, who doubled as his literary agent. But there was no will in the filing cabinet, no will to be found anywhere.

"We'd been talking about it," the lawyer said defensively. "He was going to come in. Anyway, I've spoken to the parents, and they want you to act as executor."

I called Mike and Sarah from the lawyer's office. They were frail insect voices, clouded by age and distance and despair, static from deep space. Yes, they did wish me to be Sam's executor—yes, they would be grateful if I could clean out the apartment, sort his business affairs, and get the police to release his body, as soon as the coroner's report came in. Sarah asked after my mother and father.

The report said things like *myocardial infarction* and *ventricular fibrillation; death almost certainly instant*. We buried Sam in an Astroturf cemetery in Queens, within earshot of the Van Wyck Expressway. Mike and Sarah had managed to handle the funeral arrangements from Fort Lauderdale, which proved they remembered me well enough to know that I'd likely have wound up stashing their son in a Dumpster or a recycling tin. A limousine from the mortuary brought them to the funeral: they stepped out blinking against the sharp autumn sunlight, looking pale and small, for all the years in Florida. I went over to embrace them, and we had a moment to murmur incoherently together before two men in dark suits took them away to the grave site. I followed with Marianne, because there was no one else I knew.

It didn't surprise me. I'd learned long since that Sam preferred to keep the several worlds in which he moved—music, theater, journalism, ballet classes—utterly separate from each other. I'd known the names of some of his friends and colleagues for years, without ever meeting one. By the same token, I knew myself to be the entire mysterious, vaguely glamorous West Coast world into which he vanished once in a great while. Until now, it had all suited and amused me.

An old Friday-night poker acquaintance drifted up on my left as I stood at the coffin behind Mike and Sarah and the dark suits. We shook hands, and he whispered, "Yes, I know, I got fat," while I was still trying to remember his name. I never did.

The rabbi looked like a basketball player, and he hadn't known Sam. It was a generic eulogy, no worse for the most part than many I've sat through, until he fixed his shiny blue gaze on Mike and Sarah and started in about the tragedy of living to bury an only son. I turned away, eyeing the exits. Damn, Sam, if you hadn't stuck us with these damn ringside seats, we could slide out of here right now, and be on the second beer before anyone noticed. But he had to stay, so I did too.

That was when I saw the small dark woman standing alone. Not that she was physically isolated—you couldn't be in that crowd, and still see grave and rabbi—but her solitude, her apartness, was as plain as if she had been a homeless lunatic, trundling a Safeway cart, all by herself with God. She was looking at the rabbi, but not seeing or hearing him. I patted Marianne's arm and eased away. It's okay, Sam. I see her.

Close to, she was thin, and looked paler because of her dark hair and eyes. She looked older, too—I'm bad at ages, and I'd been braced for a schoolgirl in a leather miniskirt, but this woman had to be twenty-eight or twenty-nine, surely. I said quietly, "You're Emilia. He never told me your last name."

When she turned to face me, I saw that her nose must have been broken once, and not set quite right. The effect was oddly attractive, the bumpy bridge lending strength and age to a face whose adult bone structure had not yet finished its work. Only her eyes were a full-grown woman's eyes, an old woman's eyes just now. An intelligent, ordinary face that grief had turned shockingly beautiful.

"It's Rossi," she said. "Emily Rossi." Her voice was low, with the muffled evenness that comes with fighting not to cry. "Please, is there any chance at all that you could be Jacob Holtz?"

"Sam called me Jake," I answered. "We can go now."

As we started to move away, she paused and looked back at the rabbi, who was still telling Mike and Sarah what they felt about their loss. We could smell the raw earth from where we stood. She said softly, "I imagined going up to them, talking with them, letting them know that I loved him, too, that he didn't die alone. But he did, he did, and I'd never have the courage anyway." The back of her neck seemed as vulnerable as a small child's. She said, "He always called me Emilia."

Being an executor means, finally, cleaning the place up. In a legal sense, there wasn't that much for me to do, once the police had finally unsealed the apartment and released Sam's body for burial. Bills paid off, bank account closed out, credit cards canceled, Mike and Sarah's names replacing his on God knows how many computers—how little it takes, after all, to delete us from the Great Database. A heavenly keystroke, no more.

But somebody has to clean up, and the landlord was anxious to have Sam's apartment empty, ready to be rented again for quadruple what Sam had been paying. I spent all day every day for more than three weeks at the apartment, sorting my friend's possessions into ever more meaningless heaps, then starting over with a new system for determining what went or stayed. With electricity and telephone long since cut off, the place remained cold even when the sun was shining in the windows, and tumultuous Columbus Avenue outside looked so remote, so unattainable, that I felt like an astronaut marooned on the moon.

Emily Rossi—Sam's Emilia—came all the way from New Jersey almost every day, inventing assignments for herself as a partial cover. She usually arrived at the apartment around noon; though sometimes she would bring a sleeping bag and a cassette player—and Millamant, whom Marianne was happy to relinquish—stay the night, and be at work before I got there. I was uneasy about that, but Emilia liked it. "I was always happy here," she said. "This was my safe place, with Sam. I want to be here as long as I can."

I was grateful for her presence, in part because she was far less sentimental than I about most of Sam's belongings. Not all of them: once she had been folding and setting aside clothes for donation (gangster suit apart, his wardrobe could have been worn by the average British prime minister), when I returned from one more trek through the uncharted depths of The Dark Continent to find her rocking back and forth, dry-eyed, holding a gray silk shirt tightly against her cheek.

"The first time he ever held me," she whispered. "Look," and she turned the shirt so that I could see the scattering of faded brown stains on one sleeve. "My blood," Emilia said. "It got all over him, but he never even noticed."

I stared at her. She said, "There was a man. I stopped seeing him before I ever met Sam. He followed me. He caught me on the street one day—downtown, near Port Authority." She touched her nose quickly, and then the area around her left eye. "I don't know how I got away from him. I knew somebody at *Ceilidh*, but I don't remember going there. The only thing I'm clear on, even today, is that somebody was holding me, washing my face, talking to me, so gently. It turned out to be Sam."

She kept turning the shirt in her hands, revealing other bloodstains. "He called the police, he called an ambulance, he went with me to the hospital. And when they wouldn't keep me, even overnight, he took me home with him and fed me, and gave me his bed. I stayed three days."

"It's the feeding part that awes me," I said. "I could see everything else, but Sam didn't cook for anybody. Sam didn't even make coffee."

"Chinese takeout. Mexican takeout. For a special treat, sushi." She smiled then, sniffling only slightly. "He took care of me, Jake. I wasn't used to it, it made me really nervous for a while." She turned sharply away from me, looking toward the corner where the bed had stood. "I was getting used to it, though. Tell me some more about how he was in high school."

So I told her more, day by day, as we worked, and the apartment grew emptier and even colder, and somehow smaller. I told her about writing songs, doing homework together, playing silly board games late at night, and about trying to sneak into jazz clubs when we were too young to be admitted legally. I told her everything I could about what it was like to see him dance at seventeen. In return, Emilia told me about Adventures:

"The phone would ring late at night, and I'd hear this hissing, sinister, Bulgarian secret-service voice telling me to be at Penn Station or Grand Central with a rose in my teeth at nine the next morning, and to look for a man in dark glasses carrying an umbrella, a rubber duck, and a rolled-up copy of *Der Spiegel*. And we'd each skulk around the station, with people staring at us, until we met, and wind up taking

Amtrak to anywhere—to Tarrytown or Rhinecliff or Annandale—still being spies on the Orient Express the whole way. We'd spend the night, go out on a river tour, visit the old estates and museums, buy really dumb souvenirs, and never once break character until we walked out of the station again—back in the city, back in real life. And that was an Adventure."

Her eyes never filled when she talked to me about their outings, but they stopped seeing me, stopped seeing Millamant roaming her old home step by crouching step, stalking ghosts. Emilia's eyes were doing just the same. "We took turns—one time I rented a car and took him to the caverns in Schoharie County, up near Cobleskill. We were agents who didn't speak each other's language, so we had to make up other ways to communicate." Millamant climbed into her lap, batted at her chin, bit it lightly, and put her paws on Emilia's shoulders. Emilia put her aside, but she kept coming back, meowing fiercely.

It lasted almost a year and a half, counting two separate weeks of vacation: one spent being international spies in Saratoga Springs, and one being contract assassins trailing a famously vicious theater critic who lived in Kingston. "We were always aliens, one way or another, always foreigners, outsiders, Martians. That was the whole thing about Adventures—just having each other, and our secret mission."

On the last day, with everything of Sam's packed up, sold, given away, donated or dumped, and the apartment echoing, even with our breath, we made one last pass through the shrunken Dark Continent in search of Sam's guitar. We never found it. I still worry over that, at very odd hours, wondering whether he might have given it up because of what I said to him on that bad night long ago. I swept the floor while Emilia picked up our own debris and shoehorned an unusually recalcitrant Millamant into her traveling case. Then we hugged each other goodbye, and stood back, awkward and unhappy, in that cold, empty place.

"Write," she said. "Please." I nodded, and Emily said, "There's only you for me to talk to about him now."

I hugged her again. Inside the case Millamant was making a sound like a jammed garbage disposal, and Emilia laughed, bending to admonish her through the wire mesh. Her dark hair was gray with dust, but she looked very young in that moment, even her eyes.

For the next year—almost two—we wrote more letters than I've ever exchanged with anyone except Sam, and that includes anybody I ever married. How Emilia managed to balance her output against her newspaper work, I can't guess; it was tricky enough for me—especially once Christmas Carol rehearsals started—to drag myself out of Bob Cratchit's intolerably benign consciousness back into my own sullen grief. And after wretched Cratchit came Canon Chasuble, Mr. Peachum, Grandpa Vanderhof, St. Joan's Earl of Warwick . . . actually that wasn't a bad run of roles, thinking about it. Though I should have at least read for Macheath.

But I still wrote to Emilia two and three times a week, unearthing for her sake, and my own, moments as long forgotten as Sam's youthful terror of FBI agents coming back to interrogate his father once more about Mike's ten-minute membership in the Communist Party. I rooted through tattered, filthy cardboard boxes to find fragments of the songs we'd written together. I even woke her up one night, calling with a remembrance of our one attempt at fishing, out on Sheepshead Bay, that couldn't wait until morning. Irrational, surely, but I was suddenly afraid of forgetting for another forty years.

Emilia wrote to me about living without Adventures. She wrote about answering the phone at work or at home, knowing that she might hear any voice on the planet except the whisper of the mad Bulgarian spy, enticing her away to ridiculous escapades in the dark wilds of the Catskills.

But I don't believe it, any of it, either way. I don't believe that

> *it'll be him on the phone, but at the same time I still can't believe that I won't ever hear him again. Nothing makes sense. I do my work, and I go home, and I cook my meals and eat them, and I pick up the phone when it rings, but I'm really always waiting for the call after this one....*

Once she wrote, "Thank you for always calling me Emilia. I liked her so much—she was so passionate and adventurous, so different from Emily. I was sure Emilia died with Sam, but now I don't know. Maybe not."

For my part, writing usually at night, often when rehearsals had run late and I was weary enough that memory and language both tangled with dream, the stories I told of Sam and myself were as true as phoenixes, as imaginary as computers. Things we had done flowed together with things we had always meant to do, things that I think I felt we would have done, once Emilia believed them. I recalled for her the time that Sam had withered a school bully with a retort so eviscerating that it would have gotten us both killed had it ever actually been spoken. I even dredged up a certain Adventure of our own, in which we tracked a celebrated Russian poet (recognized crossing Ninth Avenue by Sam, of course) back to his hotel, and then—at Sam's insistence—returned early the next morning to haunt the elevator until he came down to breakfast, which we wound up sharing with him. "He defected a few days later, and got a university gig in San Diego. Sam always felt it was the Froot Loops that did it." Well, Sam did spot the poet on the street, and we did follow him until we lost him in Macy's. And Russian poets did defect, and maybe it all practically happened just that way. Why shouldn't it have?

What Emilia was after in my memories of Sam, what she needed to live on, was no different from what I needed still: not facts, but the accuracy under and around and beyond facts. Not a recital of events—not even honesty—but truth. Résumés have their place, but there's no nourishment in them.

Emilia arrived weary at the Oakland Airport, looking as small and windblown as she had at Sam's funeral. But her eyes were bright, and when she smiled to recognize me I saw her meeting my friend, her lover, in Penn Station to embark on one more Adventure. It wasn't entirely meant for me, that smile.

Millamant herself had apparently been quite docile on the flight from New York—even banging around on the luggage conveyor belt didn't seem to have fazed her. Uncaged in my house, she didn't exhibit any of the usual edginess of a cat in strange surroundings: she stretched here, strolled there, leisurely investigated this and that, as though getting reacquainted, and finally curled herself in the one good chair, plainly waiting for the floor show to begin. I looked at Emilia, who shrugged and said, "Like the washing machine when the repairman arrives. Wait. You'll see."

"See what? What the Baptist hell are we waiting for?"

"Dinner," Emilia said firmly. "Take me out to that Caribbean place—I don't know the name. The one where you took Sam."

I hadn't been back since the time we celebrated his being down to two cigarettes a day. I ordered the *ropa vieja* again. I don't remember what Emilia had. We talked about Sam, and about her work for the Bergen County newspaper—she'd recently won a state journalism award for a series on day-care facilities—and I went into serious detail regarding the technical and social inadequacies of the Pacific Rep's new artistic director. We didn't discuss Millamant at all.

The evening was warm, and there was one of those glossy, perfect half-moons that seem too brilliant for their size. We walked home the long way, so that I could show Emilia the little park where Sam had told me about her. We sat on the swings, as I'd done with Sam, and she told me then, "He lied about his age, you know. I didn't realize it until you told me you were two months younger. He'd been taking seven years off, all the time I knew him. As though it would have mattered to me."

I'd had a second margarita with dinner. I said, "He was two months and eleven days older than I am. We were both born just after three in the morning, did he ever tell you that? I was about an ounce and a half heavier." And *whoosh,* I was crying. I didn't *start* to cry—I was crying, and I was always going to be crying. Emilia held me without a word, as I'd once held Sam when he wept just as hopelessly, just as endlessly. I have no idea how long it went on. When it stopped, we walked the rest of the way in silence, but Emilia tucked her arm through mine.

Back home, we settled in the kitchen (which is bigger and more comfortable than my living room) with a couple of cappuccinos. The director ex-wife took the piano, but I hung on to the espresso machine. Emilia said, "I was thinking on the flight—you and I have already known each other longer than I knew Sam. We had such a short time."

"You learned things about him I never bothered to find out in forty years. I thought we had forever."

Emilia was silent for a while, sipping her coffee. Then she said, very softly, not looking at me, "You see, I never thought that. Some way, I always understood that there wasn't going to be a happy ending for us. I never said it to myself, but I *knew.*" She did look straight at me then, her eyes clear and unmisted, but her mouth too straight, too determinedly under control. "I think he did, too."

I couldn't think of an answer to that. We chatted a little while longer, and then Emilia went to bed. I stayed up late, reading *Heartbreak House* one more time—no one's ever likely to ask me to play Captain Shotover, but the readiness is all—had one last futile look-around for Millamant, and turned in myself. I slept deeply and contentedly for what seemed like a good fifteen minutes before Emilia shook me out of one of the rare dreams where I know my lines, whispering frantically, "Jake—Jake come and see, hurry, you have to see! Jake, hurry, it's her!"

The half-moon was shining so brightly on the kitchen table that I could see the little sticky rings where our coffee cups had been. I remember that, just as I remember the shuddery hum of the refrigerator and the *bloop* of the leaky faucet, and a faint scratching sound that I couldn't place right away. Just as I remember Millamant dancing.

It's a large table, older than I am, and it lurches if you lean on it, let alone dance. I don't know how Millamant even climbed up, arthritic back leg and all, but there she floated, there she spun, tumbling this way, sailing that, one minute a kitten, the next a kite; moving so lightly, and with such precision, that the table never rocked once, but seemed to be the one moving impossibly fast, while Millamant drifted over it as slowly as she chose, hanging in the air for exactly as long as she chose. She was so old that her back claws no longer retracted entirely—that was the scratching noise—but she danced the way human beings have always dreamed of dancing, and never have, not the best of them. No one has ever danced like Millamant.

Neither of us could look away, but Emilia leaned close and whispered, "I've seen her three times. I couldn't talk about it on the phone." Her face was absolutely without color.

Millamant stopped so suddenly that both Emilia and I leaned toward her, as though it had been the planet that halted. Millamant dropped down onto all fours, paced to the edge of the table and stood looking at us out of once-golden eyes gone almost tea-brown with age. She was breathing rapidly, and trembling all over. She said, "Emilia. Jake."

How can I say what it was like? To hear a cat speak—to hear a cat speak our names—to hear a cat speak them in a voice that was unmistakably Sam's voice, and yet not Sam's, not a voice at all. Her mouth remained slightly open, but her jaws did not move: the words were coming through her, not out of her, without inflection, without any sort of cadence, without any trace of a homemade English accent. Millamant said, "Jake. Clean your glasses."

I wear glasses, except onstage, and the lenses are always messier than I ever notice. It used to drive Sam crazy. I took them off. Millamant—or what was using Millamant—said, "I love you, Emilia."

Beside me, Emilia's breath simply stopped. I didn't dare look at her. I had all I could do to babble idiotically, "Sam? Sam? Where have you been? Sam, are you really in there?"

At that Millamant actually seemed to raise an eyebrow, which was unlikely, since cats don't have eyebrows. She—Sam—*it* said quite clearly, "You want I should wave?" And she did raise a front paw to gesture in my direction. Her ears were flicking and crumpling strangely, as though someone who didn't know how a cat's ears work were trying to lay them back. "As to where I've been—" the toneless march of syllables faltered a little "—it comes and goes. Talk to me."

Emilia's face was still so pale that the color on her cheekbones stood out like tribal scars. I don't know what I looked like, but I couldn't make a sound. Emilia took a step forward, her hands out, but Millamant immediately backed away. "Talk to me. Please, talk to me. Tell me why we're all here, tell me anything. Please."

So we sat in the kitchen, Emilia and I, talking to an old cat as we would have talked to our dear lost friend, solemnly telling her our commonplace news of work and family, of small travels and travails, of his parents in Miami, of how it had been for us in the last two years. Our voices stumbled over each other, often crumbling into tears of still-untrusted joy, then immediately skidding off into broken giggles to hear ourselves earnestly assuring Millamant, "It's been a miserable couple of theater seasons—absolutely nothing you'd have liked." Millamant looked from one to the other of us, her eyes fiercely attentive, sometimes nodding like a marionette. Emilia clutched my hand painfully tightly, but she was smiling. I have never seen a smile like that one of Emilia's ever again.

She was saying, "And Jake and I have been writing and writing to each other, talking on the phone, telling each other everything we remember—things we didn't know we remembered. Things *you* maybe wouldn't remember. Sam, we missed you so. I missed you." When she reached out again, Millamant avoided her touch for a moment; then suddenly yielded and let herself rest between Emilia's hands. The arid, rasping voice said, "Behind the ears. Finally, a body I can dance in, but I can't figure out about scratching."

Nobody said anything for a while. Emilia was totally involved in caressing Millamant, and I was feeling more and more like the most flagrant voyeur. I didn't have to look at Emilia's face, or listen to Millamant's purring; merely to watch those yearning hands at work in the thin, patchy fur was to spy on an altogether private matter. I make jokes when I'm edgy. I said to Emilia, "Be careful—he could be a *dybbuk*. It'd be just like him."

Emilia, not knowing the Yiddish word, looked puzzled; but Millamant let out a brief, contemptuous yowl, a feline equivalent of Sam's old *Oh,* good *night!* snort of disdain. "Of course, I'm not a bloody *dybbuk*! Don't you read Singer? A *dybbuk*'s a wandering soul, demons chasing it all around the universe—it needs a body, a place to hide. Not me—nobody's chasing me." The voice hesitated slightly for a second time. "Except maybe you two."

I looked at Emilia, expecting her to say something. When she didn't, I finally mumbled—just as lamely as it reads—"We needed to talk about you. We didn't have anyone else to talk to."

"If not for Jake," Emilia said. "Sam, if it weren't for Jake, if he hadn't known me at your funeral—" she caught her breath only momentarily on the word "—Sam, I would have disappeared. I'd have gone right on, like always, like everybody else, but I would have disappeared."

Millamant hardly seemed to be listening. She said thoughtfully, "I'll be damned. I'm hungry."

"I'll make you a *quesadilla,*" I said, eager to be doing something practical. "Cheese and scallions and Ortega diced chilies—I've still got a can from the last time you were here. Take me ten minutes."

The look both Millamant and Emilia gave me was pure cat. I said, "Oh. Right. Wet or dry?"

Nothing in life—nothing even in Shakespeare—adequately prepares you for the experience of opening a can of Whiskas with Bits O' Beef for your closest friend, who's been dead for two years. Millamant ambled over to the battered stoneware dish that Emilia had brought with her from New York, sniffed once, then dug in with a voracity I'd never seen in either Sam or her. She went through that red-brown glop like a snowplow, and looked around for more.

Scraping the rest into her dish, I couldn't help asking, "How can you be hungry, anyway? Are you the one actually tasting this stuff, or is it all Millamant?"

"Interesting point." The Abyssinian had Whiskas on her nose. "It's Millamant who needs to eat—it's Millamant getting the nourishment—but I think I'm beginning to see why she likes it. Very odd. Sort of the phantom of a memory of taste. A touch of nutmeg would help."

She dived back into her dinner, obliviously, leaving Emilia and me staring at each other in confusion so identical that there was no need to speak, possibly ever again. Emilia finally managed to ask, "What do we do now?" and I answered, "Like a divorce. We work out who gets custody, and who gets visiting rights."

Emilia said, "She doesn't belong to us. She was Sam's cat, and he's . . . returned."

"To take possession, as you might say. Right. We can't even be certain that she's exactly a cat anymore, what with Sam in residence." I realized that I was just this side of hysterical, and closing fast. "Emilia, you'd better take him—her—them—home with you. I'm an actor, I pretend for a living, and this is altogether too much reality for me. You take Millamant home—what I'll do, I'll just call on the weekends, the way we used to do. Sam and I."

I don't know what Emilia would have said—her eyes were definitely voting for scooping up Millamant that very moment and heading for the airport—but the cat herself looked up from an empty dish at that moment to remark, in the mechanical tone I was already coming to accept as Sam, "Calm down, Jake. You're overplaying again."

It happens to be one of my strengths as an actor that I never overplay. The man saw me act exactly three times after high school, and that makes him an expert on my style. I was still spluttering as Millamant sat down in the kitchen doorway, curling her tail around her hind legs.

"Well," the voice said. "I'm back. Where I'm back *from*—" and it faltered momentarily, while Millamant's old eyes seemed to lose all definition between iris and pupil "—where I'm back from doesn't go into words. I don't know what it really is, or where—or when. I don't know whether I'm a ghost, or a zombie, or just some kind of seriously perturbed spirit. If I were a *dybbuk,* at least I'd know I was a *dybbuk,* that would be something." Millamant licked the bit of Whiskas off her nose. "But here I am anyway, ready or not. I can talk, I can dance—my God, I can *dance*—and I'm reunited with the only two people in the world who could have summoned me. Or whatever it was you did."

Abruptly she began washing her face, making such a deliberate job of it that I was about to say something pointed about extended dramatic pauses, when Sam spoke again. "But for how long? I could be gone any minute, or I could last as long as Millamant lasts—and she could go any minute herself. What happens then? Do I go off to kitty heaven with her—or do I find myself in Jake's blender? One of Emilia's angelfish? What happens then?"

Nobody answered. Millamant sat up higher on her haunches, until she looked like the classic Egyptian statue of Bastet, the cat goddess. Out of her mouth Sam said very quietly, "We don't know. We have no idea. I certainly wish somebody had read the instruction manual."

"There wasn't any manual," I said. "We didn't know we were summoning you—we didn't know we were doing anything except missing you, and trying to comfort ourselves the best we could." I was calming down, and paradoxically irritable with it. "Not everybody has people wishing for him so hard that they snatch him right back from death. I'm sorry if we woke you."

"Oh, I was awake." The cold voice was still soft and faraway. "Or maybe not truly awake, but you can't quite get to sleep, either. Jake . . . Emilia . . . I can't tell you what it's like. I'm not even sure whether it's death—or maybe that's it, that's just it, that's really the way death is. I can't tell you."

"Don't," Emilia whispered. She picked Millamant up again and held her close against her breast, not petting her.

Sam said, "It's like the snow on a TV set, when the cable's out. People just sit watching the screen, expecting the picture to come back—they'll sit there for an hour, more, waiting for all those whirling, crackling white particles to shape themselves back into a face, a car, a box of cereal—*something*. Try to think how it might feel to be one of those particles." He said nothing more for a moment, and then added, "It's not like that but try to imagine it anyway."

Whereupon Millamant fell asleep in Emilia's arms, and was carried off to bed in the guest room. She sauntered out the next morning, looking demurely pleased with herself, shared Emilia's yogurt, topped that off with an entire can of Chunky Chicken, went back to sleep on a fragrant pile of new-dried laundry, woke presently, and came to find me in the living room, settle briskly onto my lap and issue instructions. Fondling your best friend's tummy and scratching his vibrating throat for a solid hour at a time may possibly be weirder than responding to his demand for more kibble. I'm still not sure.

Presently he remarked, in that voice that wasn't him and wasn't human, and was yet somehow Sam, "In case I haven't said it, I'm very happy to see you, Jake."

"I'm happy to see you, too." I stopped petting him once we were talking: it felt wrong. "I just wish I could . . . *see* you."

Sam didn't laugh—I don't think he could—but a sort of odd grumbly ripple ran through Millamant's body. "You surprise me. You didn't actually plan to have me come back with fleas and hair balls?"

"Just like old times," I said, and Millamant did the ripple thing again. "Truth is, I think it's easier to accept you like this than it would be if you'd showed up in some other person's body. You always had a lot in common with Millamant."

"Did, didn't I?" For a moment the words were almost lost in Millamant's deep purr. "We both love peach yogurt, and having things on our own terms. But I couldn't dance like Millamant the best day I ever saw. Jake, you don't *know*—when she was a kitten, pouncing and skittering around the apartment, I used to watch her for hours, wondering if it wasn't too late, if I could still make my body learn something from her that it never could learn from anyone else. Even now, old as she is, you can't imagine how it feels. . . ." He was silent for so long that I thought Millamant must have fallen asleep once more; but then he said suddenly, "Jake. Maybe you should send me back."

Emilia was in the guest bedroom, talking on the phone to her editor in New Jersey, so there was just me to be flabbergasted. When I had words again, I said, "Send you? We don't even know how you got here in the first place, and you don't know where *back* is. We couldn't send you anywhere the BMT doesn't run." No furry ripple out of Millamant. "Why would you want to? To leave us again?"

"I don't ever want to leave." Millamant's dull claws dug harder into my leg than they should have been able to. "If I were in a rat's body, a cockroach's body, I'd want to stay here with you, with Emilia. But it feels strange here. Not wrong, but not—not *proper.* I don't mean me inhabiting a cat—I mean me still being me, Sam Kagan still aware that I'm Sam Kagan. However you look at it, this is a damn afterlife, Jake, and I don't believe in an afterlife. Dead or alive, I don't."

"And being part of the snow on a television screen, that's an improvement? That's proper?"

Sam didn't answer for a time. Millamant purred drowsily between my hands, and my Betty Boop clock ticked (at certain times of day, you can almost pretend she's dancing the Charleston), and in the guest bedroom Emilia laughed at something. Finally Sam said, "You see, I don't think I was always going to be TV snow. There was more to it. I can't tell you how I knew that. I just did."

I unhooked a rear claw from my thigh. "Purgatory as a function of the cable system. Makes sense, in a really dumb way."

Sam said, "There was more. I don't know that I missed anything much, but there was more coming. And if it's an afterlife, then the word means something they never told us about. I don't think there is a word for it—what I was waiting for. But it wasn't this."

Emilia hung up and came out to us then, and Millamant stopped talking. Instead, she leaped down from my lap, landing with the precise abandon of a cat ten years younger, and began to dance. Last night it had been for herself—at least, until we showed up—this time the dance was entirely for us, Sam showing off joyously, taking the whole room as his stage, as Millamant swam in the air from chair to bookcase and flashed like a dragonfly between bookcase and stereo, setting a rack of tape cassettes vibrating like castanets. Partnering my furniture, she swung around my three-foot-high Yoruba fetish, mimicking Gene Kelly in *Singin' in the Rain*; then whirled across the room by spinning bounds, only to slow to a liquidly sensuous cat—waltz in and out of the striped shadows of my window blinds. I couldn't remember ever seeing Sam dance like that: so much in authority that he could afford to release his body on its own recognizance. Millamant finished with a sudden astonishing flare of pirouettes from a standing start, and jetéed her way into Emilia's lap, where she purred and panted and said nothing. Emilia petted her and looked at me, and we didn't say anything either.

Neither of us said anything after that about Emilia's taking Sam home with her. She spent all ten days of her leave like an inheritance at my house. Sly smiles, grotesquely rolled eyes and hasty thumbs-up signs from my neighbors made their opinion of my new little fling eminently clear. I really can't blame them: we almost never went out, except for a meal or a brief walk, and we must have seemed completely absorbed in one another when they saw us at all. But what they'd have thought of the hours we passed, day and night, watching an old Abyssinian cat dance all over my house, let alone arguing with the cat about afterlives and the last World Series . . . no, it would have broken their hearts if I'd told them. Mine is a very dull neighborhood.

There was never a chance of anything happening between us, Emilia and me. We had grown far too close to be lovers: we were almost brother and sister in Sam, if that makes any sense at all. Once, midway through her visit, she was ironing her clothes in the kitchen when I came in to fill the cat dish and the water bowl. She watched in silence until I was done, and then she said with a sudden half-strangled violence, "I hate this! I can't bear to see you doing that, putting food down for him. It's not—" and she seemed to be fighting her own throat for a word "—it's not honest!"

We stared at each other across the ironing board. I said slowly, "Honest? How did honesty get into this?"

"Did I say that?" She scrubbed absently at her forehead with the back of her hand. "I don't know, I don't know what I meant. If he's Sam, then he shouldn't be eating on the floor, and if he's Millamant, then he shouldn't be making her dance all the time. She's old, Jake, and she's got arthritis, and Sam's dancing her like a child making his toys fly and fight. And it's so beautiful, and he's so *happy*—and I never saw him dance, the way you did, and I can't believe how beautiful . . ."

She didn't start to cry. Emilia doesn't cry. What happens is that she loses speech—when Sam died, she couldn't speak for three days—and the few sounds she does make are not your business or mine. I went to her then, and she buried her face in the ruinous gray cardigan I wear around the house, and we just stood together without speaking. And yes, all right, there was an instant when she held me hard, tilting her head back so we could look at each other. I felt very cold, and my lips started to tingle most painfully. But neither of us moved. We stood there, very deliberately letting the moment pass, feeling it pass, more united in that wordless choice than we could have been in any other way. Emilia went back to folding her ironing, and I took the garbage out and paid some bills.

Then I spent some time studying Millamant. The cat didn't seem to be suffering, nor to object to being sported and soared and exalted all around my house, day and night. But the bad back leg was plainly lamer than ever; her eyes were streaked and her claws ragged and broken, and for all the serious eating she was doing, she was thinner than she had arrived, if you looked. Playing host to Sam—playing barre and floor, costume, makeup, mirror to Sam, more accurately—was literally consuming her. I couldn't know whether she understood that or not. It didn't matter to me. That was the terrible thing, and all I can say is that at least I knew it was terrible.

The next evening was a warm one, pleasantly poignant with the smell of my next-door neighbor's jasmine, and of distant rain. Sam/Millamant hadn't danced at all that day, but had spent it necking and nuzzling with Emilia, taking naps with her and exchanging murmured *do-you-remembers*. We sat together on my front steps: a perfectly ordinary couple with a drowsy old cat in the long California twilight. I made small talk, fixed small snacks, felt my throat getting smaller and smaller, and finally blurted, "You were right. I can't say if it's honest or not, but it's no good. What do we do about it?"

Emilia petted Millamant and didn't meet my eyes. Three high school boys ambled past, slamming a basketball into one another's chests by turns, their talk as incomprehensible as Czech or Tamil, and strangely more foreign. I said again, "Sam, it's no good. I don't mean for Millamant—I mean for you, for your *ka* or your karma, or whatever I'm talking to right now. This can't be what you're supposed to be . . . doing, I guess. Emilia made me see."

In a very small voice, still not looking at me, Emilia said, "I changed my mind." I remember to this day how sad she sounded, and how neither Sam nor I paid any attention to her. An errant Irish setter, outrunning his jogger mistress, wandered up to say hello to everybody's crotch, but Millamant spat viciously and scratched his nose as Sam said, "I told you you ought to send me back. I did tell you, Jake."

I started to answer him, but Emilia interrupted. "No," she said, much louder now. "No, I don't care, I *can't*, never mind what I said. I don't care about Millamant, I don't care about anybody except Sam. I just want Sam back, any way I can have him. *Any* way. It's disgraceful, I know it's disgraceful, and I don't care."

She bent over Millamant, who slipped away from her as a yellow-haired young man in a Grateful Dead T-shirt and Bermuda shorts strode by, pumping his arms like a power-walker, totally absorbed in laughing, comradely conversation with his Walkman. I still see him, most days—it's been years now. Sometimes he's quite angry with the Walkman, but mostly he laughs.

Very gently for a voice out of a P.A. system in bad repair, Sam said, "He's right, Emilia. And you were right the first time. I have to go."

"Go where?" she cried. "You don't even know, you said so yourself. You could end up someplace worse than your damn TV screen—you could lose yourself for good, no Sam anymore, in the whole universe, not the least bit of Sam, not ever, not ever." She stopped herself with a jolt that was actually audible—you could hear it in her chest. Newspaper reporters probably aren't allowed hysterics. With actors it's part of the Equity contract.

"Maybe that's the idea." Millamant sat down and scratched—very professionally, I noticed. "Maybe that's it—maybe you're not supposed to come back as the least bit of yourself, but to be completely scattered, diffused, starting over as someone utterly different. I almost like that." And the mechanical voice sounded in that moment more like my Sam—thoughtful, amused, truly savoring doubt—than it ever had.

Emilia was hugging herself, rocking herself slightly. She said, "I couldn't bear to lose you twice. I'm telling you now, I have no shame, I don't care. I don't care if you show up as a—an electric can opener. Don't leave me again, Sam."

Only a few of the cars going by had turned their headlights on, but all the porch lights were lit now, and the lawn sprinklers hissing to life, and I could smell Vietnamese cooking two houses down, and Indian cooking clear across the street. Two young women in identical jogging suits walked past, each carrying a pizza box and a six-pack. Millamant walked slowly to Emilia, climbed into her lap and stood up—surprisingly firm on the bad back leg—to put her paws on each side of Emilia's neck.

"Matter can neither be created nor destroyed," Sam said. "Didn't they teach you that in high school, out in frontier Metuchen? *Listen!*" for she had turned her head away and would not even touch Millamant. "*Listen*—when I was a speck, a dot, nothing but a flicker of TV snow, I knew you. Do you understand me? By the time you and Jake got me back here, I had already forgotten my own name, I'd forgotten that there was ever such an idea as Sam Kagan. But I was a speck that remembered Emilia Rossi's birthday, remembered that Emilia Rossi loves cantaloupe and roast potatoes and bittersweet chocolate, and absolutely cannot abide football, her cousin Teddy, or Wagner. There's no way in this universe that I could be reduced to something so microscopic, so anonymous that it wouldn't know *Emilia Rossi.* If they give my atoms a fast shuffle and shake most of them out on some other planet, there'll still be one or two atoms madly determined to evolve into something that can carve Emilia Rossi on a tree. Or whatever they've got on the damn planet. I promise you, that's the truth. Are you listening to me, Emilia?"

"I'm listening," she said dully. She still would not look at Millamant. "You'll never forget me, wherever you are—or *whatever.* Wonderful. But you're leaving."

Millamant bumped her head hard against Emilia's chin, forcing her to turn her head. Sam said, "I don't belong here. You knew it before Jake did—probably before I knew myself. It's all I want in any world, but it's not right. Let me go, Emilia."

"Let you go?" Emilia was so outraged that she stood up, dumping Millamant off her lap. "What hold did I ever have on you, living or dead? What about Jake? Why don't you ask Jake if he'd be so kind as to . . ." And her voice went. Completely. I told you it happens with Emilia.

I put my arms around her. An old couple passing by nodded benignly at us through the dusk. I looked at my friend in the ancient eyes of a cat, and I said, "She's not going to understand. If you're going, go."

"You'll explain to her?" The robot voice couldn't possibly sound desperate, any more than it could convey anger or love, but I felt Sam's grief in my body, even so. "You'll make her see?"

"I won't make her do anything." I ached for Sam, but I was holding Emilia. "I'll do the best I can. Go already."

Millamant didn't approach Emilia again, so she never saw the last look that Sam gave her. But I did, and I told her about it afterward. Then Millamant scampered up the steps, lightly as a kitten, and began to dance.

My front porch could be better described as a catwalk with a railing. You can't even rock on it in comfort—your feet keep hitting things—and it's the last place you'd imagine as a dance floor, even for a small domestic animal. But Sam used to tell me, when we were young and I'd been awed by the flamboyance of some performer's style, "Good *night,* Jake, anybody can throw himself around Lincoln Center—all that takes is space and a little energy. The real ones can dance in a broom closet; they can stand on line at a checkout counter and be dancing right there. The real ones." And Millamant was a real dancer, that one last time on my checkout line of a porch.

I can't be sure of what I saw through the gathering dark then and the gathering years now. Millamant seemed to me to be moving almost on point, if you can imagine that in a cat, but moving with a kind of ardent restraint in which every stillness implied a leap at the throat, and violence trembled in the shadow of rigor. At moments she appeared to be standing completely motionless, letting the twilight dance around her, courting her like a proper partner. There should have been a moon, but there wasn't: only my rust-colored bug light to catch the glitter of her eyes and the ripple of her fur: So the one thing I am certain about, even at this dim distance, is that that dance was entirely for Emilia. Not for me, not for Emilia and me together, like that first time. Emilia.

She wouldn't look at first. She turned her head completely away, staring blindly back at the street, one hand clenching white on a fold of my sweater. So something else I can't say is just when the dance took hold of her, drawing her gently home to what Sam and Millamant, Millamant, too—were telling her forever. All I know is that she was crouched beside me, paying such attention, *paying,* as I never paid to my wives, my directors, or to Sam himself, at the moment when someone's headlights played briefly over us and it was only Millamant there, limping down the steps to clamber heavily into Emilia's lap and lie there, not purring. Only old Abyssinian Millamant, tired and lame, and uninhabited.

I also don't remember when it was that I said, "He made us let him go. He danced us away from thinking about him, holding him. Just for that little, but it was all he needed." Emilia didn't answer. The lighted kitchens along my street were long dark when I finally got her into the house and put her to bed.

That was long ago. Emilia went back to New Jersey with Millamant and married a nice special-education teacher named Philip, some years later. She didn't write to me for some time after her return, but she telephoned when Millamant died. Gradually we took up our correspondence again, though Sam was as notably absent from it as he had once been its prime mover. I sent a gift when the boy was born: a complete Shakespeare and a *Baseball Encyclopedia*. If those don't cover a growing child's major emotional needs, he's on his own.

Me, I haven't yet been summoned to play Captain Shotover—or Lear, either—but the Falstaffs have started coming lately, and the James Tyrones, and I did do a bloody good Uncle Vanya in Ashland one summer. And I got to New York for the first time in decades, for a get-killed-early role in a big-budget thing where they blew up the Holland Tunnel at the climax. I rather liked that one.

I stayed with Emilia and Philip over a weekend after my part of the shooting was over. They live in an old two-family house in a working-class neighborhood of Secaucus. Secaucus still has one of those, a working class. The place could use a new roof, and there's a draft in the kitchen that Philip hasn't been able to trace down yet. It's a good house, with a black kitten named Rita, for Rita Hayworth. Philip loves old movies and early music.

On the day I left, Emilia and I sat in the kitchen while she gave Alex his lunch. Alex was ten-and-a-half months old then, with a rapturous smile and the table manners of a Hell's Angel. But today he was in one of his dreamy, contemplative moods, and made no difficulties over the brown stuff, which he normally despised, or the green stuff, which he preferred to play with. I sat in a patch of sunlight, watching the two of them. Emilia's gained a little weight, but on her it looks good, and there's a warmth under her pale skin. Marriage suits her. Secaucus suits her.

I think I was actually half-asleep when she turned suddenly to me and said, "You think I don't think about him."

"Actually, I hope you don't," I said, rather feebly. "I try not to, myself."

"There isn't a day," Emilia said. "Not one." She wiped Alex's mouth and took advantage of his meditations to slip some of the yellow stuff into him. "Philip always knows, but he doesn't mind. He's a good man."

"Does he know the whole story? What can happen when you think too much about someone?"

She shook her head without answering. When Alex had reached capacity and was looking remarkably like Sydney Greenstreet in the noonday sun of Casablanca, she took him to his crib, singing "This Time the Dream's on Me" softly as she set him down, already asleep. It was one of Sam's favorite old songs, and she knew I knew. I looked down at Alex and said, "Nice legs. You think there might be a dancer at the other end of them?"

Emilia shook her head quickly. "No, absolutely. He's very much Philip's child. He'll probably play football and grow up to be an ACLU lawyer, and a good thing, too. I'm not going to make him into my dreams of Sam." We tiptoed out of the room, and she gave me one of the heavy black beers for which Philip and I—and Sam, too, for that matter—shared a taste. She said clearly and firmly, "Alex is real. Philip is real. Sam is dead. My dreams are my own business. I can live with them."

"And you never wonder—"

She cut me off immediately, her eyes steady on mine, but her mouth going tight. "I don't wonder, Jake. I can't afford it."

She seemed about to say something more, but the doorbell interrupted her. When she answered it, there stood a small brown girl, no older than five or six, on the step, asking eagerly before the door was fully open, "Miz Larsen, can I play with Alex now?" She looked Filipina, and she was dressed, not in the T-shirt and jeans which children are born wearing these days, but in a white blouse and a dark woolen skirt, as though she were going to church or to visit grandparents. But her accent was unadulterated New Jersey, born and bred.

Emilia smiled at her. "He's having his nap, Luz. Come back in an hour or so. Do you know how long an hour is?"

"My brother knows hours," Luz said proudly. "Okay. 'Bye." She turned away, and Emilia closed the door, still smiling.

"Luz lives a block down from us," she said softly. "She's been crazy about Alex from the day he was born, and he adores her. She's over here almost every day, after school, talking to him, carrying him, inventing games to make him laugh. I'm sure the first real word he says will be *Luz*."

She was talking fast, almost chattering, which is not something Emilia does. We looked at each other in a way that we hadn't since I'd been there. Emilia turned away, and then stood quite still, staring through a front window. Without turning, she beckoned, and I joined her.

On the sidewalk in front of the house, little Luz was dancing.

Not ballet, of course; not the self-consciousness that suggested lessons of any sort. Her movements were just this side of the jump-and-whirl of hopscotch, and there were moments when she might have been skipping double-Dutch without the ropes. But it was dancing, pure and private, and there was music to it—you had only to look at the intense brown face for that. Luz was hearing music, and to watch her for even a little time was to hear it too.

"Every day," Emilia said. "Her parents don't know—I asked them. She waits for Alex to wake up, and while she waits she dances. Nowhere else, just here. I hoped you'd see."

Luz never looked up toward the house, toward us.

I said, "She doesn't dance like Millamant." Emilia didn't bother to answer anything that dumb. We watched a while longer before I said, "He told you, whatever became of him—his soul, his spirit, his molecules—he'd always know you. But he didn't say whether you'd know him."

"It doesn't matter," Emilia said. She took my arm, hugging it tightly, and her face was as bright and young as the child's. "Jake, Jake, it doesn't matter whether I know him or not. It doesn't *matter.*"

Luz was still dancing on the sidewalk when the taxi came to take me to the train station. I said goodbye as I walked past her, trying not to stare. But she danced me escort to the cab door, and I looked into her eyes as I got in, and as we drove away. And what I think I know, I think I know, and it doesn't matter at all.

About Peter S. Beagle

Peter Soyer Beagle is the internationally bestselling and much-beloved author of numerous classic fantasy novels and collections, including *The Last Unicorn, Tamsin, The Line Between, Sleight of Hand, Summerlong, In Calabria,* and, most recently, *The Overneath.* He is the editor of *The Secret History of Fantasy* and the co-editor of *The Urban Fantasy Anthology.*

Beagle published his first novel, *A Fine and Private Place,* at nineteen, while still completing his degree in creative writing. Beagle's follow-up, *The Last Unicorn,* is widely considered one of the great works of fantasy. It has been made into a feature-length animated film, a stage play, and a graphic novel. He has written widely for both stage and screen, including the screenplay adaptations for *The Last Unicorn,* the animated film of *The Lord of the Rings,* and the well-known "Sarek" episode of *Star Trek.*

As one of the fantasy genre's most-lauded authors, Beagle has received the Hugo, Nebula, Mythopoeic, and Locus Awards as well as the Grand Prix de l'Imaginaire. He has also been honored with the World Fantasy Life Achievement Award and the Comic-Con International Inkpot Award. In 2017, he was named 34th Damon Knight Grand Master of the Science Fiction and Fantasy Writers Association for his contributions to fantasy and science fiction.

Beagle lives in Richmond, California.

About Jane Yolen

Jane Yolen's (*Owl Moon, The Midnight Circus,* the How Do Dinosaurs series) four hundredth book came out in 2020, and she is starting the new count with *Arch of Bone*—with her eye on five hundred! She has been writing and publishing since the early 1960s, when she sold her first book (about female pirates) on her twenty-second birthday. But Yolen began her publishing career as a journalist (short-lived) and as an editor (longer-lived) for Knopf and Harcourt, in the children's department.

Yolen graduated from Smith College in Northampton, Massachusetts, with a master's degree in education from the University of Massachusetts, Amherst. She has six honorary doctorates for her body of work. She was the first woman to give the Andrew Lang lecture at St Andrews University in Scotland, in a lecture series that began in 1927. Yolen was also president for two years of the Science Fiction Writers of America, and she served on the board of the Society of Children's Book Writers and Illustrators for forty-five years.

Yolen's books and stories have won three World Fantasy Awards, two Nebula Awards, three Mythopoeic Awards, two Christopher Medals, three SCBWI Awards, the Massachusetts Book Center Award, two Golden Kite Awards, and a Caldecott Medal, as well as many others. She was nominated in 2020 by the United States for the Astrid Lindgren Award. She was the first Western Mass author to win a New England Public Radio Arts and Humanities Award.

Yolen has also received awards from both the Jewish Book Council and the Catholic Book Council, making her very ecumenical. Her award from the Boston Science Fiction Association set her good coat on fire, which she takes as a lesson about the dangers of awards.

Yolen lives in Western Massachusetts and St Andrews, Scotland.

About the Artist

Stephanie Law's work is an exploration of mythology mixed with her personal symbolism. Her art journeys through surreal otherworlds, populated by dreamlike figures, masked creatures, and winged shadows. In her early career, she worked with various fantasy game, magazine, and book publishers as an illustrator. She created the Shadowscapes Tarot, a best-selling deck that has been translated into more than a dozen languages, and she is the author of the watercolor technique book series *Dreamscapes*. She currently focuses on working with galleries for showcasing her personal work and with botanical gardens and environmental organizations for her botanical art, while continuing to publish such projects as her recent art book *Descants & Cadences*, which features her aesthetics of mythos woven with movement and the natural world, and *Succulent Dragons*, which combines her love of the intricate patterns of nature and whimsical fantastical creatures.

Law lives in the San Francisco Bay Area.